Sophie Pembroke has been dreaming, reading and writing romance ever since she read her first Mills & Boon as part of her English Literature degree at Lancaster University, so getting to write romantic fiction for a living really is a dream come true! Born in Abu Dhabi, Sophie grew up in Wales and now lives in a little Hertfordshire market town with her scientist husband, her incredibly imaginative and creative daughter and her adventurous, adorable little boy. In Sophie's world, happy *is* for ever after, everything stops for tea, and there's always time for one more page…

Joanna Sims is proud to pen contemporary romance for Mills & Boon. Joanna's series, The Brands of Montana, features hardworking characters with hometown values. You are cordially invited to join the Brands of Montana as they wrangle their own happily-ever-afters. And, as always, Joanna welcomes you to visit her at her website, joannasimsromance.com

Discover more at millsandboon.co.uk

SECOND CHANCE FOR THE SINGLE MUM

SOPHIE PEMBROKE

HER SECOND FOREVER

JOANNA SIMS

MILLS & BOON

First Published in Great Britain 2020
by Mills & Boon, an imprint of HarperCollinsPublishers,
1 London Bridge Street, London, SE1 9GF

Second Chance For The Single Mum © 2020 Sophie Pembroke
Her Second Forever © 2020 Joanna Sims

Special thanks and acknowledgement are given to Joanna Sims for her
contribution to the *The Brands of Montana* series.

ISBN: 978-0-263-27880-4

0520

MIX
Paper from
responsible sources
FSC™ C007454

This book is produced from independently certified FSC™
paper to ensure responsible forest management.

For more information visit: www.harpercollins.co.uk/green

Printed and bound in Spain
by CPI, Barcelona

SECOND CHANCE FOR THE SINGLE MUM

SOPHIE PEMBROKE

For my brilliant, rugby-loving editor, Megan.

CHAPTER ONE

GWEN PHILLIPS HELD her breath as around her the sound of the crowd built. Less than a minute left on the clock, and just a few too many metres between the Welsh team and the try line. But they had the ball in hand. If they could just break through the Irish defence, the game could be theirs.

Not just the game. The tournament. The championship.

Four points in it, that was all. One try, and it would all be over.

Then suddenly Williams broke free, sidestepped the defender lunging for him, and he was through and launching himself towards the ground, the ball just millimetres over the line, grasped tight in his arms.

They'd done it. They'd bloody well done it.

Around her, the stadium erupted with noise. Cheers and stamping and—of course—singing. Joy and jubilation rang through the air, along with strains of 'Bread of Heaven'.

'Feed me till I want no more!' the crowd sang. And what more was there? For Welsh rugby, right now, this was the dream. And even Gwen, with her mixed feelings on the sport, couldn't help but grin, caught up in the moment.

Beside her, Joe grabbed her and lifted her in a tight hug, whooping in her ear, before turning to do the same to the stranger on his other side.

But as her feet touched the ground again, all Gwen could think was, *George would have loved this.* Her smile slipped away.

As if the thought had made the memory of her late husband real, Gwen looked down at the players on the pitch, slapping backs and hugging, and saw, impossibly, a familiar dark head atop memorable broad and muscled shoulders. He wasn't in the team strip but wearing one of the team hoodies instead. He hadn't been playing, he'd been sitting on the side, behind the subs benches, watching, she guessed. That was why she hadn't spotted him before.

George.

It couldn't be, of course. George had been dead for almost two years now. She'd seen his body, identified it after that terrible call from the police. Buried it. Cried with his parents. Explained to their daughter that Daddy wasn't coming home. That Daddy had been a hero, stopping a knife fight in a pub.

Told Evie anything but the truth, to keep her faith in and love for her father alive. To keep the memory of George one that his friends and family treasured.

They wouldn't, if they knew the truth.

Gwen shook her head to clear the memories, but she couldn't look away from the figure on the pitch.

Then the man looked up, a beaming smile across his face as he reached out to hug another player, and she realised, the truth hitting her hard in the chest.

Not George.

Ryan.

Ryan Phillips. Her brother-in-law, two years younger and with a reputation for being five times wilder than the respected, beloved captain of the Welsh team, George. The man who had actually introduced her to her husband, been best man at their wedding, a doting uncle to Evie for the first year, at least. And, until this moment, commonly understood to be living and playing rugby in France, ever since his shocking departure three years ago.

When did he come home? And why?

Would she find out? Or would his return remain as mysterious as his reasons for leaving in the first place?

'What is it?' Joe had apparently finished hugging every spectator he could reach—which, with his six-foot-plus ex-rugby player's build, was quite some way—and noticed her distraction. 'What's the matter?'

'Who do you see down there on the field?' she asked. 'The one in the grey hoodie, hugging Dewi right now?'

Joe leaned past her to get a good view, then swore. 'No wonder you're shaken up. For a moment there even I thought it was— Wait, is that *Ryan*?'

'Looks like it.' Gwen swallowed, and made herself look away. 'You didn't know he was back in the country either, then?' She'd hoped not; if he'd known and not told her, she'd have been properly miffed.

Joe shook his head. 'No idea. But if he's down there with the team, I'd place money he's planning on coming back to play.'

'Which means a new team, here in Wales.' Welsh rugby rules meant that, because he hadn't played enough games for the national team before he'd transferred to play club rugby in France, Ryan had been ineligible to play for Wales for nearly three years now. But if he'd transferred back to a Welsh club…

'They kept that bloody quiet,' Joe said. 'Well. I promised the boys I'd stop by the hotel later, stand them a pint. I'll find out what's going on for you.'

But the possibilities were already swirling around Gwen's brain.

George's death had been a tragedy, everyone agreed with that. His accident, six months before he'd died, had been a shocking loss to the world of rugby too. Cut off in his prime, so to speak. Even now, commentators still speculated on what the team might be if he hadn't been forced to give up the game so young—although maybe less so after this tournament.

That Ryan had left the country just two games before the one that had injured George had been a talking point too. Could George's little brother have protected him if he'd been playing there at his side, as normal? They'd always had a strange synchronicity on the pitch, an uncanny ability to know where the other was at all times. It had led to Ryan supporting George to try after try, either by passing him the ball at the critical moment, or distracting defenders and keeping them away.

No one had quite believed it when Ryan had declared he was leaving Wales. George least of all. Gwen remembered the yelling, the slammed doors as Ryan had walked out for the last time. And as she'd heard the names George had called his brother, she'd wondered, for the first time, if maybe Ryan hadn't got the right idea.

Maybe it was time to get out.

Everyone in Wales remembered George as a hero, especially his family. Well, everyone except Gwen, and Joe. But they weren't telling.

Evie knew her father was a hero, and that was what mattered most. Gwen would do anything to keep that illusion alive. The little girl had lost so much already, the last thing Gwen wanted was for her to have to face the truth about her father before she was old enough to understand it.

George had been a good man, and a hero of Welsh rugby, and that was how he should be remembered. Not as the man he'd become, especially after his accident.

It was bad enough that Gwen had to remember that man, rather than the loving, supportive one she'd married. People changed, she knew that. But legacies didn't.

And it was to that end that Gwen had set up the George Phillips Trust, helping those who'd suffered life-changing brain injuries, in sport or otherwise. George had always had a healthy life insurance policy, and the pay-out had meant that money was at least one thing Gwen didn't need to worry about. Building up the trust—fundraising, learning from experts, trying to educate the public—that felt worthwhile. Like she was making a difference.

It was the legacy she wished George had really left for her and for Evie. And since he couldn't, she would.

But the George Phillips Trust was one more charitable cause in a world full of those in need. Getting the attention she required to raise the money that was so desperately needed was almost impossible.

Unless she had a platform. A kind of celebrity that brought its own attention, wherever it went.

Already she could hear those in the stalls around her murmuring, wondering, as they noticed the new figure on the field—the way she had. Ryan Phillips was a name too—maybe not as big as his brother's, and perhaps fading a little in the collective memory before now, but still a name. And this unexpected return to his home country would be bound to raise his star a few notches.

Ryan had always been the tabloid favourite anyway. With their stunning looks, the Phillips brothers had been photogenic, they'd been friends with celebs, and they had been at the top of their game. And while George had settled down with her, had Evie, and given up the headline-inducing lifestyle, Ryan had done the opposite. It was a rare weekend that didn't yield a photo of him drunk with some teammates, falling out of cars, or with a soap star or pop singer hanging off his arm. His parents had despaired of him, of the embarrassment and shame he brought with every new headline.

'Why can't you be more like your brother?' his mother had used to ask, shoving the newspapers into the recycling bin.

Ryan had always just shrugged, smiled and gone his own way again.

He had been the wild-child brother to George's golden boy. That was just who they'd been.

But now…. Now that wild-child reputation could be good for something at last. People knew his name, liked his face. They'd pay attention to what he said.

Ryan could get her the publicity she needed to put the trust on the map. To cement George's legacy. To enable her to help others, so maybe they didn't have to go through what she had. What George had. What Evie had.

She just had to persuade him to help and not hinder the operation.

Which probably would have been easier if she'd spoken to him since the funeral. And if he hadn't fallen out with every other member of his family in such dramatic style the day they'd buried George.

But just because it might be hard it didn't mean it wasn't worth trying.

Straightening her shoulders, she turned to Joe. Two long years she'd been away from the rugby scene. But apparently it was time to head back in.

However scary that sounded.

'You're going to the team hotel?' she asked. 'Great. Then I'll go with you.'

'That was incredible, mate!' Ryan wrapped his arms around Dewi and smacked a kiss to the side of his head. 'The championship-winning try. I knew you had it in you!'

Back when Ryan had still played for Wales, his last season there in fact, Dewi had been the new boy on the team—barely nineteen and had hardly played for a club before, let alone his country. He'd been so wet behind the ears Ryan had taken him under his wing, just to make sure he survived all the training-camp pranks the rest of the team liked to pull.

And now he was the tournament-winning try-scorer.

Ryan ignored the part of his heart that ached at not being out there on that field today, the way it always did when Wales played, especially at home at the stadium in Cardiff.

Maybe, this time next year, he'd be out on the pitch with them. Sooner, he hoped.

He was ready for it, he knew that. It was why he'd decided to come back. Why he'd asked his agent to put feelers out for any offers from a Welsh club, however much of a drop in salary he had to take.

People thought he'd sold out to play in France for the money. They couldn't have been more wrong, but at least the cash meant he could do whatever he wanted now, regardless of the pay.

It had taken him three years, but he was ready to be back in Wales again, playing for his country.

Now he just had to persuade them to give him the chance.

'You coming back to the hotel?' Dewi asked. 'Celebrate with us?'

'Wouldn't miss it,' Ryan said, with an easy smile. They'd all be so far into their cups within half an hour they'd never notice his switch to non-alcoholic beer, rather than the pints of bitter he used to prefer. It wasn't the not drinking he minded, just the questions that always went with it. He didn't want to start explaining himself, or who he'd decided to be now, until he'd settled in a little more.

He wasn't the Ryan Phillips they all remembered, and that was a good thing, he hoped.

The hotel was nearby, so Ryan left the team showering and changing, doing interviews and signing daffodil hats and dragon banners. He'd head over, get changed, and meet them all in the bar.

But first there was one last person he needed to congratulate, still out in the stadium.

'That was one hell of a game, boss,' he said, as he caught up with Freddie Yates, the Welsh coach.

Freddie turned, his weathered face cracking into something that almost resembled a smile. 'Wasn't bad, was it?'

'That must make it, what? Your fourth championship title?' It was Freddie's third in charge of the team, Ryan knew, but a little flattery never went amiss in situations like this.

'Third, as you well remember,' Freddie replied. 'Who

knows? You play your cards right this season, you could be on the pitch for the fourth, next spring.'

'That's what I came back for,' Ryan said, with an easy shrug, even as the thrill of the possibility ran through him.

His words were true, even if it wasn't the full story. The lure of playing for his country had never gone away, despite his choice to forfeit it for a time. He knew that his teammates had never understood his decision—they knew he wasn't in it for the money, even if the rest of the country didn't. But that just made it more inexplicable for them. What could Ryan possibly get in France that he couldn't have here in Wales? And why would he give up on them, their team, his own brother, and playing together?

Ryan hadn't even bothered to try and explain. They couldn't ever understand. Because they'd never had the perfect George Phillips as an older brother.

When they'd been younger, he'd thought the two of them were their own team. Then as George had got older, stronger, better, all Ryan had wanted was to follow the trail he'd blazed. And he had. Same training regime, same youth team, same agent, same opportunities—although he'd been sure to work for a different position on the team, so he'd never be in direct competition with his big brother.

Even growing up, Ryan had known that George was the star, the one his mother had bragged about to anyone who would listen. But back then he'd believed that if he did the same, she'd feel the same way about him.

Except that had never happened. Even when he'd started playing professionally, got selected for the Welsh team for the first time…she had been more concerned with how many tries George had scored, or whether he'd get to be captain.

And Ryan had known, for sure, that he'd never live up to George's reputation. So he'd decided to stop even trying. He'd chosen instead to be the opposite of George's shining example.

The wild brother, the troublemaker. The disappointment.

At least his mother acknowledged his existence when she complained about him being photographed falling out of another taxi, drunk, with some soap star. And, really, why bother trying when he was never going to be enough for anyone?

Eventually, though, he'd had to admit that even that didn't fill the hole inside him. He'd stopped trying to be George, only to switch to playing the anti-George instead. His whole world had still centred around his golden-boy brother. The realisation, too late to change anything, he'd thought, had burned through him, and filled him with resentment.

Until one morning he'd woken up, hung-over and late for training, with a woman he hadn't even recognised in his bed, and something inside him had just said—

Enough.

He'd never be able to find his own path, decide who he really wanted to be, reach his full potential, while he was living in his brother's looming six-foot-four shadow. In Wales, he'd always be the younger, lesser Phillips brother. They couldn't see him any other way.

In France, they might let him play as himself. Live as himself.

He'd called his agent that evening and asked him to

find him another team, on the Continent. And he'd taken the first offer he'd received.

It wasn't perfect, and it had cost him a lot—cost him his family in the end. If he'd seen that coming, he might have thought again. If he'd known that in just two games' time George would be injured. That in a year and a half he'd be dead...would he still have gone? Ryan didn't know.

But if he hadn't, then he wouldn't be the person he was now. And today's Ryan Phillips was a hell of a lot more comfortable in his own skin than he'd ever been before.

That was what had made him feel able to come home, at last.

This time, he'd woken up alone, in his house in France, well rested and early for training. He was in peak physical condition, playing the rugby of his life...but he'd known, suddenly, he was in the wrong place.

It was time. Time to put the past behind him. George's accident, his death, the awful row with his parents, Gwen...everything.

He wanted his family back. His country back. His future back.

And he intended to get them.

Playing rugby in Wales again was only the start. Playing *for* Wales would be a big step.

But rugby wasn't what had brought him home.

He'd come home for his family. To show them the man he'd been meant to be all along.

It was just that the rugby was the easier part to start with.

Freddie clapped a hand against his shoulder, still hard enough to smart even now, when it had to be thirty years since the coach had played a rugby match.

'You keep your nose clean, lad, and maybe you'll get out there sooner than I think.' There was a seriousness in Freddie's gaze that calmed Ryan's excitement at the words. 'It's time to put your past in the past, son.'

'That's the other thing I came back for.' Ryan held the older man's gaze, no hint of flippancy in his voice.

Freddie studied him for a moment, then nodded. 'Good.' Then he smiled; a real, honest, actual smile. Something Ryan was certain he'd never seen on the coach's face before. 'Very good.'

Ryan's chest felt lighter instantly. As if one small segment of the weight he'd been carrying around on his heart had lifted.

He was doing the right thing. He could come home. He could move on, past everything that had happened before. One person believed in him, and that made the world of difference, it seemed.

Put the past in the past.

For the first time in three years that actually felt possible.

He looked up, as another cheer went around the stadium, and he saw that the screens were replaying the moment Wales had won, in reactions from fans around the stadium this time, instead of what had happened on the pitch. Apparently one camera had managed to zoom in on the legendary Joe Evans—the Welsh scrum half who'd captained the team for years and had retired the season before Ryan had got called up to play for Wales. He'd been a friend of George's, though, when they'd played together.

He smiled at the sight of him on the screen, larger than life, arms raised in a cheer, mouth wide and yelling, jumping to his feet as the magic happened.

But his smile slipped away as her realised who was sitting next to him, fists against her mouth, watching as if she didn't believe it could be true.

Gwen.

The other reason he'd left Wales, although he'd never admitted that. Not even to himself, until he'd been hundreds of miles away, and a long way further down his path to understanding why he did the things he did.

His brother's wife. The one woman in the world he couldn't, shouldn't want.

And the only one he desperately did.

Back then, he'd assumed it was just another case of wanting what came so easily to George. He'd had the fame, the glory, the adoration of a nation, the willpower and self-control not to screw it all up, like Ryan tended to. His suspension after starting a brawl with the opposing team was still a low point in Ryan's personal and professional history. As was the red card in the World Cup quarter-finals, for that matter.

But being Wales's golden boy hadn't been enough for George. He'd had to marry the most perfect woman too. The ideal rugby player's wife—supportive, loving, beautiful, intelligent, and she genuinely loved the game. Any bloke would be a little envious, right?

And the worst part was that Ryan had met her first. *He'd* been the one who'd spotted her with her friends in the bar. The one who'd bought her a drink and tried to chat her up. The one who might have succeeded if he hadn't been lured away by the promise of shots with the guys, promising Gwen he'd be right back…

Of course, by the time he'd returned, George had already swooped in, his usual, charming self. More charming, more handsome, and definitely more sober than

Ryan. Was it any surprise that George had been the one to get her number at the end of the night?

At the time, Ryan had rolled his eyes and moved on. It had only been once he'd got to know Gwen properly, spent time with her as family, that he'd realised how much more he'd given up that night.

Realised how much more she meant to him, as well as George.

He'd been right to leave, he'd never doubted that, even when the rest of the nation had.

But now he was back…he wondered if there was one piece of his past, of the person he'd been, that he'd never be able to put behind him, however hard he tried. A part that would always call to him, no matter where he went or what he did.

Gwen.

'Are you really sure you want to do this?' Joe asked, as he handed her the gin and tonic he'd ordered for her. 'I can find out what's going on. You don't have to be here.'

The security around the exclusive Cardiff hotel where the Welsh team was staying had been hefty, but Joe's famous face had got them in with no trouble. Now they were sitting in the fancy bar, waiting for the boys to show up in their suits and ties, all the mud washed away, even if the bruises remained.

Any minute now, Gwen told herself as she watched the door. Any minute now they'd all flood in.

'It will be nice to see them all again.' It wasn't really a lie; a lot of the guys on the team had played with George, and even the ones who hadn't had known him. She'd attended parties and team barbeques and awards ceremonies with plenty of them. They were the people she needed to keep in touch with, to help with the George Phillips Trust. This was good. It was work.

It was also a little bit terrifying.

When George had been injured, when he'd realised the damage to his arm and shoulder meant he'd never play again, he'd pulled away from all his old friends. For a time, they'd tried to visit, to see how he was doing. But Gwen had known he'd hate any of them to *really* know how he was—depressed, angry, reckless and irrational. At least, the old George would have. The new George hadn't seemed to care.

She'd cared. So she'd stage managed those visits as best as she could, keeping everything calm and relaxed, steering the conversation away from any of George's flash points, the topics that would send him into a rage without warning.

It had been exhausting.

But as the weeks had passed, the number of flash points had seemed to grow and grow, until they'd encompassed almost everything.

Joe had been there when she'd finally lost control of the situation, and George had blown up at her, at Evie for crying, even at Joe for being there at all. The raging, the yelling, the thrown mug crashed against the wall with tea dripping down the paintwork… Joe had seen it all.

He was the only one who knew the truth.

'It's not really him talking,' she'd tried to explain, after George had stormed out. *'It's the injury. It wasn't just his arm and shoulder he injured when he fell, you know. The blow to the head was the more worrying thing. Head injuries…they're funny beasts, his doctor says. And this was such a bad one. He can't… He just can't go back to the man he was before. His brain won't let him.'*

The man she'd married had been gentle, kind, however rough he'd been out on the pitch. And whatever problems they'd had in their marriage in the last months or year before his accident, he'd never been like *that* before. Then she'd been able to tell herself that it was the stress of the captaincy weighing on him, or being parent to a young child. That all marriages went through rough patches.

Now she didn't bother lying to herself. This was who he was.

She'd married George for better or for worse, in sickness and in health.

She just hadn't imagined that the sickness could make him a different person entirely.

Gwen shook away the memory. None of the boys on that pitch today knew what George had become, and she intended to keep it that way. To protect his memory. To them, she was still the sad widow who had lost the love of her life.

They didn't know he'd died the day that tackle had gone wrong, and the man she'd lived with for eighteen months after that had been someone else altogether.

Not even his own brother knew that.

Joe was giving her a sceptical look, like he knew exactly where her thoughts had gone. But then he straightened up, his attention diverted to the door. 'Here he is.'

Ryan hadn't been playing, of course, so had made it back before the rest of the team. But it seemed he'd still taken the opportunity to smarten up before the evening's festivities. Probably hoping to score with one of the many rugby groupies, knowing Ryan—unless he had his own minor celeb in tow, ready for the tabloid shots. Circulation figures for some of Britain's best-known gossip mags must have gone down since Ryan Phillips had stopped gracing their pages, she was sure.

His grey suit fitted him perfectly, as always, skimming over the heavy muscles she knew were underneath. She'd seen him play on the telly only once since he'd moved to his club in France—and that had been by accident, when trying to find English children's television for Evie in a French hotel room on holiday. He hadn't lost any form—or muscle—since his transfer, she'd seen enough to know that. If anything, reports had said he was playing better than ever.

Ryan's sharp blue eyes flashed as he glanced around the room, obviously looking for someone worth seeing and landing on Joe. With a smile, he began to cross the bar towards them. From where she was sitting, Gwen realised he probably couldn't see her, hidden in the shadow of the bulky ex-captain. But she knew the moment he spotted her. His stride faltered, just for a second, but it was enough.

She'd never really understood what had driven Ryan away from his homeland, but she knew why he'd never come back. What had changed? Why was he here now? She knew she wouldn't rest until she understood. Despite everything, Ryan was family. And that mattered to her.

When she and George had first started dating, Ryan and his parents had been welcoming and friendly. When they'd married, she'd been accepted into the family as if she'd always been there. With her own parents dead, that had meant the world to her. And when Evie had come along, everyone had been thrilled. She'd teased Ryan about settling down one day too, and he'd laughed and said that they all had George for that. Everything had been perfect.

The fractures in their happy family unit had started before George's accident, though. They'd begun the day Ryan had announced he was signing with a French club and leaving Cardiff. No one had understood why, and he wouldn't or couldn't explain. Even George hadn't been able to get his reasoning out of him, although they'd argued until the small hours.

Gwen remembered curling up in bed alone, praying they wouldn't wake Evie. That George wouldn't disappear out again when they were done, the way he'd taken to doing over the last few months, never telling her where he was going.

Ryan had left, and two games later George had been injured. And the first thing his mother Meredith had said was, *'This wouldn't have happened if Ryan had been on that pitch to protect him.'*

She remembered being so taken aback at that. Gwen had always thought that big brothers were supposed to look after their younger siblings. But in the Phillips family it was different—even if it had never been said so starkly before. George was supposed to shine, and Ryan was needed to clear his path and keep him safe. The day he'd left, she remembered George yelling, 'But I need you on my flank! I don't trust anyone else there!'

Looking at him now as he crossed the bar, Gwen wondered if *that* was the real reason Ryan had left. Maybe he'd been sick of always playing back-up to his big brother.

But now he was the only Phillips brother left.

There had been a moment at the funeral—one she didn't think anyone else had seen. A moment when Ryan had leaned over the coffin, after everyone else had gone, and had said, so softly she'd strained to hear, 'I'm sorry. I should have been there on your flank.'

And from the stricken expression on his face when he looked at her now, Gwen knew instantly that, fairly or not, he still blamed himself for not being there to save George. Not on the pitch, and not in that Cardiff bar eighteen months later when George had been stabbed in a knife fight and had bled out before the paramedics even reached him.

'He was all on his own,' Meredith had sobbed into Gwen's shoulder at the hospital. *'Where were his friends? Where was his brother? My golden boy...'*

He hadn't been alone, Gwen knew. He'd been with another woman, for a start. One who'd sobbed and screamed dramatically—but had then disappeared when the police started to ask questions, apparently. But Meredith didn't need to know that. No one did.

'Joe.' Ryan reached the table and held out a hand. 'And Gwen. I saw you both on the big screen at the game, but I didn't expect to see you here.'

Gwen got to her feet and moved to hug her brother-in-law. 'We could say the same about you, you know. Do your mam and dad even know you're back in the country?'

Ryan returned the hug tentatively, as if afraid he might break her. Or maybe just unsure of his welcome here.

He gave her a lopsided smile. 'I thought it would be a surprise.'

Not a *nice* surprise, she noted. Just a surprise. 'I imagine it will.'

'And you two.' Ryan motioned between Gwen and Joe. 'Are you two...?'

It took her a moment to realise what he was asking. Joe got it first, and laughed.

'I think my husband would disapprove,' he said lightly, although Gwen knew how much those words cost him. How he expected to be judged still, every time. 'But Ben has no interest in rugby. He's always grateful when Gwen takes me out, because it means he doesn't have to come.'

Ryan's smile was genuine, and Gwen felt something relax inside her. 'I didn't know you were married. Congratulations.'

'Thanks.' Joe's shoulders relaxed too, Gwen was glad to see. 'What are you drinking? I'll get the pints in.' He drained his own and waited for Ryan to answer.

'Ah, whatever's on draught, please, mate,' he said, after a long moment where Gwen almost expected him to say something else—although what, she had no idea. Ryan had never been one to turn down a pint.

She motioned to the spare seat at their table, and he took it as Joe ambled off towards the bar.

'So you here to congratulate the team?' Ryan asked. 'It was a great game, huh?'

'Amazing,' Gwen agreed. But she wasn't thinking about the game. She was thinking about the George Phillips Trust. About Evie, and the father she deserved to remember. This was her chance. So she took a deep breath and said, 'Actually… I saw you at the stadium and, well, when Joe said he was coming here I decided to come too. Because I wanted to talk to you.'

CHAPTER TWO

OKAY, HE HADN'T expected that. To be honest, he didn't really know what he'd expected. For her to ignore him perhaps? To walk out the moment she saw him? Or maybe just an awkward sort of reunion that would end as soon as they could both leave.

Ryan wasn't under any illusion that his return to Wales would be good news in all quarters. Quite apart from the fans and teammates who felt betrayed, he knew he had a long way to go to make up with his parents after the events of George's funeral. He'd expected a lot of apologising and begging to get any of his family to even speak with him. But if Gwen was willing—no, wanting—to talk to him, maybe things weren't all that hopeless after all.

When he'd seen Joe sitting there in the bar he hadn't imagined for a moment that Gwen would be there with him. Time was she would always have been there with George, but Ryan didn't think he'd seen Gwen out with the team since Evie was born. But then he'd turned towards their table and seen her—and suddenly all those old feelings had come flooding back. The ones he'd moved across the Channel to get away from.

God. Lusting after his brother's wife. He really was the lowest of the low—even if she was now technically his brother's widow. She hadn't been when he'd fallen for her. And now…even thinking about Gwen that way felt like he was *glad* that his brother was dead.

He wasn't. Whatever his nightmares told him sometimes.

'You wanted to talk to *me*?' he asked, just to check he'd heard her right. It wasn't the first time his imagination had told him she was saying something she wasn't. Luckily, he'd always been very clear on the reality of the situation, and he knew his brain was a lying creature.

She nodded. 'I've been working on a new project. One I was hoping you might be able to help me with.'

She needed help? His help?

A war was starting in Ryan's head. Part of him knew he do anything Gwen needed, anything she asked for. Another part knew that was probably the worst option available to him. He'd wanted to come home to Wales to be closer to his family, but now he was here he could already see perils that lay ahead on that path. Reconnecting with his family meant reconnecting with Gwen too. And that could be fine, as long as it was in a sisterly, see her on birthdays and holidays kind of relationship. One that centred around him being Uncle Ryan to Evie, perhaps.

Anything more…that was just asking for his own personal, miserable hell.

He'd forgotten. No, not forgotten. He'd thought he must be imagining it. Over the years away he'd convinced himself that the kind of connection he felt with Gwen couldn't be a strong as he remembered. He'd thought it must have faded over time. That she'd have changed, or he would have.

But here, now, he knew that nothing had changed.

In fact, nothing had changed since that first night he'd seen her across the bar and pushed his way through the crowd to meet her. Except now he wouldn't let anything tempt him away from her for a second, if he had that chance again. And certainly not a tray of shots with the boys.

'What project could need an aging rugby player?' he asked. 'And, actually, if that's what you need, I reckon Joe would be a much better bet.'

'If you don't want to help—' Gwen started, and Ryan instantly felt guilty. He knew how much it must have cost her to come here to this place, with all these memories, and ask him for his help. Gwen was a proud woman, and she wouldn't ask if it wasn't important.

'No! I didn't say that,' Ryan said. He shook his head, partly to support his point and partly to try and shake away all the wrong thoughts he had about the woman in front of him. 'What is it? What do you need? Is it Evie?' Horrible thoughts filled his head. What if it was Evie? What if while he'd been away, dealing with all his issues, Gwen had been needing him and unable to ask? He'd never forgive himself for that. For letting his family down again by not being where they needed him.

'No, no. It's nothing like that. Evie is fine.'

'I should have asked. I mean, I've been thinking about her. And you.' Was he giving too much away? Ryan couldn't tell. Suddenly it felt important that she know he hadn't just forgotten all about them and moved away, even if that was how it had seemed. 'How are you?'

'I'll be better if you agree to help me,' she said.

Her smile was too bright. Ryan watched her carefully she waited for his answer. There was something behind her eyes he didn't think he'd ever seen before. Darkness, almost. Darkness that certainly hadn't been there when he'd left.

But before he could question it, Joe returned from the bar with their drinks, plonking them on the table with a nod towards the door. 'Incoming,' he said.

Ryan looked up and saw the victorious team making their way into the bar, suited and booted and ready to drink. He grinned as Dewi headed straight for him, his blond hair still wet from the shower. He wasn't alone either. Even after so long away he still had plenty of mates on the team, ones who remembered exactly how good he was at celebrating—or commiserating when it came to it.

'Ryan! You ready for another pint yet?' Dewi clapped him on the shoulder.

'I haven't had a chance to start this one yet,' he pointed out. Across the table, the darkness behind Gwen's eyes had only grown. Joe had taken his seat beside her, sitting close, almost protectively. Shielding her from the crowd with his body.

All the same, Dewi spotted their companion and his eyes widened. 'Gwen! I didn't see you there. Were you at the game? Here, let me get you a drink. Guys! Look who's here!'

As the rest the boys headed over towards the table, drawn not just by the presence of Ryan and Joe but by the unexpected addition of Gwen Phillips in her role as tragic widow, Ryan watched Gwen shrink in on herself. He'd wondered if perhaps going to games with Joe and meeting up with the team afterwards was something she'd done more of while he'd been away. But he thought now this really was a one-off. She'd come here to see him, and now she had to face the entire Welsh rugby team.

Whatever she needed from him must be really important.

Ryan got his feet and, with an easy charm he'd almost forgotten he possessed, managed to steer the team towards the bar instead of Gwen. 'That was quite some match, guys. Only thing that could have made that victory better was if I'd been on the field with you. Now, how about I get the first round in to celebrate?'

Handing his credit card over to Dewi, Ryan left them placing their orders at the bar. Then, when he was sure that none of them were watching, he slipped back to the table, gave Joe a nod he knew the older man would understand, and took Gwen's arm.

'Come on,' he said. 'I think we need somewhere quieter for this conversation, don't you?'

Gwen glanced at Joe too, as if for approval, and then nodded.

The whole hotel was buzzing with fans, press and other hangers-on. Ryan kept his head down as he led Gwen towards the small hidden nook he'd found the night before. The table and two small bench seats were nicely hidden from the rest of the bar and the crowds.

Gwen's shoulders started to relax the moment she sat down, and Ryan could see the darkness behind her eyes starting to fade.

'Better?' he asked.

Gwen gave him a sheepish smile. 'I don't like crowds so much these days.'

'And that wasn't just any old crowd,' he joked. 'You haven't seen them much since…' Ryan trailed off, not wanting to have to say the words.

'No. Not since the funeral.'

She didn't have to say anything else. Ryan knew they

both remembered the events of that day well enough without hashing them out all over again.

Time to change the subject. 'So? You wanted to talk to me about something?'

'Yes.' She straightened little in her seat, and suddenly Ryan was reminded of all the disciplinary panels he'd ever had to attend. At least this time he was fairly sure he hadn't actually done anything wrong. Well, not recently, anyway. 'Late last year, I decided to start a trust in George's memory. Evie and I... We had the insurance money, plus our savings, and the house. We were really lucky. But I know a lot of people who suffer the sort of life-changing injuries George did—the sort that mean giving up a job they love, or needing help at home and so on—wouldn't be so lucky. And I thought if we could help them maybe that would help me... I don't know. Find meaning in what happened, maybe.'

'That makes sense,' Ryan said. Although he didn't see what it had to do with him, or how he could possibly help. He hadn't even been there when George had got injured. Helping people was clearly not his strong point. 'What you want me to do?'

'I know you have been away a while, but you're still a name over here. And that's what I need. I need the kind of people involved who can raise the trust's profile. Joe is helping, of course. But it's not going to be enough. And you... You have a personal connection, as well as the, well, shall we say public appeal.'

'You mean the tabloid appeal.' Ryan remembered all too well all those headlines, all those awful photos. They felt like another life now, but to Gwen that was still who he was. And not just to Gwen. To everyone who had known him back then—including his parents.

And if he didn't do something to change that, that was who he would always be. To his family, his friends and everyone out there who read those papers. He'd come home to start over, to try and do things right this time. But he saw now that before he could do any of that he had to put to bed the person he had been.

So far, he hadn't even been able to ask for non-alcoholic beer rather than a pint when Joe asked. Or put his feelings about his brother's wife behind him.

He'd thought he'd made all the changes he needed to while he'd been in France. He'd thought he was ready to come home and show them who he was.

But now he realised that being the man he wanted to be *here*, at home in Wales, was just his next challenge.

And Gwen was giving him the chance to rise to it. Charity work, especially in his brother's memory, could be the first step to rehabilitating his character. Not just that, but if he helped Gwen…

'I'll do it,' he said, the words out of his mouth before he could think better of them. 'But on one condition. I need your help with something too.'

'My help?' Gwen stared at her brother-in-law across the table. The brief flare of elation she'd felt when he'd agreed to help faded rapidly. She couldn't imagine what Ryan could possibly need, but she was almost certain it was something she wouldn't be able to provide.

She didn't have much left to give these days. And what she had certainly hadn't been enough for his brother.

'Yeah.' Ryan looked down at the table, his voice rough. Gwen frowned. There was something about this Ryan she didn't recognise. They'd been reasonably close before he'd left, and she'd thought she'd known all there really was to know about George's little brother. But perhaps the years apart—or even his brother's death—had changed him more than she'd expected. 'I didn't just come back to Wales to play rugby for my country.'

'I thought rugby was what mattered most in the world to the Phillips boys,' Gwen joked.

Ryan didn't even smile. Instead he raised his head to meet her gaze. 'Not the only thing. Don't you remember what George used to say?'

She did, of course she did. 'Family, country, and rugby. The holy trinity of George Phillips.' Blasphemous, perhaps, but a rule he'd tried to live by when she'd met him. And while his marriage might have faded in importance as the strains and stresses had got to him, the rest of it had stuck. Until his accident, anyway.

'Exactly.' Ryan tapped fingers against the practically untouched pint in front of him. God, things must be serious if he wasn't even drinking. 'Coming home, talking to the coach today, I think I've got the last two sorted. It's the first I need your help with.'

Family. Of course.

The other thing Ryan had left behind when he'd chosen to leave the country. Gwen couldn't help but wonder what had happened to make him remember their existence now.

She studied him again in the dim light allowed by the pale wall sconces around them. He looked older, she realised. Could she hope for wiser? Probably not. George had always joked that Ryan would never change—not least because he didn't want to.

But there was a different air about him today. And that pint glass was still full.

Maybe he really was serious about this.

'What do you want me to do?' she asked, cautiously. 'No promises.'

Even that was enough to raise a tiny smile from him. 'I want to be part of Evie's life as she grows up. With George gone… I should have been there for her, and for you. A girl needs her Uncle Ryan when times are tough, right?'

'Why now?' He hadn't been here when George had been injured. When he'd changed into someone she'd barely recognised thanks to one too many bumps on the head over the years. When she'd had to hide who he'd become from their family, their friends. From Evie.

She could have used his help then. Maybe she'd even have let him see the truth.

'I… It felt like time,' he said lamely. 'I've been away long enough. And Evie's growing up—'

'Evie's been just fine the last few years,' Gwen told him bluntly. 'She doesn't even remember you, Ryan.'

'Yeah, I know. That's what made me realise… I hate the idea of her growing up not knowing me.' He stared mournfully at his pint again. 'And honestly? Maybe her Uncle Ryan needs her. And her mum. And…and her grandparents.' The pause before the last part told her he knew *exactly* how much he was asking there.

'You want me to fix things between you and your parents?' Gwen shook her head. 'I think that's *way* above my pay grade.'

'Fixing it isn't your job, Gwen. It's mine. I just need you to help me get the opportunity to do it.'

He sounded so serious, so unlike the Ryan she remembered, Gwen couldn't help but believe he truly wanted to mend fences and bring their family back together again.

But he still hadn't answered the most important question she had.

'Why, Ryan? I'm serious. Why now?'

His shoulders slumped slightly at her enquiry. 'Because I can't turn back time and do it three years ago? Gwen… I've regretted how I left things here from the moment I got on that plane to France. Not leaving the team—that was the right decision for my career and my rugby skills. I learned a lot playing over there, and I'm excited to bring that knowledge back to my new team here.

'Not even leaving the country—I missed Wales, of course I did, but France has given me a lot too. So, yeah. I know I made the right decision going. But I hate how I left things here. I still have nightmares about my last conversation with my brother; he didn't understand why I needed to go and I didn't have the words to explain it to him.'

'I remember,' Gwen said softly. 'He was so angry. He thought you were leaving because of him.' He'd come upstairs and ranted for a while after Ryan had left. And when Gwen had told him that maybe it was time for Ryan to get out on his own, he'd stormed out again into the night. Gwen didn't like to think about where he'd gone, but she knew that wherever it was wore a perfume she still couldn't smell without feeling nauseous.

Ryan's silence to the accusation that he'd left because of his brother was telling, she thought. *Had* George been the reason he'd left? It couldn't have been a lot of fun living in the shadow of Wales's golden boy his whole life.

'I hate that I wasn't here when he got hurt.' Ryan's words were barely more than a whisper. 'I know that I should have been. And I hope—no, I *know*—that if I'd been on that pitch that day I'd have protected him.'

'That's what your mum always said.' Back when she'd talked about her youngest son at all. These days she seemed happiest pretending he didn't exist. At least she wasn't just complaining about his latest stint in the tabloids, Gwen supposed.

'But I wasn't. And I can't change that now.' He took a breath and straightened his shoulders, like he was preparing to defend himself. 'I can't change the things Mum and I said to each other at George's funeral either. I can't take any of it back. The past happened, and I can't change it. But I'd like to change the future, if I can.'

He sounded so earnest, so hopeful, Gwen couldn't bring herself to spell out the probable reception the idea would get back at the cottage George had bought for his parents with the proceeds of a sponsorship deal years ago.

Ryan had earned plenty with similar deals, she remembered. As far as she knew, the only beneficiaries of that money had been Cardiff's bars and clubs.

'I…I need to think about this, Ryan. Figure out the best way to approach them with this. Your parents… they're still hurting. You leaving, George's accident, then his death…it's been a lot.'

'I know.' He swallowed so hard she saw his Adam's apple bob. 'But you'll try?'

'No promises,' she said.

He shrugged. 'I'll take what I can get.'

'Okay.' She glanced down at her phone, registering the time with surprise. It was later than she'd imagined. 'But right now I need to go. I need to get home to Evie.'

'Of course.' He stood up, moving out of the booth and glancing around the bar. 'Want me to go and get Joe for you?'

She shook her head as she eased herself out of her seat. 'I'll text him. He'll understand.'

'Okay.' Hands in his pockets, he ducked his head, looking for a moment like the young man she'd first met in a Cardiff bar all those years ago, just before George had walked into her life. Except he was no fresh-faced twenty-year-old any more. He'd filled out and grown up and was all man now. Something she was trying not to notice. 'And…thanks, Gwen. Anything I can do to help with the trust I will, of course. For George. And for you and Evie.'

'I appreciate that.' She picked up her bag to leave, then paused. She didn't want to leave without giving him something. Some hope.

Ryan was right. The past was in the past and they couldn't change it. Wasn't she doing the same as him, trying to rewrite the stories that defined their lives? She was working for a better future with the trust. Didn't Ryan deserve the same chance?

'And, Ryan…' He looked up at her words, hopeful like a puppy wanting treats.

An insanely hot and muscled puppy, but still. It helped to focus on the cute factor, rather than the sexy one. One rugby player—one Phillips brother—was quite enough for one lifetime, in Gwen's opinion.

'I can't speak for your parents, or tell you how they're going to react,' she started, the words coming slowly as she thought about what she really wanted to say. 'But if you're serious about rebuilding bridges…you'll always be family to me, and to Evie. So if you want to see her, spend time with us…we can do that.'

The smile that spread across his face was every bit as bright as George's had been the day she'd said yes to the engagement ring he'd offered her.

'Really? When?'

'Um…' It had been more of a gesture than a concrete plan, but now she thought about it Gwen couldn't think of any good reason not to agree a time at least. 'Saturday?' She'd promised Evie they'd do something special together. Meeting her long lost uncle probably counted, right?

'It's a date,' Ryan said, still grinning, and Gwen ignored the way her stomach lurched at his words.

It definitely wasn't that.

She handed him her phone. 'Put your number in there. I'll text you the details.'

'And you'll talk to my parents?' he asked, as his fingers flew over the touchscreen.

'I'll try.'

'That's all any of us can do,' he replied, a wistful smile on his face.

Ryan checked the small parcel in the inside pocket of his coat one last time, and paced over to the railings to see if he could see Gwen and Evie approaching.

The text had come through late the night before, and Ryan didn't like to admit how often he'd checked his phone in the intervening days, waiting for it. He'd had a busy week of training with his new squad, settling into the new flat he'd rented, and trying to set up life back in the country of his birth. Most things—bank accounts, driving licence, et cetera—had carried on from before he'd left, but setting up a new flat and changing his address *everywhere* took more time than he'd imagined it could.

The distraction had been welcome, though. His new team played a mere twenty miles away from the Cardiff suburb where he'd grown up, and closer still to where he knew his parents now lived. The temptation to revisit old haunts was great, and the one to show up on his parents' doorstep unannounced and try to make things right was even greater.

But he'd made a plan. He'd enlisted Gwen's help. Now he had to be guided by her on the right way to do this.

Still, when he'd received her text he'd felt a thrill go through him.

Caerphilly Castle, ten a.m. Bring chocolate buttons.

Something was happening at last. He was moving forward, not just wading through his past.

He leaned against the railings that surrounded the castle and scanned the paths around it for Gwen and Evie. It was still only just before ten; he'd been half an hour early in his eagerness. But Gwen was never late—his own tardy nature was one of the things that had driven her mad about him in the past. George had always laughed it off as just the way he was, but Gwen had been properly annoyed by it.

He couldn't risk doing *anything* to annoy her now. Well, apart from spoiling his niece a little bit too much maybe. He wondered what the gift shop had to offer…

Finally, Gwen's sleek caramel hair came into view, next to a small girl with fluffy blonde locks. Ryan felt his chest tighten at the sight; already, Evie looked so grown up compared to the baby he'd left behind. He wondered if her hair would darken to be like her dad's, in time. Wondered if she'd remember him at all. If she even remembered George.

Gwen looked up suddenly, and pointed as she spoke to Evie. The little girl looked up too, and even at such a distance Ryan saw the challenge in her bright blue eyes. George's eyes. His eyes, even.

His family.

Ryan loped down the path to meet them, his smile painfully wide as they grew closer.

'Hi.' Maybe Gwen read his nervousness—she'd always been perceptive that way—because she returned his grin with a gentle, welcoming smile of her own. Then she stepped forward, put her arms around him and hugged him.

God, she smelled good. And he knew he wasn't supposed to notice that, knew that at the least his affection for her wasn't what this day was about—even if it wasn't just all levels of wrong anyway. But he couldn't stop himself noticing it.

Ryan pulled away.

Gwen crouched down beside her daughter. 'Evie, this is your Uncle Ryan. He was your daddy's brother.'

'Hi, Evie.' Ryan gave her an awkward wave. One thing he hadn't considered in his grand plan was that he had absolutely no idea how to behave around children. In his general experience of the world, it was one thing that just hadn't come up.

Fortunately, Gwen had given him some guidance— namely the instruction to bring chocolate buttons. He'd figured that if chocolate was good, presents had to be better. And that was one thing he had actually planned ahead for.

Pulling the wrapped package from inside his coat, he held it out to Evie. 'I don't know if your mum told you, but I've been living in France the last few years. And while I was there I saw this, and it made me think of you. So I came back here to Wales to give it to you.'

Evie's eyes widened. Bouncing on her toes, she took the present from Ryan's hands, and looked up at her mother for approval.

'Yes, okay, go on, then.' Gwen rolled her eyes as Evie attacked the wrapping paper. 'You always did know how to charm the girls, Ryan.'

'This isn't actually how I used to do it,' he muttered back to her in an undertone, surprising a laugh from Gwen.

'No, I don't imagine it is.' She flashed him a look that, just for a brief moment, Ryan almost believed was flirtatious.

'It's a bunny!' Evie held the small stuffed toy up towards Gwen, who studied its fluffy little ears and stripy navy and white T-shirt with great interest.

'Not just that,' she said. 'Evie, I do believe this might be a special *French* bunny.'

Evie gasped in amazement. 'Is it, Uncle Ryan? Is it *really*?'

What the difference was between special French stuffed bunnies and regular ones, Ryan had absolutely no idea. But the little girl seemed so excited at the prospect that the only thing for it was to go along with it.

'It is. He's called Jean Paul Lapin,' he improvised.

Evie hugged the bunny close. 'I love him. Thank you, Uncle Ryan.'

'You're very welcome.' The tight feeling in his chest was familiar, Ryan thought. It felt similar, but not quite the same, to the way his body reacted when Gwen smiled at him. Like something important had just happened, even if the rest of the world never noticed.

'Shall we head up to the castle?' Gwen asked, taking Evie's hand. 'You can show Monsieur Lapin around.'

Evie's nose crinkled up in confusion. Ryan had to admit, it was kind of adorable. 'Monsor? What does that mean?'

'It's French for Mr,' Ryan explained. 'So Monsieur Lapin means Mr Rabbit.'

'Oh!' Evie's face brightened. 'Yes, I want to show Monsor Lapin my castle. And I want to show Uncle Ryan too.'

Ryan and Gwen shared a look, one that filled him with warmth and maybe, just maybe, the start of acceptance.

This, right here, was what he'd come home for.

Evie let go of her mother's hand and, Monsieur Lapin dangling from the other, grabbed Ryan's fingers instead. 'Come on,' she ordered.

Ryan had a feeling he was going to be doing what he was told a lot around Evie. 'After you, princess.'

Two hours later, and Ryan had been fully educated in every aspect of Caerphilly Castle, its history, and the best spots for playing hide and seek. Evie's energy never seemed to run out. Ryan had thought he was in peak physical condition, but apparently he had nothing on an excited almost-five-year-old.

Eventually, even Evie needed a break—and the biggest slab of chocolate brownie Ryan had ever seen. He gazed at it wistfully as he drank his herbal tea.

Gwen laughed at him. 'You know, you could have one too.'

'Not on the team diet sheet,' he said mournfully.

That made her eyebrows shoot up. 'Since when has that ever stopped *you*?'

'Since...' When had he started caring about what he needed to do for the good of the team? In France, for sure. But the changes had come so gradually it was hard to pinpoint a single moment. He shrugged. 'A while, now.'

It would have been easier if there *had* been one defining moment. One event—George's accident, perhaps, or leaving home—that had changed him. Instead, he'd had to change himself.

It was a harder road, and it took longer. But maybe he valued it more because he'd had to work for it. He hoped so.

He hoped others might too. Starting with Gwen.

Evie was fully engrossed in telling Monsieur Lapin through a spray of brownie crumbs all about the chocolate brownie and how he couldn't have any because it was bad for his teeth, and how a bunny really *needed* his teeth.

Ryan took the brief break from entertaining her— or being entertained by her, more often—to study her mother again.

Gwen had been quiet today. He'd assumed that their meeting in the hotel had been awkward because it had been the first time in so long, because they had both been asking something of the other, because it was all about the rugby—and he was sure there'd been a lot of memories of George floating around for both of them that day. But she'd been exactly the same today, quiet, reserved, almost...brittle. The Gwen he remembered had been so in love, so full of life, she'd made the world around her more colourful.

But that was before she'd lost the love of her life, of course. Stupid of him not to imagine the ways that widowhood would have changed her.

They didn't make her any less wonderful in his admittedly biased eyes, though. If anything, she was more elegant, more beautiful now, as much as he hated to think that, given what had caused it. And the depth of love in her eyes when she watched Evie… He knew that the Gwen he'd known was still there inside too.

And it did his soul so much good to see her again.

One afternoon wasn't enough, though it was a start. He was greedy. He always wanted more.

Self-restraint had been the hardest of many lessons he'd needed to learn. And in some areas he was still learning.

'I think this went well, don't you?' he asked, watching Evie as she relented and let the bunny try 'just a *tiny, tiny* bit' of the brownie. 'Us hanging out, I mean. Me being Uncle Ryan.'

'It did,' Gwen admitted. 'Better than I'd thought it would.'

'So we can do it again sometime?' He didn't want to beg, but he was sure she heard the desperation under his words all the same.

'I…' Gwen glanced between him and Evie. 'I guess that would depend on lots of things. Including how long you're around for.'

Evie's head shot up at that. 'You're not going back to France now, are you, Uncle Ryan?

'I'm not going anywhere, Evie,' he said firmly. 'I have a contract. I'm staying here, where I can be close to my family.'

'And me?' Evie asked.

He grinned at her. 'Evie, you're the most important family I have.'

And then he tickled her, and Monsieur Lapin, for good measure.

'If she's sick, you have to clear it up,' Gwen said, dryly, but he could already tell he'd won her over.

'Next weekend, then?' he suggested, when Evie's giggles had subsided.

Gwen raised an eyebrow. 'Don't you have a match on Saturday?'

Damn. He did. His first with his new team, and not something he'd usually forget. 'I thought Sunday? I'll choose the activity this time.' Some of his new teammates had kids. He'd ask for suggestions.

She watched him for a moment, but he knew he had her. George had always said she was a soft touch when it came to underdogs—and he was definitely that.

'Okay, fine. Sunday it is.'

CHAPTER THREE

EVIE DIDN'T LET go of Monsieur Lapin for the next two days.

It wasn't too much of a problem until Tuesday, when Gwen needed to go into Cardiff for a meeting with a potential sponsor and Evie was going to spend the day with her grandparents.

'Are you sure Monsieur Lapin wouldn't be happier at home?' Gwen asked, desperation leaking out in her words.

But Evie was her father's daughter, and as stubborn as hell when it mattered to her. 'He's my best friend. He has to come with me. Besides, I want him to meet Nain and Taid.'

Nain and Taid—the Welsh names George's mother and father had chosen for themselves as grandparents when Gwen had still been pregnant with Evie. And the two main reasons she didn't want Evie to take Monsieur Lapin, whatever excuses she'd made about worrying about him getting lost.

Her parents-in-law were totally engaged and invested in their granddaughter's life, which normally she was thrilled about. But today it would mean them noticing that Evie had a new favourite toy and asking her about it, and inevitably hearing all about Uncle Ryan.

Which was a problem. Because Gwen hadn't quite found the right way to talk to them about their prodigal son's return just yet.

They might already know, she'd reasoned. They kept up with the sport their sons loved even now. They might have been watching the championship final. In fact, she knew they had, because they'd texted to say they'd seen her with Joe on the big screen afterwards. Maybe they'd spotted Ryan too. Or maybe they'd seen the announcement of his transfer back to Wales in the press the next day.

But they hadn't mentioned it if they had. Which meant that, even if they knew, they were trying to ignore it.

Perhaps they were waiting for him to come to them, but Gwen doubted it.

She loved her in-laws dearly. But she also knew they were wrong about Ryan.

There was nothing for it now, anyway. She had to get to her meeting, and Evie wasn't going anywhere without Monsieur Lapin.

She dropped Evie off with her nain and taid with only the barest greeting and farewell—and the promise to stay for dinner when she got back to make up for it. As the front door closed behind her, she heard her mother-in-law saying, 'And who is this fine fellow, now?' and winced.

Then she put the whole thing out of her head until later. She had business to do, meetings to concentrate on. And thinking about Ryan Phillips was not good for her concentration, it seemed.

But as she pulled her car into Meredith and Dylan Phillips' driveway later that afternoon, she knew she couldn't ignore any of it any longer. She'd made an agreement with Ryan, and she had to hold up her part of it. Especially after today's meetings.

'How did it go?' her father-in-law, Dylan, asked as he opened the door to her. Another point in their favour, they were totally supportive of her work setting up George's trust. It was enough to make her feel guilty for even *talking* to Ryan again. Which was insane. Whatever Meredith said, however much they resented the fact that Ryan had left, George's accident hadn't been his fault. And his death certainly hadn't been.

'So-so.' She shrugged off her coat. 'People like the idea, they want to help, but they need more visibility before they'll help me become more visible. If that makes any sense at all.'

'Not much,' Dylan said cheerfully. 'Come on, love. There's Bolognese on the stove, and I'll pour you a glass of wine. That'll make it all look better.'

'How's Evie been?' she asked, as they moved through the hallway towards the lounge at the back of the house.

'Fine, fine.' But he shot her a quick look as he said it that suggested that it hadn't all been quite as *fine* as he said. 'I think her nain is looking at some old albums with her right now. She wanted to see her Uncle Ryan apparently.'

Gwen's chest tightened. Here it was, time to come clean. But, really, what was there to say other than Ryan was in town and had asked to see Evie? She hadn't done anything wrong.

So why did it feel like she had?

Dylan grabbed a wine glass from the kitchen on the way past and pressed it into her hand, filling it with wine almost to the brim.

'Thanks.' She had a feeling she was going to need it.

'I'd better stir the Bolognese,' he said, retreating. Dylan never had liked conflict.

George and Ryan both got their fighting spirit from their mother, it seemed.

Taking a swig of the wine, Gwen moved to the doorway to the lounge to watch Evie and her nain.

'And this is your daddy scoring his first try for his country,' Meredith was saying, as she turned the page of an old-fashioned photo album. 'Do you remember how many he scored altogether, *cariad bach*?'

'Thirty-two,' Evie recited dutifully. 'That's right, isn't it, Nain?'

'It is,' Meredith said proudly.

'How many did Uncle Ryan score?' Evie asked, and Gwen watched Meredith's expression darken.

Time to intervene.

'Hello, you two! Have you been having fun today?'

'Mummy!' Evie spun around and launched herself at Gwen. 'Monsieur Lapin missed you!'

'Did he? How about you? Did you miss me?' She pressed a kiss to Evie's soft, blonde hair.

'A little bit,' Evie said, after some consideration. 'But I was having fun with Nain and Taid.' She dropped her voice. 'I don't think Nain likes Monsieur Lapin, though.'

Of course she didn't. 'Why don't you go and help Taid in the kitchen?' she suggested to Evie. 'You know he always stirs the sauce the wrong way.'

'And never grates enough cheese!' Evie agreed, skipping off to correct her grandfather's culinary mistakes.

In her chair, Meredith slammed the photo album closed. 'So. You've seen Ryan, I hear?'

Okay, so there was no gentling into this conversation, then. Gwen dropped into the nearest chair, and took another gulp of wine. From the tone of her mother-in-law's voice, she was going to need it.

'I bumped into him at the match,' she started, leaving out the part where she'd actually gone to the bar to seek him out. 'He's moved back to Wales for good, did you know?'

'His father might have seen something about it on the internet,' Meredith admitted. 'But since he didn't let us know himself, we weren't sure it was true.'

'He wanted to see Evie,' Gwen told her. 'And he wanted me to talk to you and Dylan before he came to see you both.'

Meredith stiffened at that. 'He can't face his own parents like a man and apologise for what he did?'

What he did? Or what he said? Gwen wondered. Was Meredith really still angry about the things they'd said to each other at George's funeral, or just still unable to forgive Ryan for leaving in the first place, for not being there to protect his brother on the pitch? She suspected the latter.

'He wants to come and see you and apologise. Rebuild bridges, he said. Would you be open to that?'

Meredith looked down at the album in her hands, spreading it open again to a page filled with press photographs and newspaper clippings. All about George, of course. Gwen suspected there must be a similar album for Ryan somewhere, but she'd certainly never seen it since he'd left.

'What kind of mother would I be if I didn't see my son?' she asked softly. But she was still staring at the photos of George, tracing his face with her finger.

Gwen bit the inside of her cheek, uncertain. This didn't look like forgiveness. This looked like punishment.

George's parents still clung so tightly to the past—to who George had been before his accident. Maybe she'd hidden the changes in him afterwards too well. Or maybe they just hadn't wanted to see it. Wilful, blissful ignorance.

But not everyone was willing or able to do that. She'd hidden it well from the people close to her, but George had had other friends, other acquaintances, that she'd never known. Like the woman with the heavy perfume, or the people who had been with him the night he'd died. She'd never met any of them.

There were enough people out there who knew the truth about who George had become, and who had no loyalty to her to hide it. She lived in fear of an exposé one day, on the anniversary of his death perhaps. Evie was learning to read now. If there were headlines, with photos of her father, and she saw them...

Maybe she couldn't keep the truth from her for ever, but she could change the story. Make it about the good that came from tragedy. With Ryan's help.

And he needed her help too. She'd seen that the other day, at the castle. The desperately hopeful smile on his face as he'd handed Evie the bunny had told her all she needed to know.

Helping Ryan, and Ryan helping her, was the right thing to do. No matter how difficult it might be to start with.

Meredith was still staring at the photos of George.

'I'll arrange with Ryan to get together one day soon, then, shall I?' she asked.

Meredith didn't look up. 'Whatever you think best, dear.'

Fine. That's what she'd been doing ever since even before George's accident. She'd just keep on going, and hope for the best.

What else was there to do?

* * *

When Ryan saw the text message from Gwen a mere two days later, his heart lurched in his chest.

'Message from your girlfriend, Ry?' Dewi asked, across the changing room. Being in the same club as his friend had played a large part in Ryan's decision to sign on with the Selkies, rather than one of the other, more famous Welsh teams, but for the first time he was starting to regret it. Dewi was a notorious gossip, and if he thought there was something interesting going on in Ryan's life, he wouldn't stop asking until he found out what it was.

Ryan slipped his phone into his pocket, planning to reply to the message later. 'Nothing half as interesting, I'm afraid, mate. Just a family obligation.'

His parents weren't the sort to air dirty laundry in public—one of the things his mum had hated most about his wilder days was how they had been documented on-line and in print, so everyone knew exactly what disgraceful behaviour he'd been up to, and with whom. Ryan felt pretty sure that the extent of his estrangement from his family wouldn't be common knowledge because he hadn't told anyone—and he couldn't imagine his parents doing so. If he got his way it would all be mended before anyone ever had to know about it. All the same, it felt wrong describing Gwen as an obligation.

At least until he actually read the text message, and realised what she was asking him to do.

He met her at the hospital the next day anyway, just as she'd asked. Because apparently he was still no good at saying no to Gwen.

'Care to tell me exactly what we're doing here?' he asked, as they strode through the hospital corridors. He tried to guess where they were going from signage on the walls, but the place was so large and sprawling she could have been leading him anywhere.

'You'll see,' she replied.

Ryan tried to hold in a shudder as the hospital smell became overwhelming, the deeper they got. As a rugby player, he was no stranger to hospital wards, although he'd been lucky enough to mostly be patched up by the team doctors. Not many rugby players could get as far in their careers as he had without succumbing to some sort of major injury—the sort that put a player out for months, a whole season, a year, or for ever. George certainly hadn't.

'As long as you're not taking me to the STI clinic,' he joked, trying to lighten the mood. Ever since they'd met in the car park Gwen had been quiet and reserved, in a way he'd hoped they'd moved past at the castle on Saturday. Apparently not.

She shot him a scathing glance. 'Of course that's the only part of the hospital you're familiar with.'

It wasn't true, though, was it? Ryan thought, striding alongside her down the endless corridors. Quite aside from his own injuries, he'd been in this very hospital when George had been hurt. Sat terrified by his brother's bed, waiting to see if he'd wake up.

He'd been in France when the accident had happened, watching his home team play on a foreign television screen, cheering them on all the way. Even his teammates, who might normally have favoured Italy over Wales, had been shouting support for the boys in red. The room had been rowdy and alive—and had fallen instantly silent the moment George had been tackled.

It wasn't even an illegal tackle, that was the hardest

thing to process. It was a perfectly normal, run-of-the-mill tackle, the sort George dodged or survived every game, multiple times. The sort Ryan himself made regularly. The exact sort he was known for, actually.

But rugby was a contact sport, and every player knew the risks. He'd played with a lad once, in the under-eighteens team, who'd fallen badly after a tackle and severed his spinal cord. Left with no feeling in his legs at all.

They all knew the risks.

But they all also, secretly, believed that they were too good to fall. That the training, the hard work, the drive and the ambition would keep them alive. They couldn't play if they didn't.

George was luckier than some. He slammed into the ground at a bad angle, unable to turn, gripping the ball too tightly to put his hands out to save himself. He landed awkwardly on his arm and shoulder—they could all see that from the camera angles. Then his head had bounced off the turf—no mud and rain to soften it, for once—and his eyes had rolled back.

Over in France, Ryan had been on in his feet in an instant, and on a plane home almost before the full-time whistle blew.

Ryan shook the memories away, and focussed on where Gwen was taking him. The corridors were familiar, the doors, the artwork… He realised belatedly she was leading him towards the department where they'd sat with George's doctor after the accident, learning about what to expect next.

Gwen knocked on the door, and he recognised the name, printed on a brass plaque. A. Chowdhury. The surgeon who'd treated George. Not the one who'd put the bolts in his arm to hold it together. The one who'd dealt with his head injury.

'Gwen! So good to see you.' The woman who opened the door and embraced Gwen was petite, quick moving and, on their previous acquaintance, the smartest person Ryan had ever met. 'How is Evie?'

She motioned them inside, smiling at Ryan as she indicated for them both to sit.

'Evie's great, thanks. Currently obsessed with a toy rabbit her Uncle Ryan brought her from France.'

'Ah, yes.' Anita Chowdhury turned her chocolate-brown eyes towards him, and Ryan tried not to squirm under the directness of her gaze. It was hard to make his six-foot-two frame inconspicuous, though, especially in such a small room. 'George's brother Ryan. I remember you.'

'Thank you for everything you did for my brother,' he said.

The doctor inclined her head in acceptance. 'George's injury was terribly unfortunate. But it brought Gwen into our world. And I think she's going to make a real difference to a lot of other people's lives.' She turned back to Gwen. 'You wanted to run over the details for the fundraiser?'

Gwen shook her head. 'It's all in hand, I think. You have your invitations?'

'And my party frock sorted,' Anita confirmed. 'But if not the fundraiser, why did you want to see me?'

Gwen glanced across at him, and suddenly Ryan knew. This was about him.

'I was hoping you could talk to my brother-in-law here about the work you do, and the impact we want the trust to have. He's moving home to Wales, so I'm hoping he can help us raise our profile—but that means he has to know what he's talking about.'

Ryan frowned, and twisted to face her, speaking in an undertone. 'I didn't sign up for some medical crash course, Gwen. I know about head injuries—every rugby player does. And even if they didn't, I saw what happened to George.'

It hadn't just been the head injury, of course, although that had been the scariest part. It had been the damage to his arm and shoulder that had put an end to his rugby career. If a player couldn't catch a ball reliably, he was no good out on the field. And George's range of movement had been so limited by his injury, no one had seriously believed he could play again.

'Did you?' Anita asked, her eyebrows raised under her dark, curly hair. 'You saw him unconscious, yes? But I imagine that once he awoke, you assumed he was back to normal again?'

Beside him, Gwen stiffened slightly, but before Ryan could figure out what had triggered her reaction the doctor was talking again.

'I see more than my share of rugby players here, and most of them seem to feel that taking five minutes off the pitch for the head injury assessment is more than adequate for protecting players. It isn't.'

'Most of us *do* know that,' Ryan put in. 'There just isn't much we can do about it.'

Frustration coloured Anita's expression. 'Well, there *should* be. Even a mild concussion has serious consequences. Repeated concussions, not to mention more severe head injuries…' She shook her head. 'The list of effects is too long for me to list them all. But let's start with the possibility of severe brain damage, affecting neurocognitive deficits, and work backwards through delusions, weakness of limbs, loss of co-ordination, personality changes, aggression, convulsions, slurred speech, confusion, amnesia—'

'Okay, okay. I get it,' Ryan said. 'Brain injuries aren't something to be taken lightly. That's why Gwen is trying to raise money for people who suffer them, right?'

'It's a life-changing injury,' Gwen said softly. 'In so many ways, and for everyone around the person. People need support—and I want to give it to them.'

That darkness was back behind her eyes. How hard had it been for her, supporting George's recovery, looking after Evie, dealing with their parents…? Ryan had been back on the plane to France as soon as they'd known that George would live. But now he wondered: had his brother been more affected by his injuries than he knew? And how?

Having to give up the career he loved must have been impossibly hard for George. But dealing with a body that wouldn't do what he wanted? Ryan knew from past injuries how frustrating that could be too.

But he'd had Gwen to support him. Not everyone could be that lucky. George had always been the lucky one. But had Gwen?

'Then I want to help you.' Ryan held her gaze, and she nodded. Then he turned back to the doctor. 'Okay. I'm listening. What else do I need to know?'

Three days later, Gwen fastened the diamond necklace that George had given her the day he'd got called up for the Lions tour around her neck, then sighed at her reflection in the mirror of her hotel room.

She looked tired. She knew she looked tired, and there

was only so much that concealer could do. George's parents had mentioned it when she'd dropped Evie off for her sleepover. And that meant that Ryan was bound to notice, and comment on it. Her brother-in-law had never had much in the way of tact.

But what was she supposed to tell him? *I can't sleep because I'm having nightmares about you and your brother.*

Except that wasn't technically true. However wildly inappropriate the dreams might be, she couldn't really classify them as nightmares.

They'd started the day Ryan had come back into her life, and they'd only intensified with every extra minute they spent together. As if he was worming his way into her subconscious somehow.

The first night she'd dreamt of the day they'd met—that Cardiff bar she'd visited with friends. Ryan had burst across the room to sit with her, flirt with her, before getting distracted by a tray of shots his friend had been offering and wandering off again. He'd been a whirlwind of charm and good looks and the kind of smile that had made things inside her melt—but even then Gwen had never considered him anything but a few minutes' entertainment on a night out.

In reality, George had approached her moments later, apologising for his brother's lack of manners. He'd bought her a drink, they'd talked all evening—and the rest was history.

Her dreams didn't seem to accept that, though. In her dreams it wasn't George who came over but this new Ryan, returned from France, older and steadier—and, she had to admit, even hotter than he'd been as a careless young twenty-year-old.

The first few nights she'd woken up when she'd realised the man sitting down with her wasn't George.
Then one night she hadn't. And after that the dreams
had changed.

Now, when she dreamt, she was always lying somewhere warm and cosy, firelight in the background, blankets around her. And she was naked. She blushed at the
memory. Always naked.

Then she'd feel someone behind her—someone who
made her feel safe, warm and loved. He'd run his hands
up over her bare skin, skirting over every inch of her sensitive body, his lips against her shoulder, her neck, her
ear. Her whole body would tremble with need as she'd
feel him hard against her lower back. *I need you,* she'd
whisper. And he'd comply.

His hands at her breasts, he'd push gently inside her,
filling her, making her whole body clench around him. As
they moved together, she'd feel everything in her growing tighter, closer…

And then, just before she reached her peak, she'd turn
to look at the man behind her. She'd twist and see the
dark hair, the blue eyes she knew so very well. *George.*
Then the firelight would flicker and she'd realise she
was wrong.

It was Ryan. It always turned out to be Ryan.

That shock woke her up, every time. She'd come to,
sitting upright in her bed, alone, her body tight with desperate want, cursing her unconscious brain.

Why? Why was she dreaming of *Ryan*?

She didn't want to give too much power, or meaning, to dreams. Ryan was almost a carbon copy of his
older brother—an inch or two shorter, perhaps, a little
broader in the shoulder, carrying a little more muscle.

His eyes sparkled with more amusement at the world than George's ever had, but otherwise they were alike enough to be confused on and off the pitch, unless a person could see their shirt number.

Maybe it just meant it had been too long since she'd had sex—with anybody. Maybe it meant she had a type—dark hair, blue eyes, built like a rugby player. Because since that very first night they'd met she knew she'd never looked at Ryan this way. Not once, when George had been alive.

But now, after these dreams, it was getting so much harder not to. Hard to remember him as her reckless, unreliable brother-in-law.

Especially since he'd been neither of those things since he'd returned.

Gwen didn't know quite *who* he was now. But she could at least admit to herself that she wanted to find out.

She took a deep breath, threaded the matching diamond earrings through her lobes, and gave herself one last smile in the mirror. Her caramel highlighted hair sat neatly against her collar bone, above the draping neckline of her gold evening dress.

She looked exactly like what she supposed she was. A wealthy widow looking to find a way to make a positive impact on the world. To matter. To provide her husband with the legacy she hoped he deserved.

She just didn't look all that much like Gwen Phillips, the woman she had been, before everything had changed. The woman she still hoped she was, inside.

Tonight was the night of the charity fundraiser she'd set up in conjunction with the hospital, and another charity focussing on head injuries. Gwen knew there was often competition between charities for donors and support, but in her mind as long as the money was getting to the people that needed it she was doing her job right. The George Phillips Trust was more about helping people than anything else, using the profile the name gave them to reach people who might not otherwise have engaged with the problem.

Ryan, at least, seemed engaged. She'd worried if she was doing the right thing, taking him to see Anita. If the doctor had let something slip, let on about the personality changes George had suffered…she didn't want Ryan burdened with that knowledge too. Let him remember his brother as he was—the golden, shining man they'd both loved.

But Anita had known what she was doing. She'd patiently taken him through the work she did, and some anonymous case studies of patients who'd suffered traumatic brain injuries of all levels, and with various effects. Ryan, to his credit, had listened attentively, nodding along and only speaking to ask insightful questions that provided more clarity. Even Gwen, who'd been studying the subject for years now, had felt more educated after the session.

'Okay,' he'd said, as Anita had brought things to an end so she could get back to her *actual* work. 'I get it. Well, I mean, I know I have a hell of a lot more to learn, but I understand the importance, I think. And I definitely want to help. So what can I do?'

'Well,' Anita had replied, 'we do need one more volunteer for our charity fundraiser.'

'I'll do it,' Ryan had agreed easily, apparently unaware of the mischievous look Anita had shot Gwen's way. Or the panic that had surged through Gwen at the very idea.

Still, neither of them had enlightened Ryan as to the actual nature of the fundraiser. Gwen figured she'd save that for when he was already there, and couldn't run away. He would, she had to admit, make the perfect addition to their bachelor auction line up.

But imagining that was when the dreams had changed from the bar to the fireside, damn it. Which was why Gwen had decided to blame Anita for the whole thing—even if she wasn't telling her friend about them. Or anyone else, for that matter.

There was a knock on the hotel-room door, and Gwen crossed to open it, with just one last glance at the mirror to check how bad the shadows under her eyes really looked.

'Hey, are you okay?' Ryan asked, the minute she opened the door. Which told her more than the mirror ever could.

'Just tired. Evie's been waking up at night. Nightmares, I think.' She felt bad lying to him, and worse for using her daughter as an excuse, but really it had to be better than confessing the truth, right?

I can't sleep because every time I close my eyes I imagine you naked.

Not a great conversation starter. At least, not when the subject of it was her brother-in-law.

However desperate her body apparently was for some physical human contact, Ryan was the last man she could consider asking to scratch that itch.

'Well, a glass of wine and a bit of a party should perk you right up.' Ryan offered her his arm. 'If you're ready, my lady.'

Gwen checked her room key in her clutch bag, then took his arm.

'So, what's my job tonight?' Ryan asked, as they waited for the elevator. 'Do you want me schmoozing the rich kids for donations? Or am I here as a cautionary tale about the risks of too many hits to the head playing rugby?'

Gwen winced. This was probably the time to tell about the bachelor auction, she supposed.

'Actually...' she started, but then the elevator door opened, revealing Anita Chowdhury in a gorgeous red and gold evening gown. She was accompanied by several women that Gwen recognised from hospital wards.

'Ah, here he is, ladies.' Anita reached out to grab Ryan's arm and yank him into the elevator. 'The star of our bachelor auction tonight.'

Ryan's eyebrows jumped towards his hairline. Gwen stepped into the elevator behind him and pressed the button for the lobby.

'Bachelor auction?' Ryan asked, his voice a little higher and squeakier than normal.

'I was about to tell you,' Gwen said. The elevator started to move as the other occupants began peppering Ryan with questions—about his rugby career, about France, and his relationship status.

He was out of the elevator the minute the doors opened again. Gwen turned to Anita and rolled her eyes. Anita just smirked.

'Oh, dear,' she said. 'I hope you brought your purse, Gwen. Looks like you might need to save our reluctant bachelor.'

Gwen looked towards Ryan, already most of the way to the bar and chatting with a selection of hangers-on she recognised from the rugby circuit. 'I think he can manage just fine on his own.'

'I'm sure he can,' Anita said. 'But I'm pretty certain

there's only one woman here he wants bidding on him tonight.'

Gwen jerked her head round to stare at her friend. 'What do you mean?'

'The way you look tonight? You can't tell me you haven't noticed the way he's been staring at you.'

'He thinks I look tired. Besides, we were in a tiny cramped elevator. Where else is he supposed to look?' But saying it didn't make Gwen forget the way his eyes had roamed over her dress as she'd answered the door. Or the way that every time she'd looked at him lately he'd always seemed to be looking back.

Maybe he was suffering from hugely inappropriate dreams too.

'Fine. Deny it if you want. But you can't tell me that man sat in my office and listened to the gory details of traumatic brain injuries for the sake of his own health.' Anita raised one perfectly arched eyebrow at her. 'Or even for his brother's memory. Trust me, Gwen, if he's doing this, he's doing it for you.'

Gwen shook her head. 'You're wrong. He's doing this for his family—or rather to get his family back. I'm just the means to an end.'

Then Ryan turned around and smiled at her, and Gwen felt all the same heat she remembered from her dreams flooding through her as his gaze locked onto hers.

Anita looked between them. 'Yeah. Of course he is.' She patted Gwen gently on the arm. 'You just keep telling yourself that. Now, let's go get a glass of nice, cold champagne. You look like you need cooling down.'

CHAPTER FOUR

A BACHELOR AUCTION. Of course.

Time was, Ryan would have seen this as an opportunity. A chance to bask in the attention of women who wanted him—rather than the one who didn't. Maybe even the chance to catch the eye of someone to take home for the night.

Today, though, there was only one woman he wanted bidding on him. And she categorically wasn't.

He was up fourth in a line-up of six. After him there was a reality TV star and a celebrity chef; before him a local councillor, a runner up from a TV talent show, a well-known business star and the best-looking surgeon the hospital had been able to talk into taking part. Which at least let Ryan know where he was in the scale of bid-dability.

Except all the others clearly had people in the crowd there to drive their bidding up. Ryan only had Gwen who, when it was his turn on stage, stood with her arms folded over her chest, staring at the auctioneer rather than him.

Great.

His monkey suit felt too tight around his neck, the bow-tie too flashy, the shirt too starched. He had a match to play tomorrow. He should be home preparing, resting. Not standing on stage being bid for like an expensive antique vase.

Except Gwen needed him to. So there he was.

'And next up we have a very special addition to our line-up!' The auctioneer—a woman in a tight black dress and skyscraper heels who seemed to be having far too much fun at their expense—flashed another naughty smile at the crowd. 'I'm sure all you rugby fans out there know who he is without introduction, but for the rest of you, let me introduce Ryan Phillips!' A smattering of applause—and a whoop Ryan suspected came from Anita Chowdhury.

'Ex-Wales player, he's been over in France playing his rugby for the last few years, but now he's back! And we were lucky enough to snag him before even the Welsh rugby team could.' She glanced down at her notes. 'Ryan says he likes sharing a bottle of wine by candlelight, nights out on the town, and going for a run on the beach.'

Ryan had most definitely never said any of those things. He suspected Gwen's hand behind those words. He shot her a look and found her, for once, looking at him—at least until she caught his eye and looked away rapidly.

'Shall we start the bidding at fifty pounds? Who will pay fifty for a night out with this fine gentleman?'

She wasn't entirely wrong either, Ryan mused, as the bidding started. He *did* like running on the beach—Gwen would have remembered that from back when he and George had trained together. And back then, a night out on the town had been the highlight of his week, even when George had turned them down because of training. She wouldn't know that he'd changed, in that respect. That he'd finally learned the lesson his brother had spent years trying to teach him—that if he wanted to be the best he had to give everything to the game, to his training. And that meant following the rules and sacrificing some fun sometimes.

But it was the first item on the list that interested him most. Sharing a bottle of wine by candlelight? He could almost imagine it now—that kind of private, intimate evening with Gwen. Had she been imagining it when she'd written that?

He sneaked another look at her. She was staring at her phone.

No. He couldn't let himself start hoping for that kind of attention from Gwen. She'd probably been thinking of George when she'd written it. She'd never even seen him drink wine.

Probably wouldn't now, given how rarely he drank anything alcoholic at all.

'And sold!' the auctioneer said. 'At one thousand, three hundred pounds, to the lady in the *beautiful* purple frock.'

Not a bad number, Ryan decided. More than the businessman had gone for, and the surgeon. He glanced over at the woman who'd won him, celebrating with her friends. He sighed. She was no Gwen, but for charity he could definitely manage a nice evening out for her. He'd have to go talk to her, find out what sort of thing she liked.

Then he was going to find Gwen.

The lady in purple—Rachel, it transpired—was an avid rugby fan.

'I mean, I loved your brother—God rest his soul—and I wish I'd got to meet him. But a night out with you is pretty great too!'

Of course. Had he ever been anything but a poor substitute for his brother?

'I'm looking forward to it too,' Ryan lied, with a smile. 'Now, why don't you let me have your number and I'll call to make plans soon. That way you can enjoy the rest of your evening with your friends.' He indicated the gaggle of giggling women behind her.

They giggled some more.

'Maybe we can all join you for your night out,' one of them suggested.

Rachel scowled. 'Not unless you want to pay your share!'

'I'll let you ladies decide this between yourselves,' Ryan said, and slipped away.

The ballroom of the hotel was decked out with lights and ribbons, along with some banners for the charity, and information tables. It certainly wasn't the swankiest or highest-profile fundraiser he'd ever been to, but it did at least have plenty of connections to and information on the cause it was raising money for. And it had Gwen, which made it hit his top ten automatically.

He found her loitering by an information stand, where Anita Chowdhury was talking at length with two attendees. He smiled as he recognised one of the two men—Joe and, he assumed, his husband.

Gwen didn't seem too involved in the conversation, though, so he figured he could wait and greet Joe and Ben later. He wanted to talk to her alone first.

Moving behind her, he touched one hand to Gwen's waist. She flinched.

Swallowing his disappointment at her reaction, Ryan said, 'Come get a drink with me?'

She nodded, and together they moved towards the bar

outside the ballroom on the other side of the hotel lobby. It was quieter there, and he'd noticed she preferred that these days. Even in the crowded ballroom, at a fundraiser she'd organised, she'd clung to the walls.

Presumably that was why she needed people like him involved. To talk to donors when she wouldn't.

'So,' he said, as she hopped up onto the stool at the farthest end of the bar, 'apparently I'm having dinner with Rachel in the purple dress, and possibly several of her friends, soon. She'd have preferred George, she tells me, but under the circumstances it seems that I'll do.'

Gwen looked down at the bar, but he could tell that she was smiling. 'Sorry.'

'No, you're not,' he challenged. 'You think it's hilarious.' Because it *was* hilarious, in lots of ways.

Or it would be, if it were happening to somebody else.

She peeked up from under her eyelashes, and he saw amusement dancing in her eyes. Good. At least he could still make her laugh, that was something.

'I hope it's not too awful,' she said.

Ryan shrugged. 'I'll have been on worse dates, I'm sure.'

They ordered drinks—gin and tonic for her, an alcohol-free beer for him—and waited for the bartender to move away again before they started talking.

'So you're not too cross with me for offering you up as a sacrifice to the auction gods and goddesses?' Gwen took a sip of her drink.

'I never could stay cross with you,' he admitted.

She flashed him a quick smile. 'I'd have thought that dozens of beautiful women bidding for your time and your body was basically your dream, isn't it?'

'It might have been once,' Ryan admitted. 'But I'm not the same man I was when I left Wales, you know.'

The smile slipped away from her face as she looked up at him. 'No,' she said, thoughtfully. 'I don't think you are, are you?'

His heartbeat stuttered at her words. Did she really believe that?

He knew she hadn't thought it when they'd first met again. She'd assumed he'd be exactly the same Ryan who'd left them all behind years ago.

Ryan hoped—knew—that he'd changed. But knowing it wasn't the same as other people believing it. But if Gwen believed, maybe others could too.

Maybe even his parents.

His mother had never been able to see past the golden boy George to notice *him*—not really. And the more he'd gone out of his way to *make* her pay him attention, the less he'd been the son she'd wanted at all. He'd seen that, finally, even if it had taken him a while.

But things were different now. Weren't they? *He* was different.

'Moving to France, it gave me a chance to re-evaluate a lot of things.' Ryan toyed with the neck of his beer bottle. He wondered if she'd even noticed the zero per cent alcohol label. Probably not. People, in his experience, seemed to see exactly what they expected to see. Quitting drinking almost completely was just one more change he'd made to try and become the man he wanted to be. Focussed on his training, sharp of mind. Not to mention the fact that the hangovers got more killer the older he got. 'I mean, I didn't speak the language, I was in a strange country where I didn't know anybody. Kind of gave me a lot of time to think, you know?'

'I know.' Gwen stared down at her drink. 'In some ways… It was the same after George's accident, and again after he died. More so after the funeral. In between there was so much to deal with—hospital appointments, physio exercises, helping Evie understand what was going on. And even after his death there was the funeral to arrange, newspapers banging on the door, and the police investigation. But once that was all over… It was just me, and Evie, and your parents, trying to figure out how to live now. Friends didn't know what say, so they didn't say anything at all. And you weren't here…'

'I'm sorry about that.' Ryan reached across the table and grabbed her hand. 'If it had happened before I moved to France, maybe it would have changed things. But I was committed, I had contracts, obligations. And I was building a new life for myself.'

Gwen's gaze flickered up to meet his. 'Your mother thought it must be a woman keeping you over there, you know?'

Ryan barked a laugh. The sad thing was, in a way his mother was right. Except he hadn't been running back to a woman in France. He'd been running away from what he couldn't have, right here in Wales.

He dropped Gwen's hand.

One he still couldn't have.

She was so close right now, anyone watching them must think they were couple—or at least on their way to becoming one. If this were a date he'd lean across the table and tuck her hair behind her ear. He'd speak softly so she'd move closer to hear. He'd angle his head just right so all she had to do was move in and they'd be kissing.

And for a moment, sitting there, he could almost believe that she would.

Maybe. One day. Soon?

No. He couldn't let his hopes rise that way, even if she gave him cause. Gwen belonged to George and she always would. He could handle being a poor second prize to his brother for Rachel in the purple dress.

It would break him to be that consolation price for Gwen. He couldn't even let himself consider it. The temptation—to be anything she wanted, even a George substitute if it meant he got to touch her, kiss her, stay in her life—was too great. And he'd worked too hard to be his own person.

He couldn't give that up now just because his heart stopped when she smiled at him.

Ryan picked up his beer and got to his feet. 'Come on. We're missing the party.' He was done tormenting himself with things he couldn't have.

Gwen fastened Evie's coat right to the top, then shoved her own hands in her pockets. The stadium might be packed, but it was still freezing in the cold March wind. Beside her, she could hear Meredith muttering about why they had to be there. Gwen didn't think they'd been to a rugby match since George's accident, although she knew they still watched them all on the telly. George's accident might have been career ending, but as far as they were concerned it hadn't been the cause of his death. Rugby was rugby, and nothing would change that for them.

However differently she might feel about the repercussions of that accident, Gwen couldn't deny the thrill that still went through her as she saw the teams running out from the tunnel. Ryan's first match starting for his new team, the Selkies. It seemed as good a time as any to reintroduce him to his parents.

She'd never fully understood the relationship between

Ryan and his parents—especially his mother. Over the years when Ryan had still lived in Wales, Meredith had cried and despaired of her youngest son's exploits, and the disrepute he'd brought on the family name. Gwen would have thought that Ryan taking his bad behaviour and reputation overseas would be a good thing, in some ways—but it had only made Meredith more furious.

Gwen remembered asking George about it at the time, but he'd only shrugged, his own anger with his brother still raw.

'He's supposed to be here, with us,' he'd said simply. *'He's part of the team. His place is out there on the pitch with me.'*

She'd known what he'd meant by that. Ryan's job on the team was setting up tries for George to score, turning over the ball then passing it to his brother to take the glory. They had worked so well together, in perfect synchronicity. Always had.

But how had it felt for Ryan to always be the one in the background? To be the disappointment, the black sheep? She'd always thought he'd revelled in it a bit. But now, seeing the man he'd become outside his brother's shadow, she wondered.

She had missed him, of course, while he'd been away. As she and George had become serious about each other, Ryan had been a big part of her life, along with his parents. He was the younger brother who'd steal extra pudding with her after Sunday lunch, who she'd find asleep on their sofa after a team night out. He'd made a great cooked breakfast, and had always had time to listen to her over a cup of tea when she'd been worried about George, or Evie, or anything.

He'd gone out and bought an 'I have the world's best

uncle' onesie for Evie, the day they'd told him they were expecting. He'd always, always been there, and she'd felt the loss of him desperately when he'd gone away.

But she'd never been angry about it. It wasn't her place to make choices for him after all. She had no hold over Ryan, never had. And neither did anyone else.

Even after George's accident, after Ryan's flying visit home, she'd not been angry. There had been nights when she'd wished, desperately, that he was still there—that she could call him to come round for a cup of tea and offload everything onto his broad shoulders. That he could come back and be the brother he'd always been to them, part of the team.

But as George's behaviour had become more erratic, angrier and even more hurtful, part of her had been glad Ryan hadn't been there to see it.

'There's Uncle Ryan!' Evie shouted now. Around them, people turned to see who had a relative out there on the pitch. Meredith looked a little flustered and embarrassed, but Ryan's dad stood a little straighter, a little prouder. Having a rugby player in the family, especially a professional one, still meant an awful lot here in Wales.

'I can see him,' Gwen said to her daughter.

'Do you think if I wave he'll see me?' Evie asked.

Gwen looked around at the crowds. It wasn't like an international match, where every seat was filled with fans singing and chanting, but there was still a decent crowd here to see the boys play. 'You can try, but Uncle Ryan has to focus on his game.'

Behind her, Gwen heard a man snigger and mutter, 'Can't see why he'd start now, when he never bothered before. Don't know why the coach signed him.' Apparently Ryan's reputation as a wild card still carried around here.

Gwen's jaw tightened as she resisted the urge to respond, to tell the guy he didn't know what he was talking about.

Even before he'd left for France, Ryan had cared about his rugby. He might not have had the dedication of his brother or the single-minded focus his coach would have liked, but he'd cared. And since he'd come back, well, even Gwen had to admit he seemed to have grown up a lot. Just talking to him last night at the fundraiser had shown her that. He genuinely wanted to help her with the trust, and was dedicated enough to learn, to listen, and even to date Rachel in the purple dress.

It had shown her other things too, but Gwen wasn't thinking about those right now. Definitely not that moment when she'd thought, for a second, that he'd been about to kiss her.

That way madness lay.

Better to focus on the game ahead of them. And how she was going to reconcile Ryan with his parents afterwards.

Meredith had been reluctant when she'd suggested meeting Ryan for lunch after the match, but Dylan had agreed for both of them—one of the few times in Gwen's memory that he'd made a decision without deferring to his wife first. That gave her hope. Even if Meredith was still angry with Ryan—an anger Gwen didn't fully understand—at least his father seemed open to a reconciliation.

As long as the right Ryan showed up for lunch. That was her main concern. The man she'd got to know again since his return was ready to mend fences and fix the broken relationship—and she had faith he could do it. But there had always been something about the relationship between Ryan and his mother that brought out the worst in him. She'd seen it too often at family dinners over the years before he'd left. Meredith would say something to needle him—usually comparing him to George—and Ryan would blow up. They'd argue—or, more often, he'd drain his wine glass and head straight out after dinner to the pub, or a club, or somewhere else his mother wouldn't approve of.

Would Ryan be able to hold onto his new, grown-up persona in the face of the one person who'd always, always got under his skin?

That last question distracted Gwen through a lot of the game. She was always torn watching rugby matches anyway, braced for something terrible to happen at the same time as her blood heated and she felt the excitement coursing through her body. And this, from what she could focus on, was a great game. By half-time, even the guy behind her who'd mocked Gwen's words about Ryan seemed to be rethinking his stance—especially after Ryan put the ball over the line for his team's second try.

'I guess he learned some new tricks, playing in France,' the guy said, as he headed to the bar for another pint. 'Might be worth having after all.'

Gwen grinned. If a random stranger could be convinced of Ryan's worth on the pitch, hopefully his parents could be convinced of the same off it.

The second half flew by, as Ryan's team—the Selkies—slipped past their opponents' defence again and again. Evie cheered every time her uncle caught the ball and ran with it, which seemed to be more than anyone else on the pitch. He didn't score any more tries, but, from what Gwen could see, he was instrumental in helping others score them all.

And when, after the final whistle blew, Ryan was dragged onto camera by a TV interviewer, appearing on the large screen, a huge cheer went up through the whole stadium.

'Well!' the interviewer said, as the noise started to abate. 'That was quite a welcome back to Wales, Ryan. How does it feel to be home again?'

He must have known where they were sitting, Gwen realised. Because, as he answered, he looked up directly at them.

'It's great to be back where I belong,' he said, still out of breath from the match. On the screen, Gwen could see sweat dripping down his neck, his dark hair even darker than normal with wetness. His kit was muddy and grass-stained, he had white strapping wrapped around his right thigh, but his smile was jubilant. 'Home with the people I love, especially.'

And in that moment, just for a second, Gwen was sure, so sure, that he was only looking at her.

Ryan ducked out of the interview before the pundit could ask him, inevitably, about George. He wanted to ride this high a bit longer, before the post-game crash hit. His brother would always be a part of his life, his soul—his missing piece now. He'd never had it in him to resent George for being the player, the man, he could never quite be. His big brother had always been his idol, and walking away from playing beside him had been one of the hardest things he'd ever done.

But George was gone, and Ryan needed to think about the future, not the past. *His* future.

Right now, he was on top of the world. He'd proved he deserved the place on the team, had made a great enough showing to put him in serious contention for the national team again, and hopefully to quieten some of the critics who'd been posting on social media, complaining about his signing.

He'd proved to Gwen, he hoped, that he wasn't the same man he'd been when he'd left for France. And that, maybe, he could be part of her family again. An uncle to Evie. A friend to her if she needed it—and somehow he suspected she did.

Most importantly, right now, he hoped he'd made his parents proud of him again. Maybe proud enough to forgive him for the way they'd left things at George's funeral.

He rode that high into the changing rooms, through the throng of celebrating teammates, showering and changing and preparing to celebrate.

'Great game, mate.'

'Good to have you back!'

'Nice to have someone competent at my side again.'

The compliments and back slaps felt good, of course they did. But today was bigger than any game of rugby.

Ryan showered quickly, and shrugged off requests to join the others down the pub to celebrate.

'Sorry, I need to go find my family,' he told them, hoping his grin didn't give him away too much.

His parents. For the first time in two years he'd see his parents.

And Gwen and Evie. No wonder he was grinning like a mad thing.

Everything was going to be okay.

Gwen had booked them a table for an early dinner at a gastro pub nearby, one that must have sprung up while he'd been overseas but which Gwen seemed familiar with. He'd told her that he'd meet them there, not wanting them to have to hang around at the grounds for him to shower and change. Now it meant that he got to observe them all together, a family, before they realised he had arrived.

They were sitting at a long table in the window, brittle late-March sunshine lighting them up through the glass. He took a moment to watch them, unobserved, and take in the changes—especially in his parents.

They looked older—that was his first thought. Much older than the mere couple of years that had passed should have made them. The sort of older that came with losing a child, he supposed—even if that child had been a grown man.

No one was supposed to outlive their children.

Guilt clutched at his chest, not for the first time, as he thought again that he should have been there for them all. To support them, grieve with them. Even if they hadn't wanted him there.

But despite everything, they looked happy now. He watched as his father made a cloth napkin do tricks for Evie, giving up pennies and sweets when it should have been empty. He'd done the same for him and George. Ryan remembered spending days trying to figure out how the trick was done.

Even his mother looked contented, watching their antics, sipping her wine, and making conversation with Gwen. If he hadn't known her so well, he probably wouldn't have noticed the tension in her shoulders, or the way her gaze darted around the pub anxiously once or twice.

Time to make himself known.

He stepped forward, out of the shadows, and Gwen looked up instantly, as if she were attuned to him.

'Ryan.' She smiled, gentle and soft, and he felt his

heart contract at the sight. *Friends*, he reminded himself. *Family.* That was what this was all about. Nothing more.

Then his legs got rugby tackled and, taken by surprise, he actually had to take a step backwards.

'Uncle Ryan!' Evie yelled against his kneecaps. 'You came!'

'Of course I came!' He knelt down to give her a proper hug. 'I said I would, didn't I?'

'Yes, but…' She cast a worried glance back towards her grandmother. 'Nain said not to get my hopes up,' she whispered. 'She said you were…' her nose crinkled up as she tried to find the word '…unreliable.'

'Of course she did,' Ryan muttered. Because he had been. The man he had been would have had a fifty-fifty shot of showing up for this lunch, depending on what other offers he got. His mother wasn't wrong.

But that she'd said it to Evie still hurt. Was Mum even going to give him a chance? Or was her mind made up already?

Well, if it was, it was up to him to change it. That was something else he'd forced himself to learn in France. Grit.

This mattered. So he wouldn't give up. Not ever.

Straightening up to stand again, he took Evie's hand and crossed to the table. Gwen was already standing, and reached over to hug him.

'You were fantastic out there today,' she said, as he re-sisted the urge to hold her against him for the rest of the day. *Just friends.* 'What an incredible match! The Selkies must be thrilled to have you home again.'

She pulled away, and he felt the loss of her warmth and her support instantly.

'Yeah, I think they're pretty happy,' he said. Then he

turned to the other occupants of the table. 'Mum. Dad. It's wonderful to see you. Thanks for coming.'

His mouth was too dry; it was hard to get the words out. He meant it, every word, but he still worried it came out sarcastically or wrong somehow. His parents exchanged a glance, and Ryan felt a squeeze on his hand. Evie, giving him *her* support, even if she didn't really know why he needed it—he was certain Gwen wouldn't have told the little girl the story of his falling out with his family. But she was a perceptive little thing. And she, at least, was happy to have him there. That counted for a lot.

After too long a pause, his father stepped forward. Dylan Phillips was still tall, still more slender than either of his rugby-playing sons had ever been, and still smiling.

'Ryan. It's good to see you, son.' The knot in Ryan's stomach started to loosen as his father reached out to shake his hand, and pat his shoulder. From him, that was an emotional welcome, Ryan knew. One he'd take happily.

'It's good to be home. I missed you all.' He turned to his mother. 'Mum.'

'Ryan.' She nodded her head stiffly, but didn't get up. 'Sit down. You must be hungry after that match, and this place takes for ever to serve the food.'

Ryan allowed himself a small smile as he sat. It might not sound like much, but if his mum was worried about his stomach, that was the first step back to normality. She might make Dad do the cooking, but she had always been concerned about his and George's appetites, and whether they were eating enough to offset all the training and exercise they did. It was one small area in which both brothers had been even in their mother's eyes.

It wasn't much, but he'd take it.

Sitting down, with Evie on one side of him and Gwen on the other, facing his parents on the opposite side of the table, Ryan reached for the menu. His mother was right: as always after a match, Ryan was starving so he ordered the full Sunday roast without hesitation. Evie, he noticed, asked for the same—even when Gwen pointed out she didn't actually like roast beef.

'Maybe I do now,' she said defiantly, and Gwen ordered her the kids' portion.

'And a drink for you, sir?' the waitress asked.

'Just an orange juice, please,' he replied, trying not to feel self-conscious. The other adults all had wine, of course. But he'd worked too hard to backslide into old habits now.

'No beer?' his mother asked, one eyebrow raised. 'Even George would have a pint after a match.'

Ryan shrugged. 'Didn't fancy it.' But Gwen, he realised, was watching him carefully.

Conversation over lunch was stilted, with Gwen desperately trying to keep things flowing. But it was progress. He knew that whenever his mother gave him a certain look she was remembering the funeral—probably remembering the words he'd thrown at her, carelessly, hurtfully and, yes, drunkenly.

'I was never just here on earth to play back-up to my brother! Why couldn't you let me be my own person too? Why is this my fault? I wasn't even there!'

'Exactly,' his mother had replied. *'You should have been there. You left us. And you know that if you'd been there none of this would ever have happened.'*

It had been building ever since the accident, and the funeral had pushed them all over the edge. The worst part was knowing that she was right. On the field and off it, he and George had always looked out for each other. George might have been the one to shine brightest, their golden boy, but he'd needed Ryan there for back-up too. They'd trained together, played together, gone out together... And George had looked out for him too. Making sure he got home after a wild night out— or at least as far as George and Gwen's sofa. Defending him to the coach, and other players, when they'd said Ryan wasn't committed to rugby the way he needed to be. Helping him make sure he was in shape for a game when he'd been slacking off.

George had been his best friend, his whole life. Even when Ryan knew he'd never make it out of his shadow if he stayed.

So he'd left, and George had died. And their mother blamed him.

But now they had to try and come back from that. To build a family again.

'So, how was playing in France different to playing here in Wales, Ryan?' his father asked casually, as they waited for the food.

Rugby. Common ground, and about as neutral as they were going to get. Ryan jumped on the question and answered at length. One question led to another—about France as a country, the people, the places he'd been.

'And is there anybody special waiting for you over there?' Meredith didn't exactly smile as she asked the question, but it *was* the first she'd asked herself. That counted for something. And apparently meant that Gwen was right—she thought he'd left for a woman.

'No,' Ryan said, carefully not looking at Gwen for fear that his eyes would give too much away. 'I was focussing on my rugby almost entirely. Well, that and learning the language. And a charity I was involved in, helping dis-advantaged kids get involved in sport.'

'Really?' Gwen asked. 'Tell me more about that. Maybe there are some ideas we can use at the trust.'

Ryan smiled. Perhaps there was a place for him here, after all. 'What do you want to know?'

After lunch, his parents said their goodbyes outside the front of the pub—a stilted hug from his mother and an-other handshake from his dad. They took Evie off to-wards the car—with the promise of stopping at the playground on the way—giving him a moment alone with Gwen.

'Thank you,' he said. 'For organising this.'

'I'm sorry.' Gwen sighed. 'I'd hoped your mother would be more…'

'Not like Mum?' he finished for her. Taking her hand in his, he turned her to face him. 'It's okay, Gwen. I know my parents. This was always going to be a long road back. But you've helped me to make a start, and that's all I could have asked for.'

She looked up then, her gaze locking on his and mak-ing his heart beat just that little bit faster. 'That's all you wanted from me?'

God, no. He wanted everything. Anything she'd give him. He wanted her close, always. He wanted to hold her at night. He wanted to kiss her, right now…

But she could never know that.

'No.' The denial came out as a hoarse whisper.

'Then what? What else did you come back for, Ryan?'

He couldn't look away from her eyes. In his mind, he imagined swaying closer, an arm around her waist, hauling her against him to kiss her, long and deep and everything…

Everything he couldn't have.

'I want… I want us to be friends again. The way we were before I left. I know… I know I wasn't here when you needed me. When George got hurt, or even after he died. I wasn't here for you or Evie, because I needed to be somewhere else. I needed to go away and become the person you need in your life, as your friend.'

Just friends. That was what he had to focus on. He had to protect himself from the way she made him feel. He could never be George for her, he knew that better than anybody. Even if she wanted him—and he had no evidence that she did—he couldn't let himself fall.

He'd dragged himself out of George's shadow once, made himself the person he wanted to be.

He couldn't risk slipping again now.

'I could… I could really use a friend, as it happens,' Gwen said.

Ryan smiled. 'Then you have one.'

CHAPTER FIVE

GWEN HURRIED ACROSS the road to the playground, praying that Evie and her in-laws hadn't been watching that last interlude between her and Ryan. Although, really, what would they have seen? Nothing had happened. Nothing consequential.

He'd asked for them to be friends again, that was all.

So why did it feel more important than that?

Why had it felt, for just a moment, like he'd been about to kiss her?

She shook her head to banish the thought. It was just those dreams, getting to her. Knowing every night that she'd see Ryan in her sleep. Kissing her. Touching her. Making love to her.

It was driving her insane.

He wanted to be friends, that was all. And that was all she wanted too.

It was absolutely the best thing for both of them.

But that look in his eye…

If they were going to be friends, she needed to get these ridiculous thoughts and dreams about Ryan out of her head. Time to be brutally honest with herself, and face the facts. All the reasons that thinking about Ryan this way was just insane.

Which meant she needed a friend who'd hold her to account and make her do that.

Pulling her phone from her pocket, she texted Joe.

Come over tonight? I need wine and sensible conversation. Just had lunch with Ryan and his parents.

He'd understand enough of the undertones of that without her having to explain—even if she expected that the dream part would come as a bit of a surprise. Unless she'd been far less subtle than she imagined.

Having retrieved Evie from the playground, they waved goodbye to Dylan and Meredith, and Gwen allowed herself to relax just a little. Ryan was right, it was a small first step, but nobody had stormed out, no one had shouted, and everyone had been basically civil. That was all they could have asked for today.

By the time they reached home, it was almost time for Evie's bath and bedtime. Gwen answered the door to Joe as Evie splashed around in her bath, serving bubbly pretend coffee in plastic teacups.

'Come in,' she said. 'You're just in time to help with bedtime stories.'

'As long as you don't want me to do lullabies,' Joe said, handing her a bottle of white wine, already chilled. 'She didn't enjoy my rendition of "Bread of Heaven" last time.'

'I'll do the lullabies, if you pour the wine.'

It took a while to get Evie settled after such an exciting day, and Gwen could hear her daughter telling Joe all about lunch with Uncle Ryan, when she should have been listening to her story. Still, eventually she was asleep, and Gwen could settle down on the sofa with Joe and a glass of that chilled white wine, and try to unpack all her thoughts about the day.

'So, lunch with Ryan and his parents. That must have been interesting.' Joe knew all about the estrangement between Ryan and his parents. Even if he hadn't acted as her confidant the last couple of years, he'd been there at the funeral, right at the end of the week when Ryan and Meredith had let slip the careful control they had all tried to show over the last hours, days, and weeks. When everything they had both not been saying ever since George's accident, or even long before that, had come out in the worst possible way.

'Actually, everyone was surprisingly well behaved.' She remembered how the afternoon had almost ended, and felt the heat flood to her cheeks. 'Well, mostly.' Apart from her imagination.

Joe raised his eyebrows over his wineglass as he took a sip. 'Mostly? Let me guess, Ryan had one too many beers with with meal and said something he shouldn't.'

'Ryan drank orange juice at lunch.' Gwen met Joe's eyes, knowing he'd understand how unusual that was, especially after a match, and one the team had won, as well.

'Because he was trying to impress his parents, or you?' Joe asked, his question right on the nose as usual.

Gwen sighed. 'I wish I knew. Both, maybe? You know, I don't think I've seen him actually drink since he came home. And he's trying so hard with Evie, and with his parents. He didn't start anything with his mother at lunch. Add to that everything he is doing to help me with the trust… He's not the Ryan I remember.'

'And isn't that a good thing?' Joe said. 'Sounds to me like George's little brother has grown up.'

'Maybe. I just can't shake the feeling that...' She trailed off, unable to find the words.

'That he's trying too hard?' Joe guessed.

'That he's trying to be George.' Gwen looked down at her glass, swirling the wine around, watching it cling to the sides. 'There was a moment today when I thought... I honestly thought he was about to kiss me. That's crazy, right? Then he told me he wanted us to be friends again. Like we used to be. Except...everything feels different this time round.'

That made Joe put down his glass on the coffee table and lean forward with interest. 'Okay, now this is getting better. I wondered at you calling me over here just because you'd had lunch with the family. Clearly, you've been holding out on me since Ryan came home. Tell me everything.'

So she did. Hands covering her face for most of it, Gwen recounted everything that had led up to the kiss that wasn't that afternoon—including a rather redacted version of her dreams.

'Hmm.' Joe leaned back against the sofa, his arm flung along the back of the cushions, wearing his thinking face. Gwen knew that face, and knew that her friend wouldn't speak again until he'd marshalled all his thoughts, worked through the options and reached his own conclusions on how best to help her.

So, in the meantime, she topped up their wine glasses.

'The way I see it,' he said, eventually, 'there are three questions here.'

'Only three?' Gwen quipped.

Joe ignored her. 'The first is: did you want him to kiss you and were you disappointed when he didn't? No, don't bother answering that one. I can see from your bright red cheeks that you did. So let's move on to the second: why do you believe that it's a bad thing? Because that's just as obvious from the way you called me over here in a panic.'

Gwen sighed. 'I'd have thought the reasons were obvious too.' Putting down her glass, she ticked them off on her fingers. 'One, I have absolutely no evidence he's even interested in me. It could all be in my head, just my dreams messing with me. He said he wanted to be friends, that's all. Two, he's my brother-in-law. His family would hate the idea of the two of us getting involved. Three, it would be super confusing for Evie. Four, it feels like betraying George, even after everything, and even now he's gone. And five…' She trailed off.

'You think he only wants you to prove he can be as good as George.' Joe completed the thought for her. 'That's what you mean when you said he was trying to be George, right?'

Gwen nodded mutely.

'Hmm,' Joe said, again, unhelpfully.

'You think so too, then?' Gwen asked.

'Oh, hell, no.' Joe flashed her a smile. 'Gwen, the way Ryan looks at you—the way he looked at you when you were still married to his brother, for that matter— I'd never say he only wanted you to prove he could be as good as George. That man adores you, and wants you, don't question that.'

The way he looked at her? *Did* he look at her that way? Anita had said the same thing, but Gwen hadn't let herself believe it.

'But?' There was always a but, wasn't there?

'But that doesn't mean he doesn't *also* want to prove that.'

Gwen slumped back on the sofa. 'I knew I was right.'

'No, listen to me.' Moving closer, Joe put a finger under her chin and forced her to look at him. 'The man wants you. And I reckon you want him too. Otherwise this wouldn't be getting to you this way.'

Biting the inside of her cheek, Gwen searched for words to articulate her feelings, and failed. They were too confusing, there were too many of them, racing around her brain like players on a rugby pitch, all chasing the same ball—her decision on what to do next.

'I… It's like there's something drawing me to him, all the time. I thought it would be awkward, him being back here, after everything that happened with his parents. But I don't think I realised how much I… God, how much I missed just having him here. Just coming around for a cup of tea, or showing up for breakfast. Ryan was the one who always, always listened to me, you know? He *was* my friend, and I *do* want that back. It's just…'

'You're looking at him differently now,' Joe finished for her.

Gwen nodded. She'd assumed it was just his similarity to George, to start with. She had a type, it seemed.

But George…he hadn't been the man she'd fallen in love with, at the end. After Ryan had left, that was when things had started to go really wrong. More arguments. More nights alone. Then the accident, and the brain injury that had turned him into another person altogether…

George had been changed by circumstances beyond his control. Ryan… He wouldn't even need the head injury. All it would take was for him to give up his attempts to mimic his brother's golden ways, and he'd be back to the Ryan she remembered—drinking too much, a new woman every week, taking nothing in life seriously. Everything George had become after his accident.

Gwen couldn't deny that the Ryan who had come home again had changed, for the better. But she knew how easily people could change again. Would Ryan keep up his good behaviour if he didn't get picked for Wales? If he got injured, like George had?

Once he'd proved he could have everything George had, would he stop trying? Or would he even leave again?

She couldn't risk that. Not for herself, and certainly not for Evie.

It was safer to keep things as friends, just like Ryan had said. Especially for her heart.

'I guess you have a decision to make,' Joe said, his expression serious as he looked down at her. 'You need to decide if it's worth the risk to talk to Ryan about this. To see if there's something there between you.'

She met his gaze with her own troubled one. 'I don't see how it can be.'

She just wished that realisation didn't make her heart ache so much.

Two steps forward, one step back, that was how life seemed to Ryan.

Every time he thought he was getting somewhere—bonding with Evie, making small talk with his parents, winning a rugby match, overcoming his primal instincts and agreeing to be friends with Gwen—the universe would do something to knock him back again. Like Gwen cancelling their plans to get together on Sunday.

Well, the universe clearly hadn't been paying enough attention to his form on the rugby pitch, or it would know that the worse the tackle, the more determined he became to get back to his feet and score the next try.

The try, in this case, would be getting Gwen to answer

his calls—which she had steadfastly been refusing to do since the text she sent telling him their Sunday plans were off.

Friends answered the phone when friends called, right? Or at least responded to their text messages. Even messaging her about fundraising for the trust hadn't garnered him a response.

She was *definitely* avoiding him. And he needed to know why.

After four days he caved in, and sought advice from the one person who might be able to tell him what was going through Gwen's brain.

'Oh, no.' Joe said, as he exited the studios where he recorded his weekly rugby round-up radio show. Ryan hadn't had his address or his phone number, but finding out when he'd be at the studios had been a very minor piece of detective work—he'd just asked a mate who'd been interviewed on the show the week before. 'I'm not doing this.'

'Doing what?' Ryan asked innocently. 'I just wondered if you'd like to grab a pint, or something. For old times' sake.'

Joe eyed him suspiciously, then sighed. 'Fine. But I thought you were on the wagon.'

Ryan shrugged. 'Let's say I've learned the fine art of moderation.'

That earned a barked laugh from Joe. 'I'll believe it when I see it.'

'That's the idea,' Ryan mumbled.

Joe knew a pub around the corner, so they headed there. Ryan pulled his wallet out as they approached the bar.

'What're you having?' he asked, as he signalled for the barman's attention.

'Pint of bitter, thanks.'

'Why don't you find us a table?' Ryan suggested, and when he joined Joe at the table a few minutes later he pretended he didn't see the older man's raised eyebrows at the zero per cent label on Ryan's beer bottle.

Joe took a long pull of his pint, then put the glass down. 'So. You want to talk about Gwen.'

'However did you guess?' Ryan asked, dryly.

'Because all *she's* been wanting to talk about this week is *you*.' Joe shook his head. 'I hope you both realise that just because I'm gay it doesn't mean I want to act as your own personal agony aunt.'

'That's not why we turn to you,' Ryan told him.

'Oh?' Joe steepled his fingers as he rested his elbows on the table. 'Enlighten me.'

'We come to you because you've got it all figured out. Life, I mean. You're happy, you're married, you're in love.'

'Gwen had all those things once too,' Joe pointed out.

Ryan held back a wince as he peeled the edge of the label away from his bottle. 'Yeah. But now she's alone again.' And he hated that. Hated seeing her so quiet, clinging to the edges of any crowd, working so hard in the background for the trust but letting others—and especially George's name—take the limelight.

'So you figure you can step into your big brother's shoes for her?' Joe suggested. 'Because I can tell you now, you can't. George was her first love. A one in a million. You can quit drinking, claim you've cleaned up your act, play with her daughter—but you can't be George for her, however hard you pretend.'

What? Ryan looked up, stunned. 'Is that what she truly thinks? That I'm trying to be George?'

'Aren't you?'

'No.' That much he knew for sure. 'I'd never try to replace my brother in her heart. I loved him too, remember.' The words came out hard and sure, and when he met Joe's gaze he tried to put all his belief into it.

After a moment, Joe nodded. 'Okay. So what *are* you doing?'

He knew what he *should* say: that he was trying to rebuild his friendship with Gwen. To be there for her now in a way he hadn't been when she'd needed him most—when George had died. And all of that was true.

It just wasn't the whole story.

Ryan sighed. 'I wish I knew.'

Joe watched him for a moment, then stood up. 'Wait here. This looks like it's going to take a while, and in that case, I need sustenance. You figure out your answers, and I'll be back in a minute.'

While he was gone, Ryan tried to get his thinking straight in his head, but it was hard. So much of the facts and the logic were overruled by his feelings. *George never had that problem.* George had been able to see to the heart of any problem and fix it.

George had never let his heart rule his head, except perhaps when it had come to Gwen.

He wanted them to be friends again. He wanted to be part of the family again. That was the main reason he'd come home, and none of that had changed.

But something else hadn't changed either. He'd thought that his feelings for Gwen, that overwhelming attraction, would have faded while he was away. But it hadn't. And, worse, when he looked at her now, when he met her eye, when she smiled at him…he could almost believe she felt it too.

Before, George would always have been between them. But even now he was dead Ryan knew his brother's shadow was still too long for him to escape. He couldn't be George for Gwen, and he wouldn't be a poor second choice either. Which meant keeping his distance.

However hard that was.

The question was, could he really ever be in Gwen's life and *not* want to be with her? Not want *everything* with her?

Ryan didn't know.

Joe sank heavily back into the chair opposite him. 'Right. I've ordered chips.' He handed Ryan another bottle of alcohol-free beer, and put his own second pint of bitter down on the table. 'Time to talk. Gwen is my friend, and so was your brother. So I'll ask you again. What do you think you're doing?'

As if that wasn't the question he was asking himself every moment these days.

'When I moved to France,' Ryan started, still finding the words even as he talked, 'I was looking for something. A chance to be myself, perhaps, not just George Phillips's younger brother. I wanted out of his shadow, for the first time since we were kids. Since the moment we started playing rugby, in fact. But that wasn't the only reason I left. There was something else I had to get away from here too.'

'Gwen.' Joe shook his head and reached for his pint. 'I knew it. The way you used to look at her...'

'And that's why I left,' Ryan said. 'I had to, before anybody else noticed that. Joe, I loved my brother. I never, for a single moment, actually intended to do anything about my feelings for Gwen. Not even let her know that I had them.'

'I believe you,' Joe said. 'But now you're back and you're starting to think things are different.'

'Aren't they?' Just not as different as Ryan would like.

'Of course,' Joe said with a shrug. 'Gwen's life hasn't been the same since that tackle that took George down. And as much as she's tried to move past it, I'm not really sure she ever has. She is not the same person you knew, Ryan.'

'She is, though. That's half the problem.'

Joe shook his head. 'She's been through too much. You can't just imagine she's going to open her arms and welcome you in, not now. And definitely not you.'

Ouch. That hurt.

'Because I'm George's brother? Or because she doesn't think she can trust me? I told you, I've changed.' And he'd thought that Gwen believed that too. What had made her doubt him again?

'Honestly? It's probably a bit of both.' Joe gave him apologetic smile, which went no way at all to taking the sting out of his words.

'She doesn't believe I can change.'

'Oh, I don't think that's the problem. Gwen knows better than anybody how people can change. The question is, who have you changed for, and how long can it last?'

Ryan stared at Joe. God, he was sick of being stuck in the past, being forced to play the part he always had. He wanted to move on. Why wouldn't others let him? And most of all, how could he convince Gwen that this was the real him now?

However much he tried to protect his heart from Gwen, her not believing in him would always, always hurt.

Draining his bottle, Ryan got to his feet. 'Thanks, Joe. You've cleared a lot of things up for me.'

'Ryan…' Joe stood up too, but Ryan backed away before he could try and stop him.

'No, I mean it. I'm serious about this—about all of this. About who I am now. About Gwen and being a part of her life—and Evie's—however she'll have me. About reconciling with my parents. About playing great rugby. These are the things that matter to me, and I'm going to make them happen. I'm done being stuck in the past—being George Phillips's lesser little brother. Being the one who can't settle down, who can't commit, who can't give anybody what they need. I'm done. And I need Gwen to believe that too.'

Otherwise what had it all been for? He'd thought he was ready for this, ready to come home and prove he was a new man. Now he was here, he wasn't sure he was ready at all. But it was too late. He was committed to the tackle, he had to go through with it.

He had to be the man he knew he could be. For Gwen and Evie, and for himself.

'Because you're in love with her.'

'Because she's my friend. This is my family. I lost them all once, and I won't do it again,' Ryan corrected him.

Which meant not giving up.

Slamming his empty bottle down on the table, he walked out, and went to find Gwen.

If anyone had asked—which they hadn't—Gwen would have told them that of course she wasn't avoiding her brother-in-law. He was family. They were friends. Why would she do that?

Evie, the only one who *did* ask after Ryan, mostly wanted to know when her uncle was coming to play again as apparently Monsieur Lapin missed him. Somehow he'd made quite an impact on her. Gwen supposed it was something to do with similar levels of childishness between the pair of them.

But, still, when the knock came on her door on Friday night, her heart skipped a beat. And she knew, without answering it, exactly who'd come to call.

Steeling herself, she took her vegetable stir-fry off the heat, and went to answer the door.

'Ryan.'

'Gwen.'

For a long moment they just looked at each other, and she wondered if his thoughts had strayed the way hers had. Back to her dreams. And back to that moment when they'd almost kissed…

God, he looked good. That dark hair, curling over one brow. Those bright blue eyes, watchful and wanting. Those shoulders, almost filling her doorway.

People talked about how alike the Phillips brothers were but, looking at Ryan now, Gwen could only see the differences. The tiny scar that cut across Ryan's left eyebrow. The way that, although he still stood a head taller than her, the couple of inches he lacked on George's height meant she could stare right up into his eyes. The slightly fuller lips. The even more muscled forearms. The way he wore his polo shirt untucked and with the collar open.

The heat in his eyes that she hadn't seen in George's since even before his accident. She couldn't be imagining that, could she?

Maybe Joe was right. Maybe Ryan really was as tormented by this attraction as she was.

'Can I come in?' His voice rumbled low, and she felt

it in her blood. She nodded, and stepped aside to let him enter.

'Are you hungry?' she asked, as she crossed back towards the kitchen. 'I was just making dinner. There's enough for two.' She'd planned on eating it again tomorrow night—cooking for one wasn't interesting enough for her to want to do it more than every other night. Sometimes she and Evie ate together, but Gwen's appetite rarely fancied fish fingers at five p.m.

'Always,' Ryan answered, closer than she'd expected. She took a breath. 'Great. Come on, then.'

He sat on the stool at her kitchen counter, taking in the surroundings, while she finished off the stir-fry. Sneaking glances at him as she cooked, she saw his gaze linger on Evie's drawings on the fridge, on the school dinner menu pinned to the notice-board, and skip over the large canvas picture of her wedding day by the door.

They managed some small talk while they ate, at least—about how Evie was getting on in reception class, when his next match was and who it was against, how training was going, final figures from the fundraiser and what she had planned next for the trust.

It was only once the dishes were in the dishwasher and they'd moved through to the lounge that Gwen finally found the courage to ask what she really wanted to know.

'Ryan. Why did you come here tonight?'

Lounging against the end of her sofa, too large and too solid in her pretty front room, Ryan gave her a slow smile. 'Would you believe me if I told you I just couldn't keep away?'

Meeting his gaze, she thought, *Yes*. Because she could see the truth there in his eyes.

He was as caught up in this connection between them as she was.

But then he shifted, sitting straighter, and carried on. 'Truth be told…you were avoiding me, and I figured this was one place you couldn't just run away from. Not with Evie here.'

'So you wanted to corner me? Why?'

'Because I have a proposition for you.'

She suppressed a shiver at the word. 'I'm not sure I like the sound of that.'

'You will.' His voice was firm, certain, and he inched a little closer as he spoke.

Gwen didn't move away as he continued.

'I have an opportunity for you. For the trust, really.'

That…wasn't what she'd been expecting.

'What sort of an opportunity?' she asked, curious. Was he *really* here about the trust? Or was that just an excuse?

'There's a fundraiser coming up for a charity I used to be involved with. The one I told you about at lunch last week? It's kind of a big deal—lots of great contacts there, and I could introduce you to my friends who set the charity up too. I thought we might be able to get some ideas for the trust over here.'

'Sounds fantastic! When is it? And where?' This she was on solid ground with. She and Ryan working together to promote and build the George Phillips Trust, that she could do. They could push aside anything else that was getting between them, complicating matters, and focus on what was really important. This was great.

But Ryan winced. 'That's the only catch. It's over in France, the weekend after next. Do you think Evie would be okay with my parents for a couple of nights?'

A couple of nights. That meant she'd be with Ryan, abroad, in some hotel or another, for two nights. Trying not to think about kissing him. Or dream about him naked.

Oh, there were so many ways that this could go wrong.

But it was for the trust…

'I'll ask them,' Gwen said, and hoped she wouldn't regret it later.

CHAPTER SIX

RYAN COLLECTED GWEN from his parents' house the next Friday morning. It felt strange, pulling up outside their driveway, seeing the house—not the one where he'd grown up, but the one he had helped to move them into after George had bought it for them.

He didn't want to push his luck, so he lingered in the hallway while Gwen said her goodbyes. Her bag was already in the car, ready to go. As she ran through Evie's routine one last time with his mother, Ryan looked around him at the frames on the wall. His parents' wedding day, George and Gwen's wedding day, plenty of photos of Evie, even more of George, mostly wearing his Wales kit. But not one of him. He wasn't even surprised.

'Okay,' Gwen said. 'Are we ready?'

'When you are.' Half of him still believed she was going to pull out at the last second. That he couldn't truly be so lucky as to get a second chance with this woman, even as friends. That, one way or another, he was going to hell for this. Coveting his brother's wife, even after that brother was dead.

Evie tackled his knees again and he crouched down to hug her. 'So, are you going to be in charge of your grandparents while your mum is away?' Evie laughed.

'I'm serious! Who knows what kind of trouble they'd get into without you here to look after them?'

'I think we'll all muddle along quite nicely together,' his father said, coming to pick Evie up and rest her against his hip. 'You two just relax and enjoy yourselves. It's been a long time since Gwen had a holiday.' He gave Ryan a pointed look, a look Ryan knew meant that he was on its way to having his father's approval—as long as he could make Gwen happy.

Good thing that was just exactly what he intended.

'It's not a holiday, Dylan,' Gwen said, picking up her bag. 'It's work. For the trust.'

'Of course it is, love,' his father replied mildly. Ryan wondered exactly what sort of a trip he really thought this was, but he didn't dare ask.

Or hope.

With one last hug and a kiss from Evie, Ryan guided Gwen into the car, and drove them towards the station. She was quiet this morning, but he supposed that was to be expected. This was new territory for both of them.

He just hoped it gave them more than a few good contacts for the trust.

By the time they reached the Eurostar at King's Cross, Ryan thought he might have just about convinced Gwen that this was a good idea again. She'd changed her mind halfway to London, but by then it had been too late to turn back and she'd known it.

'I know I'm being silly,' she said as they took their seats on the train. 'I've just never been a different country from my daughter before.'

Ryan winced. He hadn't thought about it like that. Obviously there was a steep learning curve involved if he really wanted to be part of this family. 'Honestly? Where we are going could be closer than you would have been if I'd taken you to Scotland.'

Gwen laughed. 'I suppose so. Like I said, I'm being silly.'

'No.' Ryan reached across the table between them to take her hand. 'You're being a mum.'

The train pulled away from the station, and they both sat and watched the city passing by, becoming countryside.

'What made you pick France?' Gwen asked, apropos of nothing.

'Uh…' He'd expected to have this conversation at some point over the next couple of days. Just not quite yet. His motives for moving to France had been so tied up with the woman opposite him, it was hard to even discuss it without confessing the secret he'd held so long in his heart.

'I mean, wouldn't it have been easier to stay in the country at least?' Gwen went on. 'I'm sure there were English teams desperate for you to move to them. Why France?'

Relief surged through him. This was about practicalities, not the emotional side of his decision. That he could answer.

'I guess I figured that if I was going to make the move, it might as well be a big one.' Ryan shrugged. 'Growing up, training was such a huge part of our lives it didn't leave a lot of time for anything else. School holidays were just an opportunity to train more. Travel, holidays—they weren't really on the cards for us. You must know that from George. Anyway, I guess I figured if I was going to leave Wales I might as well go somewhere completely different. And they play some great rugby over there.' Getting better at his sport, more serious about it, had been a big part of his decision too.

'Did you like France, then?' Gwen asked.

'More than I thought I would even,' Ryan said with a smile. 'Nowhere will ever beat Wales for beauty, friendliness, and just feeling like home. But France gave me something else. Something I don't think I even knew I needed until I got there.'

They sat back as the train continued its journey, ducking down into the tunnel under the Channel, leaving rain-splattered England behind. The silence between them was comfortable, companionable, the way it always had been with the two of them.

After a while, Gwen turned back to him. 'Can I ask where we'll be staying?' She took a sip of the coffee she'd ordered. 'I mean, is it a hotel, are we by the beach…?'

The next, slightly awkward point. 'Actually, we're going to stay at my house.'

Gwen's eyebrows shot up over her coffee cup. 'You bought a house? And you kept it, even though you moved home?'

He knew it wasn't what she'd have expected from him, but he hoped it was just further proof of the man he was now. Not the Ryan who'd spent all his sponsorship money on cars and in bars, while George had been buying their parents a house.

These days he owned property. He had an investment plan, a pension, an actual financial advisor.

'Yeah. Buying it wasn't exactly in the grand plan when I moved over there. But, trust me, you'll understand when you see the house.'

She looked intrigued now. Good. He'd given her

something else to focus on, other than leaving Evie behind, and the idea of it being just the two of them in his home for the next two days.

Even if he knew that was definitely all he was going to be thinking about, at least until they arrived.

'Okay, that is not a house.' Gwen stared up at the building Ryan had brought her to. She'd been expecting some sort of townhouse or apartment, perhaps a tumbledown holiday cottage at best. But this place, Ryan's home...

It blew her away. Despite the sign at the end of the driveway saying 'Le Manoir', it looked more like an ancient castle than a manor house. The sort where fairy tales might come true. It even had a turret, for heaven's sake. The front door was made of heavy oak, and the windows were mostly arches carved out of the stone. Apart from the extension, that was. It was off to the side of the older house, a glass and wood extension, tied into the original structure by the huge glass windows that filled must what must've once been a high arched passageway for horses, perhaps.

'That's where the swimming pool is,' Ryan told her. He looked amused at her open-mouthed reaction.

'Of course you have a swimming pool,' she muttered.

'It's good for my muscles after a game.' Ryan grabbed her hand, holding her suitcase with the other. 'Come on, let me show you around inside.'

The inside was no less impressive than the exterior. A large modern kitchen led to a dining hall with the sort of long wooden table Gwen could imagine being used for banquets. The living space featured large comfortable sofas that fitted perfectly in the oversized room. It was the fireplace that caught Gwen's attention, though.

It was late spring, and warmer here than at home. They would probably have no need to light it while she was there. But just looking at it reminded her of all the dreams that Ryan had featured in recently.

Fighting a blush, she turned her back to it. 'Upstairs?' Then, at Ryan's smirk, she realised the connotation of her request, and the heat hit her cheeks with full force.

'Absolutely,' Ryan said, turning to lead her towards the stairs.

The stairs were the first thing about Ryan's *manoir* that she didn't actually like. As she climbed them gingerly, Ryan tried to reassure her.

'I mean, the staircase has lasted four hundred years—I don't reckon it's about to give way now. And, actually, spirals are a very secure shape for a staircase.'

Gwen looked through the gaps between the steps, and felt the uneven surfaces of the wood under her feet, the oak so hard it had almost petrified into rock, and shuddered. Instead, she focussed on Ryan's broad back as they climbed. As distractions went, it was one of the more pleasant ones she could think of.

'I thought you might like this room,' he said, motioning to one of the doorways as they reached the landing at last.

'I'm sure it'll be fine,' Gwen said, secretly slightly relieved that he hadn't picked her a room up the next flight of stairs.

Then he pushed the door open, and she saw inside. 'Oh. Wow.'

The bedroom was huge, probably as big as the first flat she and George had shared together in Cardiff. It had windows on two walls, looking out over the extensive grounds surrounding Le Manoir. The floor was stone, smoothed by the ages, and covered with warm, fluffy rugs. Another fireplace took up a large portion of wall here, with a sheepskin rug on the floor in front of it, just as she'd imagined in her dreams. But turning away from that didn't help, because it only led her to look at the other focal point of the room—a giant four-poster bed, laden with blankets and cushions and a satin eiderdown.

'Do you like it?' Ryan asked, sounding concerned. 'There's an en suite bathroom through that door just there. And it shouldn't get too cold at night now, but if it does I can always light the fire. If you don't like it—'

'I love it,' Gwen admitted. 'It's...like something from a dream.' A filthy dream. One she'd been trying to pretend she wasn't still having every single night.

Ryan's smile relaxed. 'Great. Do you want to see the other bedrooms? You might see one you prefer.' But he left her suitcase by the bed before they headed back out to explore the other rooms. It was clear he'd chosen this one for her, and Gwen thought he'd chosen well.

'How many bedrooms are there?' she asked, after they'd inspected the other two bedrooms on the same floor—one another double, one a twin—and he was leading her up another terrifying spiral staircase to the top floor.

'Five, in total,' he replied. 'There's two more up here. Mine and, well, another.'

She was surprised, and grateful, that he hadn't put her in the room next to his—if only because it saved her from having to climb that second staircase. Not to mention that putting temptation a little further out of her grasp seemed like a good idea.

But when he opened the door to that second bedroom, she saw why instantly.

It was a child's room. Oh, it was neutral enough—a simple wooden bed with fresh cotton sheets and a small dressing table or desk and a stool. The walls were painted a light cream rather than left as exposed stone like most of the house. The pale curtains fluttered in a slight breeze, and Gwen crossed to the window to look out over a meadow of wildflowers. She turned back to take in the rest of the room: the toy chest by the antique wardrobe; the small collection of soft toys on the pillow—including another Monsieur Lapin, or perhaps Mademoiselle Lapin since this one was wearing a pink tutu.

Most telling, though, was the print that hung over the desk. In elaborate fonts, it read *'Though she be but little, she is fierce.'*

'Shakespeare?' Gwen asked, pointing to it.

Ryan shrugged sheepishly. 'It seemed appropriate. I mean, she's the daughter of a rugby legend. She's hardly going to let herself be pushed around, is she? Especially not with you as her mother.'

Stunned, Gwen spun to face him. 'You made this room for *Evie*?'

'How many other little girls do you think I know?' Ryan asked, with a laugh. Then he must have seen her troubled expression, because he crossed the room to her and grabbed her hands. 'Gwen. Whatever you're thinking, stop. I had this room decorated ages ago—not long after George's accident, actually. I figured that the three of you…well, I knew things would be more difficult for you all. So I figured that maybe you might all want to get away from things at home for a while sometime. I'd thought that you might all come and stay one day. You and George were to have the master suite next door, and Evie could stay here.'

He'd been planning on making amends with George, with all of them, for a while, then. That was good to know. Except…

'And where would you have been?' Gwen asked, looking up into those bright blue eyes. So like George's, and yet not.

Ryan couldn't have known how truly terrible things had been for them after the accident. In fact, she'd made sure that he hadn't. But all the same he'd planned this place as a getaway for them if they'd needed it—as much as a getaway for himself. But what had he been escaping from?

Ryan just shrugged again, and turned away towards the door. 'I think that would have depended on whether you and George wanted me around. I'd hoped…well, it doesn't matter now.'

'That you two could have been friends again?' Gwen guessed.

Ryan nodded. 'I…I hate that he died, not having forgiven me for moving away. For not being on the pitch that day he was hit. Even after his accident, I left before he was properly awake. Our last conversation was that argument before I moved to France.'

Biting the inside of her cheek, Gwen desperately tried to control all the emotions surging through her. She wanted to say something—anything that could make this all better. But how could she?

The truth was, George never *had* forgiven his brother before he died. It was another bitterness that had soured his last years. But another truth was that, if he had been himself after that accident, she liked to hope he *would* have done, long before his death. Because the George she'd married hadn't held a grudge, although the George he'd become, especially after his accident, might well have done. But how could she explain that to Ryan without tarnishing his memory of his golden brother for ever?

Not to mention that if Ryan knew the truth, that was one more person in on the secret she was desperate to keep. And there were already too many people who knew for her to be comfortable risking one more.

So instead she rested a hand against his arm, her head against his shoulder, and whispered, 'I know.'

She did. All the ugly words she and George had thrown at each other those last months. Every time she'd been unable to keep her temper, even though she'd *known* it wasn't her husband speaking but the injury.

They'd become one and the same, in the end.

There'd been no love left there at all, and that had eaten away at the inside of her for too long now. She'd hate Ryan to feel that too. To know that his brother had died hating him—because he'd hated everything by the end.

'Come on. Show me this bachelor pad master suite, then.' She flashed him a smile, and he returned it, although his never reached his eyes. Probably hers didn't either.

But he shook off his mood, all the same. For her.

'Okay. And then, if you're not too scared to make it down the stairs, I'll make you dinner.'

Dinner was simple—pasta with chicken and sauce, from the hamper he'd ordered to be delivered prior to their arrival, served with a good white wine he even allowed himself half a glass of—but Gwen seemed to enjoy it. Well, mostly she just seemed amazed at the idea of him cooking at all, and by the house.

Good. That meant he was defying her expectations. Proving she wasn't the man she thought he was.

And that was why he'd brought her there. Well, that and the fundraiser tomorrow night.

He had to keep his focus on that. They were here for work. Otherwise it would be far too easy to let himself believe that Gwen had come to France purely because she wanted to spend time with him.

'Keep your head on straight, Ryan.' That was what his friend Julienne had used to say to him whenever he had got distracted in training or worked up on the pitch.

And it was what he needed to do now. Keep his head on straight and protect his heart.

After dinner they retired to the living room, glasses in hand—although he'd switched to water, and talked some more. Outside, the sun was sinking, the sky fading from blue to orange, to pink, to navy, all the way to black.

'It's beautiful here,' Gwen said, perched on the window seat as she stared out at the night. 'And the stars! I don't think I've ever seen so many of them. Not even in the valleys back home.'

'It's one of the things I loved most about this place when I bought it.' Ryan moved from the sofa to sit on the other end of the window seat, just to be close to her. God, he had it bad. 'You can sit here and feel like you're the only person around for miles.'

That made her shift her attention from the sky to him. 'You see, that surprises me. Back home, you always wanted to be where the people were.'

He shrugged. 'Like I said, I changed.'

'Yes…but you didn't tell me why.' Wrapping her arms around her knees, she tilted her head to the side as she watched him. 'Will you? Now?'

Why he'd changed? As if it was a decision he'd made one day, rather than something that had just sort of happened to him.

'I…I moved to France to get out of George's shadow, in large part. To find out who I could be if I wasn't George Phillips's younger brother.' His brother's name still felt heavy in his mouth after all this time. 'It wasn't because I resented him, or didn't love him. I just… I needed to know. Does that make sense?'

Gwen's smile was gentle. 'It does. George was…well, his reputation, his presence could be overwhelming at times.'

She must have felt it too, he realised. She'd spent most of her adult life as 'George Phillips's wife'. An appendage to his greatness. Supporting him, loving him—but what had she given up to do so? What dreams had she had before it had become clear that being George's wife was a full-time job in itself?

Not now, though. Now she was forging her own path with the trust—even if she was still hiding behind his name, to a degree. She was doing the work because she believed in it, and she was doing it well.

Ryan's heart ached with pride for her. And the realisation that she really was the only other person in the world who could understand exactly how he'd felt.

'When I got here, I didn't know anybody, and my schoolboy French was pretty lousy at the best of times. That first night, sleeping in some motel room near the training grounds, alone, with a dog barking outside keeping me awake—although my own nerves were doing that anyway—I started wondering if I'd made a mistake. George, my parents, even my agent—not to mention the managers of Welsh rugby—had tried to convince me to stay in Wales, to get more caps for my country before I looked overseas. So I was lying there, thinking that they were probably right.'

'What changed your mind?' Gwen asked. 'I mean, I assume if you'd kept thinking that way you'd have come home before now.'

'Yeah.' Ryan tipped his head back against the wall behind him, remembering the horrors of his first day at training. Sleep-deprived, slow, and unable to understand half of his teammates—unless they wanted him to—he'd struggled. 'It was hard, to start with. Then after the first week or so I figured... I chose this. I made this decision. And even if I hadn't, it was what I had. So now I had to figure out a way to make it work.'

'And you did.'

'And I did.' She was still watching him, studying him, and Ryan smiled a self-deprecating smile to try and distract her. 'It was just little things to start with. Making an effort to talk to a new teammate every day, doing extra training with them when I could. Working on my French in the evenings rather than going out to the pub. The language barrier meant I really had to listen when the team were discussing strategies and plays—even though everyone's English was far better than my French.

'Suddenly I was more focussed and more sober than ever before. And my rugby started to improve. A lot. So I kept going. Until one day I woke up and realised I wasn't the same person who'd moved here. I wasn't thinking about myself in comparison to George any longer. I was just me—and I liked the person I'd become.'

'I like him too,' Gwen whispered.

He couldn't look away from her eyes. Not when, for

the first time, he saw everything he'd ever hoped or dreamed he might see there in the depths of them.

Possibility. The smallest chance that she might feel the same way about him as he did about her. As he'd been feeling for so long now.

He wanted to kiss her, the desire and the need to welling up in him until it was almost impossible to think about anything else. But then, all of a sudden, Gwen jumped up from the window seat and held out a hand to him.

'Come on,' she said. 'I want to go swimming.'

The swimming pool was one of the few things he had added to the original building, and something he'd never regretted for a moment. Built inside what had originally been a courtyard used to bring horses and carriages through to the stables behind Le Manoir, it benefited from stone walls on two sides, huge archways now covered with glass on the other two and, his favourite feature, a glass roof.

Watching Gwen float on her back in the moonlit water, staring up at the stars overhead, Ryan knew this was exactly why he'd brought her here. She looked so relaxed, her arms stretched out to the sides, her caramel hair darkened into a halo around her head. Apart from the occasional lazy kick of her feet to keep herself afloat, she was entirely at peace.

Ryan lowered himself into the water, grateful that the pool was heated, and pushed off from the side towards her. The pool wasn't huge, but it was certainly big enough for two.

'This is so beautiful,' Gwen said, lowering her legs until she was upright again. She swept her damp hair back, away from her face, and smiled at him. 'How did you ever manage to leave here and come home to Wales?'

He looked at her, standing waist deep in the water, her plain navy swimsuit clinging to every one of her curves, her skin shimmering with water droplets in the moonlight. And he couldn't not say it. Couldn't hide from her a moment longer. Not in this place, at this moment.

'There were even more beautiful sights back home,' he told her, knowing his eyes would leave her in no doubt exactly which sights he was talking about.

'Ryan...'

He stepped closer, until he could place one hand at the curve of her waist. She didn't back away.

'Gwen, you know why I brought you here—to help you with the trust. But also because... I wanted to show you this place. Show you completely who I became here.'

'I know.'

She was so close now he'd barely have to move to kiss her. To have her whole body pressed against his, exactly how he wanted it.

But he couldn't. Not without saying something more.

'But there was another reason too,' he went on. 'I brought you here because I'm selfish, and however much I know there can't be anything between us, I just wanted to spend this time with you, the two of us. Alone.'

'Why?' she asked, looking up at him, her eyes serious in the moonlight. 'What did you hope we could do here we couldn't do at home?'

Oh, she was killing him. There was knowledge in her eyes. And she was standing close enough to him that she had to be able to *feel* exactly what he wanted, almost.

But she was going to make him say it.

Fine. Then he was going to say it all.

'Gwen. You have to know by now how much I want you. How goddamn tempted I am by you every second we're together. And I don't know if you feel the same way—'

She gave a low, throaty chuckle at that. 'Don't you? Ryan…ever since you came back… I've been *dreaming* of you. Of us. Imagining what it could be like…'

That knowledge sent all the blood in his body directly to one place, which was no help at all in figuring out what the hell to say next. She dreamed of him. She *wanted* him.

'This might be the worst idea in the world…' He leaned in closer, until his lips were almost brushing hers. 'But I really, really need to kiss you right now.'

He waited, just millimetres away. He needed it to be her choice. For her, and for him.

He needed to know he truly wasn't alone in this. Not any more.

The moment that followed seemed to last for ever. Above the stars carried on twinkling, around them the night grew only darker. He could feel her breath against his mouth, the thump of her heart in her chest, too rapid for her to pretend this wasn't affecting her at all.

And then, just when he was about to give up hope, Gwen let out a small, breathy sound of surrender and, stretching up on tiptoe, she wrapped one hand around the back of his neck and dragged his mouth to hers.

Ryan felt the kiss in every cell of his body. He reached around, lifting her until her long bare legs wrapped around his waist. God, she was so hot against him, so soft, so everything he'd dreamed of. Her mouth never left his, and he never wanted it to.

He wanted to take her, here, now, just like this. Wanted to sink into her and stay there until the unbearable longing he'd felt for her for so long was assuaged—at least for now.

And from her kiss, her touch, she wanted it too. At least, her body did.

But Ryan wanted more than just her body. He knew that now.

He'd tried to pretend that what he felt for Gwen was purely physical, that moving away would remove the torment of wanting something he couldn't have. But it had never stopped him thinking about her.

Because this wasn't lust. It was love.

For him, anyway.

And maybe it never would be for her. But he needed it to be something more than a passion-filled moment she'd regret in the morning.

He wanted *so* much more than that.

Gently, reluctantly, he sat her on the side of the pool, drawing away from the kiss with slow, exquisitely painful movements. Gwen followed him, pressing light, teasing kisses against his lips until he thought he'd give in entirely—or they'd both fall back into the pool.

'Gwen. Sweetheart, we have to stop.' God, how he hated saying those words.

'What?' Her eyes were dazed with lust, and Ryan couldn't help but smile at the sight. 'Why?'

'Because... I won't rush into this. If we're going to do this at all, I need to know it's something more than just one night. One incredible, mind-blowing night.'

He swayed forward and kissed her again. He knew it would be—both incredible and mind-blowing.

Which also meant it was worth waiting for.

'You're right.' Gwen pulled away, but not before kissing him back. 'There's too much at stake here. Evie, your family, the trust...'

'Yeah.' And more than any of that, Ryan needed to

know that he meant more to her than just a stand-in for George. That she wanted the man he was now. And that meant showing her all of him.

Starting with the fundraiser tomorrow night. He needed to show her his life in France. To prove to her that this change wasn't just for a season, or for a chance to play rugby in Wales.

It was who he was now. And he hoped that man might be someone she could love.

They stayed, foreheads resting against each other, her sitting on the edge of the pool, him waist deep in the water and willing his body to calm down and behave, both of them breathing too heavily to pretend this was anything other than torture. And all the time, that hope battered at the bars he'd put around his heart to stop her getting in, back when she had still been his brother's wife.

He wasn't ready to believe, just yet, that she could really be his.

'Are you okay getting back to your room?' he asked, and Gwen nodded.

Pulling up her legs, she got to her feet and padded over to where he'd left a stack of fluffy towels for them. 'I'll see you in the morning?' she asked, looking back over her shoulder.

'I'll make you breakfast,' he promised.

Ryan watched her go, through the doors back into Le Manoir proper. Then he swallowed, pushed off from the side, and forced himself to swim a few lengths.

There was no way he was sleeping tonight without *some* sort of exertion. Even if it wasn't the one he desperately wanted.

CHAPTER SEVEN

GWEN WOKE UP still dreaming of that kiss.

For a moment she lay starfished in her four-poster bed, trying to untangle what had really happened from the dreams that had kept her tossing and turning all night. In the end, she decided that the ratio of dream to reality was far too weighted on the dream side. She'd need to do something to correct that…

Except Ryan was right. This wasn't something that could be rushed into. This attraction between them was so new, so unexpected, she couldn't just jump in without considering all the options. Without remembering all the reasons she shouldn't jump at all.

But on the other hand…this wasn't going away. Not her dreams, not the chemistry between them. In fact, she was willing to bet that now she knew for sure he wanted this too, the pull towards him was only going to get worse.

While she'd been able to tell herself that this was just one-sided, that it was a misplaced attraction based on him fulfilling her obvious type, and the fact that she'd missed him and his support while he'd been away, she'd still had a chance at keeping things between them friends only.

Now…she knew, in her gut, it was only a matter of

time before she gave in. To the dreams, the chemistry, the pull…to everything she wanted.

She just needed to get it all straight in her head first. They had another couple of days here in France. She needed to use that time wisely, to figure out what she wanted from Ryan. Because it was clear that just one night, to get rid of these dreams, wasn't on offer. Ryan had always been an all or nothing sort of man.

And now she was pretty sure he wanted everything. She just wasn't sure she could give it, not while keeping her own secrets.

Not to mention that the idea of giving everything of herself again, after George had thrown it all back in her face at the end, was kind of terrifying.

God, the whole thing was a mess. But perhaps, for now, she could just take it one step at a time. Starting with breakfast.

Forcing herself from the comfort of the bed, Gwen showered and dressed, and headed downstairs in search of the food she'd been promised.

Ryan was already up, flipping through a pile of post that had obviously arrived for him while he'd been gone, the coffee-maker bubbling away behind him.

'Apparently I screwed up the mail redirection,' he said, motioning to the pile of post. 'But the coffee is brewing and I have the oven warming for pastries. *Pain au chocolat*, *pain au raisins*, croissants, or all three?'

Gwen grinned. 'All three, please.'

'An excellent choice.'

He got up from his stool and headed for the stack of bakery bags on the counter, pausing on the way to press a kiss to the very corner of her mouth. Gwen resisted the urge to turn her head and make the kiss something deeper—but only just.

Really, with her body and her subconscious betraying her like this, how was her mind supposed to keep them in check until she'd had a chance to fully decide how she wanted to proceed?

To distract herself from more kissing thoughts, she picked up her phone and tapped out a quick good-morning message to Evie, via her grandmother's phone. She'd call later, after breakfast.

Then she scrolled through her emails and spotted one from Joe. She frowned. That was unusual; he normally texted or even called. But when she opened it, she saw why. He'd forwarded her a link to an online news and gossip magazine featuring a full-size photo of her and Ryan, standing together at the trust fundraiser the previous month.

'Looks like you can't keep out of the British papers, even when you *are* on your best behaviour,' she joked, holding the screen up for him to see. Ryan just rolled his eyes.

Amused, and a little distracted by quite how much like a couple they looked through the photographer's lens, Gwen started to read out the copy that went with the image.

'"Wild boy of rugby Ryan Phillips is back in the country—and stepping out with a new woman on his arm! Only this time it's his sister-in-law, Gwen Phillips, tragic widow of the late George. The pair was attending a fundraiser for the George Phillips Trust, raising money for people who suffer life-changing brain injuries. But we couldn't help but notice just how *happy* the two of them seemed to be together…"'

Trailing off, Gwen looked again at the photo. In it, she was looking up at Ryan, laughing as he smiled down at her. Their gazes were locked on each other, she realised. Like there was no one else in the room.

No wonder they hadn't seen the photographer.

'It was a fun night,' Ryan said, nonchalantly, as he put the baking tray of pastries in the oven. 'Of course we were having a good time.'

Gwen turned back to the article. '"Speaking to an old friend and teammate of Ryan's, we heard that the lovable rogue—"' Ryan snorted at that '"—might have been carrying a flame for his brother's wife for longer than we thought. 'Ryan always fancied Gwen,' our source told us. 'But she only ever had eyes for George.'"' She put the paper down. 'Well, that bit's rubbish, anyway.'

Except Ryan had gone very still over by the oven.

'I wonder who gave them that quote.'

His voice sounded strange too.

'Ryan?' Gwen stared at him. 'They just made it up, right? Nothing to worry about.'

Except Ryan just sighed and slowly turned around. 'I don't know who said it,' he told her. 'But I'm not entirely surprised that someone did. Even Joe told me it was obvious—that I, well, was attracted to you.'

'But now, right? Not back then.' How could he have? She'd been George's wife.

The idea that he could have been wanting her all those years ago…it made her stomach feel uneasy. Apart from that night they'd met, in the bar, he'd never even given her a *hint* that he'd found her attractive, let alone anything else.

But he wouldn't have, would he? Because she had been with George. And whatever anyone might say about

Ryan's morals—and they did—he would never had done anything to hurt his brother. She knew that.

Crossing to the counter where she sat, he laid his palms flat on the surface, leaning across to look her in the eyes. A soft smile lingered around the corners of his mouth. 'Gwen, I've never been able to look at you and not want you. Not since that first night I met you in that bar.'

His words caught her in the solar plexus. In an instant her whole history unravelled and re-formed from that night, except this time it was Ryan who took her number at closing time. Ryan who called and asked her out. Ryan she fell in love with, not George.

How different might her life have been if things had happened that way?

'The number of times I cursed myself for a damn idiot for leaving you for a second that night. For giving George the chance to sweep in and charm you.' He shook his head, his smile rueful. 'But in the end I figure that the past is the one thing you can't change. And, in truth, I wouldn't even want to.'

'You wouldn't?' she asked quietly. But in her head the reasons were already falling into place.

Ryan had been a hot mess back then. Reckless, unreliable, and definitely not one for settling down. At best, they'd have had a couple of nights together before he'd moved on. And then she might never have met George. And no matter how horribly it had all ended, she'd never have wanted that. They had been happy, for a time. And more than that…

If she'd never met George that night, she'd never have had Evie. And that was unthinkable.

'I wasn't the right person for you back then,' Ryan said, echoing her thoughts. 'Maybe I could have been—

God knows you'd have been worth changing for. But given my track record, odds are good I'd have screwed it up somehow. And besides...'

He trailed off, and Gwen found herself leaning closer. She needed to hear this, however hard it was. 'What?'

'George loved you so much. And you loved him. I'd never want to deny either of you that.' He looked away. 'Especially given how short the time you had together was.'

Of course he wouldn't. He wasn't that kind of man. Which only made her like him more.

But it also brought another, horrible thought to the front of her mind.

He'd said he was attracted to her. That he wanted her. But after last night in the pool, the things he'd said then... she wondered if it was more. How hard it had been for him to watch her and George together if he wanted more from her than just a night in her bed.

'I need to know it's something more than just one night,' he'd said. How much more?

She needed to know the truth. 'Be honest with me. Was that...? I mean, was *I* the reason why you left Wales?'

'One of the reasons,' Ryan admitted. 'I'd never have done anything about it, you understand. I never even wanted you to know. George was my brother, and I loved him. I'd never do anything to hurt him, you know that. But that couldn't change how I felt about you.'

'Lust,' she said, giving him one last way out of this. 'That's what you felt.'

His gaze was almost pitying. 'I tried to tell myself that too. It was just my body making demands. Just a crush even. Wanting what my brother had, perhaps. I figured that moving miles away, with a whole new nation of women for me to flirt with, would solve the problem.'

'And did it?'

'Not for a second.'

Gwen gasped in a huge lungful of air. 'Am I…? Am I why you came back? Did you have this planned from the start?'

Ryan shook his head. 'No. No, Gwen…' He swerved around the counter to her side and picked up one of her hands, holding it close to his chest. 'I came home for all the reasons I told you. I never lied about that. I wanted to play rugby for Wales again. I wanted to make up with my parents, if that's even possible. But more than anything I needed… I needed a family again—you and Evie. But I only ever imagined it could be as Uncle Ryan, nothing more. Not until…'

'Until?'

'Until that night at the fundraiser. When you looked up at me like you're doing in that photo. And I saw something in your eyes that gave me…hope, I guess.'

'I'd been dreaming about you.' Ryan's smile spread across his face until it could only be classified as a smug grin.

'You said that last night, and I was too busy kissing you to ask you to elaborate. So, tell me more about this…'

'No.' Gwen knew she was blushing; her cheeks felt fiery hot. 'I just… Before you left, I'd never thought of you that way. Not after that night we met, when you were just some good-looking stranger. From that day on, you were George's brother. And I loved you as family, but it never even occurred to me…'

'Of course it didn't,' Ryan said easily. 'I never imagined it would. You loved George with everything that you were. Nothing that happens now that he's gone will ever change that.'

She *had* loved George. Until he'd become someone she hadn't even recognised.

'But since you came back…' She risked looking up, and found nothing but understanding in his eyes. Well, understanding and an underlying core of heat. Want. One that she knew was echoed in her own gaze. 'I *see* you. All of you.'

'That's all I ever wanted.'

It wasn't exactly how Ryan had intended to confess to Gwen that he'd been crazy about her for years, but actually it hadn't worked out too badly. He hadn't said the L word, at least. That would be far too much, too fast, too soon. And besides, Ryan wasn't sure he really knew what love looked like—except that he'd known it when he'd seen it between Gwen and George. *They* weren't there yet, however fast he could feel his own heart hurtling towards it.

He'd always known that if he let himself feel, let himself fall, he'd be head over heels for Gwen in seconds flat. That was one of the reasons he'd held back, the moment he'd seen her smiling at his brother at that bar, as Ryan had downed another shot he didn't need. From that moment, seeing how happy she made George, he'd vowed to put as much distance as he could between them. Wanting his brother's wife was bad enough. Loving her? That would be unbearable. Especially when he knew she didn't even see him.

Still, as he held her gaze and basked in the warmth of it, he knew she wasn't entirely comfortable with this new revelation just yet. He'd told her last night he'd wait until she was ready for this to mean something more than just one night, but he hadn't admitted how much more he really wanted. He thought she knew now. And it made sense that it would take her a little time to adjust to it.

So he'd give her that time, and change the subject.

Flicking through the pile of post that had arrived while he'd been away in Wales, he pulled out the one he was looking for. Thick, creamy card stock with scrolling gold text, laid over the image of the Château des Ducs de Bretagne in Nantes. An invitation…one he might well have refused if it hadn't given him the opportunity to take Gwen.

He'd responded to the email invite from Julienne, but it seemed he'd been sent the real thing, as well. He handed it to Gwen.

'If that photo hasn't put you off fundraisers and me for life, this is the event we're going to tonight.' He handed over the invitation, and let her take it in.

'At the Château des Ducs de Bretagne?' Gwen's brow creased in concentration as she tried to translate the French on the invitation. 'That sounds a lot fancier than the local chain hotel I was expecting. I'm rather out of practice at the high society thing, and I'm really not sure I packed for an actual castle.'

The oven beeped, and he removed the pastries, placing one of each on a plate and handing it to her.

'It's not *actually* a duke's castle any more,' Ryan explained. 'It's basically a museum. Think of it like Caerphilly Castle—just in better condition. I'm sure whatever you brought to wear will be perfect.' Maybe it was that gold dress from the last fundraiser. He had so many fantasies about slipping that dress from her shoulders, down her body…

Gwen didn't look convinced, so he carried on.

'But if you're really worried, why don't we spend the day in Nantes today? I've booked a hotel there for tonight anyway, so we don't have to drive back after the fundraiser. We can go check in, scope out the château and do a little shopping. Nantes has some beautiful shops. I'm sure we could find something new to wear tonight, if you'd like.' And then they could stop for lunch. Maybe even at that little chocolatier he'd visited last time he was there… Normally, he was careful with his diet these days—but as a rugby player he needed a ridiculous number of calories anyway. This weekend he figured he could let himself indulge a little.

Gwen picked up her *pain au chocolat*. 'You want to take me shopping?'

He smiled. 'I want to show you Nantes. And if I get to see you in beautiful dresses too, that's just an added bonus in my book.'

She considered for a moment, then nodded. 'Okay, then.'

Traffic in Nantes was stop-start, and he'd forgotten how tight the multi-storey car park was for his four-by-four, but once they were parked they were close to everything that mattered—lunch, shops and the château.

'We'll have a little wander around first,' he told Gwen, as they climbed out of the car. 'It's a pretty town to spend time in. I think you'll like it.'

He hoped she would, anyway. Even if things didn't work out between them, he'd meant what he'd said about her and Evie using his home. Maybe they'd even visit with his parents. There were beaches not too far a drive away, and a farm that had llamas and goats and giant rabbits he thought Evie would love…

They walked up the street towards Nantes Cathedral first. Ryan had never been much of one for architecture, or religion when it came down to it. But there was something about that place that sent a shiver down his back—as if he was close to a world other than his own. He'd wandered in there one of his first days off alone in France, exploring Nantes as a way to stop obsessing about everything he'd left behind, and had somehow found himself sitting in one of the wooden pews for almost an hour, just thinking.

Looking back, that was probably the moment his changes had started.

He owed a lot to that lump of stone and stained glass.

'It's beautiful,' Gwen said, as they approached the steps. 'Do you think we could go in?'

He nodded. 'Of course.'

Inside, he let Gwen explore the columns and the smaller chapels, the stained glass and the tombs, while he took a seat and just soaked up the atmosphere. They'd been together constantly—apart from while they'd slept— since they'd left Wales. Maybe she needed a little alone time.

As far as he knew, Gwen wasn't really very religious either, but he watched her light a candle all the same. For George, he supposed.

The cathedral was peaceful and calm, but the war inside Ryan still raged. The part that told him he wasn't good enough to even *look* at Gwen. The part that hated himself for wanting his brother's wife. For thinking he could ever be a good enough man to have her for his own.

He wasn't George. He'd never be George. George had been golden and perfect and naturally everything Ryan had needed to fight and scrape to become. And even then he knew he wasn't close to George's level.

He didn't blame his parents for cutting him out of their lives after the funeral, especially given the hurtful words they'd thrown at each other. George had been their perfect son, and Ryan hadn't been there to save him from the accident that had ended his career. He hadn't been there to help him recover. He hadn't been in the bar that night when George had played hero, stepping in to stop a fight, and been stabbed. And given which one of them had more normally been in Cardiff bars... Ryan had never really understood why George had been there at all. But he knew that his brother would always be the one to stop a fight, not join in, like *he* would have done back then. George had made them proud. *He*'d only let them down, over and over again.

He could never replace George—for Gwen or for his parents. But he hoped the person he'd grown up into might find his own place in their hearts.

Gwen slipped into the pew beside him, looking up at the altar. 'This is a special place, isn't it?'

'Yeah.' His voice sounded raspy, even to his own ears.

Suddenly, Gwen's hand was in his, squeezing tight. And Ryan knew, at that moment, that he was closer than ever to being the man he hoped to be.

A man worthy of his brother's memory.

Nantes was beautiful.

From the cathedral, where Ryan sat so peacefully while she explored, to the cobbled streets they walked

down, filled with antique shops and jewellery shops, towards the Château des Ducs de Bretagne, so she could
see where she'd be partying that evening.

'Wow.' She'd been impressed by Ryan's 'little *manoir*',
but this place was something else, and she was more certain than ever that the gold dress she'd brought—the same
one she'd worn for every fundraiser she'd attended that
year—wasn't fancy enough for an event here.

From the street outside the stone walls and towers
dominated, their fairy-tale turrets pointed against the
bright blue, late spring sky. The château was alive with
visitors, exploring the grounds, sitting in the late spring
sunshine on the grass by the side of the moat. Gwen could
have just leaned against the wall and people-watched
for hours.

'Come on.' Ryan grabbed her hand again—something
he'd been doing on and off since the cathedral, when
she'd taken his. She wasn't going to deny the tiny thrill
that raced through her every time his fingers wrapped
around hers. 'Let's look inside.'

As they crossed the stone bridge over the moat, something silver glinted in the sunshine. Gwen stopped and
stared. 'Is that…is that a slide?'

Ryan laughed. 'Yep. It runs from the walls to down
by the moat. Want to try it?'

'Uh…no, thanks.' The height of the thing was terrifying. 'Let's just go in, yeah?'

Inside the château's walls, the stonework was all
painted a blinding white. The courtyard housed an old
well, a museum and a gift shop, and there were steps up
to the walls for visitors to walk around. Gwen took in
the sheer scale of the place and tried to imagine how it
would look tonight for the fundraiser.

She couldn't.

They wandered around the outside of the courtyard, then out through another gate over the moat, where Gwen was delighted to find a small family of turtles sunning themselves on the rocks. Then they headed around the moat and back into the city to find her something to wear.

Realistically, Gwen knew that hardly anybody would be paying attention to what she wore tonight. The gold dress—familiar, comfortable, and something she knew she looked good in—would probably be fine. That was why she'd packed it, after all.

But now she was here in France, with Ryan, it just didn't feel…enough. She wanted to wear something that gave her the kind of confidence that had never come naturally to her. Something she felt beautiful in.

Something that would turn Ryan speechless, for preference.

'Don't worry,' Ryan had said, as they'd walked through the streets of Nantes, back past the antiques shops and craft shops and tourist shops—and no dress shops. 'I know just the place.'

Gwen had, to be honest, doubted him. In her experience of the women who appeared on Ryan's arm—mostly seen through the papers, she had to admit—they were more often dressed for a hen night in Cardiff than a swanky fundraiser in a château.

But as she stood looking up at the nineteenth-century interior of the Passage Pommeraye, she conceded she might have been wrong to prejudge him—again.

The arching glass roof, the columns, the balconies, the sweeping staircase, the black railings against the white stone, and boutique after boutique selling everything she could possibly need—and a lot of things she wouldn't.

'Okay,' she said, turning around to get a good look at everything. 'This should work.'

It took them a mere three shops to find a dress she thought might be appropriate for the occasion. Ryan had tried to persuade her to try things on in the previous two shops, but Gwen knew what suited her, and what she liked. There was no point trying something different.

But this dress…this dress was worth a try.

She shimmied into it in the small, curtained dressing room, smoothing it over her curves as she studied herself in the mirror.

The dress was a creamy, almost buttery colour, with beading across the bodice that shimmered in the lights. The skirts were chiffon, falling in a waterfall of layers down to her ankles.

Yes, this would do very nicely indeed.

The look in Ryan's eyes when she stepped out in it only confirmed her decision. *This* was what she'd wanted to go dress shopping for. The confidence she felt when Ryan couldn't look away from her.

She'd spent the last few years building up her own confidence in herself, her competence, and the ability to keep everything—life, family, work, Evie—going by herself. But here, in France, she didn't have to do it alone any more. She could have Ryan at her side, looking at her like she was the only woman in the world.

She had to admit it was more than tempting to try and take that back home with her too.

'You're so beautiful.' He stepped forward, seemingly automatically to put his hands at her waist.

'Think I'll do?' she asked, smiling up at him.

In response, he bent his head and kissed her, slow and deep and filled with longing.

He finally broke away as a shop assistant cleared her throat, and Gwen grinned.

'Better find some matching shoes then,' she said.

CHAPTER EIGHT

THE COURTYARD OF the Château des Ducs de Bretagne
sparkled in the fading sunlight. Fairy lights had been
wrapped around potted trees that circled the open space,
with a larger centrepiece of greenery and lights in the
middle. The spaces in between were filled with French
rugby royalty, and the sort of local prominent citizens
who could be counted on to donate the big bucks.

Stalls had been set up serving drinks and waiters in
bow-ties circulated with trays of champagne and canapés. Larger lights lined the upper walls, sparkling off
the decorations that hung across the stonework.

But the brightest thing in the whole castle was Gwen
Phillips, and Ryan could not keep his eyes off her.

They'd had a perfect day. From talking over breakfast
to exploring Nantes to dress shopping to lunch at a little
café on the square, listening to a violinist while they'd
eaten and chatted some more. Every moment in her company was a joy, and Ryan didn't want it to end.

Not least because he didn't know exactly what they'd
be to each other when they returned to Wales. He had a
feeling this easy companionship between them might not
translate back across the Channel, when there was Evie,
his parents, rugby, and the national press to worry about.

For tonight, though, he just wanted to enjoy being with Gwen. Memorising every moment, in case they were the only ones he got.

To think he'd honestly believed he could protect his heart around her. Even if he was never anything more than her friend from today onwards, Ryan knew now it wouldn't make any difference.

He was hers. Whether she wanted him or not.

'This is so gorgeous!' Gwen's hazel eyes were wide as she stared around them. 'Do you know many people here?'

How could he tell? He'd barely even looked at anyone else since she'd walked out of her bedroom in the hotel suite he'd booked. Now he glanced around and realised that, yes, he knew these people. Lots of them, anyway.

'Uh, yeah. Want me to introduce you to some?'

She grinned. 'Absolutely. See if I can get the real story of what you were up to in France from your friends.'

She was teasing, he knew that. But, actually, that was exactly what he wanted her to do.

He wanted her to believe in the man he was now. Wanted her to want him, the way he needed her.

Spotting his friend Julienne across the courtyard, deep in conversation with a striking blonde he recognised as his wife, Marie, Ryan took Gwen's hand and led her across, snagging her a glass of champagne on the way.

'Ryan!' Julienne saw him coming and broke off his conversation to open his arms and welcome him. 'It's so good to see you, my friend! I hoped my invitation would tempt you back over the water. You see, I got roped into taking your place on the charity board...'

'I did! And it's good to see you too.' Ryan hugged him tight, then turned to Gwen. 'Julienne was one of my first friends on the team over here,' he explained. 'Julienne, this is Gwen. My...' What was she, exactly? He couldn't say sister-in-law without opening up a whole lot of questions. Although there was an outside chance people here might even recognise George's wife...was it better to be honest?

'Date,' Gwen finished for him, holding a hand out for Julienne to shake. He took it, then pulled her close to kiss both cheeks.

Date. Yeah, that worked. Why hadn't he thought of that?

Because he was nervous, he realised. He'd thought he was years past pre-game nerves or even self-doubt around women. But with Gwen, everything was different. He doubted himself, and his luck, every moment they were together.

Julienne introduced his wife, Marie, and the four of them took a tour of the courtyard, sampling canapés and enjoying the sight of the entertainers brought in for the occasion. While the other three stood raptly watching a magician doing incredible sleight of hand, Julienne disappeared to fetch drinks for them all. When he returned with three glasses of champagne and one orange juice, and handed the latter to Ryan, he caught Gwen frowning.

'Ah, our good Welsh chapel boy,' Julienne said, in a terrible impression of a Welsh accent. 'Hardly ever touches a drop these days. Didn't you know?'

Gwen laughed at the impression. 'No, I knew. I just... I don't know.'

Ryan did, though. She was surprised that everyone else knew. Back home in Wales he hadn't advertised it, but over here in France it was just part of who he was.

'I wouldn't say never a drop,' Ryan put in lightly. 'I had champagne at your wedding.'

'Half a glass, and only because you were making the toast,' Marie said, laughing. 'He was Julienne's best man, you know. He'd only known him a year, but apparently the bond between rugby boys is unbreakable.'

Julienne shrugged. 'My stag night was three days before a summer show match the powers that be arranged at the last minute. I needed someone I could trust to make sure we all made it back alive—and in a fit state to play!'

'And you picked Ryan?' Gwen asked, sounding faintly incredulous. Ryan knew without asking that she had to be remembering George's stag do in Bristol, when she'd had to come and bail them all out at four in the morning, before the papers got hold of it.

'Of course!' Julienne threw an arm around his shoulders, and Ryan remembered exactly why he and the Frenchman had become such good friends, so quickly. Julienne let him be whoever he wanted to be, and believed him when he showed that to be the real him. He'd never met anyone in Britain who did that—probably because they all knew too much of his past.

But he hoped that Gwen might be starting to, at last.

'Who else but the Great Abstainer for keeping us all in line?' Julienne joked, making them all laugh. 'Now, come on. I want to see the tumblers over there. Also, I heard that they're opening the slide later...'

'No way that could end badly,' Ryan muttered, but he was smiling as he followed them all the same.

It was gone midnight before they made it back to the hotel suite Ryan had booked for them for the night. Gwen slipped her high heels from her aching feet, glad that they didn't have the drive back to his house ahead of them— although, given that Ryan had stayed on orange juice all night, he could have driven them.

All the same, a night in a fancy hotel followed by room-service breakfast was the sort of treat she hadn't experienced since Evie was born. And it gave her the chance to consider all she'd learned about Ryan over the course of the evening at the Château des Ducs de Bretagne.

She'd half wondered, at first, if Julienne's view of Ryan was skewed because he was even more of a rogue than Ryan had been in his heyday. But spending time with him and his wife had made it clear that wasn't the case.

Gwen had known, logically, that Ryan had changed while he'd been in France. But seeing the person he was through another's eyes made that change all the more real.

And it wasn't just Julienne and Marie. Every person she'd met that night talked about a Ryan she hadn't truly dared believe existed. A responsible, respectable Ryan. The one who others turned to in order to keep his team- mates in line. One who cared about his reputation, about his friends, more than he cared about his own entertain- ment or even well-being.

'The number of times he threw himself across the field to defend somebody. Or pulled a teammate out of a fight in a pub and got them to sober up and go home...' Julienne shook his head. 'There'd definitely have been more injuries and more police records among our team if he hadn't joined us.'

She'd wished, at that moment, that Ryan had never

left. No, not that, because then he'd never have changed at all. Never grown up.

But she'd wished that he'd been there to save George that night, not for the first time. That he'd known how his brother had struggled after his accident, and come home to help him, maybe. That he'd been in that pub and stopped George from starting whatever stupid fight he'd begun, before his opponent had ever pulled the knife that had killed him.

But he hadn't been. And there was no point raking over that past any more. No reason to tarnish Ryan's memory of his brother now it could do no good.

Gwen was done with living in the past. She'd spent the last three years stuck as Gwen Phillips, wife of golden boy George Phillips, then his widow. Pretending to the world that her marriage hadn't been broken, even before her husband had been. Masquerading as a perfect wife, taking care of her injured husband, when most days she'd just been trying to dodge his furious rages, or keep Evie out of the firing line. Ignoring the other women who'd burst into their marriage. Before the accident, she'd suspected he'd been unfaithful. Afterwards, his shifting personality hadn't even bothered to try and hide it.

Three years pretending, playing the part of a woman she wasn't any longer.

She was ready to move into the future at last.

Ryan had changed his whole self. Maybe she could too.

And she knew exactly how to start.

Ryan had left her to change in her own bedroom of the suite when they'd returned, knowing she was exhausted. But she could hear him puttering around in the lounge area, and suddenly a burst of fresh energy surged through her.

Barefoot, she padded back out of her bedroom door, leaning against the frame to watch Ryan fixing a cup of something at the suite's kitchenette. He'd taken off his jacket and tie, and his white shirt was untucked and open over his dark trousers, showing off muscles she'd only dreamed about before that night in the swimming pool.

Now she remembered how they'd felt under her fingertips, hard and defined as she'd run her hands over his bare, wet skin.

She wanted to touch him again. Tonight.

She wanted everything he'd stopped them having the night before.

Ryan turned, a cup and saucer in his hand, and visibly started to find him watching her.

'I…I made you a peppermint tea,' he said. 'Thought it might help you sleep after a busy night. You said your ears were still ringing from the noise…'

He trailed off as she pushed away from the doorframe and crossed the room towards him.

'That's sweet,' she said, taking the cup and placing it on the counter. 'But I can think of other ways you could help me to sleep well tonight.'

She held her hand against his chest, palm to muscle, and felt him tense.

'Gwen…' There was caution in his eyes. Or was it concern? For her? Or for him?

Either way, she intended to dispel it. They'd both been waiting for this long enough.

Raising herself up on tiptoe, she tilted her head up to place a kiss against his mouth, then along his jawline and running down his throat. 'Ryan,' she murmured. 'You wanted to say something?'

She felt his Adam's apple bob under her mouth as she kissed across it, then down towards his chest.

'I… We…'

'*We* want this,' she finished for him. 'Don't we?'

She only had to look up into his eyes to see the truth of it. The depths of want there made her shiver, but only in the good way.

'Yes,' he breathed. 'God, yes. But Gwen—'

That was all she needed to know. Hands on his shoulders, she pulled herself up to kiss him again, deep and hard and desperate.

'You wanted me to be sure, to know that this wasn't just one night, right? I know that now, Ryan. So will you please just take me to bed?'

She didn't need to ask twice. Sweeping her up into his arms so fast that the whole room spun, Ryan headed straight for her bedroom again, Gwen grinning against his bare chest.

Finally, she'd have reality to test those dreams of hers against.

She had a feeling that reality would win by a mile.

The hotel bed wasn't as spectacular as the four-poster back at Le Manoir, but Gwen didn't care. The view, as Ryan placed her on the bed and knelt over her, his shirt falling open at her sides, was far superior.

His mouth was on hers again the moment she lay down, hungry and wanting, as if he'd been dreaming of this as much as she had. Perhaps he had. Gwen lost herself in his kiss, pushing his shirt from his shoulders as she rose up to meet him.

Ryan's fingers were at work divesting her of her

clothes too, pulling the beautiful dress she'd chosen down her body and letting it pool on the floor before returning to slip her bra straps from her shoulders too. He kissed his way down her collarbone, to the swell of her breast, his tongue swirling around one nipple as the lace of her bra lost the battle to keep her covered. Gwen arched her back, pressing her body closer to his, wanting, needing, every inch of them to be touching.

The weeks she'd been dreaming of this felt like months, years even. Like wanting Ryan had taken over every inch of her brain, and her body.

And now she was here, she didn't want to waste a moment of it.

Her bra was gone completely now, and one of Ryan's large hands covered her right breast, while his mouth was back at her left. Sweeping her palms up the skin of his back, she fisted one hand in his dark hair as the sensations he was eliciting raced through her.

'Is this okay?' he asked, the words mumbled against her skin.

'Just don't stop,' Gwen gasped back.

For a second Ryan raised his head and shot her a wicked smile. 'As you wish,' he said.

Then he kissed a burning trail down the hollow between her breasts, over her stomach, all the way down to between her thighs—and Gwen stopped thinking altogether.

Waking up with Gwen in his arms was, quite possibly, the best new experience Ryan had ever had the good fortune to undertake.

He didn't know how last night had matched up to the dreams she'd confessed to having about them, but it had blown his imaginings clear out of the water. The way she'd felt against him, the way they'd moved together... he'd never felt as in tune with another person, ever.

Like every barrier, every secret, every worry between them had just disappeared.

Unfortunately, there was still the real world to deal with when she woke up.

He knew the moment she came awake, because she tensed in his arms for a second before looking up at his face and relaxing.

'Sorry,' she said, pressing a kiss to his shoulder. 'It's been an awfully long time since I've woken up like this.'

Ryan held her tighter. 'That's okay. But I have to warn you, I could definitely get used to it.'

She smiled at that, but it quickly faded. 'So could I. But we've only got one more night at Le Manoir. Then it will be back to the real world.'

'We'll still be the same people in the real world that we are right now,' Ryan pointed out.

'I suppose so.'

The hesitation in her voice pricked his heart. He'd been so sure last night that this was what she wanted—that *he* was what she wanted. Not just for one night at a fancy fundraiser, or a weekend away in France. But for good, the way he wanted her.

The way he realised now that he'd *always* wanted her.

He knew relationships took more than a couple of nights away from reality. He knew that the real world posed more challenges than they'd found here in France. He just didn't think that was a reason not to try.

Of course, he'd never really managed a proper, grown-up relationship before. He'd been more of a fast fling kind of guy. But that was before Gwen.

Hunkering down under the covers, Ryan turned on his side, until his nose was almost touching hers and he could see straight into her eyes. 'Tell me what's going on in there,' he said, smoothing a hand over her caramel hair.

'Nothing,' she said, but he knew she was lying.

'Is it Evie? My parents?'

Sighing, Gwen twisted to bury her head in the pillow. 'Both?'

Ryan flopped onto his back again, and ran a hand up and down her spine. 'That's fair. I know there's a lot of things we'll need to figure out. But I have faith that we can do it.'

There was no other option for him. He wanted the life he'd been dreaming of for too long now. He'd earned it. Not Gwen. She wasn't something to be earned, exactly. She was something he hoped he'd prove worthy of every day, ideally for the rest of his life. Not that he tell her that just yet. Still too soon.

But he wanted his home back. He wanted his family back. And even he had to admit that being with Gwen would make all those things easier.

She hadn't answered him, though. 'Do you?'

'Do I what?' Gwen asked, peeking up from the pillow.

'Have faith. In us.' He was holding his breath, Ryan realised. This answer mattered, for him, and for their future.

But Gwen gave him a wicked smile, and suddenly he felt her hands running low over his body. 'I have complete faith that you can make me scream again before it's time to check out.'

And as much as he wanted to continue the conversation, as much as he feared there was something she wasn't telling him—something that mattered a lot—his body overruled his mind as she grabbed the part of him that always tended to do the thinking in situations like this.

They had the whole drive back to Le Manoir, not to mention the journey back to Wales, to talk. He was probably overthinking things, anyway. Rushing her. She just needed time to adjust to things between them, that was probably it. After all, he'd been thinking about this a lot longer than she had.

George had been the love of her life, and it took time to move from that. But Ryan knew, deep down, that his brother would want Gwen to be happy. That he wouldn't want her to be alone for the rest of her life.

He hoped George might even want the same for him.

But those were conversations for other, less interesting times. Right now, they just needed to enjoy this time together.

They'd figure out all the rest of it later.

CHAPTER NINE

THEIR LAST TWENTY-FOUR hours in France were positively blissful.

They missed breakfast at the hotel, but given what they were doing instead Gwen decided she could live with that. Besides, they stopped at a lovely little café for a late brunch before the drive back to Ryan's *manoir*.

There, they made the most of their last hours together in style. And in the swimming pool. And on the sheepskin rug in front of the fire. And most definitely in her four-poster bed. And his.

Gwen had got dressed only for the purpose of video-calling Evie. Otherwise clothing had definitely been surplus to requirements.

Best of all, she'd managed to distract Ryan from any more deep and meaningful conversations about their future together. Oh, she knew they were coming, but she didn't want to waste time on them now. Not when she knew how much harder it would be to get this kind of time alone once they were home in Wales again.

A couple of days away with Uncle Ryan, to attend an important fundraiser to help with the trust, was something Evie could just about understand—and Gwen's parents-in-law too, for that matter. Uncle Ryan staying

over in Mummy and Daddy's bed was a whole different matter. And if she as much as saw them kiss Gwen
knew she'd report it to her grandparents in no time. And
why shouldn't she? It was her life and she got to share
the things that happened in it. Gwen would never ask her
daughter to lie or keep secrets for her.

But now she was on the Eurostar back home again,
she couldn't help but let the worries fill her. If she was
honest, she'd been concerned about it ever since Joe had
sent her that photo of her and Ryan at the bachelor auction in Cardiff, although she'd managed to push it aside
for a day or so.

The problems were obvious. Yes, her time here in
France had shown her that Ryan had changed, and that
his friends and colleagues here respected and trusted him
to be the man they'd needed him to be. And she genuinely believed that she could too.

Back home in Wales, though, no one else would believe that.

Everyone there—Ryan's parents included—would still
see the man they used to know. The one from all those
awful tabloid photos, and the disciplinary hearings that
had followed. And so they'd be talked about, followed,
photographed. Eventually, Gwen was sure they'd come
to see the truth that she had—that Ryan wasn't the same
man who'd left the country three years ago. But seeing
that would take time.

And in the meantime she didn't want Evie exposed to
that sort of publicity and propaganda. She didn't want her
to hear that talk. Couldn't risk the gossip and the scandal
of her being involved with her former brother-in-law—
because didn't that just play into what people already

believed about him? That he'd steal his brother's wife? Never mind that she went willingly…

She knew that Ryan would understand all that if she explained. Maybe he'd even be willing to take things slowly enough to mitigate some of the fallout. She hoped so.

But that didn't solve her biggest mental block.

George.

Not just the idea of moving on from her husband, let alone with his brother. That much she'd managed— probably helped along by the fact that in the last couple of years of their marriage there hadn't been much of a marriage between them at all.

But Ryan didn't know that. To him, George was still perfect. His idol and hero. The man he wanted to live up to. And if they were really going to do this, be a couple, eventually she was going to have to tell him the truth.

She *really* didn't want to tell him the truth. Didn't want him to know the man his hero had become, even if the bulk of the blame for it lay with a brain injury he couldn't have helped. She didn't want to be the one to shatter his illusions.

She'd hidden the reality of George's personality change from everyone she could, especially those who would be hurt by it, like Evie and his parents. She'd told herself she was doing it for their own good, to protect them. But now she worried that wasn't her only reason.

She'd been protecting her pride too.

However much Anita Chowdhury taught her about the impact and consequences of brain injuries, their effect on a sufferer's personality, and however much Gwen understood, intellectually, that it wasn't her fault, or George's, it didn't stop the way it made her feel.

She hadn't been enough to bring George back from the place his accident had taken him. That was what it came down to. And while she knew logically that most of those changes—the rages, the affairs, the cruel words—had been brought around by his accident, deep in her heart she knew that wasn't the whole of it.

Because the part she'd never told anyone, not even Joe, was that the end of her marriage had started before the tackle that had ended his career. If he hadn't been injured, she didn't know now if they'd even still be married.

She shook the thought away, not wanting to remember those arguments, the way he'd given everything to rugby, his training, his team, and kept nothing back for them. How she'd honestly believed all those nights out with the boys had been genuinely about team building and nothing more—until she'd found the first of the text messages from a woman he'd spent the night with.

George had been the golden boy of rugby. And maybe he'd hidden his flaws better than his brother ever had. But he hadn't been perfect.

Even if her pride wouldn't allow her to let other people see that. She didn't want pity now he was dead, and she hadn't wanted it then either.

She couldn't bear to see the pain and disappointment—and probably disbelief—in Meredith and Dylan's eyes. Couldn't think of Evie growing up thinking her father had been anything but a hero.

Knowing that he'd started the fight that had killed him, over a woman who hadn't been his wife.

And she wouldn't see Ryan cursing his brother for hurting her, or wondering why she'd stayed.

Or worse…she hated herself for even thinking it, but she knew there was another fear inside her too.

She knew people could change—and she believed Ryan had. But George had changed, as well. And she couldn't help the small part of her that worried that, if Ryan had changed once, he could change back again.

'You're thinking hard over there,' Ryan said, from the train seat opposite her. 'Anything you want to share?'

She flashed him a smile she hoped looked authentic, and shook her head. 'Just wool-gathering,' she said, returning to staring out of the window.

The problem was, soon, she was going to have to do something with all that wool.

They'd caught the very early train back to England, and hit Kings Cross St Pancras station just as everyone else was starting their working day. The minute they stepped out onto the platform, though, Gwen's phone started pinging. She reached for it—but then spotted a newspaper stand carrying the daily free paper for London, and realised she didn't need to read the messages.

She already knew what they'd be about.

There, on the front cover, was a photo of her late husband. Beside him a photo of a woman she didn't recognise holding a small child.

And the headline: *'Golden Boy of Rugby Fathered My Baby!'*

Apparently the time for wool-gathering was over.

She needed to make some decisions. And fast.

Ryan took a couple of steps before he realised that Gwen wasn't beside him. Frowning, he turned to find her standing stock still behind him on the platform, staring at something.

'Gwen? Are you okay?' He was by her side in an instant, and only once she nodded did he turn to find out what she was staring at.

Golden Boy of Rugby Fathered My Baby!

Ryan barked a laugh at the ridiculousness of it. Anyone who'd known George knew he'd been besotted with his wife, and obsessed with doing the right thing. The very idea that he'd strayed was absurd.

Only Gwen wasn't laughing.

'Gwen? Don't even waste time looking at it. You knew George better than anyone. He wouldn't do something like that. It's just someone fishing for a pay-out from the tabloids, that's all.'

'It…it might not be,' she said, her voice slow and shocked. Then she turned to him, jerky but fast. 'We need to get home, Ryan. We need to get to your parents before they see this.'

He stared at her too-pale face. She genuinely believed this. And that…that put doubt in his heart too.

There had to be a simple explanation. He just couldn't imagine right now what it could be.

'Okay. We'll grab a cab to Paddington.' Practical planning, that was what they needed now. 'But, Gwen… I'm going to need you to explain this.' If there even *was* a reasonable explanation for the impossible.

How could it possibly be true? Ryan had *known* his brother. Had spent his whole life trying to be half the man he was. This *couldn't* be true.

Dragging their cases behind them, they headed for the outside world and the taxi rank. Almost as an afterthought, Ryan grabbed a copy of the paper on his way.

He needed to understand this.

'Okay,' he said, as soon as they were settled in the cab, with their luggage in the boot, and on their way to Paddington station. 'Tell me what's going on that could possibly make you believe this is true.'

He held up the newspaper and she tugged it away, placing it face down on the seat next to her and casting a nervous glance at the driver.

The driver, who was swearing at someone who'd just pulled out in front of them, couldn't have cared less, Ryan was pretty certain. But the fact that Gwen was worried that he would concerned him.

'Gwen. Talk to me.' Glad he'd taken one of the fold-down, rear-facing seats in the black cab, he reached across to hold her hands. She had to look at him here, couldn't hide.

And he had a feeling he needed to see her face as she told him this story.

'George…after the accident, he wasn't the same. He couldn't play rugby, which he hated, and the rehabilitation on his arm was slow, even getting him back to normal function was a struggle.'

'I remember.' He'd hated seeing his brother that way, stuck in a hospital bed at first, then fighting to gain full mobility back in his badly broken arm. He'd mostly got reports on his rehabilitation from Gwen, or his mother, back when they were both still speaking to him. George had been too proud to show that kind of weakness to the brother he still resented for leaving.

Gwen worried her lower lip with her teeth. 'But it wasn't just the break. The head injury…that was more of a problem.'

'It was?' Ryan frowned. As far as he recalled, there'd been no mention of that, once the initial fear and concussion had passed. He knew there was *always* concern about repeated head injuries in rugby—and rightly so, given when he'd learned from Anita Chowdhury. The terrifying hours when George hadn't regained consciousness had seemed to last for ever. But once George had come round and they'd set his arm he'd assumed the danger had passed.

'He… His personality changed. Well, perhaps intensified is a better word. We'd… Oh, God.' Closing her eyes, she tipped her head back against the seat. 'I've never told anyone this. But…we'd been having some problems even before his accident.'

'What sort of problems?' Every muscle in his body felt too tense to move. Gwen and George had been the perfect couple. If *they'd* had problems, what hope was there for *him* and Gwen?

'He… Rugby was everything to him—especially after he was made captain. I was home with Evie and feeling neglected, I guess. I nagged him, asked him to put us first for a change—but he only started staying out longer, and more often. Then I started finding text messages from other women on his phone—'

'God, Gwen, no. There must have been an explanation! George loved you! He wouldn't….'

Oh, God, but what if he had?

'His explanation was that I was a nightmare to be married to, apparently.' She gave a small shrug, her whole expression so beaten down that Ryan couldn't help but shift to the seat next to her and wrap his arms around her. 'I was about to confront him after the match, the day he had his accident. But after that…how could I? All I cared about was getting him well again. I figured if we stuck together through it, I'd get my husband back.'

'What happened next?' Ryan asked, knowing, instinctively, that this story wasn't over. It didn't end until his brother's funeral. Or until an unknown woman appeared in the papers claiming she'd had George Phillips's son.

Outside, London traffic was sluggish, and the cab stop-started its way to Paddington. There was no way they could get back to Cardiff before his parents saw the papers, or before one of them called them. He thought Gwen must realise that. But, still, she looked anxiously out of the window at the slow-moving traffic.

'He was so angry—about the tackle, about his arm. And then when he realised his career in international rugby was over, and that he might never even make it back to playing for his team... I mean, of course he was furious and frustrated. And it took a while for me to even realise that some of the...changes in his personality were to do with his head injury, rather than just what had happened to him.'

Ryan shook his head. 'When I spoke to friends who'd visited...they said he just seemed like himself. Annoyed to be stuck recovering, but he was always like that after an injury. Couldn't wait to get back out on the pitch.'

'That's what I wanted people to believe. I...I wanted people to remember George as he was. As I hoped he would be again.'

'But then he went and threw himself into stopping that fight—' Something in her expression cut him off.

George had been stabbed trying to stop a fight. That was what he'd been told. What everyone had been told. What he'd believed.

But, then, he'd believed that Gwen and George had had the perfect marriage too.

'Gwen. What happened the night George died?'

She wouldn't look at him. 'He…he stormed out to go to the pub that night. I don't even know who with— I don't think it was any of the boys from the team. But he'd started making all sorts of new friends by then. He never introduced me to any of them.' She swallowed, so hard he could watch her throat move. 'The police said… witnesses told them he started a fight with some guy over a comment he made about a woman, I think. Just… launched himself at him. People started piling in, some-one called the police, and…'

'Someone else pulled a knife.'

That could have been him. That was the only thought in Ryan's head for a moment. That if he'd carried on the way he'd started in Cardiff, if he hadn't moved to France, that could so easily have been him.

His second thought was, *I should have been there to stop him.*

No wonder his mother hated him so. Wait… 'Do Mum and Dad know the truth?'

'Which part?'

'Any of it?' Because Ryan had a suspicion he wasn't the only one she'd been keeping the truth about his brother from.

Her wince confirmed it. 'They loved him so much. I couldn't take that away from them. They'd already lost him, Ryan, I didn't see what good it would do.'

But as the taxi pulled up outside Paddington station, the truth of what it might have done hit him, hard, in the chest.

It might have made his parents able to love *him* again.

Gwen's heart hurt, reliving those terrible few years. And telling it all to Ryan…well, that hurt a hell of a lot more.

She'd been holding in all these truths for so long it was hard to let them out. Even Joe, who knew how George had been after his accident, didn't understand that it had started earlier. In so many ways it had been easier to blame the head injury for making George the man he'd become. And she knew that a lot of it—the angry flashes he hadn't been able to control, the lashing out, the irrational rages—had been due to that.

But the cheating on her... That had come earlier. That couldn't be blamed on anything other than George being human and flawed.

Something she'd worked so hard to never admit, before now.

She saw it—the moment Ryan realised what she'd done. And she recognised it too, because in that same moment *she* realised the depth of it.

The echoes of George's behaviour and her own choices, ricocheting into the future to ruin this new happiness they'd found together.

She hadn't just knocked George off his pedestal when she'd shown Ryan the reality of his brother as a man, not a god. She'd taken away part of Ryan's belief system, and the reasoning behind so much of his life. The choices he'd made, the person he'd become, so much of that had been tied up in who his brother was.

And now he knew that George had never been that person at all.

What would that do to a man?

But it went deeper than that, she knew. Ryan hadn't just spent his whole life either trying to live up to or be the opposite of his brother. He'd spent it in his shadow, unable to climb out of the darkness it had cast.

He'd been compared to George from the day he was born, and not generally favourably.

If his parents had known the truth about George, might they have looked more kindly on their younger son? Could they have reconciled much sooner than now? It was too late to know. But she was damn sure that Ryan was thinking it.

Ryan paid the taxi driver without looking at her, and Gwen climbed out of the car and waited to retrieve her suitcase. She left the newspaper lying on the seat behind her. She didn't need the reminder. Her heart was reminder enough. The tattered remnants of it anyway. The ones that had just started to mend, under Ryan's gentle care.

But she couldn't think about that now. This was bigger than a fledgling romance that made her feel wanted for the first time in ages. It was bigger than her heart and what *she* wanted.

This was about her family.

She had to get back to Cardiff before Evie heard something she shouldn't about her dad. Before she had to deal with reporters at the door or calling incessantly, the way they had after his death.

The man was dead and buried. Why couldn't people let him rest?

Why couldn't they let *her* rest? Or at least move on with her life. Maybe even find some happiness somewhere.

But not with Ryan, she could see that now. Saw it in the lines of his back as he stalked towards their platform. In the set of his shoulders as they took their seats. In the way he couldn't quite meet her eyes as the train around them filled with other passengers.

Oh, this journey was going to be absolute hell.

Just this morning, he'd been kissing every inch of her body, worshipping her with his mouth, his hands.

Now he couldn't even look at her. And she couldn't blame him either.

She wanted to believe he was just processing everything she'd told him. But she tried to make a point of not lying to herself, even if she wasn't always entirely honest with the other people in her life.

It was over for them. Before it had really even started.

Because her actions had ruined any chance he had of reconciling with his parents before now. Because she'd lied to him, and to everyone else.

But mostly because she still couldn't bring herself to let Evie have her image of her perfect dad ruined by the truth.

CHAPTER TEN

THE ENGLISH COUNTRYSIDE sped past the train windows, rain splattered and endlessly green. Ryan longed for the rugged purple mountains and rugged coastline of Wales, but even racing towards it didn't feel entirely like going home.

Home was where George was, except George was gone, and somehow hadn't ever been the man he imagined. Home was where his parents were, except they still loved a fiction and refused to see the real man Ryan had become.

Home, he'd have said last night, was in Gwen's arms. Now he could hardly look at her. Not until he'd sorted through this whole mess in his head.

It wasn't her fault, he knew that. She'd been trying to save her marriage, to look after her family. To protect Evie. He couldn't blame her for any of that.

Except, deep down, he knew he did.

How different might the last few years have been for him if he'd known the truth? If he'd suspected for a moment that George wasn't the perfect golden boy everyone believed him to be? If his *parents* had known that?

He might never have left Wales. He might have helped his brother—even saved him. He might not have fallen out so hideously with his parents at George's funeral, at least.

Everything could have been different.

He could have been different.

Would he have still acted up so dreadfully, desperate for his parents' attention, if George hadn't been so impossibly perfect? Would he have grown to be something other than the black sheep of the family if George hadn't been so white?

Finally, he turned to find Gwen watching him, owlishly, looking like a bird about to take flight if he made a loud noise. She was scared, he realised. Not of him, he hoped, but of the truths she'd shared.

'Okay, what I need to know is this,' he started—but her eyes widened in alarm and she tipped her head towards the woman sitting across the aisle from them. The one reading another newspaper with George's face plastered on the front. As Ryan looked over, the woman glanced up, her eyes narrowing as she saw him, as if trying to place his face.

He turned away, angling his face towards the window.

'So we're not going to talk about this,' he murmured softly.

'Not here,' she whispered back, urgency in her voice. 'Please, Ryan. Not here.'

He nodded sharply. 'In that case, I'm going to go find the buffet car. I need a drink.'

He didn't ask if she wanted anything, didn't wait to see if she would come with him. He just stalked in what he hoped was the right direction, taking all his fury with him.

He needed time to process this. And by his reckoning, he had until they reached Cardiff to do so. Because then they needed to face his parents—and he needed to know what she was going to do next.

They'd have seen the news, the accusations—there was no way they could avoid it. Too many of Mum's 'friends' would have called to check she had, under the guise of wanting to make sure she was okay. And that was before you got to the local journalists calling to try their luck.

Would Gwen tell them the same truths she'd told him? Or would she keep lying? Keep the fiction of his perfect brother alive, even now he was gone?

He didn't know.

He reached the buffet car at last, and stared at the miniature bottles of spirits and single glasses of wine behind the counter. Then he ordered a coffee, because he needed to drive when they reached Cardiff, and if ever he needed his wits about him it was today.

Ryan put the suitcases in the boot of his car in silence, then climbed into the driver's seat. It was hard to imagine that just a few days ago they'd been setting off with such hope. Now, as he pulled away and began the familiar drive to his parents' house, it was all about damage limitation.

'I need to know what you're going to tell my parents.'

'What they already believe,' Gwen replied, staring out of the opposite window. 'That it's a load of rubbish intended to stir up trouble and we mustn't let Evie get wind of it and become distressed.'

'Have you heard from them this morning?'

'Your mum sent a text first thing. Said not to read the papers today as she didn't want me upset.' Gwen sounded guilty just saying it.

'Trying to protect you the same way you're protecting them, huh?'

'I guess so.'

They spent the rest of the drive the way they'd spent their train journey—in silence. He hated it. But right now he honestly had no idea what to say.

All these years, he'd imagined what might have happened if he hadn't left Gwen at the bar to go take that shot. If George hadn't swooped in and charmed her.

But now he was revisiting all the major events of his life from another, different 'what if.'

What if he'd known George wasn't so perfect? What if his parents had?

It was as different a life as the one in which he got Gwen's number that night, instead of George.

When they pulled up outside his parents' house, they sat in silence for a moment, just staring out the windscreen at the falling rain. Earlier, he'd imagined that this would be the moment they returned to reality after their perfect days away. The moment he hoped they'd decide to force reality to suit *them*, to allow them to be together.

Now he realised that reality had barged in and ruined things, far sooner than either of them had been ready for.

'We'd better go in,' he said, unfastening his seat belt.

But Gwen paused. 'Are you sure you want to? I mean, it might not be the best time…'

'Right. Of course.' Heaven forbid he visit his *own parents*. Because they still believed he was the black sheep, the bad son, the one who had let his brother die alone because he'd left the country to try and find himself, away from the golden boy's shadow.

Because that was what Gwen *wanted* them to believe.

If Gwen got her way he would *always* be the black

sheep. The disappointment. The son who let them all down. No matter how much good he did now, however hard he worked to overcome his past transgressions, none of it would matter.

They'd been assigned their roles, and Gwen would make sure they stuck to them. George, the hero. Her, the tragic widow. And him…

No. He couldn't be that person any more. Not even for her.

He turned to face her, hoping the rain hid them from view if there were any nosy paparazzi floating around out there, braving the weather. The two of them wouldn't make the front pages of the papers, not like the allegations about George, but they'd be on the local gossip websites for sure.

'Gwen, how long do you think you can keep this up?'

'As long as I have to.' She was so *stubborn*. Why hadn't he remembered that when he'd been idealising her over in France?

'You can't! Mum and Dad have to know the truth, deep down. Enough of these stories surface…now this one's out there, you can't tell me there won't be more. People love a bandwagon like this to jump on. Soon it won't matter if they're real or not! And someone is bound to come out with the real story about how George died sooner or later. Isn't it better to just tell them the truth now? Get it over with?'

'No!' Gwen cried, twisting round towards him. 'Because if I admit it, even once, that makes it real. And if it's real then Evie will have to know eventually. And she *idolises* her father. Your mum has shown her news clippings and videos and photos of him every day since he died, talking about what a great man he was. If she loses that... She's already lost the man himself. Can't she keep the memory?'

'But it's not real! And you know no person is perfect, Gwen. Not even George.' He'd thought *she* was, but he should have known better.

'Don't you think I know that?' she yelled. Her hands were clenched into fists on her thighs, and he reached out to cover them with his own. He figured he had one last chance to get through to her.

One more attempt to make her see sense. To accept the past and move on to the future—with him.

He just hoped to heaven that it worked.

Frustration oozed out of Ryan, from the tension in his shoulders to the fists clenched against his thighs.

'Gwen, think about it. If this woman really did have George's child, there are ways she can prove it. She could try to claim money from his insurance pay-out. She might want Evie to know her half-sibling—then what will you do?'

Why wouldn't he just stop? Why not just walk away and give up on all of this? Why did he keep trying to *reason* with her, of all things?

Because he's in love with you.

He'd never said the words, but Gwen knew it all the same. She'd finally recognised that look behind his eyes, the one that had been there since the day he'd returned from France. The one that had practically glowed out of him the morning they'd woken up together in Nantes.

He loved her.

Even worse, she knew she was falling in love with him too.

And she was going to tear it all apart to protect Evie, and her own damn pride.

'Then I would deal with it,' she said flatly. 'Somehow.'

'Gwen—'

'No, Ryan. Listen. I know what I'm doing here, okay?' *Don't believe me*, her mind screamed. *I have no idea!*

But she'd set this plan so long ago, and she didn't know what to do but to follow it now. To keep living the life a past version of herself had decided on. Even if things had changed.

She took a breath, and kept talking. 'If I can make the George Phillips Trust a success, then it won't matter what people say about him any more. His name will be out there, representing good things, making the world a better place. A safer place, even.'

'And even if things do come out you can blame it all on his head injury, and claim that's why you're working so hard to help others in the same situation.' Ryan shook his head, a look of disbelief on his face. 'God, I should have seen this so much sooner. You're trying to rewrite the past.'

'And aren't you? Going abroad and starting again as a whole new person—and now you're trying to come back here pretending that nothing you did before even happened!' It was a low blow, and she knew it. But she was on the defensive now, and she couldn't stop herself.

'That's not what I'm doing! I came back to prove— Oh, what does it even matter now?' He raked a hand through his hair. 'Gwen, I came back because I've finally put my past behind me. I'm ready to move on with the rest of my life. With being the man I always hoped I could be but somehow could never find. I think I've found him now. And if you'll let me, I'll spend the rest of my life being that man for you because—'

'Don't say it,' she interrupted, trying to stop him. But it was no good.

'Because I love you, Gwen Phillips.'

She'd already known it, but it hit her like a punch to the gut all the same. Like a heavy tackle, bringing her to the ground until she saw stars.

And the worst part was that it couldn't matter any more.

'I love you, and I want to be with you,' Ryan went on, each word strong and deliberate. 'But I can't live in the past with you. I can't live, pretending. I've worked too hard to find who I am and what I want to be to start now. If you want another George—'

'No! I don't. Ryan, please…' The last thing she wanted was to rehash her last relationship. When it had been good, it had been everything. But when things had changed…

Ryan had already changed. He'd become the person he was meant to be, she could see that now.

She just wasn't sure that *she* had yet.

'If you want another George, I can't be him. I can't be anyone other than who I am.' He met her gaze head on, and she knew he meant every word. 'If that's enough for you, you know where to find me.' He opened the door and stepped out into the rain to open the boot and retrieve her suitcase.

And just like that, it was over. Because how could she tell him he *was* enough when she couldn't be open about their relationship, not if she wanted to protect George's legacy?

Climbing out of the car, she pulled her hood up over

her hair and half her face, and took her suitcase from him. There was no kiss goodbye, not even a hug. Instead, he just gave her a sad smile as she turned and headed into the house.

And everything about it felt wrong.

Her mother-in-law was waiting with the door open before Gwen could knock, before Ryan had even got back in his car and driven away through the pouring rain.

'What were you doing, sitting out there with Ryan so long?' Meredith stripped the wet coat from her shoulders and hung it to dry, fussing around Gwen and shepherding her towards the lounge. 'I know he's helping you with the trust but, really, Gwen. You want to be careful, you know. People will talk. Especially with all this nonsense in the papers about George. They love to look for a scandal, don't they? And, heaven knows, Ryan's brought enough of them to our door already. I know you think he can be a good man like his brother, and you're a good person for thinking so, but, Gwen, I think you need to reconsider including him in the fundraising for George's trust. He's my own son, and I'll always love him, but you can't ignore the fact he only ever seems to bring trouble.'

Except this time the trouble was all George and Gwen. And she couldn't even tell Meredith that. Would she ever be able to see the new man Ryan had become?

'Where's Evie?' Gwen asked, casting around for her daughter. Normally she'd have been climbing all over her by now, and more than anything Gwen wanted to hug her, hold her close, and remind herself what she was doing all this for. *Who* she was doing it for.

'Oh, she fell asleep on the sofa with Taid, watching some movie about pirates or something. Now, about

Ryan.' There was an awkward pause as Meredith gave her a meaningful look. 'I really do think that you spending time with him will only bring up more horrible rumours about George. We both know that he wasn't…quite himself after his accident. It's not fair to his memory to let these people say these things, though. Have you spoken to his lawyer yet?'

Wasn't quite himself.

Understatement of the century and yet…it was still the very first time Gwen had heard Meredith admit that George had ever been less than perfect. And Meredith had told her not to read the papers—but obviously knew she would have. Perhaps even knew that Gwen wouldn't be surprised by the stories.

Gwen stared at her, blinking away a fog that seemed to have descended too many years ago. But suddenly she saw things more clearly. Saw the panic behind Meredith's eyes, the tremor in her fingers.

And she knew.

'You…you're worried these stories are true, aren't you?' she said. 'Why? What do you know?'

'Of course they're not true!' Meredith said indignantly. But she changed course and steered Gwen into the kitchen where they couldn't be overheard. 'Not this little hussy claiming George gave her a baby, and none of the others either.'

'What…what others?'

Meredith waved a hand. 'Oh, barely a week goes by without someone telling me some dreadful story about my sons. It always used to be Ryan, but since he left they moved on to George. The difference is that when they were about Ryan I believed them. Now, when they're about George, I know better.'

'Do you?' Gwen watched her mother-in-law carefully. She knew Meredith's tells, knew when she was lying about how much sugar she'd given Evie in an afternoon, or why things had to be done the way she wanted.

'Well, George would never do such a thing, would he?' Her gaze darted around the room as she answered, flying past a photo of George and her on the wall, and Gwen knew instantly she was lying.

'Meredith.'

'And even if they were true, what does it matter now? He's dead, isn't he? Can't they let us have his memory?' Her voice grew higher with every word, a desperation in it Gwen hadn't heard since the funeral. 'He was my perfect boy!'

'Nobody is perfect, Meredith,' Gwen said slowly. 'Not even George.'

He'd hated being held to that standard, Gwen remembered now. Resented that he could never put a foot wrong without uproar, while Ryan got away with it every week. If the brothers had ever talked about it, maybe they'd have realised that *neither* of them had had it all that easy. It was no excuse for either of their behaviours, but perhaps they'd have been better brothers for realising it.

George had wanted a freedom that the golden boy, the perfect son, had never been allowed—but he'd taken it anyway. Ryan had wanted the recognition, to be a person in his own right, not just in his brother's shadow— so he'd acted up, been the anti-George so people had to at least acknowledge him.

Both of them hurting and wanting what they couldn't have.

And now one of them was gone, and still Ryan was being compared to his brother.

And she was facilitating that. Keeping him in George's perfect shadow.

No wonder he'd driven away without looking back.

'Meredith,' she started again, as her mother-in-law busied herself fetching wine glasses and getting the bottle out of the fridge. 'I think we need to talk about George and Ryan. Don't you?'

At her words, Meredith slumped against the fridge door. 'I can't hear it, Gwen. I don't want to know. Can't I keep my memories?'

Her chest hurt. She didn't want to do this. She'd never wanted to do this.

'You can remember George however you want. He was a good man, and a good husband to me for a number of years.' Not all of them, but his mother didn't want to know that. 'But you have another son too. One who is alive, and who wants to be part of your life—who has worked so damn hard to turn his own life around, to be someone you and he can be proud of. If your memories of George are keeping you from loving Ryan…then I don't think that's right. Do you?'

Meredith turned slowly. She looked a decade older, Gwen realised, all in the space of a few seconds.

'You won't tell Evie? I don't want her to grow up hating her father.'

'She won't,' Gwen promised. 'But I won't lie to her either. When she's older, if she has questions, I'll answer them honestly. I'll tell her the great things about him as well as the harder things. Because she'll hear them from other people otherwise. And I want her to know what's true.'

Certainty filled her as she spoke the words. And for the first time since George's accident she knew, without a shadow of a doubt, that she was on the right track. At last.

It was a harder path, she had no doubt. But she didn't want to be Meredith in twenty years' time, still insisting on perfection from someone who could never reach it.

She wanted to live in the real world. Where there was love and trust and support—and where she appreciated it all the more because she knew it wasn't automatic. It was something you worked for.

She wanted that for her daughter too.

And for herself…

'Meredith, I'm going to be spending more time with Ryan. These allegations about George won't change that. I hope you can find a way to make peace with him.'

'He's the only son I have left,' she whispered. 'I suppose—'

'Mummy!' Evie bounded into the room, fully awake from her nap, and wrapped her little arms around Gwen as she lifted her into her embrace. 'Where's Uncle Ryan?'

'He had to go, sweetie.' Gwen met Meredith's gaze over Evie's head, and she nodded. Finally, some acceptance. A first step, at least. 'But I'll take you to see him again very soon, I promise.'

Just as soon as she'd figured out a way to make everything right again.

CHAPTER ELEVEN

IT HAD BEEN almost two weeks. Practically half a month since he'd seen Gwen, kissed her, held her.

And, God, did he miss her.

As he grabbed his bag and his headphones for the bus ride from the team hotel to the stadium, Ryan tried to put her out of his head, but all he could think about was waking up beside her that first precious morning. Knowing that at last he was where he was meant to be.

Except apparently she didn't agree.

'Hey, Phillips. You got your game head on?' His captain, Alwyn, stopped him halfway to the door.

'Course I have,' Ryan replied automatically.

It was his first game back for Wales, and the coach was taking a huge chance on him just putting him on the bench for it, even for a theoretically friendly warm-up match before the summer tour. He couldn't risk not having his head in the game.

Even if his heart was still with Gwen, in Nantes.

'Good.' Alwyn slapped him on the back and let him continue on his way.

Ryan pulled his headphones over his ears, just like the other lads, blocking out the world and letting him focus on the challenge ahead as he climbed onto the bus.

In just a couple of hours they'd be out there on the field. Well, he'd be on the side-lines, waiting to see if he was needed. But he was in Wales, playing for Wales again. Back where he belonged.

Everything he'd wanted was coming together.

He'd sent his parents his complimentary tickets for the game. Whether they'd come, he had no idea. But he figured he had to try. He had to *keep* trying.

Gwen he had to let work things through on her own. But his parents…maybe there was still hope there. And he wouldn't give up, as long as there was hope.

Preparing for the match happened more or less on autopilot. Ryan went through his usual rituals and routines, as if this were just any other match. By the time it came to run out of the tunnel onto the grass of the stadium, and sing the national anthem, it was too late to worry about the immensity of the situation anyway.

Lining up, he slung his arms around his teammates' waists on either side of him as the band started to play. First, the English national anthem—as the visitors they got to go first. The Welsh male voice choir sang it well, supported by the team and their fans. But it didn't touch Ryan's heart—not really.

But then the first strains of the Welsh anthem 'Land of my Fathers' sounded and Ryan's heart started to beat in time.

'Mae hen wlad fy nhadau yn annwyl i mi…'

The familiar words filled the air as the tune lifted the stadium. The roof was open today, the torrential rain of earlier in the week having cleared at last and the pitch mostly dried out.

'Gwlad beirdd a chantorion, enwogion o fri…'

Ryan lifted his chin, the words coming from memory,

learned so long ago. He smiled as he remembered George teaching him the lyrics, before his first proper Wales match as a spectator, so he could sing along. Whatever his brother had done or become in later years, whatever had come between them, they'd been close once. He wouldn't give up that memory either.

'Ei gwrol ryfelwyr, gwladgarwyr tra mad...'

He risked a glance up at the crowds surrounding them. A sea of red shirts and daffodil and dragon hats on one side. On the other, the white shirts and red and white flags of the English supporters. He couldn't make out individual faces at this distance, especially not through face paint and hats and flag waving. But he hoped his parents were up there somewhere.

'Dros ryddid collasant eu gwaed...'

His attention strayed to the men around him—good men, solid teammates, trusted, guys he hoped would become good friends. Not all natural singers, bless them, whatever people said about the Welsh, but they were belting the anthem out all the same.

They were there with him, believing in the same thing. That they could be better than they had been before. That they could keep working to improve. Not just to win— although that definitely mattered too, especially against England. But just to be *better*. To strive towards being the best they could.

'Gwlad, gwlad! Pleidiol wyf i'm gwlad...'

As they hit the refrain, the cry of love for their nation, Ryan looked up at the huge screen at the end of the pitch, the cameras scanning the Welsh crowds as they sang their hearts out.

And then his own words dried up in his mouth as the camera lingered on two particular faces.

'Tra môr yn fur, i'r bur hoff bau...'

Gwen. Gwen and Evie. Both singing along. Evie had a small red dragon painted on her face, and was standing on her seat to sing.

She was here. *They* were here.

And Ryan would have a full eighty minutes—plus half-time and post-game talks—to figure out what that meant.

'O bydded i'r hen iaith barhau.'

The camera swooped away, back to the team, as the anthem came to an end. And then it was time to play, and Ryan had to focus on the game, even from the bench. He forced himself to push Gwen from his mind.

But when Gareth was injured twenty minutes in, with England five points ahead, and Ryan had to run onto the pitch to take his place, all he could think was, *Please let me play well. Play my best, even. For the team. For the coach. For Wales. For me. For Mum and Dad.*

For George's memory.

For Gwen.

And for Evie.

She'd forgotten how nerve-racking it was, having someone she loved out on that pitch, until Ryan came on as an injury replacement in the twenty-first minute. Knowing that every tackle, every hit could break him. That he might come off that field a different man from the one he'd been when he went on.

But she also remembered now the exhilaration and pride. How a whole nation was placing its hopes on his shoulders.

She knew how much it meant to Ryan to be out there today, and her heart was ready to burst with pride for him now he'd achieved it. He'd worked so hard—not just in training, but on becoming the man he wanted to be.

She couldn't wait to tell him how much she loved him for it. And just for being exactly who he was.

But she did have to wait. At least for now.

Joe sat on Evie's other side, explaining the play to her. Gwen listened in with half an ear, but mostly she was just watching. Watching Ryan as he raced up and down the pitch. How intently he focussed on the play. How good his hands were, grabbing the ball out of the air and passing it exactly where it needed to be. How quickly he could be wherever he was needed.

And, yes, how damn good he looked in that Wales kit, with its clinging top and shorts that showed off his thighs…

'Will we see Uncle Ryan now?' Evie asked at half-time.

'Not yet,' Gwen replied. 'After the match is over. There's still another half to go.'

She wanted to, though. She wanted to race down there to the tunnel and through to the changing rooms and find Ryan and tell him everything.

Except, given that Wales were still down at the break, they were probably getting a loudly yelled half-time team talk, firing them up for the second half.

Ryan needed to focus on the game. But that didn't stop her planning out *her* full-time talk in her head.

I'm sorry. She definitely needed to start with that, right? After that, hopefully it would be easy.

Maybe she'd just kiss him. That seemed to solve—and also sometimes cause—a lot of their problems.

The second half kicked off and Wales almost closed the gap within the first five minutes. Gwen found herself sitting closer to the edge of her seat as every second ticked by, clutching Evie's hand tightly enough that she actually asked her to stop.

Gwen couldn't look away from the ball—that white shape blurring through the air from man to man, hands to hands, then flying through space off someone's boot.

Suddenly Ryan was under it, catching it and racing towards the try line, and Gwen stopped breathing altogether.

'Go, Uncle Ryan!' Evie yelled beside her, and she could hear Joe cheering too. But Gwen couldn't cheer. She couldn't do anything but watch as the huge men in white shirts bore down on him, determined to take him to ground.

The crunch of the impact was audible, and a groan of sympathy went up around the stadium. Joe, obviously sensing her distress, reached across and grabbed her hand.

'Look, Mummy, you're on the big screen!' Evie cried.

Gwen couldn't even look. She knew what it would show.

A woman afraid for the man she loved.

The referee had blown the whistle, a penalty in the ruck that had followed the tackle, and the medical team was on the pitch.

'He's sitting up,' Joe said. 'Look, Gwen. He's fine.'

One of the team handed him a water bottle and leaned in to say something. Down on the field, Ryan looked up at the big screen and smiled. Then he raised a hand and waved, and blew a kiss, and Gwen's lungs started working again.

'He's okay,' she whispered. 'He's okay.'

'Are you?' Joe asked, sounding faintly amused now the panic was over.

'I will be.' When she got to talk to him. When she told him she loved him.

When he hopefully said it back.

Just twenty more minutes left on the clock. She could make it through that. Couldn't she?

One last chance.

Less than a minute left on the clock. One last play. When the whistle blew again it would all be over.

Ryan forced himself to focus on the moment, not on Gwen up in the stands. Her face, when he'd been hit in the tackle. The worry—and the love. The hope it gave him.

Wales had a line-out, just ten metres out from the try line. If they could pull this off, get the ball over the line and score one last try, the game would be theirs.

If they couldn't, they'd lose. Simple as that.

Sometimes life came down to two options, and Ryan liked to think he'd got better at picking the right one over the last few years. Making good choices—or at least better ones. But this time it wasn't just up to him.

It was the whole team.

They lined up, the play already agreed, nerves palpable. Across the way, the English team were joking, shouting, trying to break their focus. They wouldn't succeed.

The ball flew, and Dewi caught it. Fast, he passed it back to Ryan, on to Alwyn, and on down the line. Each throw had to go backwards, but with each catch they surged forward, closer and closer. Until the ball came back to him and Ryan instinctively reacted, his feet moving before he even thought, sidestepping, dodging, twisting and then—*yes!*—running, exactly the way his big brother had taught him, so many years ago.

The English defenders were right behind him, but he

was too far now, too fast, too determined. He threw himself over the line, grounding the ball with so much force that the grass rucked up behind it—and the whistle blew.

Try.

His first try for Wales in his first game back. It was everything he'd dreamed of.

His teammates raced over to celebrate, to hug him, clap him on the back, insult him in a loving way, the usual.

There was the conversion to follow, of course, but that flew over the posts as an afterthought. The whistle blew and the game was won.

There would be team celebrations for hours. Interviews, showers, pub, the usual.

'Ryan, how did it feel to score the final try?' the TV interviewer asked on the side-line as he was pushed into the frame.

'Uh…amazing.' But Ryan only had one thing on his mind as he scanned the crowds, trying to find Gwen.

'Your first match back too!'

'Yeah, it was pretty special.'

'And there was someone special out in the crowd, watching you today, I understand?'

Ryan looked at her in surprise as she motioned to the big screen. And there, standing at the railings, just metres away from him, he realised, was Gwen, lifting Evie up as she cheered for him.

'Your niece, Evie.'

Ryan grinned. 'Yeah, she's pretty awesome. Her mum's not bad either, actually. Now, if you'll excuse me…?'

Handing the microphone back, he jogged over to where Gwen and Evie waited, Joe behind them. Climbing straight over the railings—to a cheer from the crowd—

he picked Evie up, swung her round and kissed her on the cheek.

'You were amazing, Uncle Ryan!'

'You're better,' he told her. 'And I love your dragon.' He pointed to the cuddly red dragon in her arms.

'Taid gave it to me,' she said. 'They're here somewhere too. He said he gave you and Daddy a dragon just like this when you came to your first rugby game. And Nain taught me the words for the anthem too, so I could sing along like you.'

Tears stung his eyes, but he blinked them away.

'They're really trying,' Gwen said. She took Evie from his arms and passed her over to Joe, who knew a hint when he saw one, obviously, as he distracted her by going to look at all the other players swapping shirts and signing autographs further down the pitch.

'I can't believe you came,' he said.

'Of *course* I came. I wasn't going to miss your first game back for Wales. And besides…' She took a deep breath. 'I needed to tell you I'm sorry. That I love you—who you are now, the person you were always meant to be. And I didn't ever want to push you back into George's shadow, I swear.'

'I'm sorry too,' Ryan said. 'I know how hard this must all be for you. I know how much you loved George, and I respect you wanting to protect Evie.'

'I *did* love George. But I need to move on from our past together. Find a way to forgive him for those awful last few years so I can be happy again. With you, if you'll have me.'

'Always.' Ryan wrapped his hands around her waist to lift her to him, tilting his head to kiss her as another cheer went up all around them. They were probably on the big screen again.

He didn't care.

'You're my future,' he whispered, as he set her down. 'You're everything I've been working towards all this time, even when I didn't know it. You and Evie, and my parents. I want us to have the happy future that you deserve.'

'I want that too,' she murmured back, in between kisses. 'And I know there's still a lot to work out. But… I love you. And it feels like that's a pretty good start.'

'It's the only one I need,' he replied, knowing he'd won so much more than a game of rugby that day.

Then he kissed her again, and knew in his bones that loving Gwen was the best choice he would ever make.

* * * * *

HER SECOND
FOREVER

JOANNA SIMS

Dedicated to the real Lee Macbeth...
It's the excitement of hearing about fans like you
that keeps me writing.
I hope you enjoy this one too, Lady Macbeth!

Prologue

"Mack."

Cowboy Colt Brand's head bobbed up and down as the bright Montana morning sun beat down on his bare arms.

"Hey, Mack!" Colt raised his voice a notch higher, thinking that his companion couldn't hear him. "Stop me if you've heard this one before. A miniature horse, an alpaca and a giraffe all walk into a bar. The bartender asks, what can I get you fellas to drink—" Colt paused to chuckle to himself before he continued "—and the alpaca said…"

Colt squinted and looked up to the left as if the sky would hold the words he was searching for in his mind. "Well, shoot, Mack! I forgot what the heck the alpaca *said*."

A quick siren behind him made Colt glance over his shoulder. Colt swore at the unwanted interruption, but wanted to reassure his companion. "Just keep calm and let me do the talking, Mack. I've been to this police-harassment rodeo before."

"Colt!" The police officer had pulled up beside him and had rolled down the window to his squad car. "Where in blazes are you goin'?"

"Home to Sugar Creek Ranch." Colt flung his hand forward toward the horizon.

"You're headin' the wrong way." The police officer who also happened to be a longtime friend yelled, "Pull over!"

"Tell me one thing I'm doin' wrong, Jimmy! Just name it!"

"Just pull over," the officer snapped.

Grudgingly, Colt followed the order and pulled over to the side of the road. He sighed in frustration while he waited for Jimmy to park his squad car behind him. On his way out of the car, Colt heard Jimmy say into the radio pinned to his uniform, "Tell Chief I found him."

Hands on his hips, his eyes hidden behind his mirrored sunglasses, Jimmy stood on the side of the road and frowned at him. "Darn it, Colt. I've got a heck of a lot better things to do with my time than chasing you all over God's creation! I done told you not to get caught drivin' under the influence again, didn't I?"

"I wasn't driving! *He* was." Colt pointed to Mack.

"You've already been warned time and again that you can't operate a conveyance under the influence—not a tractor, not a lawn mower, not a snowmobile and not *even if* that conveyance has four legs!" Jimmy pointed to Mack. "Riding that there horse drunk on this here highway ain't no different than driving a car drunk."

"How can you say that I was *driving* when I didn't even have my hands on the reins?" Colt had been resting his hands on the saddle horn. He held up his hands in the air for his friend to see while Mack dropped his head down to nibble a blade of grass pushing through the asphalt.

"That don't make it no better, Colt. And who's horse is this? Did you steal this horse?"

"I won him fair and square in a poker game and now I'm taking him home," Colt mumbled, his head bobbing downward. He sure was tired.

"I'm sorry, friend, but I'm going to have to take you in this time."

"Come on!" Colt grumbled. "How will Mack get home?"

"I already put in a call to your brother Gabe to bring the horse trailer." Jimmy dropped his chin and looked at him over the brim of his sunglasses with somber eyes. "Now, I promise you that this don't give me no pleasure. I can't let you off with a warning this time. I've got my orders. So climb down off of that horse—I've got to arrest you."

Chapter One

"Welcome. I'm Gilda." A slender woman with closely cropped honey-colored hair and a German accent greeted Colt at the door of the room. Life had taken a sharp left turn for Colt after his arrest and now he found himself on a Monday morning at the Strides of Strength Therapeutic Riding Center, a place where they provided equine-assisted activities and therapy for kids with disabilities.

"Guten Tag." He raised two fingers to the brim of his dusty cowboy hat and gave her a quick salute.

"Please—" she gestured to the table behind her "—fill out a name tag and sit anywhere you like. Help yourself to the coffee. Lee will arrive shortly."

Colt scrawled his name on a tag, peeled it off and slapped it onto his hat. The classroom, newly constructed and still smelling faintly of fresh paint, occupied one half of an eight-stall barn. Across the aisle, and through the large picture window, there was an unobstructed view of two draft horses sleeping with their heads hanging over their stall gates. If he weren't feeling so bitter, he might have been able to appreciate the craftsmanship in the classroom design, with its tall pitched roof, hand-carved tables long enough to sit several people and the screened-in porch off the back door that afforded sweeping views of the pastureland and snowcapped Montana mountains far off in the distance. But he *was* bitter. All he did was borrow a friend's horse to get home after a very lucrative night of poker. Next thing he knew, he was being hauled in for driving under the influence! He'd paid a hefty fine, was sentenced to unsupervised probation for six months and three months of community service. Now he was relegated to a summer of taking a bunch of kids for pony rides when he could be spending his time doing real ranch work at his family's cattle spread, Sugar Creek, or traveling to rodeos with his friends.

Colt pulled out a chair, dragging it noisily across the polished concrete floor and sat down at the back table. Not bothering to take off his hat as he was raised to do, he slumped down, put his dirt-caked boots on top of the table and yanked the brim of his hat over his eyes. As soon as this little "orientation" waste-of-his-time was over, the quicker he could get the heck out of this place. The less time he spent on this island of misfit toys, the better.

Occupational Therapist Lee Macbeth leaned with her back against barn, out of view of the classroom windows. She closed her eyes and breathed in deeply several times, always feeling a bit nervous before she spoke in front of a group of new people. It was always the same, no matter the size of the crowd—first came the horrible butterflies in her stomach followed by an outbreak of sweat on her face, hairline and neck and then finally, her heart racing in her chest like she was about to jump out of a plane without a parachute. It never got any easier, even after ten years of volunteer orientations and traveling the world as a motivational speaker. But somehow, she always managed to pull herself together and get the job done.

Lee opened the round polished yellow-gold necklace she wore on a long chain around her neck and stared at the picture tucked inside. "Here we go."

She clicked the locket shut and pushed away from the wall. She pulled down the edges of her Strides of Strength logoed red polo over her snugly fit dark blue jeans and rolled her shoulders back. Right before she walked into the classroom, she pushed her softly layered, loose mahogany hair back from her face, lifted her chin slightly, pasted a welcoming smile on her face and then pulled the door open.

"Hello, volunteers!" She waltzed through the door waving both of her hands enthusiastically, always relieved to see that the volunteers who had signed up to join the summer program actually showed on orientation day. "Welcome to summer orientation! We are so happy to have you with us!"

Lee took her spot behind the podium, her brain quickly tallying the number of warm bodies in the space. Only ten—or eleven if she counted the bored cowboy in the back of the classroom with his filthy boots dirtying up her tables, which had been carved and hand-stained to her specification from trees harvested from the property. She read the name tag slapped haphazardly on his cowboy hat but Lee already knew who the cowboy was—she had just looked at his file this morning. *Colt* hadn't bothered to look up or return her greeting.

So, ten volunteers and one pain in the hind end.

It was a much smaller crowd than she had hoped for. The summer program, which started in two short weeks, depended heavily on volunteers. With the larger than average number of clients signed up this year, it was going to be a challenge to serve the needs of all the riders and horses. The ten volunteers, as usual, were female, all in their early to mid-twenties with lineless skin on their faces and the eagerness of unencumbered youth in their eyes. She was set to turn thirty-five this year—twenty-five seemed like two lifetimes ago.

"Thank you so much for your interest in the Strides of Strength summer program." Lee did her best to ignore the cowboy, focusing her smile and energy on the volunteers who were giving her their undivided attention. "You have no idea what your time and effort will mean to the children who spend their summer with us. We aren't just providing therapy for children with disabilities—we are building self-esteem, self-confidence and memories that will last for the rest of their lives. What you do here this summer truly matters."

Soon after she began to interact with the new crop of volunteers, Lee's nerves slipped away as she moved through her standard orientation routine. First, she showed the group a PowerPoint presentation and then spent the rest of the session answering questions. Even though the volunteer pool was smaller than she would have liked, they were an enthusiastic bunch made up mainly of graduate students earning degrees in occupational therapy, physical therapy or speech language pathology. What these women lacked in numbers, Lee was certain they would make up for it in energy and dedication. Colt, on the other hand, who had hardly moved a muscle, was going to prove to be a regrettable thorn in her side.

Why did I let Judge Ackredge talk me into this?
She had never let anyone work off community service at Strides of Strength. But Judge Ackredge was
a dear friend and he had called in a favor.

"It's going to be a sincerely rewarding summer
for all of you. And, when you see how much this
program means to our kiddos, I promise the exhaus-
tion will be well worth it." Lee tucked a strand of
hair behind her ear, and as it always did when she
talked about the kids, she felt a swell of emotion
bring unshed tears to her eyes. Her hand came up
to clutch her locket—it seemed to give her strength
or steady her emotions when she needed it the most.
"Volunteers are our lifeblood and we are so grateful to have you here with us. We depend so much
on the kindness of our community and there is so
much need here. We ask that if you know of anyone who can donate materials or skilled services,
please think of us. Lord knows there's always a
fence to mend…"

Without looking up, Colt raised his hand.

Lee fought the urge to frown. "Sir? Do you have
a question?"

With one finger, Colt pushed the brim of his hat
upward so his face and eyes were exposed. For the
briefest of moments, she was captive to his brilliant
deeply set sapphire-blue eyes. Lee was struck by
what she saw in those eyes in a way she hadn't expected. Her hand tightened on the locket and she

had to take a step backward to break the eye contact first.

"I can mend a fence," Colt said with a baritone drawl that touched off a pleasure zone in her brain.

"Wonderful. I'll take you up on that." She nodded quickly, fiddling with papers on her podium, unnerved by the way his gravelly voice had made her pulse quicken. Colt had that deep roughness in his voice that was sweet music to the female reptilian brain.

Lee forced her attention back to the graduate students, but none of them were looking at her. All the young women were turned in their seats, giving their undivided attention to the cowboy. And why wouldn't they? The tenor of his voice seemed designed specifically to grab the focus of the female ear. He also had golden-tanned skin, raven-black hair that brushed across his broad shoulders, a strong chin covered in stubble and those striking blue eyes. This fox in the henhouse was going to be a problem—for all them.

"There are also fans to be installed in the barns," she continued. "So if any of you know an electrician who is willing to volunteer their time..."

Colt raised two fingers in the air. He had finally taken his boots off her new table. He was sitting forward with his arms on the tabletop, his eyes seemingly glued to her face. "I can do that. Easy fix."

It was absolutely unheard of that her mouth would suddenly lose the ability to move—she could always talk a mile a minute about any subject just about any time. And yet, here she was, temporarily dumbfounded. Lee gave him a quick nod and swallowed several times before she continued. His sudden interest in what she was saying was just as disturbing to her as when he had appeared to be completely ignoring her. Either way, he was an unwanted distraction.

"And we do have some plumbing needs so if you…"

Up went Colt's hand again.

"I know a thing or two about plumbing."

Lee tucked another strand of hair behind her ear, a bit of a nervous tick at times, annoyed that she could feel a blush on her cheeks. She met good-looking men all the time in her travels—and some had very sexy accents. Why was *this* good-looking man making her feel flustered?

"Well then." She cleared her throat. "It's good to know that we have a jack-of-all-trades with us this summer."

Lee wrapped up the session and the agitation Colt had triggered inside of her body dissipated as she circulated through the small group of volunteers, shaking hands and thanking them each personally for their time. Colt leaned against a wall in the back of the classroom, seemingly waiting for his turn with her. It didn't go unnoticed that each female volunteer paid court with the cowboy, stopping by to chat with him before heading out the door.

When she finally reached him, Colt took off his hat in a gentlemanly gesture and held out his hand to her.

"I'm Colt Brand."

"I know." Her response was snappier than she had intended. To soften her tone, she gestured to the name tag on his hat. "I can read."

Colt reached up with a quick grin, tugged the name tag off his hat and balled it up in his hand. Colt Brand was tall, lean, with corded muscles on his neck and forearms. The man smelled deliciously to her senses, like leather and saddle soap.

"I just reviewed your application this morning." She fought to keep her mind focused on business and not on how fantastic he smelled. "Why don't you come to my office and we can discuss your particular circumstances in private?"

Colt flashed straight white teeth at her. "It'd be my pleasure to accompany you, ma'am."

He was quick to move in front of her to open the door so she could walk through. Lee said, "Thank you," but scrunched up her face at the thought of being called *ma'am*. She was only in her mid-thirties! She wasn't old enough to get ma'am-ed yet by a man in his twenties, was she?

"I always know when I'm in the South or in Montana, because I get the ma'am treatment. But please try *not to* ma'am me. It makes me feel like I've got one foot in the nursing home."

Colt smiled down at her and darn it if her heartbeat didn't quicken.

"I didn't mean any disrespect."

"I know you didn't." She slipped through a cattleman's gate so they could take a shortcut through one of the pastures situated between the barn that housed the classroom and the office at the front of the facility.

The minute the mares in the pasture saw her, they headed over to greet her. This was one of the greatest pleasures of her life, her stolen moments with these beautiful and elegant animals.

"Hello, my sweet babies." Lee rubbed their noses and spent a moment giving each of the horses some individualized attention. Sweet Girl, a Thoroughbred off the racetrack, enjoyed a belly rub and Ruby, a grumpy black Shetland pony, loved to have her ears scratched. Lee knew the quirks and behaviors of every single creature on her property, from the horses to the dogs and cats. They all mattered. They all were her family.

Colt watched Lee from a couple of feet away. It was a chance to stand back and observe this woman who had caused a seismic shift in his brain without even trying. So many females—really smart, beautiful females—had tried to gain and hold his attention but none had ever succeeded. He was still a young man, not even thirty, and the thought of settling down with one woman for the rest of his life had never appealed to him. The thought of a wife and family had always been way off in the distant future—so far down the line that he couldn't even imagine it. Until now. Until Lee.

Something strange, and completely unexpected, had happened when he finally looked up to see the woman who matched the sweet, lilting voice standing at the front of the classroom. Lightning struck. One minute he was Colt Brand and the next moment he was Colt Brand in love. She had a lovely face to match that easy-on-the-ears voice and her eyes, a golden hazel-brown, held a depth of feeling and kindness he had only seen in one other woman in his life—his mother. Once he laid eyes on Lee, Colt was certain he would never want to take his eyes off her again.

That's my wife.

This was the one thought so clear in his mind when he raised his hand to gain her attention in the classroom. Colt didn't know *how* he knew that he had just fallen in love at first sight; he just knew that he had. She was so pretty, this woman, with her creamy skin, hazel eyes and a button nose housed in an oval face framed by layered brown hair. Her dark blue jeans were snugly fit to her hips and legs.

She was slender and not as curvy or busty as he typically favored. But it hadn't been her body or her hair or even her classically pretty face that had sent a bolt of lightning into his brain. It had been those eyes—so sincere, so penetrating and so honest— that had made him sit up and take notice.

As he watched her now, with the late morning sunlight touching her silky hair, and her pretty face so filled with love for her horses as she hugged them and stroked their soft noses, his stomach was tied up in knots with excitement and he had adrenaline setting off little sparks of electricity all over his body. He had just found something he didn't know was missing in his life—he had found the woman he was meant to spend the rest of his days loving.

"Seriously?" Lee gave a half laugh in surprise. She was left standing alone when Sweet Girl, and then Ruby, walked away from her to join him instead.

"What can I say? Women love me." Colt smiled at her broadly while he wrapped his arms around Sweet Girl's neck for a hug and patted her on the shoulder. Ruby nudged his hip with her muzzle and the Thoroughbred spun her large head around and pinned back her ears in jealousy.

"Okay." Lee waved her hand at him. "Let's keep moving before you cause a fight between these pasture mates who *never* fight—not even at mealtime."

Colt gave each mare one last bit of affection before he jogged a couple of steps to catch up with Lee. He had long legs and a lengthy stride but he had to work to keep pace with her. Lee was a woman of average height, which was the only thing average about her. She walked quickly, with purpose, as if she were always late for something.

"Were you able to take the tour with Hilda earlier?" Lee asked him.

"A tour? No. I missed that one."

Colt had chosen to sleep in on his last official day of freedom for the summer. He had been angry at the thought of wasting his time at Strides of Strength, babysitting a bunch of kids. Now he was convinced that his arrest and subsequent sentence had led him directly to the woman he was meant to marry.

"You built all of this?" he asked, impressed.

The facility was a major operation with five separate barns, enough fenced pastureland to accommodate a large herd of horses, hay fields for growing hay, an indoor riding arena and several buildings dedicated to different therapy disciplines.

"There was just a couple of old buildings and barbed wire fencing when I wrote the grant application to buy this place," she said, leading him into one of the barns. "It's still a work-in-progress, but we've come a long way since those days."

"I'd say."

She sent him a quick smile in between the chore of checking the water buckets in each of the stalls.

"Would you grab me that hose over there?" She pointed to the garden hose hanging up across the aisle from where she was standing. "Lift that blue handle to turn the water on."

Colt brought the hose over to her, glad to be able to help her. If anyone had told him that he would *want* to be of service to Strides of Strength just a short hour ago, he would have laughed in his or her face. But now? It felt good to help Lee. He knew instinctively that the way to this woman's heart was through her horses and her therapy program.

Lee handed the hose back to him after she filled the water bucket. "Thank you."

"Not a problem. I'm here to help." He said it and he knew that he meant it.

His companion studied his face for a moment, as if she were studying something unusual under a microscope. Her eyes were guarded as she looked around the barn. "This is the oldest barn on the property and I'm afraid it's in need of the most TLC."

"What's the list?"

She started walking again and he followed. "What *isn't* on the list? The roof needs to be patched and sealed, the entire outside needs to be stripped, primed and painted, fans need to be installed in every stall, and I wrote a grant for automatic watering systems, but we haven't had the money to hire a plumber to install them."

"I can start tackling that list tomorrow."

Lee suddenly stopped in her tracks and looked up at him again. He loved it when she looked at him and he had a chance, in that moment, to admire her pretty face.

"Are you serious?"

"Yes, ma'am." She grimaced and he quickly rephrased, "Yes, *Lee,* I'm serious. I can do everything on that list."

"Even the automatic watering systems?"

He nodded, liking the way she was looking at him in this moment. There was a flicker of respect in her eyes that hadn't been there before. She stared at him for a second or two longer before she continued walking.

"I have to say, Colt, that I didn't think this was such a great idea, having you here this summer."

"Neither did I."

"But if you're as handy as you say you are…"

"I am."

"Then perhaps this isn't the worst idea I've ever had."

Colt tilted his head back and truly laughed for the first time that day. "Is that what I was? The *worst* idea you'd ever had?"

Her bowed lips quirked up sheepishly as she

tried to stop herself from smiling too broadly. "Well, perhaps not the *worst* idea."

"But close?"

Lee's response was interrupted by the sound of a familiar squeal and his name being shouted from a nearby paddock.

"Uncle Colt! Uncle *Colt*!"

Colt saw his niece, Callie Brand, running through an open gate, her arms pumping furiously, her cheeks flushed with excitement.

"Shut the gate, Callie!" Lee called out to her.

"Oh!" Callie spun around, raced back to the open gate, shut it and then ran toward him, her face pink from exertion, until she threw herself into his arms.

"What are you d-doing here, Uncle Colt?" Callie exclaimed, her arms like a vise-grip around his torso. A young woman in her early twenties, Callie was short in stature like most people living with Down syndrome, so her head barely reached his chest.

There was one person in his life who could always make Colt smile and that was Callie. His older brother Liam had married Callie's mom, Kate, and soon after the marriage, Liam had adopted Callie, even though she was already an adult. Ironically, the same judge who had refused to drop the charges against him and assigned him to Strides of Strength for community service had officiated Callie's adoption into the Brand family.

Colt hugged his niece tightly before he looked down into her happy blue eyes.

"I'm volunteering here for the summer," he said before he asked, "What are *you* doing here?"

"I—I work here," Callie proudly told him. "I—I have a job now. And I—I get a paycheck. D-didn't you know that?"

He shook his head—why didn't he know that about his niece?

"No. I didn't. But I'm real proud of you, Callie."

Callie kept right on hugging him, her head resting on his chest. "Thank you."

Callie finally finished the hug, stepped back and held up her left hand and wiggled her ring finger for him to see a small diamond ring. "I—I'm engaged, Uncle Colt."

Colt put his hands on both of Callie's shoulders and leaned his head closer to her so she could look right into his eyes. "I know, sweet pea. I have the invitation to the engagement party on my refrigerator where I can see it every day." Colt felt Lee's eyes on them, so he kissed Callie on the top of the head, "You'd better get back to work before you get in trouble with the boss. I'll see you later."

"Okay. Bye." Callie giggled behind her hand before she spun around and headed back to the wheelbarrow she had abandoned in the paddock.

Colt waited until his niece was out of earshot

before he turned to Lee. "It's really good of you to give Callie a job."

"She *earned* her job with me." Lee stared after Callie. "I didn't *give* her anything. The Callies of the world are the reason I do what I do. Everyone deserves a chance to have purpose in this life— that's what we do here. That's *why* we exist, to help people break through barriers in their lives so they can do whatever it is they want to do."

"And if there are some barriers that they can't break through?" Colt asked, watching Callie talking to herself as she picked up manure with a fork in the paddock.

Lee was observing Callie, as well. "If they can't break through, then we get a really big piece of equipment and mow them right down." As almost an afterthought, Lee added in a lowered tone, "There's always a way."

Chapter Two

On the way back to her office, Lee gave Colt the ten-cent tour of the property and introduced him to the permanent staff. It was hard to miss that every woman who came in contact with Colt, young or old, seemed to melt just a little in his presence. Yes, he was inarguably a very handsome, appealing man. But it really did shock her that even Gail Allen, a devoted Baptist and church pianist who provided free lessons to Lee's students, seemed to take a liking to the tall cowboy. Colt was charming and polite and deferential to all the ladies, tipping his hat, giving them little compliments in that silky baritone voice of his. By the time they reached her office, which was housed in a small tin-roofed, single-story farmhouse that had been on the property since the turn of the century, some of Lee's initial worry about having him with them for the summer had lessened.

"This house was one of the few buildings we could save on the property," she said at the front door. "All of the wood planks you see on the floors inside were salvaged from the buildings we couldn't save." She let the door swing open. "It makes me feel happy that we were able to give them a new life. A new purpose."

"You're very big on giving things new purpose," Colt observed.

"Of course." She closed the door behind him. "Isn't that what it's all about?"

"I never thought about it like that." Colt removed his hat and hung it on a hat rack just inside of the door. The sight of his hat hanging on her hat rack temporarily distracted Lee. It was as if she had seen that hat hanging there before—as if it had always been there. As if it were *meant* to be there.

The sound of a familiar and comforting meow brought her mind back to the present. A twenty-two-pound dark gray feline came out of her office, tail upright with the tip slightly curled over so it looked like a question mark. The cat came directly to her and rubbed up against her leg.

As she always did whenever she saw Chester,

she smiled and leaned down to give him a scratch beneath his chin.

"This is Chester." She made the introduction.

Lee watched Colt closely to see his reaction to the cat. Her grandmother, for whom she was named, had always told her that you could tell a lot about a man by the way he acted around cats. Most men favored dogs and thought it was emasculating to like a cat; according to Grandmother Macbeth, men who could relate to a cat were simply more secure in their manhood.

Chester picked his favorite spot on the southwestern print rug that occupied the space in the entryway, flopped onto his side, trilled and yawned.

"I don't want to tell you your business," Colt said, "But you may want to consider putting Chester on a diet."

Lee frowned at him. "He *is* on a diet, thank you very much. We try not talk about his diet in front of him. Chester knows he's on a diet and he's very sensitive about it."

Chester rolled onto his back, thick cream-and-gray belly fur sticking up in the air, his hind legs flopped out to the side while he busied himself intermittently licking a front paw and rubbing it over his ear.

Colt looked at Lee with his lips quirked up in amusement. "I see that."

Lee noticed the clock on the wall and realized

that she was frittering away valuable daylight just hanging out with Colt when she needed to be having a serious discussion with him about his placement at Strides of Strength for the summer program. Even *she* had been sucked unwittingly into the charm vortex! Instead of discussing the very serious matter of his arrest and subsequent community service sentence, she was bantering with him about Chester's very successful diet!

With a shake of her head at her own susceptibility to cowboy charm, Lee ushered Colt into her nearby office, waiting for Chester to mosey his way into the room before she closed the door for privacy.

"Have a seat." Lee gestured to one of the armchairs, unmatched flea market finds, situated in front of her desk.

Colt sat down on one chair and Chester managed to hoist his hefty self into the chair next to him. Chester sat facing Colt, purring loudly and gazing at him with his large green eyes. He reached out his paw toward Colt to get his attention.

"He wants you to pet him," Lee noted, taking a seat behind her desk.

Colt obliged the feline while looking around her office, studying the framed degrees and awards and pictures she had used to fill the empty spaces of her walls. Something caught his interest and he stood up and covered the distance to the other side of the room with a couple of long-legged strides. It was a picture of her standing with her first group of riders. She had started the program with two of her own horses, one speech-language pathologist and one physical therapist. Now she had enough riders to contract three therapists in each discipline.

"You've been busy." He walked back toward the desk.

"Always." She unlocked the drawer, pulled out his file and put it on the desk.

Lee had discovered in her twenties that the best way to put the past behind her was to run as fast as she could into the future. If she was busy, her mind occupied, it was easier to forget. Unfortunately, the past had a way of sneaking up on her when she had downtime. She had learned to resent downtime.

Before Colt sat back down, he bent over, scooped up Chester who was on the floor pawing at the side of her desk and deposited him gently next to the file.

"Hi, my handsome boy." Lee couldn't resist her chubby feline. She rubbed his head. After a moment, Chester sat down contentedly, arms under his body so he looked like an oversized bread box, closing his eyes with a happy sigh.

Colt took his seat again. "He needs a ramp."

"I know," Lee agreed. "I've looked online for steps that are tall enough, but I need to have something custom-made for him. It's on the list."

Colt nodded, his hands resting on his knees,

looking too large for her flea market armchair. "I know I've heard about this place before—maybe from my brother or even Callie's mom, Kate. Now that I think about it, you must know Kate...?"

Lee nodded, her hands folded on top of his file. "She's donated some of her time to train my therapy horses. And I know your brother Liam too. He takes care of all of the horses' annual physicals and only charges me for the shots, so he's been a big asset to us ever since we opened ten years ago."

"It seems like you and I have been living our lives with just one degree of separation. It's kind of surprising that the two of us haven't run into each other before."

Lee didn't respond, smoothing her hands over the file. It didn't surprise her in the least that they hadn't crossed paths. In her experience, young cowboys like Colt weren't focused on serving others. They were focused on serving themselves and their whims—bouncing from rodeos to line dancing at the bars to hunting and fishing and then back again. It wasn't necessarily a harsh judgment against him—it was just the observable truth of the stark differences in their lives. She didn't spend her time at rodeos or line dancing in the downtown Bozeman bars. She wanted her life to have more purpose that just drifting from one amusement to the next.

"Now I wish I had paid this place a little more attention." Colt's eyes pinpointed on her face in a way that made her self-conscious enough to reach for her locket with a free hand.

"Well—" she tucked her hair behind her ear "—you're here now."

Colt nodded and his eyes seemed so intent on her face. It was impossible for Lee to ignore the natural, completely unexpected chemistry between them. He was attracted to her—she could feel it as much as see it. But what was alarming to Lee was the undeniable response she was having to this man. His attraction was not one-sided. Against the will of her own mind, her body was responding to the masculine resonance of his voice, the woody scent of his skin and the firmness of his lips. She was physically attracted to this man, bottom line. She would, of course, ignore that attraction. It was simply shocking that she had found herself attracted to *any* man—something that hadn't happened in a decade—much less a cowboy who was at her facility to serve out his community service.

Lee opened his file and scanned the contents briefly.

"Is that file about me?" he asked.

She looked up with a nod, forcing herself to focus on the facts and not how blue his eyes were. "You were arrested on Highway 84 near Four Corner for driving under the influence—" she paused for a split second before she added "—while riding a horse."

Colt grinned at her a bit sheepishly. "Mack. Great horse. Won him with a pair of twos, which is a pretty difficult thing to accomplish."

"I don't know if that rises to the level of an accomplishment," she interjected.

"My friend is an amateur poker player," he countered. "So it's not easy to get one over on him. And Mack is a really good horse. My friend still hasn't quit complaining about losing him."

When she didn't play along with him, Colt's grin faltered as he continued, "I admit it's a bit unusual to get arrested on horseback…"

"So unusual it made the six o'clock news."

"It was a slow news night, I think. And I only got arrested because I had been pulled over on my tractor a couple of times."

Lee closed the file, rested her arms on the desk in front of her, her mouth unsmiling. The topic of conversation had, thankfully, thrown a big bucket of cold water on her attraction to Colt. "I take drunk driving very seriously, Mr. Brand."

Colt's grin dropped entirely and he shifted a bit in his chair. "As do I."

"No," she returned, "you don't. Your record proves that you don't I'm afraid."

"I suppose what's in that file isn't altogether flattering."

"No. It's not," she agreed. "You could have injured or killed yourself, the horse and innocent people driving on that road if you had steered Mack into traffic."

"You're right," he acknowledged somberly. With both of his large hands, Colt pushed his unruly black hair off his handsome face. For the first time since they had entered her office, Lee believed that she was seeing a more sober, serious side of the man.

"We are both a profitable business with horse boarding and a nonprofit business with the Strides of Strength equine-assisted therapy program. This place is my life. It means the world to me. And this is the first time since opening that I have allowed anyone to fulfill their community service at my facility."

"Why now? Why me?" Colt asked, his hands threaded together and resting in front of his body.

"Judge Ackredge is a close friend of mine. He called in a favor." Lee was blunt. "I understand he has some connection to your family, as well."

"Judge Ackredge handled Callie's adoption."

"I see." Now the picture was coming more sharply into focus. Callie was the connective tissue holding together their vastly different lives. Colt's brother, Liam, had adopted his wife Kate's daughter Callie even though she was already an adult. It had been an unusual but touching moment for everyone who knew Callie, including her. Lee sat back in her chair and studied Colt. "Am I wrong to assume that this wouldn't have been your first choice of placement for your community service?"

"No," he said with a ring of honesty in his voice. "This wouldn't have been first, second or last choice, for that matter. But I've been known to be wrong about a thing or two."

There was a moment of silence between them while they studied each other.

"I need to be straight with you," Lee finally stated, breaking the silence. "I'm still on the fence about you being here this summer."

His shoulders stiffened at her words and he seemed to brace himself for something negative to follow. "I think you should give me a fair shot. You don't seem like the type to be pessimistic."

"*But*," she continued her thought, "I've seen you with the horses and the staff...how you are with Callie..." Her voice trailed off a bit. She cleared her throat and continued, "I do think this arrangement is worth giving a try, particularly with all you bring to the table as a handyman."

He nodded, his shoulders relaxing.

"I don't intend to have you working directly with our riders," she added.

"Now that's a relief!" Colt said with a big smile. "I was worried. I don't think that's for me."

"Are you uncomfortable around people with disabilities?" she asked more sharply than she had intended.

"I don't know much about it one way or the other. Callie's my only experience."

"Then you're in for a treat this summer." Lee slipped his file back into the drawer and locked it. "You're going to meet some of the most amazing kids in the world. Truly inspiring kids. But I do want something to be really clear between us, Mr. Brand." She used his surname deliberately. "I expect you to be here on time and ready to work, Monday through Friday, until your hours are fulfilled. And if you step out of line, even a *centimeter* out of line, I have Judge Ackredge on speed dial."

"I don't plan on screwing this gig up, Lee. But if I do, you'd be well within your rights to call the judge."

Lee stood up and Colt followed her lead.

"But I bet," he added with that charming smile of his that made her heart pick up the pace, "that you'll be able to burn that honey-do list by midsummer."

"Well—" she willed her heart to stop thumping so hard in her chest just because he had smiled at her like she was the only woman in the world "—we'll see. That would certainly be nice."

She came out from behind the desk, which had previously put a nice, safe distance between them. As she approached, that heady scent of leather-and-saddle soap hit her senses. When she had been discussing his past transgressions, it had been easy to suppress the odd mixture of emotions Colt's presence had been stirring in her body. But now that they were standing side by side again, it was impossible for her to ignore her own attraction to this man. It was simply undeniable. Colt was tall and handsome and kind to her most beloved cat. *And* whenever she got within a few feet of him, her body chemistry went haywire until it felt like it was about to short circuit.

"It was a pleasure to meet you." She held out her hand and soon her fingers were engulfed in his warm firm grasp.

"I thank you for your time." He held on to her hand a little longer than necessary. "It's going to work out between us just fine."

"One more thing I should have mentioned earlier, Colt."

He paused, waiting.

"It wouldn't be wise for you to mix business with pleasure while you're here." Lee felt as if she were giving this warning to herself, as well. She didn't need to mix her business with this man either. "My volunteers are vital to the summer program and I don't want any broken hearts or romantic intrigue undermining their work."

An odd twinkle entered Colt's cobalt blue eyes and he leaned his head slightly in her direction. "Lee—" he said her name in a way that sounded more intimate than before "—you don't have to worry about that. I believe my heart is already set on somebody."

* * *

Colt parked his ruby-red Ford dual-wheel truck on the narrow street and walked up the driveway to Clip Art Salon. The Clip Art Salon was owned by his older half brother Shane's wife, Rebecca, and was located in a converted garage behind their historic Victorian house in downtown Bozeman. His mind had been whirling since he left his meeting with Lee. Never in his life had he been so impacted by a woman and he knew, instinctively, that this moment in his life was different. Of course, he had been infatuated with multiple woman in his past but he had never thought *there's my wife* before. And it was freaking him out. He wasn't even thirty yet. How could he be thinking of marrying a woman he'd just met today?

On his way up the steep curved driveway, Colt noticed that Shane's fire-engine red antique truck wasn't parked behind the house, but he didn't need his brother to visit one of his favorite sisters-in-law. All four of his older half brothers were married men and Colt had a solid relationship with all of their wives. But there was something special about his connection with Rebecca—she was down-to-earth and pragmatic and she always spoke to him in unvarnished truths. Colt took a moment to lean down and pet his brother's black-and-white-spotted cat, Top, who was lounging in a sunny spot in the courtyard separating the main house from the converted garage.

"Hey there, Rebecca." Colt opened the door to the little salon.

Rebecca's face lit up when she saw him. She put down her dust rag and opened her arms wide to greet him. "Colt! Come here and give me a hug right now!"

Rebecca was five months pregnant with her third child and it was the first time her belly had really gotten in the way during a hug.

"How are you feeling?" Colt glanced down at her baby bump.

"Would you believe it?" His sister-in-law smiled, her hand on her stomach. "Wonderful. I haven't had one single day of morning sickness. This has been the easiest pregnancy of the three." She tapped her fist on her head. "Knock on wood. Let's hope it stays this way. Sit down. Sit down. Keep me company. My next client won't be here for another hour."

Colt sat down in the chair at the second station and stretched out his legs. "What's Shane up to today?"

"He took the boys fishing. They leave in a couple of days to go spend the summer with their father." Rebecca frowned slightly. "I dread it. I really do. I just have to pray that they will be back before I give birth and leave it in God's hands."

Rebecca had inherited the Victorian house from

her great-aunt and had moved her two boys, Caleb
and Carson, from New Hampshire to Montana in
hopes of resetting her life after a divorce. What she
found was true love with retired Army Sergeant
Shane Brand.

"Do we know if it's a boy or a girl?" Colt asked.

"Savannah convinced me to have a gender reveal party," Rebecca said of their sister-in-law. Savannah was married to his oldest brother, Bruce,
and she liked to find any reason to have a party at
Sugar Creek Ranch.

"Shane is rooting for a girl." Rebecca smoothed
her hands over her stomach. "The boys want another brother."

A wistful expression passed over Rebecca's face.
"I'm just praying for healthy."

"You'll get healthy," Colt quickly reassured her.

Rebecca favored him with a smile, showing off
her two front teeth that overlapped slightly. "You're
a sweet guy, Colt. Do you know that?"

He returned her smile. Rebecca had a way of
making him feel better about himself even when
he had screwed up royally. She never let him off
the hook, but she always made him feel worthy of
being loved.

"Where are you coming from?" she asked him.

"Strides of Strength."

Rebecca's brown eyebrows raised on her fair-
skinned, plump face. "Community service."

"Yep."

"Don't take this lightly, Colt."

"I won't."

"I'm serious. You've always gotten away with things because of the Brand name and everyone just shrugs and says *that's just Colt being Colt*, but you're getting too old to be pulling high school pranks."

Colt caught a glimpse of himself in the mirror. His five o'clock shadow looked like it was going on ten o'clock and his hair looked wild and unkempt.

"You're right," he agreed simply.

Rebecca sat forward a bit. "I'm *right*? You're not even going to argue your point?"

"Nope." He ran his hand over his face. "I think I could do with a shave."

"You absolutely need a shave. And a haircut."

He used his boot to push the chair around so he was fully facing the mirror. Lee Macbeth was a class act, perfectly put together. What must she have thought about his disheveled appearance?

"You feel up to a quick overhaul?"

"Do I feel up to it? Please. Why do you and Shane *always* insist on letting things get out of hand? That man of mine looked like Grizzly Adams when I first met him. Here." Rebecca handed him a plastic gown to slip over his shirt. "Put this on and come over to the sink and get your hair washed first."

Colt followed her directions and sat down in the chair in front of the sink.

"So, how did it go this morning?" she asked while she massaged the warm soapy water through his hair.

"There's a lot for me to do out there."

"Like what?"

"Painting, installing automatic watering systems and fans. Stuff like that."

"You are the most handy of the Brand brothers." She began to rinse the shampoo from his hair. "Did you have a chance to meet the owner?"

"Yes. I met her today. *Lee.*" The way he said her name did not escape Rebecca's notice. His sister-in-law was silent while she wrapped his face with a warm towel to loosen the stubble on his face so she could give him a close shave, but she had given him a sharp look when he said Lee's name.

After he was seated in Rebecca's chair and she was gently combing the knots out of his shoulder-length hair, his sister-in-law caught his eye in the mirror.

"I've seen pictures of Lee before. She's a very pretty woman."

Colt could already sense where Rebecca was heading in that kind and gentle manner of hers. Lee was older, accomplished, educated and serious. He, on the other hand, had always been the adorable bird dog who wouldn't hunt—cute but basically useless.

"I've never met anyone like her before," Colt said honestly. He could trust Rebecca with his newfound feelings. She wouldn't judge him too harshly.

Rebecca finished her chore, put her comb down and put both of her hands on his shoulders. "Colt, you know how much I love you and I believe you have so much untapped potential. But—"

"She's out of my league?"

"No," Rebecca quickly responded. "Absolutely *not*. But all I'm saying is that if this interest of yours in her is sincere, then you are going to have to stop paddling around in the kiddie pool and learn how to swim with the Olympians."

Chapter Three

Colt arrived at Strides of Strength early Monday morning. He had foregone a poker game the night before with his buddies just so he would be fresh for his first day. That morning, he'd taken a shower and put on a cotton button-down shirt, *tucked in*. He had used his electric razor to shave the stubble off his face and checked his appearance in the mirror, something he never bothered to do, twice before walking out the door. But all of this effort he had put into making a great first *second* impression on Lee had been a waste of time.

"Good morning." Gilda waved her hand with a quick smile. She had been consulting with a small group of stable hands in front of the massive covered riding arena. A woman in an English riding habit was riding a muscular bay gelding in the arena while the early morning sun bathed the mountain peaks in the distance with a brilliant gold-and-orange glow.

"Guten Morgen." Colt tipped his hat to her when she broke up the meeting, sending the workers scattering in different directions and then headed over to him.

Gilda, a slight woman in her early sixties, who was dressed exactly as she had been at orientation—riding boots, slim-fitting riding pants and a long-sleeved shirt with a Strides of Strength logo walked his way. When she walked, she leaned forward a bit, her right shoulder dipping lower than the left and her arms didn't swing freely by her sides. There was stiffness—a sternness—in her body that Colt interpreted as seriousness for her role in life. Gilda was the general manager in charge of both the non-profit side of the facility as well as the profitable boarding side of the property. She gave him another slight smile when he greeted her in German.

"Guten Morgen," she repeated his earlier greeting in German, as well.

Gilda led him to the office and Colt, for the second time in a short time, was disappointed when he discovered that neither Lee nor Chester were there. He resisted the urge to ask if Lee was on the property, not wanting to give even the slightest hint at his feelings. Yet, Lee and her pretty hazel eyes and her wispy hair and self-effacing smile had been at the forefront of his mind all weekend. Any doubt that he was completely smitten with her had been discarded. Colt was enamored, truly enamored, with a woman for the first time in his life. And the feelings he was having for Lee put into perspective all of the other infatuations he had experienced. It had been child's play, he realized. Not real. The emotion he had for Lee was confirmation that love at first sight could happen. It had just happened to him and he sure as heck wasn't sure what to do about it.

"Wait here, please." Gilda gestured to the waiting area. "I will be but a moment."

She opened the door to Lee's office and returned a moment later, closing the door gently behind her, with a piece of paper in her hand.

"Here is the list." Gilda handed him the paper. "Lee and I discussed all of the needs on the property and we have prioritized the most urgent from top to bottom. Please follow it precisely."

The list was certainly long and could be daunting for someone without his vast experience growing up on a Montana cattle spread. Sugar Creek Ranch was one of the biggest land holdings in the greater Bozeman area and they had run a thousand head of cattle before. Colt knew what it took to maintain a facility with horses and livestock. It made him happy to see that everything on Lee's list of priorities was something he could handle. And if he couldn't handle it on his own, he had a long-standing list of connections to people who could help him.

"Is this all?" Colt folded the list and tucked it into the pocket of his shirt.

Gilda's brows lifted in surprise. "You are not impressed with this list? We could add more."

Colt opened the front door for her. "I can handle my own load, now."

"We shall see," his companion said in a way that reminded him of his second-grade teacher, Mrs. Bjorn, who was always sending him to the principal's office for one reason or another.

"I will introduce you to our in-house farrier. Boot takes care of all of our horses, including most of the boarders' horses. If you need any supplies or equipment, please speak with Boot first before you speak to me. That is his area of expertise, not mine."

Just like Lee, Gilda walked with purpose and with an extended stride. Did all of the womenfolk on this property walk like they were being chased by something? He was darn near out of breath by the time he reached a small workshop on the far side of the indoor riding arena.

"Boot?" Gilda walked inside of the dusty, disorganized workshop. It was the only place on the property that appeared to be in disarray. Old tires were piled up in the corner and the shelves that lined the paneled walls were stuffed with old spray bottles, tipped over and rusty and coffee cans filled to the brim with nuts and bolts and nails. There was a half-dismantled riding lawnmower in the middle of the shop with its parts cluttering the cracked concrete floor. Colt heard a loud sneeze followed by a very loud sniff, another sneeze and then a cough coming from a small room that was tucked away in the back left corner of the shop.

"Boot?"

"Yeppers." A gravelly, rough voice preceded the man's appearance into the main part of the workshop.

"I'd like you to meet Colt Brand. He will be working for us this summer as a handyman." Colt noticed an affectionate sparkle in Gilda's guarded brown eyes when she looked at Boot. "Colt, this is Boot Macbain."

"Sir." Colt stepped forward and held out his hand to the man.

Boot Macbain was a tall man somewhere in his sixties, his head shaved bald, a prominent straight nose, snapping deep-set blue eyes and a bushy snow-white goatee. His hands, large, rough and beefy, were stained with black oil spots, presumably from years of working on farm equipment without gloves.

"I heard you were going to be providing a much-needed service here." Boot was eye to eye with him and Colt was six feet four inches in his bare feet.

"I'll leave you now." Gilda nodded to Colt and then her eyes touched on Boot one last time before she left.

"Fine lady," Boot mused openly before he turned his attention back to Colt. "I'll show you the good stuff. We've got a whole warehouse full of man's toys that's going to leave you salivating. You ever operated a backhoe?"

"Started when I was seven."

Boot smiled at him, showing an even row of Chiclet-sized teeth. "Someone raised you right, son."

Boot took him to an enormous gray metal warehouse that was filled with farm equipment—tractors, manure spreaders, aerators, bush hogs, Bobcats and different-sized trailers. It was truly a man's playground.

"Over this a way—" Boot gestured for him to follow "—is where I've stocked the power tools and just about any little gadget you might need. If we don't have it, let me know and I'll try to finagle room in the budget."

"How did you guys manage to amass all of this?" Colt stood with his hands on his hips, trying to take in all of the options at his disposal.

"Lee is a master at writing grant proposals and sweet-talking donors," Boot said as he exited the warehouse and walked to a second smaller adjacent building. "This here is where we stock our wood and posts to fix the fences."

At the end of the tour, Boot said, "Well, that should get you started."

"I'd say so," Colt agreed. And unable to resist the question that had been rattling around in his brain ever since Boot mentioned Lee, he asked, "Have you known Lee a long time?"

Boot's sharp blue eyes honed in on his face, as if he could already sense his interest in the pretty entrepreneur.

"Long time." He gave a nod. "She was married to my son."

"He drives that tractor around this property too fast, Gilda!" Lee spun her chair just in time to see Colt drive past her window on the tractor. As he always did, he looked over at her office window and caught her looking out at him. He raised his hand in greeting and smiled at her broadly. Her cheeks grew hot from being caught, *again*, watching him out of her window. Lee spun her chair back toward the desk, frown lines creasing her forehead. "The man's a menace with that tractor. Please tell him to *slow down*."

"I have," Gilda replied calmly. "I will tell him again."

"Yes." Lee nodded. "Please do. It's a safety hazard and camp starts next week."

Lee shuffled papers around on the desk, her mind temporarily scattered by the lingering image of Colt's handsome smiling face in her mind. That face—that smile—had been more of a distraction in her life than she wanted to admit to herself, much less anyone else in her life. Her life was exactly as she wanted it to be—it was as she had designed and planned and carefully constructed. A fleeting, *ridiculous* attraction to an overgrown boy masquerading as a man was not going to become a permanent dish on her menu.

"How is he doing, other than driving around here like a bat out of hell?" Lee asked.

"Very well, in fact."

Lee stopped shuffling papers, sat back in her chair and frowned. A *very well* from Gilda was high praise indeed.

"Everyone loves him," Gilda added.

Of course they do.

"He arrives early," the manager continued. "He is a hard worker."

Shocking.

"He is very helpful and polite. I've heard nothing but good things so far."

"What does Boot think of him?" Lee crossed her hands in front of her body.

"I haven't asked him directly."

"But you like him."

Gilda took a moment to mull over her exact opinion, as was her way, and then she said definitively, "Yes. I think that I do. So far."

If Lee had been looking for an ally to find a good reason to reassign Colt to a different facility, she wouldn't find one in Gilda. Having Colt at Strides of Strength made her feel uncomfortable and uneasy. Not because she thought that he was a deviant or untrustworthy—but because she felt pulled toward him in a completely organic way, against her own will, like a magnet. She had worked to avoid him on her own property, taking different out-of-the-way paths in order to not run in to him directly. It would be impossible, and completely juvenile, to behave this way for the entire summer. If she was attracted to Colt, like every other female on the property, human and animal alike, then she was just going to have to face it, deal with it, *desensitize herself* to the feelings and get on with business. Honestly, she didn't have time to be conflicted about a cowboy.

Lee pushed away from her desk. "You know what, I'll talk to Colt about the tractor. Ultimately, I'm responsible for him."

Gilda and Lee parted ways, with the manager

heading to the boarder's barn to oversee the progress of afternoon hay distribution and mucking of the stalls. Lee headed toward the pasture at the back of the property where she had spotted Colt fixing a line of fence that had been in desperate need of repairs for months. Colt had been on the property for only a week and already his handyman skills were making a difference and Lee couldn't deny that. Colt had climbed up the light pole and fixed a light at the front of the property that had been burned out for too long and now the area was flooded with light between the three barns. Almost all of the broken boards on the fences had been repaired and now Colt was replacing the split or rotten posts. Holding her locket in her hand as she approached Colt, Lee ran an internal dialogue in her mind, reminding her body that she was not going to act on any attraction she might feel for this man.

"Hello," she said.

Colt was kneeling down in front of a post he had just put into the ground, his back to her.

He was humming to himself as he worked.

"Hello?" she said more loudly when he didn't turn around.

Colt stood upright, turned around, spotted her and gave a start. He laughed, pulled ear buds out of his ears and let them dangle around his neck. "My stars! I didn't hear you come up behind me."

Unexpectedly, Lee laughed in return. "*My stars?*

That sounds like something my Grandmother Macbeth would say and she's in her nineties!"

Colt took a bandanna out of his back pocket and wiped the sweat off his face and neck. "Come to think of it, that was something my grandmother used to say."

They stood there smiling at each other, not speaking, just mindlessly enjoying the moment without thought. Finally, Lee realized that someone needed to speak and it was going to have to be her, because Colt seemed content to let the moment drag on. If she had wondered about Colt returning her attraction, she didn't have to wonder any longer. Colt *was* attracted to her. It showed in the way he studied the features of her face and in the way he gazed at her with such admiration—his attraction was unmistakable. And it simultaneously thrilled her and shook her to the core.

"How's it going?" It was a stupid question— she could see with her own eyes how it was going.

Colt didn't seem to mind. He looked over his shoulder at his own work and then turned back to her. "I've got only one more post to put in and then I can get started working on the barn."

This time, the smile was genuine. "That's wonderful news! I've been so worried about that. I've heard that we are going to have record highs this summer and I'm genuinely concerned about how hot the horses will be in that barn. Last year, they were sweating in their stalls."

Colt adjusted his cowboy hat. "Not this year."

Until that moment, Lee hadn't realized how much Colt had already added to the function of the property. She had been worried about how she was going to budget getting the fences fixed and now that problem was solved. In one week, by one industrious man. How could this same person be the reckless drunkard arrested for riding while intoxicated?

Colt's eyes were on her face when he asked, "So, you're happy with my work so far?"

"Yes." She turned her head away, not wanting to get caught up in his eyes. "So far, so good."

Her companion's smile widened with pleasure. He winked at her. "Maybe you'll put in a kind word for me and I'll get some time off for good behavior."

Colt was just kidding with her—she could see it in his face. But her stomach knotted up in the strangest way at the thought of him leaving at the end of summer.

"I don't know about that," she countered. "You've proven to be a valuable asset for us."

"That's nice to hear."

"However…"

"Uh-oh."

"I would appreciate it if you would drive on the property with more caution." This admonition came out much more tempered than she had originally intended. She had intended to be stern and firm and really put her foot down with Colt. But when she got sucked into his charming orbit, she had gotten all soft and gooey inside. Darn it if she hadn't wanted to hurt his feelings.

Colt's expression turned sheepish. "I get a little impatient to get from point A to point B."

"You need to slow your roll, Colt. The week after next, we are going to have children on this property and their safety, the safety of the horses and the staff are number one."

He lifted up his hand like he was swearing to something. "I promise to do better, boss."

Lee's hand went back to her locket. "Thank you. And thank you for the work you've already done here. It's been…more helpful than you can even imagine."

With a quick wave, Lee turned away from him, her heart pounding in her chest as if she had just run a mile. Even the simplest of exchanges with Colt got her blood pumping in a way she hadn't experienced in such a long, long time.

"Hey, Lee?"

She turned around at the sound of her name—a name that somehow sounded exotic and sexy when said in Colt's baritone voice.

"It was good to see you."

"It was good to see you too," she said honestly.

"I was beginning to think you were avoiding me."

Her brain froze for a split second before a simple excuse fought its way through the fog and out from her lips. Flatly, she said, "I've been busy."

Colt's eyes drifted down to her lips and she couldn't help but wonder how incredible it would feel to be kissed again, to be held again. To hold someone's hand again.

"Well, maybe I'll get lucky and you'll have a reason to come talk to me tomorrow." He rested his hands atop the posthole digger stuck in the ground.

"Perhaps." She pointed her finger at him, with a half-kidding, half-serious tone. "But not about the tractor."

He crossed his heart. "No. Not about the tractor."

Colt watched Lee walk away, her ponytail bouncing playfully on her back. Colt had begun to make a list of traits that he particularly admired about Lee, and one of those traits was her swinging ponytail. She always walked with happiness in her stride and that extra bounce made that ponytail swing back in forth in the most charming way. He watched all the way until she disappeared into the enclosed riding arena and then he dropped his head down onto his hands and tried to catch his breath. His heart was pounding harder than it had all day, even more than it had when he struggled to get those posts in the hard ground. Lee Macbeth

made his heart race, plain and simple. He knew—
he knew as sure as he was standing in Montana—
that Lee was the woman he was meant to marry.
He felt it in his gut and he knew it in his mind.
And yet, he could tell that Lee wasn't going to be
caught easily. He was going to have to be strategic
and patient. The news that Boot had shared with
him earlier in the week had knocked him off bal-
ance. Lee had been married before but Boot talked
about the marriage in the past tense. Lee *was* married to my son. If there had been a divorce, would
Boot still be so involved with Lee's business? Colt
wanted to ask Boot directly about the marriage, almost had done it a couple of times, but decided it
was best to hold his tongue. Lee wasn't wearing a
wedding ring; she seemed like the type of woman
who would let the world know she was married by
faithfully donning her wedding ring.

"You calling it a day, son?" Boot groaned as he
stood up from his chore of reassembling the lawn
mower.

"I think so." Colt twisted to the side to stretch
the stiff muscles in his back. "This place has worn
me out."

"This place'll do that to you," Boot agreed.
"There's never enough energy, daylight, help or
money, that's for sure. You've been a big help already, I have to say that."

"Lee scolded me about driving the tractor too fast."

Boot chuckled. "I figured she would."

"Where do want me to leave the keys for the tractor?" Colt slipped the keys out of his pocket.

"Over there on that ledge will do just fine." Boot pointed to a small shelf by the entrance.

Colt picked his way over to the shelf, dropped the keys on the ledge and then his eyes spotted an old picture, frayed at the edges with spots of sun damage blurring some of the image. It was a picture of Boot in his younger days, standing in front of a muscle car with his arm around a tall gangly young man in a graduation cap and gown.

"That's a nice ride," Colt commented. "A Cheval?"

Boot walked over to join him. "Yes, sir. That was my boy's dream car. I was so proud to be able to get it for him for graduation. My parents couldn't afford a car for me, so it was something that I could do for my own son. My wife wasn't so sure about it, but she finally agreed."

Boot hesitated for a moment and then he said, "After Michael died, I kept that old Cheval running for as long as I could."

The older man beside him smiled faintly. "My friend was a mechanic and he told me that at the end, the car had been rusting from underneath for so long that the only thing holding it together was prayers and car polish."

They stood together looking at that picture silently.

"Well." Boot patted Colt on the shoulder, turned around and disappeared into the small office. Colt leaned in to get a closer look at the man who would grow up to be Lee's husband. He looked like a nice kid, like someone he would have been a friend with in high school. After that exchange with Boot, Colt had one of his questions answered without ever having asked it. Boot had lost his son. Lee had lost her husband. He didn't know how her husband had passed away, but there wasn't a ring on her finger because Lee was a widow.

Chapter Four

The week before the summer session began was always the busiest for Lee. It was a time when her mind was so occupied by details and decisions that any personal issues she might have were shoved into the background. She didn't have time to think about her own baggage, not when she had the children to think about. During the final prep week, she had to train the volunteers as to the specific manner in which to lead the horses. The horses at Strides of Strength had so many different people handling them that they wanted to keep how they were led consistent. Lee was also in charge of teaching the volunteers how the children would mount and dismount from the specially designed mounting ramps, how to execute an emergency dismount and how to be an effective side-walker. It took three people to provide equine-assisted therapy for one child: a horse leader, a therapist and a side-walker to ensure the safety and stability of the child.

"One of the most important things that you have to remember—" Lee stood in front of the new volunteers in the covered arena "—is that you can't use the horse or the rider for support. Your arm is going to get tired, especially if you are side-walking with one of our taller horses like Sweet Girl, but it's your responsibility to stop yourself from leaning on the horse or putting pressure on the rider's leg."

Lee asked Gilda to bring one of the demonstration therapy horses forward. Callie was sitting on the back of the horse, acting as the demonstration rider. After all, Callie was one of her original riders. She was the perfect person for the volunteers to practice with before the summer session began.

"If a rider is like Callie and is more independent—" Lee gave Callie a quick smile "—you don't even have to have your hands on their leg or foot. You can walk next to the horse, without touching the rider, but always ready to perform an emergency dismount."

Lee showed the volunteers several appropriate

side-walking positions and then demonstrated the incorrect positions.

"I'm going to lean on you a bit. Okay, Callie?" she asked, resting her arm on Callie's thigh.

"Okay," Callie said with her trademark smile.

"It's easy to accidentally lean on the rider and this can cause pain and discomfort for the rider. Many of our riders are nonverbal and cannot express to you that they are in pain or uncomfortable. So, please be mindful about carrying your own weight."

After the morning session, Lee hoofed it back to the office to check in with Gail Allen, who was organizing all of the intake forms for the program to ensure that all of the riders were properly enrolled prior to the beginning of session. Their summer program had gained some notoriety after she had been nominated for a CNN Heroes award and parents would bring their children from all over the country to attend. The first official week of the program would be particularly hectic because the therapists would be getting eyes on their clients for the first time. Most of the riders arrived with previous evaluations, while some would need to move through the entire evaluation process.

"How's it going, Gail?" Lee asked anxiously as soon as she walked through the door of the main office.

Gail had been one of Lee's most faithful volunteers and a fierce advocate of the program. Gail had single-handedly begun the partnership between the First Baptist Church Bozeman, a church that was established in Bozeman 125 years earlier and prior to Montana statehood and Strides of Strength. Every year, Gail spearheaded a fund-raiser at her beloved congregation to raise money for Lee's program.

"We're doin' just fine, dahlin'," Gail said with her soft southern Georgia drawl. As was usual for Gail, her bobbed, wavy silver-white hair was perfectly quaffed, her subtle makeup was accented by the perfect shade of lipstick for her peaches-and-cream complexion and her accessories—earrings, necklace, bracelet and ring—complemented her outfit. "We are ahead of the game this summer. All the forms are in!"

Lee raised her arms up in celebration. "Yes!"

She wasn't really superstitious but she couldn't help but believe that this was a good omen for the summer session.

"Hey! Where's Chester?" Lee looked around. She was surprised her feline companion hadn't greeted her at the door, as was his habit.

"I believe you'll find him in your office." Gail nodded toward her office with a little smile on her face that gave a hint to Lee that something out of the ordinary was going on.

Lee went to her office and found Chester happily sprawled out on top of her desk. He lifted up his large gray head, blinked his eyes at her and gave her a meow that morphed into a yawn.

"How did you get up there?" She wrinkled her brow curiously. On closer inspection, she saw a set of steps custom-made specifically for the height of her desk.

"Where did these come from?" She ran her hands over the stained wood that matched her desk perfectly and the small carpet inserts that picked up the main burgundy color of the rug in the lobby.

"Gail? Where did this come from?" She asked the question, but it was largely rhetorical. This gift for Chester—this gift for *her*—had to have come from Colt.

Gail appeared in the doorway, a pleased look on her face, her hands clasped excitedly. "Isn't it wonderful? Chester followed Colt into the office, watched him set those up and walked right up them like he knew they were made just for him. It was one of the sweetest things I've ever seen. Chester sat on that top step right there, gazed at Colt as if to say thank you and reached out and touched him with his paw."

Lee couldn't stop admiring the quality of the stairs. Colt wasn't just handy—he was a very talented craftsman.

"I wish I had been here to see that."

"Colt wanted to surprise you," Gail said.

Lee nodded. "He succeeded."

"You know," the older woman mused aloud, "I believe that man has surprised all of us, just a little bit since he's been here."

Lee leaned over and kissed Chester on the head. From the therapists to the volunteers to Gilda, Gail and Boot—everyone had embraced Colt and welcomed him into the fold. It had never occurred to Lee that he would be able to fit into this world so easily. But Lee still was reserving judgment about his placement until she saw how the children and the parents responded to Colt. No, he wasn't going to be leading the horses or side-walking during sessions, but it would be unavoidable for him to interact with the children and parents at some point. Until Colt was able to pass *that* test, his position on the facility, no matter how beneficial it had been already, was not secure.

Lee gave Chester one last cuddle before she headed out the door. She checked her phone for the time before she headed to the back of the property. As good as his word, as soon as he was done repairing the fences, Colt had begun working on the main projects in the oldest barn. He was standing on the metal roof of the barn, wearing his cowboy hat, but he had taken off his shirt. Lee's heart gave a little jump at the sight of his tanned, muscular chest and arms. He was simply and undeniably a handsome man. Colt was *every* woman's type—tall, young, fit, strong chiseled features and a leading-man smile. Her attraction to him, she decided, was evidence that she was still human, nothing more.

"You're being careful up there, aren't you?" She shielded her eyes from the sun and looked up at him.

Colt stopped rolling the thick silver sealant on the metal roof and grinned down at her. "Absolutely. Don't worry about me. I love heights."

"I know," she said, remembering him climbing up the light pole like an agile cat. "But I'm still worried."

When his smile widened, as if he was interpreting her worry as a sign of a more personal connection between them, she added quickly, "Liability."

"Don't go anywhere." Colt ignored her *liability* aside and walked over to the ladder that was propped against the side of the barn.

Lee rushed over to the ladder to hold it for him. Maybe he didn't need her help, but she was going to give it to him anyway.

Colt hopped down off the ladder, his half-naked body so close to her that she could reach out and touch the sexy contours of his biceps and the ridges of his flat stomach. His skin, hot from the morning sun, smelled salty from the sweat and Lee discovered that she was even more attracted to him, not less.

"Thank you." Colt leaned over to pick up the shirt he had balled up and tossed onto his toolbox.

Lee was finding something in the distance to admire while he shrugged on his shirt and buttoned it up, instead of staring at his body as was her want.

"You can look now," he said in a teasing voice.

Embarrassed, with a blush creeping up her neck that just happened whenever she was near Colt, she tried to cover up her feelings by saying, "I think it would be best if you kept your shirt on while you worked, Colt. We're going to have a lot of parents and kids here starting next week."

"I gotcha." He nodded easily. "Come into the barn. I want to show you what I've done so far."

"Okay," Lee agreed, "But I wanted to thank you first. That's why I stopped by."

Colt adjusted his hat on his head, tipping the brim up a bit so she could see his eyes. Those eyes were smiling at her, knowing that she had seen his gift.

"And here I was hoping that you stopped by because you missed me." He frowned at her playfully.

In truth, she *had* missed him. It was a truth that she wasn't willing to admit out loud. But lately she had been finding reasons to seek him out. And if she missed seeing him during the day, she would look for his truck in the parking lot and feel a knot in her stomach when she realized that he had gone for the evening.

Lee reached for her locket and held on to it tightly. Sometimes she squeezed it so tightly that her fingers felt stiff and sore after she released the keepsake.

"Thank you for the steps. For Chester."

"You're welcome." He sent her a pleased smile. "They were a gift for the both of you. Do you like them?"

"They are so *beautifully* made, Colt. The way you matched the stain on the wood to my desk— you could put those online and sell them. A lot of cat furniture is so wobbly."

"Well, I'm glad you like them."

"I don't like them, I *love* them," she corrected. "How did you manage to pull that off without me knowing?"

"I bribed Gilda with a bag of Helmut Sachers coffee."

Lee couldn't help but laugh. Colt had a way of always making her laugh and it felt good to be around him because of it. She smiled all the time, but that smile was often a mask to make other people feel good. It wasn't a reflection of how she actually felt inside. When she was with Colt, somehow he was the one who made her feel good inside.

"Gilda is very serious about her coffee. You know, Vienna is where they first brewed coffee," Lee said.

"I think she might have mentioned something

like that to me a time or two," he said. Gilda was proud of her Austrian heritage and had bemoaned, once or twice, the taste of American coffee.

"I didn't realize Gilda could be bought off so easily," Lee mused.

"It was a larger-sized bag of coffee, if that makes you feel any better."

Lee walked beside him into the barn. "Not really."

Once inside the barn, Colt shifted gears and began showing her the plan for the two most important projects: the fans and the automatic watering systems.

"Now—" Colt led her over to the electrical panel inside of the tack room "—we don't have enough voltage coming into this barn to handle the load of the fans and the automatic watering systems."

"Meaning?"

"We've got to get an electrician out here to ramp up our capacity."

Lee immediately saw a chunk of her budget disappearing. Electricians, even at the reduced rate they usually gave her, were expensive. She took in a deep breath and let it out. He glanced over at her.

"Don't worry," he said, having read the wrinkles in her forehead correctly. "I've got a friend who's the best darn electrician in Gallatin County. He won't cut corners or do anything that isn't by the book and up to code, so we won't have to worry about anything catching fire here. He'll do everything industrial grade."

"Okay. But for how much?"

"You let me worry about that," Colt said, "Ben and I go way back and he owes me a favor or two."

"You don't mind calling in those favors for this job?"

"Nope," he said. "I don't mind at all. Now, about the watering system."

Colt led her through the particulars of installing the automatic watering systems that she had purchased six months ago. It was a much more complicated job than she had thought, much like installing the fans. But after Colt walked her through his plan, she was able to do something she rarely did—she put her faith in Colt's ability to get the job done and left her worry behind with him. Colt climbed back onto the roof while she headed over to Boot's workshop. She glanced behind her one time and found that Colt was watching her walk away. She gave him a little wave and he gave her his trademark tip of the brim of his hat.

"Hi, Boot." Lee tried her best to ignore the mess in her father-in-law's workshop. It was the one place she had agreed to use a hands-off approach but the clutter made her nuts.

Boot stood upright, stiffer than she'd like, with a groan and opened his arms to her. "Daughter."

They hugged tightly, taking a moment to lean

against each other. It seemed like they had been leaning on each other for a lifetime.

"So, you finally got this old thing put back together?" she asked of the lawn mower.

"Yeppers." Boot rubbed his hand over his head. "But she's not purring just yet."

"Boot…" She wrinkled her brow at him. "Do you really think that she's ever going to *purr* again?"

"Don't you worry yourself about it. I'll get her purring again."

"Okay." She held up her hands in surrender. "I'll wait with bated breath for the purr."

Lee walked over to the faded snapshot of Boot and her late husband. She picked up the picture and wiped the light film of dust that had covered the image. "You know, I remember this day like it was yesterday."

"Me too." There was that familiar catch in her father-in-law's voice whenever he spoke about his only son, his only child, Michael.

"He took me out after graduation in that car. He was so proud of that car. So proud." She put the picture down on the shelf, turned her back to the image and crossed her arms in front of her body. "We rolled the windows down—we still had our gowns on from the ceremony—and he took me out on one of the country roads and he drove so fast…"

Her voice trailed off for a moment. She swallowed hard a couple of times. "I can still feel the wind on my hand."

"I remember all of us parents were ticked off at the both of you for showing up to the restaurant so late."

"I know," she said quietly, pensively.

The Macbains and the Macbeths had lived across the street from each other in a middle-class suburb in upstate New York. Michael and Lee had grown up together, always being seated next to each other for every school event because of their last names. They were play buddies in elementary school, crushes in middle school and finally, they were each other's first love in high school. Michael had been her first everything—her first kiss, her first lover, her first genuine heartbreak. Nothing compared to losing Michael. It was difficult to imagine that anything ever would. She missed him every day. Her heart ached for him every day.

"But we all forgave you when we saw you walk through that door with your caps and gowns, looking so grown up. You, the valedictorian and Michael, the captain of the football team. Both of you with full-ride scholarships—we were all so proud of you."

"Magical times," Lee agreed.

Neither of their families knew at that graduation dinner that Michael had proposed to her just moments before. He hadn't had a ring yet and she wasn't ready to wear a ring then. But he had asked her to be his wife someday and she had agreed, without hesitation. Of course, she was going to marry Michael Macbain—they were going to graduate from college the same year, get married and have lots of beautiful babies together while they both had incredibly successful careers. It had always been in her mind that their eventual marriage was inevitable—it was written in the stars *and* in her diaries. That was before she realized how easy it was to dream and how difficult it was to actually make those dreams a reality.

"How're things going with the new crop?" Boot turned the subject to the volunteers, steering the conversation to emotionally neutral territory.

Lee uncrossed her arms. "They're doing great. I'm super happy with them. I put them through their paces today and everyone was on point. We don't have even one weak link this summer, thank goodness, because our rider numbers are up and our volunteer numbers are down."

"It's been a good thing to have Colt on the property," Boot added. "He's been a big help to me, I can tell you that."

This wasn't the first time Boot had sung Colt's praises. It hadn't escaped her notice that the two men had already formed a bond. Boot wasn't one to form bonds easily, not after losing Michael. When she was growing up, Boot had been the life of the party. After Michael passed away, he had shrunk back into himself, like a turtle retracting its head and legs into its protective shell. Boot had sloughed off his friends, choosing to surround himself with his broken gadgets and flea market rescues. Lee often wondered if Boot surrounded himself with broken things that couldn't seem to be completely fixed because he couldn't seem to fix himself.

"Hello." Gilda arrived, carrying a thermos.

Boot stood a hair straighter when he heard Gilda's accented greeting. "Afternoon, Gilda."

The manager seemed a bit hesitant as she stepped forward to offer the thermos to Boot.

"I brought you some authentic coffee from Vienna."

"Much appreciated." Boot took the thermos. "I could use a pick-me-up. I've got a lot of hooves to trim this afternoon."

Gilda smiled, her eyes expectantly on Boot's face, her arms crossed in front of her body in a way that struck Lee as unusual. "I hope you like strong black coffee."

"Is there any other way to drink coffee?" Boot asked, untwisting the top of the thermos and breathing in the scent of the rising steam.

"No. I don't think there is." Gilda ducked her head. "Well, I hope you enjoy it. I must return to my work."

Lee had watched the exchange between her father-in-law, a widower for nearly fifteen years, and her manager with curiosity. There was some interesting chemistry brewing between the two of them.

"What's going on there?" she asked.

Boot glanced over at her a bit shyly. "Nothing for you to bother with."

"Oh, really?"

"Gilda is a nice lady," her father-in-law said.

"Yes, she is."

"But," he added seriously, "I already had my forever."

The teasing smile dropped from her face. Boot had loved his wife to pieces—that was the truth. No matter how many times the single ladies tried to get his attention, he was steadfast in his belief that a man should only marry one woman in his lifetime.

"I understand," Lee said softly. She did understand how Boot felt—all too well, in fact. She had already had her one and only forever too.

Chapter Five

"Come on, man. What's goin' on with you? We're takin' the boat out. We're goin' fishin'. We've got enough beer to last us all day."

This was a familiar complaint from his friend Chad ever since he had begun his community service.

"I hear you, man. I just can't," Colt said. He had his phone on speaker so he could keep both of his hands on the steering wheel. Ever since his arrest, Colt had begun to take an inventory of his life and found it severely lacking. This was the last time he wanted to be on the wrong side of the law. The greater Bozeman area had been his playground.

He'd played hard and gotten away with a lot of bad behavior because of his last name and his father's connections. This was the first time he'd actually had to pay a consequence for his actions and it felt like a turning point.

"I want to get ahead of some work out at Lee's place," he added when his friend went silent on the other end of the line.

"I thought you didn't have to be out there on the weekends."

"I don't. Ben's gonna meet me out there and make a plan to get those fans installed."

There was another pause on the line. He had grown up with Chad and the rest of their crew of five tight-knit friends. Out of all of them, he had been the last holdout—the one the crew could always count on to bend the rules, act like a clown and generally make a spectacle out of himself. He had a built-in job at Sugar Creek and his father, Jock, no matter how angry and frustrated he got with him, wasn't going to fire him from the family or the ranch. So Colt had just never really bothered, or had a reason, to grow up. And then he got arrested, which brought him to Lee Macbeth's doorstep. Meeting a woman like Lee had flipped his perspective on life upside down.

"Ever since you've been hangin' out at that place, you haven't been acting like yourself, man."

Colt's hands tightened on the wheel until they

hurt—it felt like his friend was being negative about Lee's program.

"I'm gonna let you go, Chad," Colt said before he stabbed the red end-call button on his phone. "Catch a big one for me, bud."

Chad's words had put a strange knot in his gut—and it was not because his friend thought he was being lame for not drinking all day on the lake. It was something in Chad's tone that made Colt think that his friend wasn't so evolved when it came to kids with disabilities. Colt searched his own mind. Had he been one of those kids in school who made fun of children who were different? If he were honest with himself, he had to admit that he had. He teased kids—he had harassed kids—all to get a laugh from his friends. If Colt took a poll among the people he'd gone through school with, maybe even the term *bully* could have been applied to him.

"You were a jerk," Colt muttered to himself. "A real *jerk*."

The kids at Strides were Lee's entire world and it was a world Colt wanted to belong to. He knew Chad had tried to shame him into turning his truck around and heading out to the lake but it had had the opposite effect. He didn't want to be the class clown anymore. Lee's life stood for something. He wanted his life to stand for something too. And that certainly wasn't going to happen by hanging out all day getting drunk with the same group of guys he had gotten drunk with on a stolen twelve pack of beer in middle school. The time had long since passed for a change.

Colt's phone rang, breaking his brooding train of thought. It was his older brother Liam calling. Colt had seven siblings total—four older half brothers, two younger brothers and one sister, Jessie, who was the baby, the only daughter, and their father's undisputed favorite.

"You going to be around later on this afternoon?" Liam asked when he picked up the line.

"I should be. You coming out to work on the truck?"

Liam had built a cabin on Sugar Creek Ranch property but had moved to Triple K Ranch when he'd married Kate and adopted Callie. Even though Liam had moved out of the cabin, he had left his antique truck project housed in the shed. Then his brother Shane had lived in Liam's cabin for a time until he had had the good sense to marry Rebecca after a short engagement. Now, it was his turn in the cabin.

"I was thinking about tinkering with it a bit. Kate and Callie are driving me nuts with the wedding plans."

Colt laughed. "I bet. What time are you thinking about coming out?"

"I don't know. Around noon or so."

"I should be done by then. I'll meet you out there."

Colt hung up the phone and turned onto the road that would lead him to Strides. Up ahead on the lightly traveled road was a jogger. It caught Colt's attention because it wasn't typical to see anyone—much less a woman—jogging alone on a relatively deserted stretch of highway. As he pulled closer, Colt recognized a familiar swing of a ponytail. It was Lee. She was wearing shorts and a tank top. This time, it wasn't the ponytail that caught his attention and made his brain scatter for a moment while he tried to make sense of what he was seeing for the first time. Nothing could have prepared him for what he was seeing.

Colt pulled up beside Lee and rolled down the window on the passenger side. "What are you doing out here by yourself?"

Her pretty face flushed and breathing hard from the run, Lee looked at him through the open window. She pushed sweaty strands of hair back from her forehead before using the bottom part of her tank top to wipe the sweat out of her eyes.

"I'm blowing off some steam," she said with her smile. It never failed—when Lee smiled at him, he fell just a bit more in love with her. "What are *you* doing out here by yourself?"

"I'm meeting Ben at the barn. This was the only day he could get out here." Colt leaned over and pushed open the passenger door. "Hop in and ride back with me. It'd be better if you could hear what Ben's thinking about how much capacity we need for the fans and the watering systems."

Lee looked to the right toward the entrance to Strides. It wasn't far by car, but it was still a bit of a distance on foot. After a second of thought, Lee nodded.

"Okay." She grabbed the handle at the top of the door, stepped up with her right foot and then slid into the seat next to him.

While she buckled her seat belt for the short ride to the entrance to her property, Lee caught him staring at the bottom part of her left leg. He hated that she had noticed him looking, but he had to imagine that she had grown used to the stares.

"Bionic leg." She smiled at him without any self-consciousness and patted her prosthetic. Lee's left leg had been amputated below the knee.

"It's nice."

Colt winced at the idiotic comment that had just come out of his mouth. *It's nice?* What kind of thing was that to say about someone's prosthetic leg?

Good naturedly, Lee turned her head toward him, still smiling, her ponytail swinging to the right. "Thank you. I just got a great new foot for it."

The relaxed, easy way Lee dealt with her prosthetic set him at ease. How could he have not known that she was missing part of her leg? There was never any clue in the way she walked. Heck—he had just seen her jogging on the road better than he could do on his best day. He wanted to ask her what happened, but let the questions—so many of them—form and then drift away.

"I like your tattoo." Colt was seeing a completely different side to Lee. The woman riding next to him in his truck was revealing body secrets that had been hidden beneath her always crisp and professional clothing. On the top part of her left arm, she had a colorful rising phoenix tattoo.

She thanked him, looking down at her own arm. "I never thought I was a tattoo kind of girl. But I guess I am after all."

Colt glanced over at the tattoo, noticing that the phoenix only had a right leg and claw. The left leg and claw were noticeably missing. He imagined that this tattoo represented Lee—she was the rising phoenix. But rising from what pile of ashes?

"That's Ben's truck right there." Colt pointed to the white van with Gallatin Electric painted on the side.

"Perfect timing then," Lee said as he pulled his truck into a parking spot in front of the office. She opened the door, swung her legs out and hopped down to the ground. Colt resisted the urge to reach out to help her, even though he could plainly see that she didn't *need* his help.

"Let me change real quick and I'll meet you in

the barn." She clapped her hands together with a bright smile. "I'm so excited about the fans!"

In that moment, he forgot about her *bionic* leg and just focused on her sweet smile and lovely face. He'd never seen any woman get so excited about stall fans; but then again, he'd never met anyone like Lee Macbeth before.

Colt turned off his engine and watched Lee walk with that purposeful stride toward the main office. It was a shock—plain and simple—to realize that the woman he'd fallen for was missing part of her leg. He'd seen plenty of amputees when he went to the VA hospital with his brother Shane, but he'd never dated a woman with a disability before. What in the world had happened to Lee? What in the world had *happened*?

"Thanks for coming, Ben." Colt forced his brain to get back to the business of the day. Ben was in high demand. Folks always needed a reliable electrician and Ben had a reputation for being the best. Ben also happened to be one of the *crew* from his school days who had learned a trade, started a business and then drifted away, bit by bit, from the group. Come to think of it, Colt couldn't remember the last time Ben had joined them for poker night or a day of drunken fishing. It had been years, not months.

"Nice place." Ben stood with his hands on his hips, looking around at Lee's facility. "I don't have much reason to come out this way. This is a bit out-side of my area."

"I know it is. I appreciate you making the trip out here on a Saturday."

"We go way back," Ben said.

"That's a fact."

Ben was a short, stocky man with a fleshy face, unruly eyebrows, cropped brown hair and a country-boy drawl. His button-down shirt was stretched snugly over his barrel belly, but Ben could manage to find his way into all kinds of tight spaces in attics and crawl spaces even with the extra weight on him.

"Let's go take a gander at this project of yours," his old friend said.

Colt led the electrician through the property to the red barn.

"It looks like the wife is keeping you well fed, my friend," Colt teased Ben.

Ben chuckled at the good-natured ribbing with a pat on his stomach. "I tell you, I married one heck of a cook."

"How is Missy?"

"Pregnant."

Colt stopped walking for a step before he contin-ued moving forward. None of Colt's friends had be-come fathers in a community where people tended to marry and start families young. "Congratulations!"

"Five months." Ben beamed at him.

"Do you know what you're having?"

"It's a girl."

"Daddy's little girl," Colt said.

"That was the first thing I thought when I heard the news," his friend agreed.

Colt led Ben into the barn and began to take him through the plan for the fans and the watering systems. He was just wrapping up the talking points when Lee arrived, dressed in dark slim-fitting jeans, her standard Strides of Strength polo with sleeves long enough to cover the tattoo he now knew was there on her arm, and her hair was slicked back from her face. He couldn't stop himself from looking down at her left leg, trying to detect some hitch in her walk. But it wasn't there. If a person didn't know that Lee had a prosthetic leg, they wouldn't be able to figure it out just by her walk.

"Lee Macbeth," Colt made the introduction. "This is one of the best electricians you'll ever meet, Ben Campbell."

Ben greeted her respectfully, shaking her slender hand and then getting right down to business. Ben took Lee and Colt through the options to bring enough electrical power into the old structure to support the new fans and watering systems, and in a short time, Colt could see that Lee trusted the electrician's word. Ben's appearance, with his faded frayed shirts and his thread-worn jeans belied the expertise he had gained in the years he had been perfecting his craft. The minute Ben started talking, that's when Colt saw the respect grow in Lee's eyes.

Ben shifted his weight and hoisted up his sagging jeans. "It's a mighty big project and I've got a full plate at the moment."

"These horses do such important work. I wouldn't have a program without them. They mean everything to me. They mean everything to a lot of really special kids. Their comfort and their safety is the most important thing to me," Lee explained to Ben. "Colt says that you're the best. I need the best." Lee walked over to rub the nose of one of the horses in the barn. "They are my family."

If Ben was on the fence about donating his time to the project, and it seemed to Colt that he might be, then Lee's sweet personality and genuine concern and love for her horses changed his mind.

Colt saw the shift in Ben's expression—one moment he was trying to hem and haw his way out of the job and the next he was looking at his phone to find a time when he could come back to do the job.

"The soonest I can get back out here is next Saturday. That's the best I can do."

"We'll take it!" Lee clasped her hands together happily, her hazel eyes shining with excitement. "You have no idea what this means to me, Mr. Campbell."

"Ben," he corrected. "By God, when I hear Mr. Campbell, my gut twists." He looked at Colt with a grin. "Do you know how many times I sat up there in the principal's office with a pile of rocks in my gut while Principal Bennett told the secretary to call *Mr. Campbell* again? He always had to add the *again* just to make a point. I'm flat-out traumatized from it."

"One or both of us was always in the principal's office," Colt explained to Lee.

"That was darn near our second home." Ben hiked up his pants again. "That's why I'm glad that the wife and I are having a girl. Boys are too much trouble by half."

"You're having a baby?" Lee's eyes brightened. "That's wonderful!"

"Yes, ma'am."

Lee scrunched up her face. "Okay…now it's my turn. Please don't *ma'am* me. I'm not that old!"

"That's fair." Ben smiled at her. Colt could tell that his old friend liked Lee. It was the first inkling that Lee could fit into his world, something he hadn't really considered—he was too busy trying to figure out how to fit into hers.

"Do you have children?" Ben asked as they headed out of the barn.

"No," Lee said a bit wistfully to Colt's ears. "But one day—hopefully real soon—I will."

Ben and Lee went on to discuss a timeline for the project while Colt's brain was stuck on Lee's comment. Was there a boyfriend in the mix he hadn't uncovered? Or was Lee just wishful thinking out loud about children? Colt couldn't be sure, but he did know one thing without any doubt—Lee was dreaming of a child in the near future and he was the right man to make that dream come true for her.

"Hand me that wrench, will you?" Liam pointed to the toolbox next to his 1940s Ford truck he had been restoring for the past several years. Liam, a large animal veterinarian with a thriving practice and a father of three, rarely came out to work on his pet project.

Colt bent down and grabbed the wrench, handing it to his brother. His mind was still back at Strides with Lee. He couldn't get the image of seeing her with that prosthetic leg. He wished it wasn't true, but it was jarring. It had never occurred to him that Lee had experienced such an obvious trauma. He felt protective of Lee. Perhaps that just came with the territory when his heart had been stolen by her smile. Colt wished he could have been there to protect her from whatever terrible event had happened in her life that had resulted in her losing part of her limb.

"I tell you, Colt, I had no idea how much of a headache I was saving for myself when Kate and I eloped. Callie's wedding is taking over our lives."

"I still can't believe she's getting married." Callie was engaged to a young man, Tony, who lived

in California. They had met at a convention for individual's with Down syndrome; from Callie's telling of it, it was love at first sight for both of them.

"That makes two of us." Liam gritted his teeth
and tried to loosen a bolt in the engine. "Four of us,
really. Tony's parents, Kate and I are on the same
page. We've slowed this thing down to a crawl but
we can't stop them from loving each other. Tony's
parents are making the move from California to
Bozeman. We've renovated Kate's old house for
them so they can be independent but close enough
for us to support them."

Colt stood with his arms crossed in front of his
body. He mused allowed, "Callie's getting married."

"Yep," Liam said. "And I just want them to give
me the bill at the end. I don't want to discuss sil-
verware and flowers and venues. Just give me the
bill and I'll pay it. Shouldn't that be enough?" Liam
asked rhetorically. "But, no. They want me to be
involved."

Liam stood upright. "I now know more about
wedding dress silhouettes than I have ever wanted
to know."

"It's going to be pretty amazing to see you walking her down the aisle," Colt said.

That brought a smile to Liam's face. "I have to
agree with you there. She's grown up so much—
she's lived on her own, she's gotten engaged, she
has a job. She's been working on a cookbook of her

favorite recipes that she wants to self-publish. She's just exceptional. By any standards."

"From what I've seen, she does a great job out there at Lee's place."

Liam wiped some grease off his hands. "Lee is a godsend. Kate says that Lee's program made a huge difference in Callie's life. It didn't seem like therapy to her. It was just her doing some activities on a horse and Kate thinks it went a long way to build Callie's self-esteem."

Colt saw a crack in a door and he decided to just open it. "You've worked with Lee for a while now, haven't you?"

Liam grabbed two bottles of water out of his cooler and handed one to Colt. "Going on ten years now, I guess."

Colt gave a little shake of his head. Lee had been living under his nose this whole time! The woman he felt, in his gut, was the woman he was supposed to marry had been mere miles away. Where was he during this time? Why hadn't he met her before this?

"Do you know what happened to her?" Colt asked bluntly, wanting to cut through the fat and get to the meat of the matter.

If Liam suspected his question had an ulterior motive, it didn't show in his expression. "You mean to her leg?"

Colt nodded.

"Car accident," his brother told him.

Colt swallowed hard several times. The next question he asked was only posed to confirm what he seemed to already know in his gut.

"Was there anyone else involved?"

Liam finished his water, recapped the bottle and tossed the empty bottle near his cooler to retrieve later.

"I don't know all the details." His brother returned to his work on the old Ford engine. "But from what I've heard, she was driving and her husband was in the passenger seat."

Chapter Six

Lee had lived in a 1932 charming bungalow in downtown Bozeman for several years. It was the perfect house for a family because it had a large backyard with a white picket fence and a huge tree already outfitted with a tire swing. Buying this house was the first step she had taken to building the family of her dreams. Lee pulled out her savings account register, wrote down a deposit she had made the night before and then looked at the total. She had been saving for years to start her family and the numbers in her account were nearly large enough to make her dream a reality.

Lee slipped the register back into the drawer.

After she slowly the pushed the drawer shut, she picked up a crystal-framed picture of Michael and her on their wedding day. The two people in that photograph were so young. So naive.

"Almost there, my love." Lee ran her fingers over Michael's face. "A promise made is a promise kept."

She stared at that photograph for several more minutes and then closed her eyes tightly to block out the image of Colt's face that snuck into her mind without permission. Lately, her early morning thoughts, which had always been reserved for Michael, were being intermingled with thoughts of Colt. Even worse, before she went to sleep, thoughts of Colt had overtaken memories of Michael— memories that had always lulled her to sleep. She didn't *want* to think of Colt as much as she did—it angered her. Her mind was preoccupied with the man and her body was betraying her, as well. For years, she had suppressed the desire to make love. If she couldn't make love with her one and only forever, she couldn't imagine ever sharing that part of herself with anyone ever again. And yet, when she closed her eyes, thoughts of Colt's lips on her lips and his hands on her body would not be denied. Because of Colt, she was tossing and turning in bed. Because of Colt, she was experiencing something that she hadn't in such a long time that she had forgotten what it felt like—sexual frustration. Lee had finally given in to her body's demands and had begun to find ways to pleasure herself—to ease the ache in her own body. And when she did, her thoughts weren't of her dear, sweet Michael. Her thoughts were always of Colt.

"Stop it!" Lee chastised herself aloud as she replaced the photograph carefully in its honored spot on her desk. "It isn't real! It's just…"

Lee shrugged her shoulders and then shook her head, trying to come up with an explanation she could convince herself of. "It's just brain chemistry tricking me into thinking there is something more when there clearly isn't."

Determined to get through a day without dwelling on Colt, particularly when she had so much to get done before the summer session started, she leaned over to search the computer bag at her feet for her laptop. Her latest grant proposal was due in two days and with the summer program also starting in two days, she needed to finish the proposal and submit it today.

"Oh, no. *No!*" Lee rummaged through the computer bag, unzipping pockets, searching and then moving on to the next compartment. "Darn *it*!"

How could she have been so scatterbrained when she left the property? She had left her laptop at Strides! Lee grabbed the crutches that she had leaned up against the desk and made her way to the living room where she had left her prosthetic. Lee lowered herself down on the couch and slipped her crutches into the space between the couch and end table where they would be out of the way but easily accessible when she needed them again.

"Can you believe I did that? If my head wasn't attached, I swear." Lee rubbed Chester's head. The chubby gray feline trilled, blinked his eyes at her and then rolled over onto his back for a belly rub.

Lee obliged Chester, giving him a quick rub before she turned her gel prosthetic liner inside out, put the base of the liner up against the end of her leg and then rolled the liner up over her knee to her thigh. Putting on her liner was second nature now. She checked to make sure there wasn't any air between her skin and the sleeve before she bent her knee to a forty-five degree angle and gently pushed it into the socket of the prosthesis that she used for her everyday running around. Lee stood up and rolled the socket sleeve with a vibrant galaxy print up over her knee until it was snuggly fit to her upper thigh.

"I'll be back, sweet boy." Lee planted a kiss on Chester's head.

On her way out the door, she grabbed her wallet, her phone and her keys. She could imagine exactly where she left the computer. It was on her desk packed up with the extension cord wrapped neatly on top, waiting to be put in her bag. Lee walked quickly to the detached garage she had built behind her historical house and climbed behind the wheel of her putty-gray Jeep Gladiator. She put the key in the ignition, turned it and then realized that the engine wasn't turning over. She tried again, pumping her foot on the gas.

"Seriously?" Lee hit her hand on the steering wheel. "What is going *on* today?"

She didn't bother lifting up the hood because she wouldn't know what the heck to look for anyway. The next-door neighbor had jumper cables, but she knew they were out of town because she had been picking up their mail for them. The neighbors across the street had jumper cables—of course, she had watched the entire family load up their boat and leave for a day of fun on the lake. She sent her friend and neighbor Shayna Wade a text. Shayna, a university professor, responded quickly that she was on campus prepping for summer classes.

Of course she would be. Just like her, Shayna was always working.

After exhausting her neighborhood options, Lee figured that her quickest solution was to get in touch with her father-in-law rather than hunting down neighbors who may or may not have cables. For all she knew, it could be something other than the battery!

"Hey, Lee. I was just talking about you." Boot thankfully answered the phone on the second ring.

"You were?"

"I was."

"Tell Gilda hi for me." She assumed that Boot was talking to the property manager because she seemed to always find the two of them together lately. "My truck won't start, Boot, and I need to get my computer out of my office so I can finish the grant. Can you grab my computer, bring it here and see if you can figure out why my truck won't start?"

"Hold on a sec," Boot said and she could tell by the more muffled sound of his next words that he was holding the phone away from his mouth and speaking to someone nearby.

"You're about to leave, aren't you?" Boot asked the person she assumed was Gilda. "Do you mind dropping off Lee's laptop at her house? Her truck won't start."

"That would be out of Gilda's way, Boot," she interjected.

"I'm talking to Colt," Boot told her.

"He doesn't need to come to my house," she protested more loudly and strongly than she had intended. The tone in her voice sounded harsh and urgent. The man had already invaded the space in her mind—the reality of him invading her private space made her break out into an immediate sweat.

But nonetheless, she cringed at the thought of letting her conflicted feelings for Colt slip out into the world. Luckily, Boot was focused on fixing her problem and not on the odd way she had objected to Colt coming to her private world.

"Sweet Girl threw a shoe, Lee," Boot explained. He sounded just like Boot always did, which allowed her to breathe a bit easier. Her father-in-law appeared to be oblivious to her discomfort over Colt. "I need to take care of that first. If you need to have this computer right away, Colt can have it to you in ten minutes or so."

She needed her computer and she certainly didn't want to stop Boot from caring for Sweet Girl just because her feelings were topsy-turvy over Colt.

"You'll come later to look at my truck though, right?" she asked.

"Do you have jumper cables, Colt?" Boot asked and then after a short pause said, "Colt will give you a jump. If it's the battery, problem solved. If not, at least you'll have your computer."

"Okay," she said, feeling boxed in. "What's he doing there now anyway?"

"He's been helping Ben," Boot reminded her. "They've been working all morning to get enough juice into the barn for the fans. They've got a plumber friend here too, making a plan to install the watering systems."

"Oh. That's right," Lee muttered. "I forgot."

Her mind had been so cluttered with getting ready for the first week of the summer session and finishing her grant proposal to install a pool on the property for aquatic therapy on time, the fans and watering system, as important as they were to her, had taken a back seat in her brain. And if she were being honest with herself, she trusted Colt to get the job done for her. She *trusted* him.

"You've got a lot on your plate, right now, Lee," Boot said. "Just go inside the house, relax for a minute and wait for Colt. You sound tired."

"I am tired." She leaned her head back onto the driver's seat headrest and closed her eyes. So many things in life were out of her control—she had learned that hard lesson years ago. Having Colt come to her house was really a molehill and she shouldn't turn it into a mountain. "Is Sweet Girl okay?"

"She's fine. I'm going to start getting her fixed up once I hang up with you."

Lee ended the call with her father-in-law, swung her legs out of her truck and hopped down to the ground. She walked around the side of the house to the front porch and sat down on the swing. She resisted the urge to go to the bathroom to check her reflection in the mirror. She looked how she looked and she wasn't going to primp for Colt. Her hair, which hadn't been washed for a couple of days, was pulled back into a messy ponytail and she didn't change out of Michael's threadbare college NYU T-shirt or her frayed cutoff denim shorts. This was how she looked on a weekend at home. This was who she was and she didn't need to cover that up for Colt.

While she waited for Colt, she kept herself busy by answering texts and emails on her phone. Both of her parents, still married, her older sister, Tessa and her beloved grandmother, for whom she was named, all lived in Central Florida now. It was difficult to be so far away from her family but at least they had technology on their side; she video-chatted with her sister several nights a week. Lee was in the middle of sending her sister a series of recent pictures of Chester when she saw Colt's unmistakable ruby-red truck driving slowly up the road. She tucked her phone into the back pocket of her jean shorts, went down the porch steps and waved her hand to him so he would be able to more easily find her house. She felt a small jolt of excitement and nervousness when she caught sight of his handsome face—darn dopamine. It always felt good—*physically* good—to see Colt.

Colt pulled his truck into the narrow driveway beside her house, parked and shut off the engine. He gave her that million-dollar smile of his as he delivered her laptop to her.

"I haven't been on this street since high school. This is the Millers' old place, right?"

She gave him one definitive nod. "That's who I bought it from."

"You've done a lot with it," he said, still looking at her house.

"It's home." Lee wrapped her arms around her

laptop and held it in front of her body like a shield. "Thank you for my laptop."

"No problem. I was on my way back to Sugar Creek. This was on my way."

"I'm going to put this in the house." She tapped the laptop case. "Boot said that you could look at my truck?"

He nodded, taking a step backward toward his truck. "I'm going to pull my truck up to your garage."

As he had before—as most people just instinctively did—Colt glanced down at her prosthesis. She watched his face carefully, examining him closely for any sign of revulsion. It would be so easy to dismiss him if she could find one shred of evidence that her disability made him uncomfortable.

"I'll meet you out back." The sooner she got Colt out of her private world, the better off she felt she'd be. In her mind, he looked like a fish out of water standing on her manicured lawn in his cowboy gear. Her neighborhood was filled with established professionals—realtors, bankers, university professors and small business owners—not cattle folk. They lived on the outskirts of town. A reassuring thought came into her mind as she set the laptop on an antique sideboard table just inside the front door: *he doesn't belong here.*

Lee hurried to the detached garage where Colt was waiting for her. Colt had managed to maneuver his oversized Ford truck into the second parking spot in the small garage. Lee had to turn sideways so she could squeeze into her Jeep.

"Pop the hood for me, will you?" Colt asked from the front of her Jeep.

She popped the hood and then put the key in the ignition. "I've never had any trouble with it before."

Colt lifted the hood, propped it open and then scanned the engine. He connected the jumper cables between her Jeep and his truck before he started the Ford. He revved his own engine a couple of times and after several moments, he said, "Give it a try now."

Lee turned the key and the engine didn't turn over. "No."

"Is it even trying to turn over?"

She tried again. *"No!"*

Colt shut off his engine, got out of his truck and unhooked the cables.

"It's not the battery?" Lee asked, frustrated.

Colt wound up the jumper cables. "I'm not sure quite yet. I need to take your battery down to the auto-parts store, let them test it and see if it has a bad cell."

"You don't have to do that," Lee protested, wanting him to be on his way. "Boot can do that later."

Colt ignored her as he walked to the back of his truck, lifted the bed cover, threw the jumper cables in the back and grabbed a couple of wrenches

from his toolbox. Lee squeezed out from behind
the driver's seat so she could catch up with him on
his way back to the front of her Jeep.

"Did you hear me? Boot can do this. You've already done enough for me today."

Colt handed her one of the wrenches. "Hold this
for me, will you?"

"Did you hear me?" she asked again, taking the
extended wrench.

"Yes, Lee." He smiled at her, releasing happy
butterflies loose in her stomach. "I heard you."

That was the last they discussed his leaving the
job for Boot. Lee watched while Colt worked to
remove the battery, holding the wrenches when he
asked. It didn't take him much effort to free the
battery from the engine.

"It shouldn't take me too long." Colt put her battery in the back of his truck.

"You really don't have to do this," she added,
but knew that he was determined to play knight-in-
shining-armor to her damsel-in-distress.

"I want to do it." He had backed his truck out of
the garage and braked next to her. "For you."

Lee turned her head away from him and pretended to find something interesting in a nearby
tree. His eyes were too blue—too intense—too
focused on the features of her face. What was it
about Colt? Why did he make her feel so jumbled
up inside?

"Lee…" The way he said her name, with that extra bit of something that let her know she was a woman that had caught his eye, set off wonderful jolts of happiness in the pleasure center of her brain.

She brought her eyes back to his, knowing that she was going to risk getting caught up in their ocean blue.

Colt leaned his arm out of the window, his eyes admiring on her face. "I can see that I make you nervous."

Defensively, her eyebrows dropped and she frowned. "I never said you did."

"I like you. You like me," Colt continued as if he hadn't heard her. "That's a good thing."

Stunned that Colt had just put words to everything that she had been feeling building between them for weeks as if he were discussing a grocery list with her, Lee pressed her lips together and continued to frown at him wordlessly. It was so unlike her to be caught off guard to the point that she couldn't manage to form a snappy retort.

"You go do your work and let me worry about your truck." Colt grinned at her and wrapped his fist on the side of his truck as if he were adjourning a meeting.

Words finally found their way into her mouth.

"You worry about my truck and I'll worry about my proposal."

"Isn't that what I just said?" he teased her.

She raised her eyebrows and put her hands on her hips, recovering from her earlier shock. "All I see right now is a whole lot of talking and wasting of valuable time. You should already be halfway to town by now."

Instead of cowing him, Colt's grin widened, signalling that he liked to banter with her. He tipped his hat to her with a wink. "As you wish, Lady Macbeth."

Lee liked him. Colt was certain of it now. That back-and-forth exchange had confirmed it for him—for the first time since he had fallen in love at first sight with the pretty entrepreneur, a crack in the armor she had been wearing whenever he was around gave him hope that his feelings were, indeed, reciprocated.

He made the trip to the auto-parts store as quick as he could—he wanted to get back to Lee's Jeep, get it running so he could be her hero for the day and then find a way to weasel just a bit more time with her before she sent him packing. Any time he had with Lee was time well worth spent for him.

"That should be it." Colt secured the new battery into place, wiped his hands off on a spare towel he kept in his truck before he headed to the front door of the house. He rang the doorbell and waited for his ladylove to answer.

"Hi." Lee opened the door in her jean shorts. Her

thighs were slender and shapely, well muscled from riding horses and working at the stable. It was still a bit of a shock to see the prosthetic instead of the lower half of her leg, but it never detracted from how he felt about her. In fact, the colorful sleeves she wore over the upper part of the prosthetic— today it was a dynamic scene of the solar system— showed a fun side of her personality that she didn't always show when she was being Lee Macbeth, owner of Strides of Strength.

"What's the verdict?" she asked him.

"There was a bad cell in the old battery, so I got you a new one," he told her. "Get your keys and we'll see if she starts."

Lee scooped up her keys from a nearby table and rejoined him on the porch. Her hair was a bit messy, which he liked. It was nice to see that she was human and wasn't always put together perfectly. Colt also liked that her face was scrubbed clean of makeup. He could see that there were dark circles beneath her eyes and the smattering of freckles on her nose were more prominent. The more he got to know her, the more he saw the real Lee Macbeth, the more he wanted to find a way to get closer to her. Maybe he *should* try his brother Shane's move with Rebecca—Shane had started things off with a kiss and figured out the dating part later.

Colt seriously contemplated his next move with Lee as they walked together to the garage. He made sure to shorten his stride so she could keep pace with him, but she always surprised him at how naturally, and quickly, she walked with her *bionic* leg.

"Here goes nothing." Lee put the key in the ignition.

"Don't be pessimistic," Colt told her. "It's not in your nature to be pessimistic."

The Jeep immediately started and Colt watched her face through the windshield. There was a genuine smile just for him.

"You fixed it!" Lee exclaimed as she turned off the engine and stepped out of the truck. "I was worried that I was going to have get it towed and go to the dealership and get a rental car. I kept on thinking, please, not *this* week."

Colt had noticed that Lee always held herself away from him—she never touched him, even in passing. But today, that touch barrier was crossed and she put her hand on his arm and gave it a little happy shake. "Thank you. I mean it, Colt. This is one huge thing I don't have to worry about now."

"I'm glad I could help." He looked down at her beaming face and thought to capitalize on the moment. She was happy and her guard that she usually had up against him was temporarily down. But something made him hesitate. The garage wasn't private. His first kiss with Lee—and there would be a first kiss shared between them—deserved to be done in private.

Lee withdrew her hand from his arm, a confused expression flashing across her sweet face. She turned away, putting some distance between them.

"You'll have to give me a receipt so I can reimburse you," she threw over her shoulder.

Colt followed behind her, watching her ponytail swing like a jaunty pendulum, watching the swing of her shapely hips in her cutoff shorts. Lee always seemed to be running away from him like a nervous rabbit when in every other aspect of her life she sat at the head of the table—commanding, in control and in charge.

At the bottom of the porch steps, Colt pulled his wallet out of his back pocket, tugged the receipt out of one of the compartments and handed it to her.

"I'll write you a check." She plucked the receipt out of his hand.

"Don't worry about it." He wanted the battery to be a gift—a small token.

"No." Lee shook her head. "I'll write you a check."

"Whatever works for you, works for me," he said.

For a moment, Lee seemed to have a debate in her own mind before she asked, "Do you want to come inside while I grab my checkbook? I could get you something to drink."

He nodded. "I'd appreciate it." Colt followed her up the steps and through the front door. He wasn't going to pass up any opportunity to spend some one-on-one time with Lee.

"Sweetened or unsweetened?" She stood in front of the oversized refrigerator.

"Sweet." Colt looked around the kitchen, noting all of the differences—structurally and aesthetically—since he had last stood in this space when he was a teenager.

"Ice or no ice?" she asked, taking a glass out of one of the cabinets.

"No ice," he said, running his hand over the large butcher-block island. "The only thing I remember being the same is that door leading out to the backyard."

Lee poured tea into a glass with ice for her and a glass without ice for him.

"I wanted an open concept without ruining the charm of the house." She put the pitcher of tea back into the refrigerator.

The kitchen had been a small square, cut off from the living and dining rooms. Back in the day, the cabinets and countertops had been a mustard yellow reminiscent of *The Brady Bunch* house and the walls had been covered in rooster wallpaper. Lee had removed several walls, opening the kitchen up to the rest of the house.

"I kind of miss the roosters." He smiled as she handed him his glass.

Lee pulled opened a drawer, pulled out a rooster coaster and slid it toward him. "A nod to the past."

Even though she was smiling at him, there was stiffness in her shoulders and her arms that let him know she wasn't altogether comfortable with him in her house.

Wanting to put her at ease, he shifted the conversation to her passion. He held out his glass to her. "Here's to a successful summer."

"Yes." She touched her glass to his. "A successful summer."

She took a couple of sips of the beverage, then put her glass on the butcher-block countertop.

"I'll be right back." She turned her body slightly to the side to slip past him.

"Lee." This was his moment. If he didn't take it, the summer might sweep them both away without another presenting itself.

She paused next to him and looked up into his face.

Colt took off his hat, leaned his head down and let his lips hover above hers. He wanted to give her a chance to duck away from him, avoid the kiss, but she didn't. She stood as still as a statue, her breath suspended as he pressed his lips to hers. It was a short kiss, but he felt a promise of how right things could be between them in the softness, the sweetness of her lips. Colt's eyes locked with Lee's as he straightened and put his hat back on.

Her eyes wide with surprise, wordlessly, Lee swayed slightly until she was leaning back against the kitchen island. It was the first time a woman had reacted to his kisses in this way and he wasn't exactly sure how to read it. She hadn't slapped him or thrown him out of the house on his ear—so that was a positive. But she hadn't leaned into the kiss and asked for more either, which was what he had typically experienced before.

"You kissed me," she finally said.

"I did kiss you, Lee." He adjusted his hat on his head with his eyes steady on her face. "I've wanted to kiss you ever since the first moment I laid eyes on you."

Chapter Seven

This was exactly the reason why she had been avoiding Colt—this exact reason. Lee had felt the unmistakable physical chemistry between them. She was experienced enough to know when a man was attracted to her. But what hadn't happened to her in over a decade was the feeling in her own body that she was attracted to someone in return. Perhaps it had been mental, but that part of her body had been shut down since she lost her husband. She hadn't wanted to kiss or hold or touch or *make love* to any man since Michael. Until now.

"I can't apologize for it," Colt added with his eyes glued to her face.

"I didn't ask for an apology." There was an unfamiliar catch in her voice. Her heart was pounding so hard in her chest that she heard it like a loud drumbeat in her ears.

Her brain seemed to be frozen in time, her mind reliving that short, sweet, unassuming kiss. How should she react to this moment in her life? She knew how she *should* react. She should escort Colt out of the house and on Monday morning find a new placement for him. And yet, that wasn't what her heart wanted.

With her eyes locked with Colt's, Lee pushed away from the counter, reached up to put her hands on his handsome face and pressed her lips to his. She felt him inhale in surprise and a split second later, he wrapped his strong arms around her waist and deepened the kiss.

Don't do this, Lee.

This was the phrase that pounded in her brain, but the wonderful sensation of Colt's lips on her, his large hands splayed across her back, drowned out the sensible words. Still holding onto her body with one arm, Colt guided her back a step, reached behind her and pushed some papers out of his way, and then easily lifted her up and set her down on the island. He stepped between her legs, which allowed her to naturally wrap her legs around his hips.

"This isn't smart." Lee took his cowboy hat off

his head and tossed it in the direction of the living room.

"Yes, it is." Colt pressed his lips to her neck and breathed in deeply with a sigh. "This is the smartest damn thing I've ever done in my life."

"How can you say that?" Lee dug her fingers into his long hair and bit her lip hard to stop herself from moaning as he sucked on her earlobe.

Colt lifted up his head so he could give her a half smile. "Do we have to talk about this now?"

She missed his lips on her skin. She needed to feel the warmth of his body close to hers. "I don't know why you're talking at all."

Colt laughed, seeming emboldened by her words. And why wouldn't he be? That was exactly the signal she had sent him. Give me *more*!

Colt made quick work of stripping off her T-shirt, tossing it in the direction of his hat. The cool air hit her skin and it almost—almost—made her stop. But then his strong lips and warm breath replaced that cold air when he dropped a trail of kisses from her neck down to the small swell of her breast. Her nipple was hard and straining against the silky material of her bra. Her hands back in his hair, her eyes closed, her body tight with anticipation at the thought of him taking that nipple into his mouth. It had been such a long time—oh, how she needed to have this man's mouth on her skin.

"Oh." Lee's head dropped back. "Oh."

Colt had moved the thin material of her bra out of his way and had taken her breast into his hot mouth. There was nothing like that sensation, that wonderful tugging and suckling on her breast. So many jolts of excitement raced through her body. Her breath was shallow and the idea of stopping what they had started didn't seem possible. Her body was shouting at her—screaming at her—for relief. Let Colt relieve that ache. Just let him. She needed it so badly. She needed *him* so badly.

Colt's hands gripped her hips and he pulled her closer to his body. His lips were on her breast, then her neck and her ear and then on her lips. He kissed her breath away and all she could do was hold on and enjoy everything he was giving to her.

"I love you, Lee," she heard him murmur into her ear.

The merry-go-round went into slow motion as she absorbed his words. Her hands stopped moving in his hair and she felt her body stiffen.

He felt her pull away from him and he pulled away from her. Colt pushed his hair back out of his eyes, his chest rising and falling, his eyes shining bright blue with love for her. This wasn't a passing fling this man wanted—he wanted much more from her than that.

"You don't know what you're saying." It took her a moment to find enough breath to speak.

"I know exactly what I'm saying," Colt said seriously. "I love you. And you love me."

Those words hit her like a bucket of freezing water in the face. She had only loved Michael. Only Michael. She had always believed that to love another man would be a betrayal of the husband she had lost.

"No, I don't." Lee shook her head, wishing she wanted to rewind time and erase the last moments of her life. But the memory of being in Colt's arms was too precious—too sweet. She didn't want to forget it.

Colt crossed to her, took her face in his hands. "Yes, you do."

Yes, she did.

Her lips met his—it was a mutual kiss. She didn't want to love him. But she did. She loved Colt Brand.

"Hold on to me," he ordered, slipping his hands beneath her bottom.

She did his bidding, and wrapped her arms around his neck so he could scoop her up.

"Is the master bedroom in the same place?" he asked, carrying her through the living room.

She nodded. She was simply too busy nibbling on his warm salty neck to say yes.

Colt was carrying her to her bedroom and they were going to make love. All of the flashing warning signs going off in her brain were ignored for the unrelenting need building between her thighs. She had repressed that part of her for so long that now that the floodgate had been opened, there was no going back. She was a woman—he was a man—and they were going to fulfill the promise of the natural attraction that was between them.

Lee was licking Colt's earlobe when he had the inconsideration to ask an important question. "Do you have something for us to use?"

"You mean a condom?" She lifted her head.

He turned sideways so he wouldn't bump her legs on the doorjamb as they entered her bedroom.

"No," she said, sourly. How dare he be so practical at a time like this?

"You don't have anything in your truck?" she snapped, annoyed that he was the one being responsible while she was so revved up that she was about to throw caution to the wind.

He shook his head slowly. His eyes were conflicted.

"I suppose we should stop," he said right before he kissed her because her mouth was so conveniently close.

"We shouldn't have started," she pointed out.

Colt put her down on the bed and stood in front of her, his legs wide, the obvious bulge in his pants a distraction. She reached out without thought and touched him—how could she not?

"You say the word and we'll stop." Colt had a

fire in his eyes but he didn't reach for her. She knew he was waiting for her to decide their next move.

Her mind knew the correct answer but she didn't want to do what was correct. She wanted to do what was going to feel good. Colt was going to feel good.

Lee made decisions every day and she made a decision then. She hooked her finger into Colt's belt loop and pulled him toward her. She met his eyes while she unbuttoned and then unzipped his jeans. Her actions would speak louder than words to him.

Colt's fingers tugged her hair free of her loose ponytail and tipped her head backward so he could taste her lips again.

"Are you sure?" he asked against her lips.

"Do you want to keep talking? Or do you want to finish what you started, cowboy?" Lee asked.

Colt yanked off his boots and tossed them aside, then he yanked off his shirt. Wanting to speed up the process, she stood up so she could rid herself of her jean shorts, glad that she could easily slip them off over her prosthetic. In that moment, it occurred to her that she had never navigated the bedroom with a man after her amputation.

"What's wrong?" Colt asked, getting ready to rid himself of his jeans.

"I don't know if I should leave my leg on or take it off," she mused aloud.

Colt glanced down at her leg. "That's not the

body part I'm focused on, Lee. Take it off, leave it on. I don't care either way. Do what's right for you."

"I'll leave it on," she decided but pulled the shoe off the foot.

She looked up from her task to find Colt standing completely naked before her. The shoe slipped out of her hand and landed on the floor. She couldn't take her eyes off the man standing unabashedly before her.

"You are beautiful to look at," Lee said, her eyes trailing down from his muscular, tanned chest, over the flat stomach to the thick engorged shaft ready for her pleasure.

He smiled at her, completely comfortable in his own skin. And why wouldn't he be? Colt slipped off her bra and her panties and then he lifted her up in his arms so he could put her down on the bed. He quickly joined her, wrapping her up in his arms, his hands roaming her body until he found the most sensitive center of her body. She opened for him, knowing that he could feel how much she wanted him.

"I need to taste you." Colt moved down so he could replace his fingers with his mouth.

Lee closed her eyes and let Colt's hot mouth and seeking tongue take her on a journey out of her body. She opened herself to him and dug her fingers into his thick hair to keep her grounded in the moment. He was so hungry for her, feasting on her until she was arching her back and crying out from the pleasure she was receiving from him. His hands cupped her bottom and he lifted her body, supporting her, as he thrust his tongue deep inside of her.

Her eyes flew open as she felt herself climaxing in a way that had never happened before.

"Colt." She gasped his name. "Colt."

She was floating on air, suspended weightlessly in her mind while waves of tingles and chills skipped over her body followed by an electrical storm sending bolts of pleasure everywhere.

"My sweet Lady Macbeth." Colt dropped kisses on the inside of her thigh, lowering her body softly.

Still drifting on a cloud, languid and relaxed, Lee's eyes fluttered open. Colt leaned over her and kissed her open mouth just before he joined his body with hers. Their eyes locked as he seated himself completely inside of her.

"I love you, Lee." Colt kissed her again.

She wrapped her arms around him and pulled him down on top of her. She took every inch of him. She wanted every inch of him.

She heard him say, in the recesses of her mind, "God—I never knew it could feel like this."

Colt began to move inside of her, slow, steady and rhythmic while she held on for the ride. This dance, so ancient and instinctive, was natural for them. There was no learning curve, there was no need to *learn* each other. They moved in perfect harmony, matching their movements, matching pleasure for pleasure.

Lee felt the tension in his body and knew that he was about to climax. It excited her and she began to move frantically beneath him, lifting up her hips to take in more of him, raking her fingernails down his back. The thought of him coming inside of her pushed her over the edge right into a second climax of her own. She cried out his name again, rolling on the waves, as he thrust deep inside of her. She was panting and straining, wanting to take more of him in and experience the release of his essence into her body again and again and again. It wasn't until Colt had collapsed on top of her, the feeling of his weight pressing her into the mattress that the analytical part of her brain began to take charge again.

"Holy crap." Colt kept a hold of Lee as he moved to his back. He kissed her head with a satisfied sigh.

"Exactly what I was thinking." The woman in his arms sounded less thrilled than he would have expected after such an incredible lovemaking session.

Colt looked at Lee. Her arm was flung over her eyes and she had a pained expression on her face.

"Are you okay?" He pushed himself up onto his elbow. He wasn't expecting high praise but Lee was not basking in post-lovemaking bliss.

"What have I done?" Lee groaned behind her arm.

"Come on, Lee." Colt sighed. "Can't we enjoy

this for a couple of minutes before you start over-analyzing it?"

"No." She wiggled free of his arms and sat upright. "What have I done? This is a disaster."

Frustrated, Colt got out of bed. "No, Lee. This isn't a disaster. World hunger is a disaster. This was just two people who happen to love each other expressing it."

"Quit saying that I love you," Lee snapped. "And quit standing there like that. I can't think straight when you're standing there like that."

"You *do* love me or I wouldn't be here right now," he retorted. "And I'm just standing here like a normal person."

"Sure. Everyone just stands around looking like Michelangelo's David. That's perfectly normal."

Colt yanked on his jeans. "If I remember correctly, that statue looked like he had just gone swimming in really cold water. Not sure that's a compliment."

"Seriously?" Lee scooted out of the bed and quickly began to dress. "You're going to nitpick that compliment because David isn't hung like a horse?"

"It's a fair point."

Lee pushed on his arm and pointed to the door. "Just meet me in the living room."

"So we can have a talk. Is that it?" He leaned over to grab his boots off the floor.

"I know it's not in your nature to cooperate, Colt," Lee said, searching for her bra. "Please! Just this once! Cooperate!"

"You thought I was pretty damn cooperative a minute ago."

Lee slipped on her bra and then shooed him out the door. "Go."

"Fine." Colt went into the hall. "I'll go. But I'm not leaving."

Lee slammed the bedroom door shut behind him. Colt stared at the door for a moment before he walked, barefoot, toward the living room.

"Women," Colt said to Chester as he buttoned up his shirt and pulled on his socks and boots. "Am I right?"

He sat down on the couch next to Chester, his eyes focused on the shut door at the end of the hall. Colt hadn't expected to end up in bed with Lee—that thought hadn't even crossed his mind. But after they had made love, he certainly hadn't expected to be expelled from the bedroom. All of this was uncharted territory for Colt. He had no idea how to handle Lee.

The chunky gray cat rolled over, gazed at him with his wide green eyes and reached out his large paw to get him to pet his stomach.

"Why isn't Lee this easy to love?" Colt obliged Chester and rubbed his belly.

He waited for what seemed like an hour for Lee

to emerge from the bedroom, but when he checked his phone, it had only been ten minutes. Her hair was slicked back into a bun, giving her a severe look that he hadn't seen before. Her face was pale and grim and she was wearing a long-sleeve shirt and jeans. Her arms were crossed tightly in front of her body.

The kiss had been an impulse—an impulse that had led to lovemaking and he couldn't find it in his heart to regret it. He loved Lee. He meant it sincerely and with his whole being. He loved her. He wanted to make a life with her. Loving her with his body had just been a natural extension of what he had been feeling for her in his heart. He had made love to a woman—truly made love—for the first time and now that woman looked as if she regretted what had happened between them. That look on her face put a pit in his stomach that felt like a jagged mass of concrete.

Lee paced a bit in front of him, her brow furrowed.

"What's on your mind?" he asked, his tone flat. It was a way to get the ball rolling. He already had a pretty good idea what was on Lee's mind. Regret.

"I shouldn't have let that happen." She stopped pacing. "That was so irresponsible of me. So *unprofessional* of me. I don't even know who that person was…"

"You made a mistake."

"Yes," she agreed quickly. "I did. I made a mistake. And…" she paused for a second, gauging her words "…I'm…sorry."

"Well." He dropped his head down, leaning forward so his arms were resting on his thighs. "This sure as hell is a first for me."

Lee looked at him questioningly.

"I've never had anyone consider me a mistake before." Colt stood up.

"I'm not trying to make you feel badly, Colt." Lee's face flushed.

"If you aren't trying—" he found his hat on the ground by the couch and snatched it up "—you're failing."

Lee sat down heavily in a nearby chair. "What do you want me to say, Colt? That this was a great idea?"

"Yeah." He put his hat back on and adjusted it low over his eyes. "That would be a start."

"You are my *employee*," Lee said, "I crossed a line."

"I'm not your employee. I'm just a man working off my debt to society."

She stood up. "And that makes it so much better."

Colt walked over to stand before the woman he loved, wanting her to accept him in a way he wasn't sure she could. "What do you want from me, Lee? We can't go back and change what we did. And I sure as heck don't want to change it. I'm in love with you." Colt frowned. "Damn it, Lee. I want to take you out to dinner. I want you to meet my family. I want…"

Colt's words trailed off. He could see in her eyes that she wasn't ready for any of that with him.

"Forget what I want," he said. "Tell me what you want. Do you want me to call the judge and tell him to find me a new gig?"

For the first time since she came into the living room, Colt saw something real in her eyes. Fear. She took a step toward him but stopped. "No. Don't do that. You've been such a huge asset to us. Everyone is so happy you're there—don't let my mistake ruin it for the program."

"If you want me to stay on, finish my hours with Strides, then I will. I like being there with you. I feel good when I'm there. But I'll only stay on one condition—don't call what happened between us a mistake again, Lee." He swallowed hard several times. Acid was churning in his gut. He'd never felt so ill from a conversation with a woman before. If this was what love felt like, he wasn't so sure he wanted it after all. "I can't stand to hear those words coming out of your mouth."

Chapter Eight

The conversation had left Lee feeling drained.
She watched as Colt strode to the front door; she
wished she could think of something to say that
would make everything better between them, but
she knew there were no words powerful enough to
accomplish that.

Colt paused with his hand on the doorknob.
Without looking at her, he said, "This wasn't a
mistake, Lee."

Lee swallowed hard and fought the urge to disagree. There was no sense in it; she wasn't going
to convince Colt and he wasn't going to convince
her. When she didn't say anything in response, Colt

made a frustrated noise in the back of his throat and yanked open her front door. On the other side of the door, with her hand raised to knock, was her neighbor and friend, college professor Shayna Wade.

"Colt Brand!" Shayna was standing at the front door with jumper cables in her hand. "What are you doing here?"

"Just passing through," Colt said in a monotone. He gave Shayna a quick hug, glanced back at Lee with guarded eyes and then headed with that long-legged stride of his to his truck.

Lee tried not to stare at Colt as he backed out of her driveway. She had a horrible sinking sensation in her stomach—fear mixed with anxiety and shock. Lee tried to smile normally, as if the framework she had built for her life hadn't just burned to the ground, hugging her friend and inviting her inside.

"My word." Shayna sat down on a bar stool at the kitchen island. "Colt looks so much like his brother Noah I just about had a heart attack."

Lee used a rag to wipe a nonexistent spot on the counter near the sink. "Does he? I wouldn't know."

"The spitting image," Shayna mused.

"Huh." This was the only response Lee could manage. She felt disoriented and odd. Michael had been her first and only lover. After this afternoon, that was no longer true and she couldn't ever take that back.

"Are you okay?"

Lee nodded a little. "Yeah."

Shayna was staring at her with her keen violet-blue eyes and the expression on her face let Lee know that her friend wasn't convinced.

"Did Colt fix your Jeep?" her friend prodded.

Lee nodded again. She looked up at Shayna; Shayna and her sister, Tessa, were her confidantes. They were the women to whom she bared her soul.

"He fixed my Jeep," she said quietly. "And then I slept with him."

Her friend had an analytical mind and didn't speak without thinking first. Shayna's face and eyes didn't hold any shock or judgment—only contemplation.

After a moment, Shayna said, "Good."

"Good?"

"Yes," Shayna said, "Good. Why shouldn't you be loved, Lee?"

"But Michael…" Her face crumpled at the thought of her husband while unwanted tears slipped onto Lee's cheeks. She brushed them away with her fingers.

Shayna came to her side and enveloped her in a warm hug. "Michael loved you more than life itself. He would not want you to be alone for the rest of your life. It's not healthy."

Lee stepped out of her friend's hug and located

a tissue. She blew her nose loudly. "You're alone and you're fine."

Shayna lifted her eyebrows. "Define *fine*. I'm in love with a man who can't see past all of this—" her friend waved her hand over her heavyset frame "—voluptuousness. I've been firmly in the friend zone for over a decade."

"Idiot."

"Totally." Shayna's smile lit up her peaches-and-cream complexion that was offset by her glossy raven-black hair. "But I know that it's not healthy. So who am I to judge?"

"Thank you," Lee said. "I'm judging myself enough. I don't need anyone's help."

"Exactly."

After another pause, Lee continued, "I'm a planner. I make plans. I have lists. Colt Brand isn't on any of my lists."

"Maybe he should be."

"No," she said. "I made a promise to Michael, and I can't imagine someone like Colt going along with my plan."

"You never know. Colt is doing much better at Strides than you first assumed. Maybe he's more evolved than you give him credit for?"

Another shake of her head. "I don't think so. Besides, I don't even know what I'm talking about. It was one moment—one transgression. It's not like I'm thinking about a relationship with Colt."

"Lee." Shayna tilted her head to the side a bit. "You have traveled all around the world. You have been asked out on countless dates by men who have résumés to literally die for and no one has so much as crossed the start line with you. If you didn't have feelings for Colt, we wouldn't be having this conversation."

"That's what he said."

Shayna nodded her head. "See—more evolved than you might assume."

"You know—" Lee wrapped her arms around her body, suddenly feeling a chill on her skin "—if people find out that I slept with the infamous six-o'clock-news Colt Brand while he was working off his community service at my facility—the jokes write themselves, don't they?"

"I can't disagree with you there. Small town, big gossip."

"I don't want the program to suffer because I…"

"Climbed Colt Brand like a tree?" Shayna filled in the blank.

That comment made Lee laugh for the first time since she had blown through the giant warning barricades and leaped into bed with Colt.

"Look, Lee," her friend said, "I know Colt has a reputation—and he came by it honestly, I'll give him that. But one thing I know about him—he's a gentleman about women. His mother, Lilly, saw to that. He's not going to be bragging about what happened here today. Your secret is safe."

The first week of the summer session kept Lee so busy that it was easy to put her transgression with Colt out of her mind. Most of the time. Colt was busy finishing projects on the property and she was busy making sure that everything for the first week rolled out smoothly. But at the end of the day, when the volunteers were rinsing off the horses and putting hay in the stalls, and the sun was setting in the distance, and no one needed a moment of her time, Lee's mind inevitably returned to Colt.

"He certainly is good with our kids, isn't he?" Gail bustled into the room with a cup of water in her hand.

Gail caught Lee in the act of watching Colt with one of their riders. Lee quickly turned her chair around so her back was to the window.

"I've been noticing that, yes."

Gail poured the water on the wilted fern that sat on Lee's desk. The fern, a gift from her mother, was a testament to Lee's inability to sustain a plant's life. Gail had taken pity on the fern, which had recently turned a bit brown and crispy, and was making a valiant effort to revive it.

"Everyone loves him." Gail tried to fluff the brittle branches of the fern. "The kids, the parents. Everyone. God has truly blessed us this summer."

Gail stared down at the fern with motherly concern before she turned around and headed back into the reception area of the office.

It hadn't escaped Lee's notice that Colt had added something special to Strides of Strength—not only was he incredibly handy, making short work of their honey-do list—but he was a rare male role model for the boys who came to ride in their program. He was a real cowboy—one who was kind to them.

It also hadn't escaped Lee's notice that Colt was actively avoiding her. At first she thought that was a positive, but she missed him. Bottom line. She missed him popping into her office or swinging by to give her an update on his progress. And she wasn't altogether sure what she should do about it. Nothing had changed between them—she was still the head of a vital community program and he was still a man working off his community service. Yet, in her heart, everything had changed between them. She hadn't fallen into bed with Colt because she was so hard up that she couldn't control herself to be alone with a handsome cowboy. Colt had been right about her—she did love him. It was just a fact that Lee was in love for the second time in her life. It didn't make a bit of sense, but she knew herself well enough to know that it was true.

* * *

Colt had been licking his wounds for a week, avoiding Lee as much as he could. He still wanted to be close to her but he forced himself to stay away. He should have known when he looked around her house, which was set up as a bit of a shrine to her marriage to her late husband Michael, that Lee was far from ready for a relationship with him. The only thing that cheered him up—unexpectedly—were the riders who had flooded the facility for the summer session. Colt had met kids with cerebral palsy, autism, Fragile X and CHARGE syndrome. There were several riders who also had Down syndrome and he watched with pride as Callie acted as a role model for a younger generation. When he was first assigned to Strides of Strength, he had thought the court had been out of its mind. How could he be a good fit for a program like that? But he was. As it turned out, these kids were *his* people. He had a natural way with kids with disabilities—they made sense to him and he made sense to them. It didn't matter that they couldn't speak in sentences—some didn't speak at all—he understood them. And they had already become a part of his circle of friends.

"Hey there, Abigail." Colt saw one of his favorite riders walking toward him on the concrete sidewalk.

Abigail was a tiny little girl who resembled a Cabbage Patch Kids doll and she was as cute as a bug with her pink walker. Abigail was nonverbal but so determined. One of the wheels of Abigail's walker got stuck on a small rock on the sidewalk, which stopped her forward motion. Abigail scrunched up her face and pushed on the walker as hard as she could. The little girl looked back at her mom, making an angry sound, her dark brown curly pigtails swinging.

"I'll get it for you, Abigail." Colt knelt down so he was eye level with the little girl. He reached out, picked up the rock and tossed it into the nearby grass.

"Say thank you, Abigail." Abigail's mother, a woman in her mid-twenties, slender with the same dark brown curly hair as her daughter, was trailing behind. Close enough to keep an eye on her adventurous daughter, but far enough back that Abigail could have a sense of independence.

Abigail, up on her tiptoes to propel herself forward, looked up at Colt, then pushed past him as he stepped onto the grass so she had plenty of room.

"Thank you." Abigail's mom smiled at him.

"My pleasure." Colt watched Abigail for a moment longer. "She's really getting the hang of her walker."

"She's made so much progress since we've been here," she said, a pleased, relieved smile on her face. "And it's only week one."

Colt waved to the mother, then refocused his attention on the task at hand—going to see Lee. The projects in the barn were complete, which gave him a reason to break the ice with her. It was just time to tear down the wall they had erected between them. Lee wasn't ready for a relationship with him, that much he had figured out. But that didn't mean he didn't love her—that didn't mean he couldn't wait for her to be ready.

"Uncle Colt!"

On his way to Lee's office, Colt bumped into Callie.

He gave his niece a fierce hug, always so glad to see her.

"Guess what?" Callie's round face was beaming with excitement.

"What?"

"Tony's coming tomorrow!"

"He is?"

"Yes." Callie clapped her hands together joyfully. "He is. He's coming with his mom, and we are going to talk all about the engagement party, and we are going to go dress shopping, but not Tony because he can't see me in my dress, and then we are going to go to the Miss Gail's church because Tony's father is Catholic but Tony's mom isn't Catholic, she's Baptist, so we are going to get married in Miss Gail's church."

Instead of waiting for him to respond to the lengthy news dump, Callie hugged him again tightly, giggled, waved and then trotted off toward the nearby barn.

"Okay." Colt smiled after his niece.

There was a magic at Strides that he wouldn't have known about if he hadn't been forced by the courts to be there. These kids—from his niece to Abigail to all the others he had met—always gave him something to smile about. They were all struggling with disabilities that gave them challenges in life he couldn't imagine handling on a day-to-day basis and yet they made *him* feel good.

"Hi, Miss Gail." Colt took off his hat and hung it on one of the hooks on the wall.

"Hi, dahlin'," Gail said in her Georgia peach drawl.

"She in there?"

Gail nodded. "She's on the phone but you can go on in."

Colt knocked on the door softly and then opened it. He watched Lee very carefully but her face didn't register anything but happiness to see him, so he didn't feel uncomfortable entering her office when she waved him inside.

"I am so sorry to hear that, Lisa." Lee gestured for him to shut the door behind him. "We understand. Family has to come first. Take care of your father and if and when you are ready to return, our door is always open."

Colt sat down in one of the chairs opposite Lee's

desk. His mind naturally returned to the day, three short weeks ago, when he had first laid eyes on Lee Macbeth. That was the day he had fallen in love with her and the feeling had only grown stronger. Watching her with *her kids*, whether she was providing therapy directly or supporting other therapists to serve their needs, she was so beautiful on the outside, but Colt had discovered how truly beautiful she was on the inside.

"Everything okay?" he asked when she hung up the phone.

They hadn't spoken but once or twice since their intimacy at her house and they hadn't had a moment alone. Oddly, it wasn't as awkward between them as he had imagined in his mind.

"Lisa's father is in the hospital. She's flying to Baltimore tonight."

Lisa was one of the volunteers; Colt knew that Lee was always worried about having enough volunteers to run the program. Now she was down one.

"How long will she be gone?"

"She's not sure. It could be a week, it could be a month."

Colt nodded his understanding. There really wasn't anything helpful he could say.

Lee spun her chair around to look out the window for a moment, then she twisted the chair back to face him. She leaned forward and rested her elbows on the desk. The way she was looking at him, like she was in the middle of hatching an intriguing plan, got his attention.

"Everyone has been telling me how great you are with the kids," she said.

"That's nice to hear."

Lee tapped her fingernail on the desk. "I'll admit I didn't really think that you would be a good fit with our kids."

"That makes two of us."

"But you are," she added. "A good fit."

Colt smiled. No one was more surprised than he was. He simply had a knack for interacting with kids with disabilities. "I really like the riders."

Lee smiled at him—a bright, natural smile—a smile he hadn't seen on her face, directed at him, since he fixed her battery. "They really like you. Even Brent, who doesn't like anyone, actually seeks you out. That's huge for him."

"Brent's good people. I like him." Brent was a teenager with autism who spoke in short phrases and had a lot of behavior and sensory difficulties. To Colt, he was just a cool kid who liked to fist bump with him.

"When you first started working here, I really couldn't imagine you working directly with the students," Lee said with a small shrug. "I really couldn't."

Colt was relieved that when they were talking

about business, at least, things seemed pretty normal between them. "Same here."

"But I was wrong."

Colt sat up a little in his chair. "In what way?"

"I think you would be great working with the kids," Lee elaborated. "In fact, you're so tall you could actually side-walk with Sweet Girl. Most of our volunteers are too short and their arms start to get tired too quickly when they side-walk with her. And she has such great motion for kids who need to build core strength like Abigail."

"You actually want me to work with the kids?" This was a high compliment from Lee and Colt knew it. She was very particular about who worked directly with her riders and he hadn't passed muster in the beginning.

"Would you be interested?" She leaned forward a bit, her face hopeful. "We're down a volunteer."

He always wanted to impress Lee, but his response was sincere. "I think I'd like that."

Lee's apple cheeks rounded as her smile widened. "We'll have to get you trained."

"Just say when."

"I'll talk to Gilda about it. Either she will train you or I will." Lee continued to beam at him and he just allowed himself the luxury of admiring her pretty face.

After a moment, she seemed to remember that he

had come into her office without the explicit chore of becoming a volunteer.

"Did you need something in particular?" she asked.

"The barn's done," he said casually, but inside he was excited to tell her that her biggest to-do at the facility was complete and he had been the one to get it done for her.

"Are you serious?" Lee's eyes widened a bit. "All of it?"

"Every last thing on your list," he told her. "I was hoping you'd have some time today to come check it out with me."

Lee glanced down at the time on her phone. "I'm free right now."

"Then let's go." He stood up.

Colt grabbed his hat off the hook, brushed his hair away from his forehead and adjusted the hat so it fit right on his head. Out of the corner of his eye, he saw Lee staring at him. It wasn't a stretch for him to figure what might be on her mind. The last time she saw him put his hat back on, he had been picking it up off her living room floor.

"Don't get lost, you two." Miss Gail's laugh chimed in the small space like a holiday bell.

Colt held open the door for Lee and tipped his hat to Miss Gail. "I'll have her home before dark."

"See that you do, young man," the pianist said with a knowing smile. Colt had the distinct feeling that Gail had picked up on the natural chemistry between himself and Lee. It made Colt wonder how many other people at Strides could see the obvious. He wondered how many people could plainly see that they were in love.

Chapter Nine

Together, they walked through the property, much as they had on Colt's first day, but for Lee, it felt completely different. She had been dreading the time when they would have to face each other alone after their indiscretion and yet it hadn't felt uncomfortable for her in the least. He was still just Colt—respectful, easygoing, willing-to-lend-a-hand Colt.

On the other hand, she found herself looking at his lips and his hands and his legs, and finding it difficult not to remember what it felt like to be touched by him. To be kissed by him. To be fully connected to him in a way that she had only been connected to one man before. It was the oddest tug and pull in her brain—on one side she was drawn to Colt, like a magnet being pulled to a magnetic surface. On the other side, her brain couldn't even begin to process the idea of a man coming into her life in any meaningful way. Michael had been her one and only forever. How could a woman expect more than that?

On the way to the red barn, she felt Colt watching her walk. She looked over at him with a question in her eyes.

"How do you do that?" he asked her.

"Do what?"

"Walk like you have both of your legs."

The way he worded it, so bluntly, made Lee laugh. "Trust me, it wasn't always like this. My first prosthetic was terrible and it *hurt* to wear it. I didn't just jump right up and start running like I'd seen on YouTube videos, which really ticked me off because I was used to being ahead of the curve on everything in my life."

"Fake-limb honor roll."

She smiled at him. "I absolutely wanted to be on the fake-limb honor roll. But that didn't happen. It was months before I could walk on my starter prosthetic for more than an hour. But to answer your question, I had a great physical therapist for my gait training—that was really what allowed me to learn how to walk unaffected. Also, the type of foot I use really simulates the articulation of the joints of a real foot."

"I didn't know until that day I saw you jogging," Colt told her.

She nodded. "I worked hard at it."

When they entered the barn, Colt took her on the tour, showing her the final installation of the fans and the automatic waterers that, until Colt had come to their facility, had been sitting in their boxes in the warehouse.

"Colt." Lee felt herself become emotional when she walked into the barn. Perhaps to some it seemed ridiculous to get emotional over fans and watering systems or a roof that wouldn't leak. But the horses who were housed in this barn had often had rough lives before being donated to the program. They were older and had aches and pains, and gave so much to their riders—they deserved to be comfortable when they were resting.

"I can't say thank you enough." Lee walked into one of the empty stalls and activated the automatic waterer in the corner.

Colt was standing in the aisle of the barn. She noted that he was careful to keep a respectful distance. He was afraid to get too close to her and she would have thought that this would be her preference—but it wasn't.

"If you're happy, then I'm happy," Colt said, his arms loosely crossed in front of his body.

"I'm happy." She closed the stall gate behind her. "And the roof?"

"Tight as a drum. Zero leaks."

Lee rubbed her eyes to catch the tears that were forming. "I've been wanting to do this for these horses for such a long time. There has never been enough money. And then you come along and just—" she shrugged her shoulders "—fix all of it."

"It wasn't that big a deal." He took a step forward and then stopped.

She looked into his face, really looked into his eyes. "It's a very big deal to me."

They stood together in the aisle of the barn and Lee could feel that Colt wanted to reach out to her. She almost walked into his arms and hugged him for fixing the barn. She wanted to do it, but couldn't allow herself that moment. She was completely conflicted about her obvious feelings for Colt. But she wasn't conflicted about how it would look if she got involved with him while he was working off his community service.

Colt cleared his throat and something in Lee's gut seized.

"While I've got you alone, Lee," he said in a lowered voice. "I think we should clear the air a bit between us."

He was right. It was unavoidable. And at the moment, this barn was about the most private spot on the property with all of the activity centered on the open arena by the front of the facility.

Lee nodded her head and sat down on a couple bales of hay stacked just outside the stall. Colt knelt down in the aisle way in front of her and tipped the brim of his hat up so she could see his eyes.

"I've been torn up inside about how we left things the other day."

Lee clasped her hands together, wishing she hadn't made such a mess of things between them. If only she had fought her impulses more. If only she had told herself, *No you can't make love to the cowboy.*

"I'm sorry."

"No," he said in a harsh whisper. "I'm sorry. I've never…" He looked around to make sure no one was listening. "I've never done anything like that before."

Lee's brows furrowed. "You've never done anything like *what* before?"

There was no way Colt was about to confess that he was a virgin. There had been nothing virginal or inexperienced about Colt's performance in the bedroom. If anything, he had taught her several things in their one encounter.

"I've never *made love* without protection." Colt examined her face so closely. "I've never risked getting anyone pregnant before in my life. And I just want you to know, if you get in a family way, I promise I will be there for you."

Lee didn't realize that she had been holding her breath. She let it out quickly on a bit of a sigh. It was hard not to be touched by Colt. The way he looked on the outside—and his reputation for childish stunts—simply did not match the person she had gotten to know.

"Thank you, Colt," Lee said quietly. "I appreciate you saying that. Shayna's right. Your mom did raise you to be a gentleman."

Colt broke into a smile at the mention of his mother. "Lilly expects that of all her boys. I really want her to meet you."

Lee's stomach twisted tightly. "We should have been more careful."

"You're right," he agreed easily. "But sometimes—in the heat of the moment…"

"We don't make the best decisions." She nodded. "But you don't have to worry about that anymore."

"I'm not going to abandon you, Lee."

"Thank you," she said again, "But I can't—" she swallowed hard a couple of times, fighting to bring the words that were so difficult to say to her lips "—get pregnant."

Her sentence hung in the air between them while Colt stared at her face. It was as if he needed time to process her words and change the direction of his thinking, like flipping a switch from on to off.

"You can't?" he asked, as if he wasn't quite sure he believed her.

She shook her head. "No. I can't."

Colt stood up. "Then I'm sorry, Lee."

He joined her on the bale of hay and she found that the heat from his body, the feel of his cotton shirt against the skin of her arm was oddly comforting. He seemed to sense how difficult the topic was and he had moved closer to her without giving mind to the distance they had silently agreed to keep between them since he had left her house.

He didn't say anything. He was waiting for her to continue.

"We tried for years." She glanced over at his profile. "Michael and I wanted a family. That's all I ever wanted and when we couldn't get pregnant, it was devastating."

Colt was listening to her intently. His eyes were forward, his hands quiet and resting on his thighs.

"They called it infertility unspecified—but all that really meant to us was that we couldn't have a baby."

Colt looked over at her and their eyes met. "We had just started the in vitro fertilization process…" She broke the gaze and looked out the barn door to the green grass in the fields and the peaceful image of the horses grazing in the pasture. "And then the accident."

She felt Colt reach for her hand. She resisted the

urge to pull away from him. Colt didn't deserve that kind of rejection from her—not in this moment when all he wanted to do was give her some comfort.

"I'm sorry," he said simply. And it was enough.

"It was a long time ago."

"You still feel it like it was yesterday," he said.

That brought her eyes back to his, still surprised at his apparent sensitivity. "Yes. I do."

Together they sat in silence. She didn't want to talk about her struggle with infertility anymore. The fact that she hadn't been able to have a child with Michael—to have a tangible piece of him that Boot and she could hold and touch and love was still a source of deep pain. The doctors had never been able to pinpoint the reason behind her difficulty with conception. Between them, they had all the necessary elements but no baby. Losing her leg after the accident had been easy compared to losing Michael, knowing that he had never fulfilled his dream of becoming a father. Lee had always felt responsible for that. It was her failing—her cross to bear.

"Hey—do you want to see what I did to fix the windows?" Colt asked. "They don't leak even a little bit now."

Lee laughed and that laugh was exactly what she needed to move on from the sadness of the past.

"Of course, I would love to see what you did with the windows."

Colt stood up, still holding her hand, and helped her up. They walked into a nearby stall and he proudly described his handiwork to her.

"If you look here, you can see where I built a whole new frame for the window—the old frame was completely rotted so I had to replace it."

Lee found that she enjoyed listening to Colt describe his work to her in a way she never enjoyed listening to other handymen. Boot tried to describe his work process to her and she felt like falling asleep it sounded so boring. Somehow, listening to Colt talk on just about anything sounded interesting to her ears.

"Then I caulked all the edges and filled in any gaps with caulking and weather seal so it's in there nice and tight." Colt pushed open the window. "I also replaced the hinges so you can open these windows with just one finger."

"Super cool," she said, realizing that she sounded a bit like a teenage groupie watching her boyfriend's band practice.

They walked out of the stall and back into the aisle.

"Thank you, Colt. For everything you've done for us so far."

Colt smiled at her with those even white teeth of his. He looked like he could walk straight off a

Western movie set with those good looks of his. So handsome.

"I feel good being here," he said. "I like who I am here."

"I like who you are here too," she admitted honestly.

They walked together toward the barn entrance, their time alone coming to an end. There was a sense of sadness that this private moment was over between them but Lee knew that it was risky for them to be spending too much time alone on the property. Anywhere, for that matter.

"I can see that we have to be careful." Colt stopped at the barn's entrance.

"Yes," she agreed.

She could feel his eyes on her profile, so she looked up at him.

"Until I'm finished with my hours," he continued, "we have to keep our relationship…"

"Professional," she said firmly.

He gave one nod of his head. He looked off into the distance. "But when I'm done…"

"Why don't we cross that bridge when we get to it?" she was quick to ask, wanting a reprieve from dealing with what was so obviously between them. She felt it. She knew that it was there. How to handle it was beyond her ability to process at the moment.

"No, Lee," Colt said, "We need to cross it now.

"I've been thinking about things and I see now that this thing between us is kind of tough for you to navigate. It's not as simple for you as it is for me. I get that."

Lee waited for him to continue because she could see that he was determined to say his piece.

"While I'm still working off my hours, we'll just be colleagues. Friends."

"Friends without benefits." The light tease came flying out her mouth without thought.

He smiled at her again and she liked it.

"But when I'm finished with my hours, I am giving you fair warning now that I'm going to ask you out on a date."

She opened her mouth to protest but he shook his head to stop her. "A proper date. You'll say yes and then I'll pick you up at your house like regular folk do."

"And I'll say yes?" she countered. "Don't you think you should ask the question first and then let *me* do the responding?"

"That's fine. We can do it your way." Colt tugged the brim of his hat down lower over his eyes. "But you'll say yes, Lee. Because you love me the same as I love you."

On Sunday, Lee, Boot and Gilda took Colt through the training given to volunteers. Gilda taught him how to take the lead position with the horse. Even though he had a lifetime of experience leading horses, he'd never done it with a child with a disability on board. The responsibility to ensure the safety of the horse and the rider felt heavy to Colt.

"Because our horses are led by so many different people," Gilda told him, "we want them to be led in exactly the same way across hands so it's easier on them. They thrive on consistency and knowing what the expectation is. The signals we are giving them should be the same."

"Watch how Gilda is synchronizing her pace with Apollo. She's walking at his shoulder and when his hoof drops, her foot drops. Perfect control," Lee explained.

On his other side, Boot added, "What's most important to remember is that the therapist is in charge. Listen for the therapist's instruction. If she wants you to go left, you go left. If she wants you to stop, you stop."

"Gilda!" Lee called out and waved her hand. "Bring Apollo back this way, please."

"We'll always have two side-walkers," Lee told him. "The therapist will take one side of the horse and you will be on the other, if you aren't leading. It can be really tiring to side-walk a rider who isn't independent, so we might have you side-walk more than you lead."

Lee had Gilda lead Apollo, a palomino draft

horse, over to the mounting ramp to show Colt how to assist riders onto the back of the horse. Some of the riders were in wheelchairs, which required a specific method of transferring safely onto the horse.

"Once the rider is on the back of the horse," Lee said from Apollo's back, "The side-walkers need to be in place and the leader needs to be ready to walk-off immediately. Any adjustments to the equipment or the rider must be done away from the ramp."

With Boot leading Apollo, Lee pretended to be a rider while Gilda and Colt side-walked. They taught him the proper hand placement on the rider's leg or foot and then they showed him several dismounts, including an emergency dismount. Boot and Gilda performed that maneuver while Lee held the lead rope and explained what Colt was watching.

Boot lifted Gilda off the horse, under the arm-pits, and then dragged her quickly across the ground and safely away from Apollo.

"How often do you have an emergency dis-mount?" Colt asked, not liking the idea of having to do that with any of the riders he had met.

"Not too often," she explained. "Usually once or twice during a summer session. It could be due to a rider's behavior or the horse's behavior. Either way, the rider must be safely removed from the horse and the leader will remove the horse from the rider's parameter."

Colt nodded his understanding. While Lee was deep in her explanation, Colt could see Boot and Gilda over Apollo's back. Boot offered Gilda his hand, which was expected, but their hands lingered as did their gazes. How Boot looked at Gilda was exactly how he felt he must look at Lee. It was so obvious that there was something deeper than friendship between Lee's father-in-law and the Austrian manager.

"Thanks for the lesson." Colt gave Apollo a pat on the neck when the lesson ended. "You're a good instructor."

Gilda led Apollo back to the barn, leaving Boot and Lee behind with him. Boot stared after Gilda before he said, "Well, I'll be heading back to my shop unless you need me for something else."

"Thank you, Boot." Lee gave him a quick hug. "That was a huge help."

Colt offered Boot his hand. "Thank you."

Boot grasped his hand firmly, gave it one shake and then slapped him on the back. "You're gonna do just fine."

They watched Boot walk away and when he was out of earshot, Colt asked Lee, "Do you think something is going on between Boot and Gilda?"

Lee's shoulder's tensed immediately and her brow furrowed. "I know they're really good friends."

"I think it's a little more than that."

"No." His companion shook her head, her ponytail swinging emphatically. "I've asked Boot about that before and he said that he believes you only get married once."

"I didn't say anything about marriage."

It wasn't difficult to read in Lee's facial expression and tense body language that the idea of her father-in-law dating bothered her.

"Either way." Lee started walking and he followed. "Boot doesn't intend to date anyone."

"Would it bother you if he did?"

Lee glanced over at him with a frown. "I've only ever known him with Melissa 'Mama' Macbain."

"Times change," he said gently, sensing that her resistance to the idea of Boot moving on was somehow closely connected to her own resistance to moving on.

Lee's frown deepened. "It would be weird to see him with someone else. That's all. Just like it would be strange for Boot to see me with someone other than Michael."

Colt stopped in his tracks and Lee kept on walking. When she realized that he wasn't keeping pace with her, she stopped and turned around to face him.

"So, I'll see you tomorrow?" she asked. "You'll have your first rider at eight o'clock."

It was always so easy for Lee to default to the

program, particularly when she wanted to avoid a topic.

"I'll be here."

Lee's smile never returned to her face. "I'll see you then. It will be good to have you in the arena with us."

Colt stood in the middle of the arena, watching Lee walk away from him. He had a sinking feeling in the pit of his stomach whenever Lee spoke about her late husband. Michael's ghost was ever present. Colt knew how to compete and win. But how in the world was he going to be able to compete with the memory of a man Lee had loved and lost? A man enshrined as perfection in her mind. How was he ever going to truly win Lee's heart?

Chapter Ten

"Come here, my son." Lilly Hanging Cloud Brand held out her arms for her son. "I am so happy to see you."

Colt's mother was a full-blooded Chippewa Cree Native American who had been raised on the Rocky Boy's Reservation near the Bear Paw Mountains in Montana. Lilly was a kindhearted, spiritual woman who had raised eight children—seven boys and one girl—on the sprawling Sugar Creek Ranch with her husband, Jock Brand. Colt had gotten his blue eyes from Jock but the rest of his looks—from the blue-black hair to his straight, prominent nose and his chiseled cheekbones—came from Lilly and the Chippewa Cree Nation.

"I'm happy to see you, Mom." Colt leaned down and kissed his mother's soft cheek. Lilly was a beautiful woman with long pin-straight hair, black with strands of silver, and brown-black eyes.

"You look so well, Colton." Lilly reached up and touched his face. "Better than before."

It was a high compliment from his mother. She had never approved of his antics or his drifting from one mess to clean up to the next. Of all her children, he had been the son who had spent the most time with her on the reservation and she had always expected him to represent their people with dignity—not end up on the six o'clock news.

"Before we go to the others—" his mother took his hand and tucked it under her arm "—let's have a little chat, you and me."

Colt escorted his mother to her sewing room—this was Lilly's own private space in the opulent ranch house. When Jock had made his fortune, he'd insisted on building a house that would showcase his wealth. Lilly, always the bending reed of the family, agreed to the building of the mansion but insisted that she have a space in this house where she could keep herself grounded in her traditions.

"What are you working on now, Mother?" Colt sat down in Lilly's room, always fascinated by his mother's creativity.

Lilly's grandmother had taught her the traditions of making clothing and footwear and Lilly handcrafted items in the tradition of the Chippewa Cree and then sold the items so the funds could be used for the betterment of the reservation.

"I am making Callie's engagement dress." His mother smiled softly. "She wants a jingle dress like Savannah wore for her wedding."

His eldest brother, Bruce, had renewed his vows to his wife, Savannah, in an historic home in downtown Bozeman, Story Mansion, several years back and Lilly had made Savannah a traditional wedding dress for the occasion. Callie had always admired their wedding photograph when the family gathered in the main house at Sugar Creek Ranch, as they were tonight.

Colt stretched out his legs and crossed his ankles, feeling relaxed and comfortable in his mother's private space, surrounded by her reams of brightly colored material and beads.

"So—" Lilly sat down across from him and leaned forward, her face keen with interest "—what is this change I sense in you?"

Colt smiled at his mother. Nothing about him had ever escaped her notice.

"I'm feeling good about myself for the first time in a long time," he confessed. "I don't know how to explain it really, other than I feel like me finally. Like the old me was the imposter and now this person is the real deal."

His mother studied him for several long seconds before she said; "You were always my most sensitive boy."

"Whenever I took you to the reservation, the spiritual leaders would all say to me that you were special. That you had a special soul."

"You've never told me that before."

"It wasn't the right time," Lilly said. "But now I think you can understand it."

Colt pushed his hair away from his forehead and rested his hands on the top of his head. He let out a long breath and then said, "I found what I was meant to do."

"And what is this thing you have found?"

"It's not a thing," he said. "It's a who."

Colt told his mother all about Strides of Strength—about the riders and his connection to them. He told her everything except that he had fallen in love with Lee. That he kept to himself.

"I always knew that you would not be satisfied only working here on the ranch. I told your father this. Yes, you are a rancher. Yes, you work the land. Of course, this is in your blood. But this connection you have always had to the smallest birds— the birds who do not fly so easily—the birds with the broken wings—this too is also in your blood and to deny this is to deny that which makes you who you are."

Colt and Lilly left her sanctuary to join the family celebration that was unfolding—Shane and Rebecca were holding a gender reveal party in the back patio area of the ranch house. The party was serving double duty because this was the first time Callie's soon-to-be in-laws were joining them at Sugar Creek Ranch.

"Hey, big sis." Colt hugged Rebecca and then leaned down to say hello to the baby in her belly. "Hello, niece—nephew?"

"We'll know soon enough." Rebecca beamed at him happily. Pregnancy simply suited Rebecca Brand. She had a definitive baby glow and her curvy figure had somehow been enhanced by the growing baby bump.

"What's the plan? Is Shane going to jump out of a cake or something?"

Rebecca laughed. "Thankfully, no. He has planned fireworks in the color that matches the gender."

"Well," Colt mused, "it wouldn't be a Brand event if it wasn't over the top, now would it?"

"No. It wouldn't."

After he touched base with Rebecca, he then found his brother Shane to congratulate him. As he wound his way through the crowd, each one of his siblings mentioned how good he looked. Like Lilly, they were noticing a change in him. No one knew that the real change in him was the love he felt for Lee. That love had made him want to be a better person. That love made him want to fit into her more serious and philanthropic world. The connection he had to the riders at Strides served as proof—validation—that his love for Lee was good and right. Until Lee Macbeth, he had been drifting along with no direction and no real plans. Now, he was focused and motivated. These were qualities he always had but had never wanted to tap into before. His love for Lee had brought those qualities to the surface.

"It's about damn time you flew straight." Jock, a gruff rancher with deep-set blue eyes and a shock of bright white hair had never been one to temper his words. "Now finish this nonsense out at that petting zoo or whatever the heck-fire goes on out there with all of those do-gooders and get back to work here. Hunter and Bruce have been carrying your load long enough."

Jock gave Colt a little slap on the cheek. "Good to see you, son."

Liam, who was just within earshot of Jock's words of wisdom, came over right after their father left. "He leaves you with a warm fuzzy feeling, doesn't he?"

"The man is a walking Hallmark card."

Liam laughed and then nodded to the group of people nearby. "Callie has been bugging me about you. When is Uncle Colt getting here? When is Uncle Colt getting here? She wants you to meet Tony and Tony's parents."

"How are they doing?"

"The parents?"

Colt nodded.

"Total culture shock," Liam said under his breath. "California to Bozeman, Montana? We're from different planets, man."

Callie always gave him the best hugs and tonight was no exception. Callie held on tightly and then she did something that had never happened before—she let go of him and linked her arm with a young man, short in stature, with thick glasses. And like Callie, Tony had Down syndrome.

"Uncle Colt—" Callie's face was lit up with excitement "—this is my *fiancé*, Tony."

Colt shook the young man's hand and then he was introduced to Tottie, Tony's glamorous mother, who was covered in diamonds that offset her perfectly golden bobbed hair, and Tony Sr., Tony's father.

"Are you in the cattle business, Colt?" Tony Sr. asked him.

"I work on Sugar Creek with my brothers."

"That's good. That's good. Family is the most important thing." Tony Sr. nodded. "I own a chain of carpet stores. Tony's been selling for me since he was in high school."

Colt looked over to where Tony and Callie were standing, their heads close together, their hands intertwined. They looked like any other engaged couple—affectionate and enamored.

"Kate didn't expect any of this with Callie. Did you?"

Tony Sr. gave a little shake of his head. "Not at all. How could we imagine such a thing as this? We had hoped that they would be happy with their long-distance romance."

Callie rested her head on Tony's shoulder and Tony put his arm around her and hugged her tightly to him.

"We hoped it would fade," the father continued. "And yet, here we are."

"This is a big move."

"A very big move," Tony Sr. agreed. "But he is my only child." There was a catch in the man's voice and the slightest pause before he continued, "He's my son and this is his chance to have what his mother and I never thought he would have. A wife. A marriage. How can I deprive him of that? No. Kate and Liam can't move—Kate has her family ranch and all of those horses. Liam has a practice he's built. They can't move, so we move. I can travel back to California whenever I need, no problem. I can sell carpet anywhere. Who knows—perhaps Bozeman needs a new place to buy carpet."

Tony Sr. nodded as if to confirm his thought.

"I'll be fine," the man said, "I'm worried about Tottie. She's leaving all of her friends behind—she has so many—her social clubs, her charities. The only thing she'll have to keep her occupied here is

Junior and I'm not so sure that's going to be such a good thing."

Colt didn't have a chance to respond because his brother Shane had gotten up on the small stage that was a permanent fixture at Sugar Creek.

"Good evening, all." Shane stepped behind the microphone with his guitar in hand. Shane was a singer-songwriter and he had recorded an album once he had embraced a sober lifestyle and married Rebecca. Shane had faltered in his sobriety a couple of times, but he seemed to be back on track and working the program that the VA had set up for him. He looked happier now—tonight—then Colt had ever seen him look before.

"Some of you might remember that I wrote a song for my sweet Rebecca called 'Pretty Eyes.'" Shane smiled at his wife who was standing by the stage, her hand resting protectively on her baby bump. "I love you, Rebecca with the pretty eyes."

Rebecca mouthed the words *I love you* and wiped fresh tears from her cheeks as Shane played her song. During the song, Colt looked around at his family. So many of his siblings and family members had found their mates. Jock and Lilly, Bruce and Savannah, Liam and Kate, Callie and Tony— they all had found each other. His brother Gabe, a long-distance high-end horse transporter had found his true love, Bonita, and once she finished medical school, she was moving to Bozeman to start her medical practice. Now, he had finally found Lee and he hadn't even known that she was the vital piece of his life that had been missing. But she was that vital piece. On a night like tonight, when his family had gathered to celebrate the coming of the next generation of Brands, Colt knew in his gut that Lee belonged, here, by his side.

Colt joined in with the rest of the crowd, clapping for Shane as he finished his love song to his wife. Shane took off his guitar and held out his hand for Rebecca to join him on stage. With his arm around his wife, Shane said, "Green is my favorite color and Purple is Rebecca's. So, green if it's a boy and purple if it's a girl."

They all looked upward and saw glorious bursts of plum and lavender sparkling against the darkened backdrop of the night sky.

Shane's voice was the loudest when the crowd shouted, "It's a girl!"

Colt whooped and hollered with the rest of the clan, happy to welcome a girl into a family dominated by boys.

"No!" someone shouted. "It's a boy!"

Shane had his arm around his wife's shoulders, holding her tightly, when a fresh set of fireworks, this time in forest and lime green, lit up the sky.

Lilly joined her son and daughter-in-law on stage and said simply into the microphone, "It's a boy and a girl. We're having twins!"

The crowd erupted with cheers at the news; Colt was happy for his brother and sister-in-law—he was happy for his parents who always wanted more grandchildren. Until Lee, he hadn't given much thought to children. Now, the idea of becoming a father in his twenties didn't seem like such a impossibility.

"I—I want a b-baby," Colt heard Callie say to Tony Jr. "Right after we get married."

"No," Tony Jr. said with a petrified expression on his face. "I can't do that. Mom and Dad told me to get a job and take care of myself. Now I need to take care of you. Like my dad takes care of my mom."

"I—I have a job. I—I know how to cook. I—I have my own apartment." Callie frowned at her fiancé. "I—I take care of myself. I—I want to have a b-baby. If you don't want to have a b-baby, then I—I don't want to marry you!"

Realizing Callie was not going to back down from this discussion with Tony Jr., Colt gave his sister-in-law Kate a heads-up.

"I think Callie is having her first fight with Tony," Colt told Kate in a lowered voice.

"No." Kate, a slender, fit woman with sun-streaked dark brown hair and deep laugh lines around her eyes, said, "It wouldn't be the first. What are they fighting about now? Let me guess—babies?"

"Yep," Colt said. Kate and Callie were as close

as a mother and daughter could be and Kate knew her daughter better than anyone.

Kate sighed with a shake of her head. "Stubborn, just like her mother. I'll go talk to her."

Colt congratulated Shane and Rebecca, said good-night to the rest of the family and then headed to his cabin in the woods. He texted his friends back and told them that he, once again, would not be joining the poker game. He liked to drink beer when he played poker, a lot of it, and that always got him in trouble. Tomorrow was the first day Lee was going to let him work directly with the students and he wasn't going to violate that trust by showing up hungover or late. No—he was going to arrive early and well rested and ready to work. *And* he was going to log eight more hours on his service time, bringing him one day closer to being free to ask Lee out on a date. Now that was a day worth working toward.

Monday morning, Lee had to admit to herself that she was rethinking her decision to let Colt work directly with the riders. Yes, he was a favorite of the parents and the kids, and *yes*, he had proven himself to be more reliable than she originally assumed, but this was something entirely different. She was entrusting him with the safety of the riders and entrusting him to be a significant part of the program.

"Do you have the list ready?" Gilda appeared at the door of her office.

Every day, Lee created a master list, matching riders and horses with volunteers who would act as side-walkers and leaders.

"I just finished." Lee held out the list for Gilda. "I put Abigail on Sweet Girl now that we have someone tall enough to side-walk with them."

Gilda reviewed the list. "I think this will be good for Abigail. Sweet Girl has a nice narrow base of support."

"I hope so," Lee said uncertainly. "It's Colt's first session."

"Colt will do very well," Gilda ensured her, echoing the sentiments of Boot from the previous day. "Boot is very impressed with this young man."

Lee's stomach clenched a bit when Gilda brought up Boot. Wasn't she the one who suggested that Boot ask Gilda out? But now Lee felt uneasy about the growing friendship. It was like watching something inevitable happen—like the sun rising in the east—and knowing that she was powerless to stop it.

"It seems like everyone likes Colt."

"Yes," Gilda agreed. "This is so. What's not to like?"

As if to add his two cents to the conversation, Chester, who had opted to get into his carrier this morning to come to Strides, yawned and meowed at the same time.

"Well, I guess everyone is in agreement about him then." Lee leaned down and kissed the oversized gray tabby on the head.

Gilda held up the list. "Let me get started on this and I will see you out there." She turned precisely on her heel and left the office.

Even with everyone so supportive of Colt, Lee couldn't seem to settle her stomach waiting for him to arrive. She stood at the window, facing the long drive into Strides, watching for his headlights. She knew the headlights on his fire-engine red Ford truck and when she spotted his truck turning off the main road onto the gravel drive, the smile that came to her face was automatic. Why had she doubted that she could count on him to be there? He hadn't let her down so far.

"Be good." Lee dropped another kiss on Chester's head before she headed out the front door.

She met Colt at his truck.

"Good morning, my lady." Colt jumped out of his truck, his hair wet from a shower and slicked back off his forehead.

"Good morning," Lee said, feeling those pesky butterflies in her stomach that were always there whenever Colt turned that smile her way. "Are you ready?"

For the first time, she actually sensed some nervousness coming from Colt. Usually he was so confident about everything he did at the facility. But this was something new for him. He had never side-walked for a therapy session before.

"Don't worry, Colt." She reached out and put her hand on his arm, just for a brief moment. "You've got this."

Colt put his cowboy hat on. "If you believe in me, then that's saying something."

Did she believe in him? Lee had to search her own mind and her own heart for a split second. She always strove to be honest. She knew that honesty had a resonating frequency that people could hear and sense.

"Yes," she finally said, "I do believe in you."

Colt had to admit that he was scared, as all get-out, to be responsible for the safety of Lee's special-needs riders. He was human and he got scared, but it didn't happen all that often. Today, he was scared. His first rider was Abigail—tiny, nonverbal, determined, feisty Abigail.

"Are you sure you want to put her on Sweet Girl?" Colt asked under his breath to Lee, not wanting anyone to hear him doubting her plan.

Lee nodded. "Sweet Girl has the perfect movement to help loosen Abigail's abductors but no one has been tall enough to side-walk Sweet Girl."

Colt watched Abigail push her pink walker along

the perimeter of the arena to the ramp where he would help her mount.

"But now we have you," Lee added when he didn't say anything.

"You're not going anywhere." Colt rubbed his hands together to dry the nervous sweat on his palms. Abigail was so tiny—so fragile-looking—the last thing he wanted to do was accidentally hurt her.

"Just remember your training and you'll be fine," Lee tried to reassure him and he appreciated her effort. "I'll be here, Gilda will be here. You'll be fine."

"Alright." He gave her a nod so she knew he heard her.

Lee caught his eye. "Time to cowboy up, Colt."

Hearing that phrase coming out of Lee Macbeth's mouth did exactly what she had intended—it broke the tension in his body and made him smile.

When he walked up the steps to the top of the ramp and waited for one of the volunteers to lead Sweet Girl between the ramps, Colt was feeling steadier even though he felt his hands shaking a bit from the adrenaline pumping through his body. On the other side of ramp, on the left mounting side of Sweet Girl, the speech-language pathologist helped Abigail onto the Thoroughbred's back and, as he was trained, Colt was there to hold on to the little girl's right leg.

"She's never been on a horse that big before." Abigail's mom watched nervously from the ramp. "She looks so little up there."

"Sweet Girl is as gentle as they come," the therapist reassured the mom before she told the horse leader to Walk On.

With his left hand, Colt held on to Abigail's leg to ensure that she was safe on the horse's back while he walked down the stairs of the ramp and into the arena next to Sweet Girl. Julie Reed, the therapist working with Abigail, happened to be the speech-language pathologist who helped his sister-in-law Rebecca speak more clearly after her near-fatal car accident.

"We have a Stop card and a Go card." Julie Reed pointed to the two large colorful cards attached with Velcro to the saddle pad in front of Abigail.

"Let's stop," Julie instructed the leader, and the entire team halted. Colt was glad that they stopped for a moment. It was an odd sensation holding onto Abigail, working to keep her steady on the back of the horse. It was like nothing he'd ever experienced—he could already feel his arm getting fatigued and they hadn't been walking the arena for five minutes. He wondered how the women, who dominated this type of work, managed to side-walk for hours every day. It was a workout for him.

"Abigail," Julie said to the little girl on the big horse, "do you want Sweet Girl to go?"

Abigail squealed with excitement and nodded her head in a bobbly fashion that was typical for her.

"If you want Sweet Girl to go, you have to tell her. Touch this card if you want her to go." The therapist modeled what she wanted Abigail to do by touching the green Go card. When Abigail didn't reach for the card, the therapist took the girl's hand and touched the card with it and then said, "Go!"

Abigail laughed and smiled when Sweet Girl walked forward. The team repeated this action again and again and again, stopping and starting, and Colt marveled at the patience it took on the part of the team and the horse. Nothing in his life had ever taken this kind of patience. At the end of the thirty-minute session, Julie said to Abigail, "Let's tell Sweet Girl to go one last time."

As the therapist had every time, she supported Abigail reaching for the green card.

"Go!"

When Abigail's fingers touched the green card, the entire team heard her say the word *go*.

"You heard her," Colt could hear the excitement in the therapist's voice. "Let's go!"

Colt wasn't exactly sure what the excitement was about, but he could see Lee celebrating on the sideline of the arena. Abigail's mom leaned over the railing and he could see as they walked near her side of the arena that she was crying.

"Did she say *go*?" Abigail's mom called out. "Did you say *go*, Abby? Say *go*, Abby!"

Abby didn't repeat the word but she laughed and smiled at her mom as she rode by on the back of the tall Thoroughbred.

"That was her first word!" Colt overheard Abigail's mom tell Lee before they hugged. "Abby just said her first word!"

They returned to the ramp and the therapist helped Abigail dismount. Abigail's mom swooped her daughter up and they celebrated this amazing milestone Colt had just witnessed. He had been a part of Abigail saying her first word at nearly three years of age. He had done something important that day—something important for someone other than himself. Colt couldn't completely sort out the myriad of feelings he had in the moment, but he did know that he was forever changed by the experience. Forever changed.

Chapter Eleven

Three weeks after his first gig as a side-walker, Colt crossed a milestone he had been working toward since the moment he laid eyes on Lee: he had finally accumulated his court ordered hours of community service. He was officially a free man. A man who was free to date the owner of Strides of Strength without putting her in a compromising position with the community. So when he walked into Lee's office at the end of the day, he entered with the confidence of a man who knew exactly what his next steps needed to be.

Colt gave Chester a pet on the head before he sat down in the chair opposite Lee's desk. He pushed his long hair back from his face and smiled at her.

"Do you know what today is?" he asked, his eyes roaming her lovely face.

She nodded wordlessly. She didn't look as excited about this moment as he felt. That gave him pause.

"I'm a free man," he added just to confirm that they were celebrating the same event.

Lee rested her hands on top of his file—the file where she had logged his hours for the court.

The woman he loved didn't return his smile. Instead, she looked somber, an expression he didn't like to see on her face at all.

"You have done a lot of good work for us, Colt," she finally said. "There are so many things that still wouldn't be done if you hadn't been assigned to us this summer."

Now Colt was frowning. This sounded oddly like a goodbye and as far as he knew, he wasn't going anywhere. If anything, he planned on being a bigger part of Lee's life, not pull off a vanishing act. This moment, this very moment, was what he had been working so hard for. This was why he had begged off fishing and hunting and poker games with his buddies. This was why he had worked so many overtime hours. It had all been for Lee. It had all been so he could be with Lee.

"I know everyone will want to thank you, to say goodbye," Lee continued. "Gail will definitely want to throw a party."

Colt leaned forward, his brow furrowed. "What are you talking about?"

"You've fulfilled your hours, Colt," she said. "Like you said, you're a free man."

"Yeah," he agreed. "A free man who isn't planning on going anywhere."

Lee looked at him with an expression he could only read as cautiously optimistic.

"What is that expression on your face, Lee?" Colt asked with a smile meant to reassure her. "I'm not leaving the program."

"You're not?"

"Heck, no," he said, petting Chester who had climbed down into his lap and was now purring and kneading his leg. "I'm sticking around. I like it here."

Lee still didn't respond.

"That is, of course, if you want me to stay?"

His ego needed her to confirm that she still wanted him around. Here he had been planning their first date while she was thinking about his farewell party. They definitely were reading from a different sheet of music.

Lee tucked a wayward strand of hair behind her ear—he now knew her well enough to know that she did this when she was feeling a bit nervous or uncomfortable.

"I think everyone would love for you to stay on."

Her response didn't satisfy Colt's need in the least.

Colt lifted the rotund tabby off his lap and put him on the desk. Standing now, Colt caught and held Lee's eyes. "I'm interested in what you want, Lee."

Her lips parted and the pupils of her eyes enlarged, and all Colt could think about was kissing her. But there was an audience just outside the window and he couldn't risk giving Lee a reason to run away from him again.

"Do you want me to stay?" he prodded her.

"Yes," she said in a quiet voice. "I want you to stay. For as long as your schedule allows. The kids love you but we will all understand if you can't make it and…"

"Lee…"

"Yes?"

"It's okay to quit while we're ahead."

Lee threaded her fingers together and rested them on his file. "I will send your hours to the court tomorrow."

Colt sat back down. "That works for me."

"You worked off these hours a lot faster than I thought you would." She put the file into her desk drawer.

"A date with you gave me all the motivation I needed to get done quick," he said, watching her face closely. Colt sensed that Lee liked the limbo they were in—she liked the fact that they could work together while not having to address what was so obviously going on between them.

Lee blanched. Her complexion turned a grayish color and her lips pressed together tightly.

Colt leaned forward so he could talk to her in a lowered tone that she could still hear. "I told you I was going to ask you out on a date when I was done with my hours."

Lee bit her lip hard and nodded.

"And now all of the color has drained from your face."

He watched as Lee sought and then held on to the locket she always wore around her neck. "I'm sorry."

"What are you apologizing for, Lee?"

Colt now had a sick feeling in his stomach. This wasn't going at all how he had hoped—how he had imagined. Over the last three weeks, he had developed a solid working relationship with Lee and the other volunteers. They had laughed together, shared rider triumphs and achievements. All the while, Colt had believed that there was something *extra* in his interactions with Lee. He had always believed that they both were looking toward the future when they could bring their true feelings to the surface for the world to see.

"I…" She held on tight to that locket. "I'm sorry, Colt. I can't."

He waited for her to continue because he didn't want to give voice to the anger and the hurt that had erupted in his body.

"I want you to stay," she said. "I want us to be friends. But I have plans." Her voice lowered a notch. "Promises that need to be kept. And I'm finally there. I'm finally ready."

"And you won't make room in those plans for me?" Colt asked, bitterness laced in his voice. "Is that right?"

Lee swallowed hard several times, and tucked hair behind her ears that was already tucked into place. "Michael…"

When Lee said her late husband's name with all the love Colt wanted for himself, it felt just as bad as when he had the wind knocked out of him after being bucked off a horse. Colt gritted his teeth together so tightly that it hurt his jaw. He couldn't force Lee to let Michael go. He couldn't force her to move on from her first love.

Colt stood up but it took him several long seconds to finally form the words he needed to say. "I'm the one who's here, Lee."

His words hurt her and he was sorry for that. But it was the truth. He was standing before her, ready to give her all the love he had. He hadn't even known the kind of love he felt for Lee existed. And now that he knew it existed, he wanted to hold on to it. He wanted to hold on to Lee. The problem was, Lee wasn't reaching for his hand—she was holding on as tight as she could to the love she had with Michael.

There was nothing he could say to Lee—nothing that would convince her to give what they had a chance. So he did the only thing he could do—he walked away.

"Colt." Lee had come out from behind her desk.

He stopped but he didn't turn around. He didn't want to look at her face again. Not now.

"Can we…" She paused before she continued, "Can we put you on the volunteer list for Monday?"

Colt balled his hands into fists, then stretched them out several times to release the tension in his body. When he had been assigned to Strides of Strength for his community service, he couldn't have known how it would become a part of his identity to be connected to the riders and other volunteers—to Lee. But he couldn't continue to love Lee—to be in love with Lee—while she clung to the memory of her late husband. He just couldn't do it. He wasn't that type of man.

"No," he said, his hand on the door. "Go ahead and strike my name off of that list."

After Colt left her office, Lee had sat there for a long while wondering how the conversation had managed to get so far off track.

Yes, she knew that Colt wanted to ask her out

on a date—he had told her explicitly that he was going to do it. Yet, there was a part of her—a part obviously in serious denial—that had believed they could go on indefinitely as they were. She liked where they were. Colt was such a wonderful addition to the property and the program. He was so talented and so intuitive with the riders. How wrongly she had judged his book by the cover.

"Hi, Boot. Hi, Gilda," Lee called, entering her father-in-law's shop.

Boot and Gilda were sitting at an upside down barrel that Boot had turned into a makeshift table so they could share a cup of coffee.

"Could I talk to Boot alone, Gilda? Do you mind?"

"No," Gilda said easily. "I don't mind at all."

Lee slumped into the rickety lawn chair Gilda had vacated.

"I was wondering how long it would take you to show up here." Boot leaned back, his arms crossed and resting on his stomach.

Lee lifted her eyes. "Why do you say that?"

"Colt was just here returning all of my tools like he wasn't coming back."

She picked at a piece of rust on the rim of the barrel.

"So…" her father-in-law said. "What happened between the two of you?" Boot held up his hand and added, "And don't say that nothing happened because that just isn't so. Last I heard, he was planning on staying on here and now he's not. I have to suspect that has something to do with what's been going on with the two of you."

"What's been going on…?" Lee blurted out. Did everyone know that she had feelings for Colt? She had worked very hard to keep that under wraps.

"Just cut to the chase, Lee. You know I hate it when people beat around the bush."

Boot had never been big on side courses—he always just wanted the steak.

"Colt asked me out on a date."

Boot chuckled, his arms still tucked in front of his body. "Is that all? The two of you are acting like it was the end of the world."

Lee's mouth dropped open. How could Boot be so casual about her possibly dating someone after they had both tragically lost Michael?

"Colt asked me out on a date," she repeated, wondering if her father-in-law had actually missed the gravity of what she was telling him.

"I heard you," he said, "and you said no quite obviously from the looks of it."

"Of course I said no, Boot."

"Of course? Why of course?"

"You're the one who said you only get married once," she reminded him of their earlier conversation.

"Yes." Boot pointed to himself. "Me. I will only

get married once. I'm an old man. What's the point in getting married again? I had my wife. But you're still young. There's no reason for you to be alone for the rest of your life. I know how much you loved Michael—you don't have to live the rest of your life as a lonely widow to convince me of anything."

Lee was rendered speechless for several minutes. Why was every conversation going absolutely off the rails today?

"You were there, Boot. You were there the day Michael died."

"Yes, I was." Her father-in-law's voice was emotional.

"You heard what he asked me. He made me promise I would continue. I promised him. On his deathbed, Boot." Lee pushed down the tears that were forming. "I promised him."

"I remember," Boot said, his eyes intense on her face. "What does that have to do with anything we're talking about here?"

Lee sprang out of her chair like someone had pulled an ejection switch. "Am I going absolutely nuts here? Is it me? I am thirty-five years old, Boot. I'm running out of time here."

"I know that time is not on your side."

"No." She shook her head. Her voice raised a notch. "Time isn't on *our* side. I'm doing this for all of us. For you, for me, for Michael. I've been planning and saving for years and I'm finally ready.

I have enough money to try another round of IVF at the end of this summer! This is Michael's child we're talking about. This is *your* grandchild! So sure, of course—it's the *perfect* time to start dating Colt. Of course it is! I'm sure he'd love to go with me to my appointments. Heck, screw dinner, why not just go to the fertility clinic for our first date?"

"Sit down." Boot gestured to the empty seat. "You're giving me a crick in my neck."

Lee sat down heavily in the chair. She had grown up with Boot and he still filled a father-figure role. Even in her thirties, if he told her to jump, she was hardwired to listen.

"Why is your generation so determined to just vomit all of your information on social media and to each other before you've even had the first dinner together? Why does Colt even have to know about any of this on the first date? He's just asking to take you out—maybe go to a movie or grab a bite to eat. The two of you don't even know if you're compatible. Why don't you find that out first before you start a doomsday scenario?"

Boot didn't know the whole story and she wasn't about to tell him that she had already skipped first base with Colt and instead went straight for the home run. She had a feeling that it wouldn't change Boot's opinion either way if he did know. "I'm actually surprised that you aren't upset with the idea of my dating someone else."

"Well, you got that one wrong. No one, especially Michael, would want you to martyr yourself." Boot stood up. "So, no. I'm not upset one whit about that. If you want to go out on a date with that young man, don't say no on account of me. I like him—not enough to date him myself, mind you," Boot teased. "But he'd be a fine choice for someone like you. He could keep you grounded in a way not even Michael, God rest his soul, ever could."

Boot had managed to cut through the clutter in her mind and focus her thoughts in a way that she hadn't accomplished on her own. Perhaps she just needed him to be okay with her moving forward with someone other than his son. Either way, Boot's approval of her exploring a relationship with Colt gave Lee courage. She had courage in so many aspects of her life—she had overcome so much—but now she realized that she was being a coward when it came to her feelings for Colt.

"I'm glad I caught you before you left." Lee found Colt in the tack room in the red barn. She knew that he had kept a small cache of his tools there and would likely be in the process of packing them up.

Colt glanced over his shoulder at her, his face grim. "I don't have time to talk right now. I've got something to do."

Lee thought about turning around and leaving

but then thought better of it. She didn't want Colt to leave Strides—who would be better off if that were to happen? No one. And more importantly, she didn't want him to leave her. Not like this. The friendship they had built over these last weeks mattered to her.

"I'm sorry, Colt."

"There you go apologizing again," he muttered, tossing a hammer into a nearby toolbox with a clang.

"Because I am sorry," Lee said. "I'm sorry I don't have all of my feelings sorted out so neatly like you do. I'm sorry that I am worried about how people will see our relationship."

Colt spun around and glared at her. "I don't give a damn about what people think and neither should you. You either love me or you don't."

"Easy words coming from someone with nothing to lose."

"Nothing to lose?" he asked. "Nothing to lose? As far as I can tell, I've got everything to lose. For the first time in my life, I'm doing something important—I'm helping people. You gave that to me. For the first time in my life, I love something more than just myself—I love you. And you just pull the rug out from underneath me like it was nothing."

"I didn't mean to do that, Colt."

He turned his back on her again. "But you did anyway."

In an aside to herself, Lee said, "Why am I always apologizing to you?"

He didn't answer her. He kept packing up his tools.

Lee realized that she needed to show Colt something. He had been showing her how he felt and she had been hiding all of her cards. For once, Lee veered from her plan, walked up behind Colt and wrapped her arms around him. Colt didn't move. He didn't reach for her hands.

Lee leaned her head on his back and tightened her arms around him. "I should have said yes."

Colt turned in her arms. His blue eyes were stormy with emotion. "You still can."

"Then, yes..."

By the time Lee got the word *yes* out of her mouth, Colt was kissing her. His strong arms were holding her as tightly as she was holding onto him. She had been fighting the urge to kiss this man for weeks. She had been fighting the desire to join her body to his again and again and again. It had been so damn difficult to pretend that she didn't want to make love with Colt. It had been so damn taxing to pretend that her body wasn't aching for him.

Colt held on to her and walked them both backward until he reached the door to the tack room. He slammed the door shut and hooked the latch to lock them inside the small room. Lee didn't bother to protest. They both had been resisting this urge for too long as it was.

"You make me crazy." Lee pulled his belt buckle loose.

Colt kissed her neck while he pulled her shirt out of the waistband of her jeans. "Damn straight."

"All the volunteers already went home." Lee gasped when his mouth found her nipple.

"I don't care."

"Of course you don't." Those words came out on a moan of pleasure when his hand slipped inside her underwear.

"Lee?"

Colt whispered her name into her ear, sending shivers of sheer ecstasy racing across her skin.

"Yes?"

"Please stop talking."

Lee couldn't talk if she tried. She clung to Colt's arms while he slid his fingers inside of her.

"My sweet lady Macbeth." There was a smile in Colt's voice. He knew how much she wanted him now. He knew how much she needed him.

With his free hand, Colt unbuttoned his jeans and then unzipped them, freeing his erection through the opening in his boxers. Lee reached for him, holding him, wanting him to fill her body so completely as he had once before.

Colt started to remove her clothing, pushing her jeans and underwear down.

"Wait!" she whispered harshly.

He growled in frustration and his hands stopped moving. "What? *Why?*"

"These jeans are too tight at the bottom to get over my prosthetic." She looked down at her jeans.

"Then just leave one leg in," Colt said in a growly voice. "Who cares?"

Lee yanked off her right boot, pulled off one leg of her jeans and stepped out of the right hole of her underwear. "This is weird."

Navigating hot, spontaneous sex with a prosthetic did raise some interesting issues.

"Get up here." Colt was leaning back against bales of hay. He lifted her up and sat her down on his lap, not caring a bit about the fact that she was dragging half of her jeans and underwear on her left leg.

Lee wrapped her legs around him and he pushed her clothing out of their way. "Hold on to me," he said while he lowered her onto his hard-on.

"Colt." Lee said his name into his warm neck. "Colt. You are so frickin' sexy."

Colt lifted up his hips and pushed himself farther into her body. "You are so frickin' beautiful."

They kissed, long and deep and wet, their breath mingled, their bodies pumping, seeking that release.

"Come for me." Colt bit her earlobe, sending her into a frenzy of movement.

She held on to him, moving back and forth, pleasing herself with his hardness, the thickness of his body. The release came in sweet, wonderful waves, one after another while he held her tightly. He gave her that moment, sitting still while she set the pace and controlled the movement.

"You are mine, Lee," Colt said right before he exploded into her.

"I am yours." Lee gasped, wanting to hold on to Colt and never let him go. She wanted this moment to last for forever.

Chapter Twelve

Their first official date was a horseback ride on Sugar Creek Ranch. Liam's cabin was tucked back in the woods and there was a private entrance. Colt understood Lee's hesitation to broadcast their relationship to the town of Bozeman. Unlike him, Lee had much more at stake—Strides of Strength depended on community donations, and these donations came largely based on the respect and trust Lee had built in the community. So Colt didn't mind their dates being unconventional. In fact, he preferred it that way. Why spend time in a restaurant when they could have a picnic by a stream?

"This is absolutely beautiful." Lee looked out over the pastureland in the distance.

"I'm glad you like it." Colt joined her on the blanket he had packed for their afternoon picnic. As far as the eye could see and beyond, all of it was a part of his family's land holdings. Colt was proud to bring Lee to Sugar Creek. He hadn't convinced her yet to join the family for their traditional Sunday breakfast, but he was going to keep on trying. He loved Lee and he wanted her to be a part of his life the way he had become a part of hers at Strides.

Lee leaned her head back to let the late morning sun warm her face.

"You are so pretty to look at, do you know that, Lee?" Colt admired her profile.

She laughed, a sweet, lilting laugh that always sounded good to his ears. "Michael always told me I was, but I thought he was just being biased."

Colt couldn't stop himself from frowning. No matter what they did, Lee managed to work Michael into the conversation. It always felt like he was on a date with three people, not just two. And he didn't like it.

"You are beautiful," Colt told her, reaching out to touch the softness of her wavy hair. "So beautiful."

They had a light lunch and then they made love by the riverbank with the sound of the water rushing over boulders and the rustling of the wind in the tall brush mingling with their moans of pleasure. Lee had anticipated their lovemaking. She proudly showed him the wide-legged jeans she had donned so she could pull them off over her prosthetic. Colt was also prepared with protection. They had made love twice without using a condom but both of them agreed, just for the sake of habit if nothing else, that having protected sex made the most sense. They had already had the health discussion—they were both healthy and Colt didn't want to have any more discussions like that with Lee. He just wanted to love her as often as he could.

Lee was laughing and panting and holding onto him as he kissed her and nibbled on her neck and drove into her hard. She liked it hard. She liked it soft. She liked making love to him more than any other woman ever had. When he was making love to Lee, Colt felt like the luckiest man in the world. He now understood how men could fall in love with one woman and spend a lifetime never getting tired of loving her. He knew, in his heart, that this was the love he had found, as well.

Colt held off as long as he could, making sure that Lee was satisfied before he climaxed. He felt the sun beating down on his back, hearing the sound of birds flying overhead and loving the happy sounds Lee was making in his arms. After a moment to catch his own breath, Colt pushed himself up on his elbows and stared down into the dreamy face of the woman he loved.

"I love you, Lee."

Lee reached up and put her hands on either side of his face. "I love you, Colt."

Colt tilted back his head and howled like a wolf and then rolled over onto his back, taking her with him. "I knew it!"

Lee rested her head on his chest, her hand over his heart. There couldn't be a moment better than this. He had the woman he loved in his arms and she just admitted, without hesitation, without quali-fication, that she returned his love.

"Damn straight." He smiled, closing his eyes. "Now, that's what I'm talking about."

Weeks of lovemaking and horseback riding and hiking were a wonderful honeymoon period when Lee began to date Colt. His cabin hidden in the woods on Sugar Creek property was the perfect place to duck away from the demands of their lives and spend time just getting to know each other. Boot had been right; she did need to see if they were compatible before she opened up about her plans. If things didn't progress with Colt, why was it im-portant for him to know about her promise to Mi-chael? These incredible moments with Colt could just be a collection of memories and nothing more.

"Did you always want to be an occupational ther-apist?" Colt asked her. They were together in his bed, after having made love several times, and as they liked to do, they would spend several hours just talking.

Lee had donned her underwear and one of his flannel button-down shirts. She had covered her body, including her prosthetic, with the covers.

"No." Lee toyed with the hair on his arm. "I didn't even know what an occupational therapist was until after my accident."

She turned slightly toward him. "After I had to have my leg amputated, that's when I met a woman who was destined to change the course of my life. Dana. That was her name, and she was the one who helped me figure out how I was going to get around my house after the amputation. I realized that, here was this woman whose whole life was dedicated to helping people with disabilities do what they wanted to do. So, as soon as I could, I went back to school, took all of the prerequisite courses needed to qualify for the master's program in occupational therapy and after I graduated, I became involved in equine-assisted therapy." Lee gave a quick shrug of her shoulder. "The rest is pretty much history."

Colt threaded his fingers with hers. "What do you mean, help you get around your house? I've seen you get around everywhere better than I can most days."

"I don't always have my prosthetic leg on. I get around my house all kinds of different ways. I hop, I use my crutches, I use my walker—I even trialed this contraption that you strap on your thigh and it looks like a pogo stick so I can get around without my leg. Sometimes, I just flat-out crawl where I need to go."

Lee watched Colt's face and as always, he was curious but not repelled by her disability. "Every day things are still a challenge—like showering. I have to sit down on a chair to shower and then get out of there without killing myself." She laughed self-effacingly. "Anyway, Dana was so important in my recovery that I knew I wanted to be like her. And now I am."

"Now you are." Colt lifted her hand and kissed it.

Lee rolled over so she could rest her head on Colt's chest. She loved listening to his heartbeat; the strong sound of his heart comforted her.

"How come you always leave your leg on when we're together?" Colt asked.

"I suppose I don't want to gross you out."

She felt him move and she knew he was looking down at her. "Gross me out?"

"Yeah. I'm used to my stump. You've never had to deal with something like that before, have you?"

"No," he admitted. "But I'm seen every other part of you, Lee. Up close and super personal."

Lee laughed. It was true. And yet, somehow showing Colt her leg seemed more intimate than being naked in front of him or letting him put his lips anywhere on her body.

"I know. I've just never shown it to anyone other than doctors or therapists or my friends."

Colt sat up and displaced her in the process. "I think it's time you showed me."

Lee sat up, as well.

"I'm serious. I've shown you all of mine. It's time for you to show me yours."

"That's not the same thing. All of your stuff is perfection personified."

Lee preached self-confidence and self-love and self-acceptance for a living. It seemed hypocritical not to let her friend, her lover, see the real her in this moment.

"Okay. You asked for it." She rolled down her sleeve cover. "But be warned. It's weird to look at, I'm just telling you that right now."

"Nothing about you is going to bother me."

"We'll see." Lee pushed a button on the side of the prosthetic to release the air pressure that was holding her leg tightly in place. She removed the leg before she rolled the sock off her stump and then the protective silicone sleeve.

She was nervous, truly nervous, to show her leg to Colt. She ran her hand over her stump, put her arm under her thigh and then showed him what the medical community called her residual limb.

Colt leaned in and looked at it closely. "Wait. Do you have a smiley face emoji tattooed on it?"

With a laugh, Lee held her leg up higher so he could see her tattoo.

"I wanted to put something on it that would make me laugh." She smiled at the memory.

Colt examined her stump for a bit longer and then the moment passed as if it should never have been a big deal in the first place.

"What do you think?" she asked him.

"What do I think?" He frowned at the question. "I think it's a part of you. I love you, so I love your leg. Okay?"

"Okay."

Once Colt had officially been absolved of any further obligation to the court, he knew it was time to go public with their relationship. Colt was convinced, even though Lee disagreed, that people would accept their relationship as easily as he had been accepted into the Strides of Strength family.

"You're invited to Callie's engagement party at the Story Mansion. Aren't you?" Colt slowed Mack down so Lee could catch up on her horse.

"Of course." Lee trotted up beside him on his Arabian-Quarter mix named Prince.

"So, I'm going and you're going. It will be the end of summer, so you won't have the stress of the program hanging over your head."

"I know there's a point in here somewhere," Lee teased him.

"I think Callie's party will be a perfect event for us to go together," he said and then added, "As a couple."

When she didn't respond to him right away, he continued, "It would mean a lot for you to attend as my date. We'll get dressed up to the nines—trust me when I tell you that you want to be my date when you see me in a tuxedo."

"I don't doubt that."

"We'll dance—we'll eat great food. What do you say?"

"I say..." Lee was smiling back at him, about to finish her response, when a baby deer bolted across their riding path, spooking both of their horses. Prince began to prance sideways, his eyes wild, snorting and rearing.

"Whoa." Lee sunk down into the saddle and tried to keep her center of gravity from shifting.

"You okay?"

"I think so," she said, trying to keep the horse steady. "I think I just need to move him forward so he doesn't think he can spook and not listen to me."

"Be careful."

Lee was an Olympic-level rider, but Colt also knew that any horse could get any rider, no matter how experienced, off. That was the risk anyone took when they decided to ride on the back of a flight animal.

Colt hung back while Lee trotted the gelding

forward. In a flash, the mother deer bolted in front of Lee's horse while Lee was posting up in the saddle. The gelding moved to the right and Lee went flying forward.

"Lee!" Colt yelled when he saw her falling.

Colt dismounted quickly, dropping his reins and running to Lee's side. The top part of her body was on the ground but her foot was caught in the stirrup.

"My leg!" she shouted, her voice garbled from the pain. "It's stuck!"

Colt grabbed the reins to stop the horse from bolting again. If the horse had spooked, Lee would have been dragged on the ground. She could have been killed.

Lee was reaching up but her body was twisted.

"What do I do?" Colt shouted urgently.

"The release button." Lee was in so much pain she had begun to cry. "On my leg! Please. Get me free!"

Colt yanked the leg of her jeans to her knee, tugged on the socket sleeve like he had seen her do several days before and then pushed the release button. Lee's leg popped out of the prosthetic and she dropped to the ground.

"Damn it!" Colt realized that he had let her fall.

Lee rolled away from the horse's hooves, crying from the shock of falling and the pain of having her body twisted so violently. She curled up into the fetal position, rubbing the part of her leg that had just been released from the prosthetic.

Colt tied the horse to a nearby tree so he wouldn't run off and then he raced to Lee's side.

"Lee!" He called out her name, wanting to wrap his arms around her. "Lee!"

"Don't touch me!" Lee howled, pushing his hands away from her body. "Don't touch me!"

Colt sat back on his haunches and tried to catch his breath. "What can I do?"

"Don't touch me!" she yelled at him.

"I'm not touching you, Lee!" Colt snapped at her and then immediately regretted doing it. "I'm sorry. I just want to help you."

"My leg," Lee finally said, her face streaked with dirt and tears streaming from her eyes. "Get my leg."

Colt looked over his shoulder and realized that Lee's leg was still hanging from the stirrup.

"Crap." He went back to Lee's horse and worked the prosthetic foot out of the stirrup. When he returned to Lee, she had pushed herself upright and she was rocking back and forth, rubbing her stump.

"Oh, no," Lee moaned. "I think I hurt my stump."

Colt knelt down beside her, careful not to touch her but close enough that he could do her bidding.

"I have your leg," he said, holding her leg in his hands.

Lee looked up at him, and all he wanted to do was dry her tears from her face. They stared at each other and then they both started to laugh. He was, in fact, holding her leg, and it was such a strange thing to say to a person that it added a bit of levity to an otherwise horrible moment.

"Oh." Lee winced. "It hurts to laugh."

"Do you think anything's broken?" Colt asked.

She shook her head. "No. I don't think so. But I think I really did hurt my stump. I can't use my leg if I did and I'll be stuck using crutches. I can't have that happen. Not now. Not during the summer session."

"Tell me what to do," he said. "We need to get you back to the cabin."

Lee did her best to clean off the sock she was wearing, picking off twigs and clumps of dirt. "Here…" She held out her hand for the prosthetic. "I need to just put it on and see if I can stand with it."

Colt did the only thing he could do—wait and watch. Lee put her limb back into the socket and tried to use the suction valve.

"It's broken. Without the suction, my leg will just slip right out of the sleeve," Lee said and then cursed loudly. "You'll have to help me get up."

Colt helped support Lee while she pulled herself into the standing position. With her arm around his waist, Lee hopped next to him while they slowly made their way over to the horses. It was the first time Colt really understood how disabled Lee was without the prosthetic. If he hadn't been there, how would Lee have gotten back to the ranch? As it was, he wasn't exactly sure how they were going to get her back on the horse.

"Got any ideas?" Colt asked, wanting Lee to tell him how she wanted to get back on the horse. She couldn't walk to the cabin and it might hurt her even more if he tried to carry her piggyback. The horses were the best option to get her back quickly.

"Can you lift me up and sit me down in the saddle like we do the kids?" she asked. "If you get me in the saddle sideways, I think I can swing my leg over."

So that's what they did. Colt lifted her up and set her down in the saddle, then Lee swung her leg over the saddle horn and got herself situated in the center of the saddle seat.

"I'm not used to riding without my leg," Lee said, holding onto the saddle horn tightly.

"I'm going to walk us out," Colt said. "Just keep yourself in the saddle and I'll do the rest."

"Obviously easier said than done."

Colt grabbed Mack's reins and began the long hike back to his cabin. On the walk back, all he could think about was seeing Lee lying on the ground, crying. Never in his life had he been that afraid or helpless. It had never occurred to him how dangerous riding a horse could be for Lee in particular. She made everything look so easy with the prosthetic that most of the time he forgot that she had a disability. He supposed that was the point— that's why Lee had perfected her walk with the prosthetic.

"How are you doing back there?" he asked after a long stint of silence between them.

"Besides being royally pissed off," Lee said, "just fine and dandy."

"The minute we get you back to the cabin, I'm going to throw you in a hot tub with Epsom salt."

"I hope you mean throw figuratively." She laughed and then moaned. "I think I've had enough being thrown for one day."

Colt was able to take them on a shortcut, shaving a good ten minutes off their trip back to the cabin. Lee swung her leg over the saddle horn and slid down the saddle into his arms. Balanced on one leg, Lee grimaced when she tried to hold on to him.

"Just let me carry you," he said.

Lee thought for a quick second before she nodded. "Okay."

Colt dropped the reins for both horses, knowing that they would be preoccupied grazing on the grass long enough for him to get Lee inside. He would get her inside, then get the horses untacked, making sure, of course, to dislodge Lee's leg from his saddlebag.

"You scared me," Colt said as he carried her up the porch steps.

"I scared myself," Lee admitted. "I haven't fallen off since I was fifteen."

Lee reached down and turned the knob to the front door and Colt pushed it open with his foot. Colt carried her over to his couch and set her down gently.

"This is ridiculous," Lee complained. "I hate being carried around like an invalid."

"I'll be right back," Colt said. "Don't go anywhere." He cringed. "Jesus. Just pretend that you didn't just hear me say that."

It was a stupid thing to say in hindsight, but at least he had managed to make Lee laugh again. Colt quickly gathered up the horses, put them in the pasture so they could continue grazing, left all of the tack in the front yard to be dealt with later and then he retrieved Lee's leg and jogged back to the cabin.

"Are you still okay?"

She nodded, taking her leg from him and looking it over more closely.

Colt tossed his hat onto the kitchen counter on his way to the bathroom. He began to fill the bathtub with warm water and then dumped two cups of Epsom salt in.

"Let's get you in the tub," he said after he gave her a maximum dose of ibuprofen.

Colt lifted her up off the couch and took her into

the bathroom. After helping her undress, and grateful that she wasn't fighting him every step of the way, Colt lowered Lee into the warm water.

Lee sunk down into the water with a deep sigh. Colt sat down on the side of the tub and watched her.

"Is it warm enough?"

Lee opened her eyes and looked up at him. She reached for his hand on the side of the tub.

"It's perfect. Thank you."

Lee's eyes drifted closed again and Colt felt his tense muscles starting to relax. She was safe. He had her home where she belonged.

Suddenly, Lee sat up straight and felt around on her neck. "My locket. Where's my locket?"

"I haven't seen it since before you fell off."

"I've got to go back. Please take me back so I can look for it."

"*I'll* go back and look for it. You need to stay here and rest."

Colt picked Lee up out of the tub, wrapped her in a towel and then set her down on his bed.

"Please find it, Colt." Lee held on to his hand for a moment. "It's so important to me."

"I'll do my best, Lee. I promise you. I'll do my very best."

Chapter Thirteen

The Monday morning after the accident, Lee was resting in her bed at home. She hadn't been so sore since the car accident that ultimately cost her a husband and a leg. Gilda and Boot and Colt, along with the volunteers, would make sure that the program continued to run smoothly without her. But it frustrated her to be so banged up that she could hardly get out of bed.

"Hey, Tessa." Lee answered the video call, happy to see her sister's face.

"Hey. How are you?"

"I've been better," she admitted. "I'm so sore, I can only use my prosthetic for a short time and it hurts to use my crutches. Basically, I'm hobbling around here with my walker. Such a drag."

"Thank goodness Colt was with you."

"I know. I would have been in real trouble if he hadn't been there."

Tessa nodded, her dark brown curls framing her narrow face. Tessa looked back at her with her same hazel-green eyes. "I wish you would stop riding altogether."

Lee frowned. "I know. Mom and Dad said the same thing. But I'm living the horse life, Tessa. That's what I'm doing. I can't imagine never riding again. Just thinking about it makes me want to cry."

They spent an hour on the video call, covering every topic from shared childhood traumas like walking in on their parents having sex to Grandmother Macbeth's insistence on continuing with her predawn walks well into her nineties. Tessa always made her laugh and laughter was what she needed to keep her from going stir-crazy at home.

"So, what's the news on the IVF?" Tessa asked. "Are you still thinking about going through with it?"

"I have the money now," Lee said. "I can't imagine *not* trying. Michael and I were so close right before he died. The eggs are already fertilized, just waiting for me to finish the process that we started together."

Tessa's skeptical expression didn't escape Lee's

notice. Her sister had never been a fan of the death-bed promise that she had made with Michael. Tessa didn't believe it was right to bring a child into the world after the father had already passed away.

"I know how you feel about it," she said to her sister.

"Do you know how Colt feels about it?"

Her sister knew where all of her buttons were and she had pushed the largest one of all. Colt didn't know anything about her plan to go through the IVF process to have Michael's child. She had every intention of telling him when the time was right. For now, they were having a good time together—no promises were made between them. Lee knew that this time was coming to an end. She just wanted to get through the summer session and then she would sit down and have a long talk with Colt. If he couldn't handle the idea of going on the IVF journey with her, then as much as she loved Colt, she would have to let him go. Nothing—not even her love for Colt—was going to stand in her way of keeping her promise.

"You've got to tell him, Lee," Tessa told her. "The sooner the better."

"I will." She had already planned to tell him before they went to Callie's engagement party. Before Colt went through the trouble of introducing her to his family as his girlfriend, she wanted him to have all of the facts about her future plans.

"The longer you wait, the harder it's going to be on you both."

Lee hated to admit it, but Tessa was usually right. Maybe Boot hadn't given her such great advice about taking the relationship out on a test-drive before telling Colt about her plan for starting a family. Maybe she shouldn't wait until the end of summer.

"I think I'd better tell him," Lee agreed.

"Tell him now, Lee. You're not being fair to him if you don't."

It wasn't easy for Colt to split his time between his duties on the ranch and his volunteer work at Strides. He was tired but with Lee on bed rest, he knew he had to push himself to pick up the slack at Strides while holding up his end of the workload at Sugar Creek. After the last rider had their session, Colt packed up his things and headed downtown to pick up some takeout from one of Lee's favorite restaurants. On the way, he spotted the jewelry store where three of his brothers had purchased engagement rings. Acting on his gut, he pulled his truck into the jewelry store parking lot and stared at the door for several minutes before he made a decision.

I'll be there soon, he texted Lee and then got out his truck and walked into the jewelry store.

"Colton Brand!" The woman behind the counter was an old girlfriend from high school. "Are you lost?"

"Hi, Laura." Colt took off his hat and hung it on the hat rack just inside the door. "Nope. Not lost."

"Are you looking for a present for Callie? I saw her engagement announcement in the paper. I swear I was simply tickled pink about it. I still can't believe someone like her managed to get engaged before I did."

"Callie's very important to me," Colt said, his face unsmiling.

"Oh, well, of course she is," Laura exclaimed in a squeaky voice. "I just meant it was unusual, that's all."

The contrast between Laura, who obviously had some built-in bias against people like Callie, and Lee, who spent her life trying to enhance the lives of individuals with disabilities, couldn't be more clear to Colt in that moment. How his taste had improved over the years. Running into Laura—voted the prettiest girl their senior year of high school—confirmed that he was in the right place at exactly the right time.

"I'd like to see your engagement rings."

Laura laughed an insincere laugh that grated on his nerves. "Isn't that for Callie's fiancé to do for her?"

"This isn't for Callie," Colt said. "This is for the woman I intend to marry."

* * *

That night, Colt arrived at Lee's house with an engagement ring in his glove compartment. Just as he had known when he first saw Lee that she was the woman he wanted to marry—he found the perfect ring for her immediately. It certainly wasn't the right time to propose when Lee was still recovering from her fall. But he was going to propose to her as soon as the right moment presented itself. She wasn't the type who would want an elaborate proposal. It had to be something simple, something meaningful—a moment about which they could reminisce for the rest of their lives.

"Pasta primavera." Colt brought Lee's favorite dish into her room after finding a plate in her kitchen.

Lee pushed herself up on the pillows with an expectant look on her face. Her hair was a mess, she still had sleep in her eyes and he couldn't love her any more than he did in that moment. It had to be true love because he didn't care one bit if she ever shaved her legs or wore makeup. He just loved her, inside and out.

"Where's yours?" she asked, taking the plate with a look of anticipation of good tastes to come on her face.

"In the kitchen."

Colt grabbed his food and drinks for them both and then joined Lee for dinner in bed.

"What did you get?" Lee asked him, waiting impatiently for him to get settled so she could dig in.

"Spaghetti and meatballs."

"That was Michael's favorite too," Lee said offhandedly—it seemed that they couldn't get through any time together without Lee bringing up her late husband. Colt boiled a little on the inside every time Lee put him in the conversation, but this wasn't the time to raise the issue with her. This was the time to help her heal and get back on her feet.

Chester was already taking up a large bit of real estate next to Lee, so Colt had to make space for himself on her other side.

"You're the best!" Lee took a big bite of the food and then made a happy noise in the back of her throat. "You have no idea how much I've been craving this."

"Yes, I do," he said. "You've been texting me about it all day."

She laughed in between bites. "Sorry about that."

"No, you're not."

"No, I'm not."

They talked and laughed all the way through their meal, and when they were completely stuffed on Italian food, Colt gathered up their plates and got himself ready to leave.

"I'd better head out." He returned to the bedroom.

"Why?"

"My truck isn't exactly inconspicuous. The neighbors know I'm here."

"So?" Lee asked. "I'm injured and you're visiting me." She patted the bed next to her. "Don't go. Stay. We'll binge watch *Game of Thrones*."

Lee did have an ulterior motive for wanting Colt to stay. Her sister had been texting her, asking if she had spoken to Colt about her IVF plan. Now that Tessa was on the hunt, her sister wouldn't give her a break until she filled Colt in.

But as was always the case whenever she was near Colt, the TV got ignored and their attention turned to the sensation of their bodies pressed tightly together. She wasn't necessarily proud of it. Being around Colt made her hormones go haywire and all she wanted to do was strip off his clothes. It was a new experience for her. It had been different with Michael—she hadn't been in her thirties. She had been his first lover, so any experience in that department had been a shared experience. Colt brought a whole different skillset to the table, one she sincerely enjoyed.

Colt rolled on a condom and then placed her on top of him. It was odd not having her prosthetic on—that had always given her physical and mental support. When she had it on, even if she didn't look whole to other people, she *felt* whole. Without it, even after all of these years, she felt less than herself.

"Are you sure you're up to this?" Colt paused.

Lee loved the feel of her skin next to his—he was always so warm. She kissed his neck on a particular favorite spot of his.

"I feel better that you're here," she said, wanting him to focus on loving her and not her fall from the horse.

Colt stopped entirely, leaning back his head and looking at her in the eyes. "I'm serious. You've been away from Strides this week. We need you back."

She leaned her head down on the spot where his heartbeat was pounding softly and wrapped her arms around him. This man was continuously so sweet to her. He was always so concerned about her. Why couldn't she have him and her child? Maybe she was underestimating Colt again—just like she had when she met him. He loved her without her leg—why wouldn't he love her with Michael's child?

"I'm coming back tomorrow, maybe not for a full day, but I will be back."

Those were the magic words. Colt made love to her slowly, gently, kissing her all over her body, bringing her to climax so many times that she lost count. He was insatiable for her and she knew that she was insatiable when it came to him. Colt lifted himself up on his arms so he was hovering above her, their hips connected. She reached up and put her hands on his face. She loved to watch him as he found his own release. The way he growled in the back of his throat, the strength in the cords of his neck, the tension in his biceps. From granite to flesh, he was Adonis come to life and he was making love to her.

Colt dropped his head down so he could catch his breath, letting his shoulder-length hair brush across the naked skin of her breasts. He lowered himself down on top of her, letting her take his weight for just a moment before he moved over to her side.

"Dessert." She dropped a kiss on his chest before she laid her head on that spot.

He chuckled, his eyes closed, his arm possessively around her. She was so comfortable that she could have drifted off to sleep in his arms. When her phone chimed, she almost ignored it.

Have you told him?

Darn Tessa!

Lee sent her sister a severely frowning emoji and then put her phone facedown on the nightstand.

"Everything okay?" Colt murmured groggily.

"Uh-huh." She didn't want him to move—she wanted him to stay right where he was.

Then Colt's phone chirped.

Lee sat up. "Darn it! Why is everyone bugging us tonight?"

"Bad luck," Colt said, checking his phone. He groaned in frustration. "I've got to go. Gabe's got a flat on his trailer out by Four Corners. We all drew straws and I'm the closest brother to him."

Maybe this was for the best. His truck was still sitting in her driveway. Perhaps she was being ridiculous—she hadn't completely abandoned that possibility about herself—but she just wanted to get through the celebration at the end of the summer session before her relationship with Colt became public property.

Lee slipped on some loose clothing while Colt got ready to go. She grabbed her crutches from the side of the bed and followed him out to the living room.

"So, we'll see you tomorrow?" Colt asked before he kissed her.

She nodded. "Are you on the schedule for a half or whole day?"

"Half." He knelt down so he could pet Chester one last time. Colt and the chubby cat had developed a bond and Chester always sought out his attention now. "A whole day is tough with everything piling up at the ranch."

She was about to respond when she heard Tessa's special chime sound on her phone. She simply would not give up.

They kissed one last time before Colt left to help his brother. Lee moved over to her phone, grabbed it, sent her sister the text, I will! followed by five red-faced cursing emojis.

"I *will*," Lee grumbled as she tossed her phone onto the bed. "I *will* tell Colt. Tomorrow."

Her day of reckoning with Colt was upon her. She knew that nothing would ever be the same between them again and she dreaded that change. Absolutely dreaded it.

"You hungry?" She held up bags of food she'd stopped off to buy on her way to Sugar Creek. She felt almost completely healed from her fall and she had been able to use her old prosthetic all day without any difficulty. She walked with a slight, barely noticeable limp with this prosthetic but all she really cared about was being back on her feet and back at Strides.

"Absolutely." Colt greeted her at the door fresh out of the shower, shirtless, barefoot, with his jeans zipped but still unbuttoned.

Lee set the food on Colt's small dining table, glad that he couldn't see how nervous she was on the inside. All the way over to Sugar Creek, Lee's stomach was in a knot. The longer she had waited to tell Colt about her plan, the harder it seemed to tell him. Now it felt like she had been keeping something from him. That hadn't been her intention— she had been following Boot's advice and seeing if the relationship was going anywhere before she unloaded all of her baggage. For Lee, this relationship had so much potential. It was unexpected—

certainly—but that didn't change how she felt about Colt. He wanted to be a part of her life—he actively worked to be a part of her life—and she could see a future with him. She could see herself marrying him, and that was something she had really never believed would happen to her again. She had always believed that each person, if they were very lucky, was entitled to one forever. How could she be so lucky—what had made her so special—that she was entitled to a *second* forever?

They laughed, as they always did, while they shared the meal she'd brought with her. When they were finished, they went outside to the porch and sat down on the swing facing out toward the pastureland. Mack and Prince were grazing together at the top of a hill, their tails gently swishing back and forth, their ears twitching every now and then to flick off a pesky fly. Lee took a steadying breath, wishing the news she was about to share with Colt didn't seem like she was about to throw a stick of dynamite into the relationship they had been steadily building since the moment he walked onto Strides of Strength's property.

"Colt?"

"Hmm?"

"There's something that I want to share with you." Lee looked over at him.

"What's that?" He was checking his email on his phone.

"Could you put your phone down for a minute?" she asked. "I need to tell you something important."

Colt turned his phone over and put it facedown on his leg. "There. You have my undivided attention."

"Thank you."

Lee turned her body toward him. "I don't think I've been very fair to you, Colt. I thought I was doing the right thing—giving us time to see where *we* were going without oversharing. Boot thought it was a good idea…"

"Boot thought what was a good idea?"

"But sitting here today, I'm not so sure. Boot's from a different generation—I mean, he actually thought Instagram was a new way to send a telegram. So talking it through out loud, I'm really beginning to question taking his relationship advice."

Colt had a question in his eyes and she could see that he wanted her to get to the point. "Remember I told you when I met you that I had plans…?"

He nodded. She could tell by his concerned, curious expression that he had picked up that this discussion might be more serious than the many others.

"Before the accident, Michael and I were having difficulty conceiving—I told you that," she said, feeling that swell of pain that was still so strong whenever she tapped into the memory of the accident. "We had already started the IVF process…

My eggs were extracted, fertilized and now they are frozen, just waiting for me to implant them."

"Wait." Colt stopped pushing the swing back and forth with his booted foot. "What do you mean they're ready for you to implant?"

Lee lifted her chin defensively. "I made a promise to Michael. Before he died. That I would continue with the process."

"What are you trying to say, Lee? That you're planning on having Michael's child?"

Her arms were crossed in front of her body now. "Yes. That's what I'm saying. It's taken me years to save up enough money—after the accident, I was in the Grand Canyon of medical debt."

Colt's brow was furrowed and he was looking at her like she was something odd he had never seen before in his life.

"You're planning on having Michael's baby? Now?"

She nodded. "That's always been my plan. I tried to tell you that."

Colt stood up and moved away from her. "Well," he said, looking out at the horizon. "You didn't try hard enough."

Lee waited for him to continue.

Colt turned back toward her, his expression angry now. "Jesus, Lee. That's not something you wait to tell a person."

"Maybe not," she agreed. "In hindsight."

"In any frickin' sight! All this time, you've known that you're going to have your late husband's child? In what universe does it make sense not to tell me that?"

Lee stood up now too. "I didn't know if you and I were going anywhere other than the bedroom."

That was honest, even if it sounded harsh when given voice to.

"You knew I wanted more than that," Colt said angrily.

There was tense silence between them while Colt gathered his thoughts. "You're really going to do this?"

She nodded. "I made a promise to my husband."

"Is this about a promise or is this about what you want? No one, not even Michael, would hold you to that promise."

"It's what I want," Lee said. "It's what I've always wanted."

"Even now?" he asked, and she knew he was really asking, *After me?*

"I love you, Colt. But the desire to bring Michael's baby into this world is still there. I can't just flip a switch and turn that off. It's been part of me for most of my life."

Colt stared at her as if seeing her for the first time. The way he was looking at her made her feel nauseous inside. She wasn't going to be able to have it both ways—this was, as she'd always suspected—an either-or proposition.

"Now what, Lee? You drop this bomb and now what?"

"You could be with me."

"Be with you? Do you mean go through this insanity with you? Hold your hand while you have Michael's child? What about a child we could have together? What about building a family with me?"

"Why do I have to choose?" she asked, frustrated. "Why do I have to choose?"

Colt stared at her, shook his head, went into the house and then returned with a small box in his hand. He held it out to her.

Lee slowly opened the jewelry box and then covered her mouth with her hand. "Colt." She reached into the box. "You found it."

"I promised you that I would do my best to find it and I did. It took me several trips back to the mountain, but I finally found it last week."

Lee took her locket out of the box. It had been freshly polished. She closed her eyes and held it close to her heart.

"And, you got it cleaned up for me." After a moment, she opened the locket to ensure that her wedding picture was still there.

Colt was standing stiffly before her, his face grim. "Yes."

Lee clicked the locket shut, slipped the long

chain over her head and then looked up at Colt with tears of gratitude in her eyes. "Thank you."

"There have always been too many people in this relationship, Lee. Always. I know you love Michael—I know you will always love Michael— of course you will. But I expected a real shot with you—a real seat at the table. But you just can't do it. You can't be with me without still being married to him. I can't stay with you—raise Michael's child—and pretend that your whole heart is with me. That would be a damn lie, Lee. You know it and now I know it too."

Chapter Fourteen

"So, you made a mistake. Who doesn't? There's no sense beating yourself up about it for the next fifty years," Tessa told her though the speaker on her cell phone.

She was driving toward Strides. It was the final day of the summer and usually she was elated at this point. And part of her was elated. The riders had made great progress during their time in the program. Gail, as she always did, had choreographed a performance for the parents that allowed all of the riders to participate in a way they normally didn't have the opportunity to do. There was always a wide variety of food donated by the local restaurants and Callie, who was an accomplished cook, had spent the last week preparing baked goods to serve for dessert. The summer had been a triumph in all aspects but one: her relationship with Colt.

After she told him about her goal to use the fertilized eggs and bring Michael's child into the world, her relationship with Colt came to a grinding halt. It was so close to the end of the summer session, and he knew that she wouldn't be able to train a replacement for such a short length of time, so he had agreed to continue volunteering. But he refused to even speak to her about anything that wasn't related to the riders or the program. He had completely shut down and closed himself off from her. Colt was a very sensitive man—that sensitivity could turn very cold, very quickly.

"Would you do anything differently?" Tessa asked.

"Of course I would. I wouldn't let my libido set the agenda. I couldn't seem to control myself around him."

"You're in your thirties, which means you're at your sexual peak and you haven't gotten any in nearly a decade. Who wouldn't be a raving lunatic in those circumstances?"

"Maybe."

"No. *Definitely*," Tessa reiterated. "A sexual peak is no joke."

That made Lee laugh. At least nothing had changed with her sister. She could always count on that.

"I guess not," Lee said. "I just wish that I hadn't screwed things up so badly with Colt. I really miss him."

"You could always just forget IVF and focus on Colt."

It wasn't that Tessa's suggestion hadn't crossed her own mind more than once—it had. In fact, weighing her choices was all she could think about in her downtime. Every time, she landed on the side of continuing with the process. It wasn't just a promise that she needed to fill—a box she needed to check—she wanted that child. She had dreamed of that child—a boy with Michael's unruly curly hair and his lanky body. A girl with his soft brown eyes and sharp intelligence. Who was this child? She had dreamed of meeting him or her for so very long. And now that she was right at the starting line of the last leg of the marathon, she should quit to go in a totally new direction with Colt? Perhaps someone else would make a different choice. Her choice was the child she had always planned to have with Michael.

"I'll call you later, Tess," she said into the speaker.

"Love you," Tessa said.

"Love you too."

Colt had considered not showing up for the final day of the summer session. Seeing Lee now hurt like someone was cutting him with a knife. He wanted to leave Strides for good and focus all of his attention on getting over his relationship with Lee. It was the only thing he could think to do—bury his head in ranch work and reintroduce himself to his friends.

"Good afternoon, moms and dads, therapists and volunteers!" Gail Allen stood on the stage that had been erected in the music room for her pleasure, dressed in her Sunday best. "We are so thrilled to have you here with us today."

Most of the riders were on the stage. Many of them were making noises, swaying and walking in circles. Each of the participating riders had a volunteer with them to facilitate their participation. Abigail's mom was sitting on the ground in front of the stage, ready to help her daughter with her important task of ringing a bell at a key moment in the song.

Gail sat down at the piano, which had been donated by a local family and began to play the song she had been practicing with the riders all summer long. The students, with a little help from their volunteer friends, sang the song in their own special way—sometimes with words, sometimes with sounds that were word-like, all the while ringing their bells. Gail was at her happiest, as evidenced by her shining eyes and wide smile, when she was sitting behind a piano, singing with the riders.

Colt did his best to focus on Gail and her summer choir, yet his attention was inevitably pulled to Lee. She was standing near the stage, clapping her hands, smiling proudly. To his eyes, she was the most beautiful woman he had ever seen. That hadn't changed even if their relationship had. He still felt like a cartoon character that had been hit over the head with a frying pan, and he was stumbling around with stars and birds flying around a giant bump on his skull after Lee told him about her appointment with the fertility clinic. How could he have seen that one coming? How could *anyone* see that coming?

"Thank you so much for a wonderful summer." Lee took her place on the stage to address everyone who had participated in the program. "I am always so humbled by the courage and determination of our riders and the dedication of our therapists and volunteers. I count myself blessed for having known each and every one of you and I am so grateful that we were all brought together by grace. I love you all."

Lee led them in a round of applause, and Colt was reminded, once again, of Lee's talent for inspiring people just by her own determination and will to make lives better for others. Standing before them, a woman who had overcome tragedy to triumph, she had built this place with grit and willpower and sheer stubbornness. And Colt admired her for it. But it was also that same stubbornness that wouldn't allow her to let go of her past with Michael and embrace a future with him. That was also true. As if to emphasize his point, he saw Lee reach for the locket around her neck and hold on to it tightly.

"Are you staying for lunch?" Callie had found her way, as she tended to do, to his side. He put his arm around her shoulders.

"I don't think I can, sweet pea," he said, his eyes still on Lee. "Not today."

"B-but I made your favorite cookies."

"Salted caramel?"

She nodded.

"Well then. Why don't we sneak into the dining room so I can grab a couple to take with me?"

Liking the idea of sharing a secret with him, Callie walked with him to the dining room, which was decorated with congratulatory balloons and festive ribbons. Some of the volunteers had agreed to miss the presentation so that they could help the restaurant staff who had delivered the donated food set up the lunch spread for the riders and their families.

"I—I'll get you a b-baggy," Callie said. "Wait here."

"Okay, boss lady." He always had a smile for his niece, no matter what. One of the best things that had happened to the Brand family was Callie's adoption.

"Here." Callie had returned with a plastic Ziploc bag and was speaking in hushed tones. "Open it for me."

Callie stuffed as many homemade cookies she could get into the bag. "I—I'll get another b-bag."

"No." He laughed, zipping the bag shut. "I think I have enough."

"Okay." She hugged him. "I-if you say so."

He kissed the top of her head. "Thank you for thinking of me, Callie. I love you."

"I—I love you too, Uncle Colt," Callie said, still holding onto him. "Do you know what?"

"What?"

"I—I'm getting married."

"I know, sweet pea." He smiled and tightened his hold on her. "I know you are."

Lee didn't see him leave, but she knew that he had. His truck, always a big presence in the parking lot, was gone. Lee ducked into her office for a moment to collect her emotions. She closed the blinds of both windows and sat behind her desk in the dim light. She didn't have tears at the moment— she had cried so much over the last couple of days, her ducts had all but dried up. And what good were those tears anyway. She had always known that this day—Colt's last day with Strides—was coming. But it still hurt nonetheless.

After several moments alone, she stood up, squared her shoulders and forced herself to put on a cheerful smile that didn't exactly match her mood. This was a celebration and she wasn't going to dampen the occasion by sulking around the place like a kid who'd had her favorite toy taken away. No. She was going to push her sadness aside and focus on the riders. When she focused on the riders—when she focused on anyone other than herself—that was when she was at her best.

"You did a wonderful job this summer, Callie." Lee stopped by the dessert table to thank the young woman. Callie had grown up with Strides and now she was a woman engaged to be married. Callie was one of Lee's original riders and proof, at least to Lee's mind, that the program worked.

"Thank you," Callie said, fussing over her baked goods. "Are you coming to my party?"

"Absolutely I am."

"I—I really want Tony to work here with me. Can he work here with me?"

"We'll have to see, Callie. I didn't just give you this job, you know. You had to earn it."

"I—I had to have an i-interview."

"That's right."

"I—I had to prove that I could do the job."

Lee nodded.

"Tony sells carpet," Callie told her.

Lee laughed. "We don't have a lot of carpet to sell around here, Callie. But we'll see what happens when he moves here, okay? We'll all sit down together and talk about what he wants to do with himself. He might not even want to work with horses."

"He's afraid of horses."

Lee scanned the table of treats with a smile. "That might be a problem, Callie. Horses are kind of what we do here."

"Okay," Callie said in her easy way. "Do you want a cookie?" She pointed to a nearby plate. "Those are Uncle Colt's favorite cookies."

"What kind are they?"

"Salted caramel cookies," Callie said. "Try one."

Lee picked up a cookie and took a bite of the soft, gooey treat. "Hmm. That's delicious, Callie."

Callie beamed at her. "Do you like it as much as you like Uncle Colt?"

Surprised, Lee bit the inside of her cheek. She chewed the bite of cookie, swallowed and then said, with complete candor, "Well, I don't know, Callie. This is a mighty tasty cookie."

"Hey. I didn't know you were out here." Colt walked into Liam's workshop.

Liam was working on his antique truck, something he tended to do when the estrogen in the party-planning process became too overwhelming for him.

"If I thought the beginning of this whole engagement party ordeal was stressful in the beginning? Brother, you have no idea."

"That bad, huh?"

"I sincerely believe that all of this wedding stuff has shaved years off the end of my life just from stress alone."

Colt sat down in a nearby chair and crossed his arms loosely in front of his body. "Yeah, but you're making Callie happy."

Liam stopped twisting a bolt with his wrench to look over at him. "Now, that's what makes all those years I'm losing on the end of my life worth it."

"She's a good egg, that one," Colt said.

"That's the truth." Liam finished his task and turned back to him. "You know, I think about this engagement party and this wedding. This isn't a party for a woman with Down syndrome—this is a party for a young woman. Nothing else. None of us could have ever imagined this for her. But Callie imagined it for herself."

Liam paused for a moment before he continued, "I couldn't imagine what my life would be like without her in it now."

"None of us can," Colt agreed.

Liam came over to search for a tool in his tall red metal toolbox. "So, what's new with you?"

"Nothing." Colt frowned. He knew his family had some inkling that he had been dating Lee; they had seen them on the ranch on occasion. No one knew that he had ended things with her.

Liam looked up at him. "That doesn't sound like nothing."

Of all of his brothers, perhaps Liam was the one who might be able to give him some sound advice about Lee. He was, after all, the only one of them who had married a woman with a child. He was the only brother who had adopted and promised to love Callie as his own for the rest of his natural life.

"I broke up with Lee."

"I'm sorry to hear that." Liam found what he was looking for in the toolbox. "You want to talk about it?"

Colt did want to talk about it after all. He told Liam everything, including the fact that he had gone as far as to buy her an engagement ring. Liam, as he always did, listened without a word. He just listened. And then, when Colt had completely exhausted everything he had to say—angry words, hurt words, loving words—Liam took a moment to digest what he had heard. That was Liam's way.

Finally, Liam took a break from his project to share with Colt what he had been thinking.

"I'm not going to sit here and tell you that her plan isn't an unusual one."

"Unusual isn't what I would call it. Crazy and weird is more like it."

"But," Liam continued, "who's to say that she's wrong?"

"Me. I'm to say."

"Look—I can't fault you for not wanting to raise another man's child when you feel you should be starting a family of your own with Lee."

Colt nodded his agreement. Finally, Liam was talking some sense.

"But I'm raising a daughter who isn't my own biologically."

Those words were a sucker punch in the jaw for Colt. During all of his thinking, mostly angry, about Lee's desire to have Michael's child, he never connected Liam's situation with Callie to his situation with Lee. Yet, they weren't completely different.

"Could I love Callie any more if she were my own flesh and blood?" Liam asked.

Colt met his brother's eyes silently.

Liam continued, "Could you love her any more if she were a Brand by blood?"

"Hell, no," Colt retorted angrily. "That doesn't make a damn bit of difference to me."

Liam gave him a nod of approval before he asked, "Then why does it really make a damn bit of difference to you who the biological father of Lee's baby is? Wouldn't you love that child just the same as you love Callie?"

"I don't know. It seems…" Colt paused "…different to me somehow."

"Maybe how you're thinking has nothing to do with the baby and everything to do with how you think you measure up with Lee's late husband." Liam turned back to his project. "Maybe that's the real truth, brother."

One week after the end of summer session, Lee was at the Bozeman Fertility Clinic, waiting for her pelvic scan. She had already had her blood drawn and now she would have them check the thickness of her uterine walls, which was one factor in frozen embryo implantation success. Then she would see the doctor to discuss each step in the process. Lee felt surprisingly calm, considering how many years she had been working toward this moment in her life.

"Lee Macbeth." The ultrasound technician opened the door and called her name. Lee smiled and followed her into the back.

On the table, Lee watched the screen while the technician performed the ultrasound. The technicians' weren't supposed to signal anything good or bad with their expressions, but Lee could see by the extended time the technician spent on one area of her pelvis that something had caught her attention.

"Everything okay?" Lee asked, looking at the black-and-gray ultrasound screen. She couldn't see anything out of the ordinary—but then again, she didn't have a trained eye.

The technician was noncommittal, telling her that the doctor would go over the results of the ultrasound with her in a moment. Lee got dressed quickly and went back to the waiting room. Now she was nervous. Was something on the ultrasound that would stop her from moving forward with the transfer? Was her lining too thin? Lee wiggled her foot nervously, not even able to occupy her mind with a game of *Candy Crush* on her phone. All she could do was look at the door and will it to open.

The nurse called her name and she sprung out of her chair and quickly made her way to the doctor's office.

"Good morning, Ms. Macbeth," Dr. Shankar greeted her warmly. Dr. Shankar was a woman of middle age, petite with black hair. She was a well-known expert in the field of fertility and Lee felt lucky to have her as her doctor.

After Lee was seated, Dr. Shankar smiled at her. "How are you feeling?"

"I'm good," Lee was quick to say. "Never healthier. As far as I know."

"This is good to hear," the doctor said. "A mother's health is always most important for the baby."

"I agree," Lee said. "That's why I've been taking vitamins, getting plenty of rest, exercising, meditating. I am so ready to start this process, Dr. Shankar. I'm ready to transfer those embryos."

Dr. Shankar's smile didn't falter when she said, "I'm afraid that isn't possible at this time, Ms. Macbeth."

For a moment, Lee felt as if she were falling backward. She felt dizzy and sweaty and woozy. She swallowed a mouth full of bile down and winced as it burned her throat.

"Why not?" she asked the doctor.

"Because your ultrasound and your blood work show us that you are already pregnant."

Lee stopped breathing for a split second. She stared at the doctor, stunned.

"I'm pregnant?"

"Yes." Dr. Shankar nodded. "Have you not been experiencing symptoms?"

Lee looked down at her hands, thinking. Yes, she had been a bit queasy, but stress always made her stomach feel wonky. Yes, she had put on some weight but she had naturally assumed it was all of the pasta primavera she had been binging on since ending things with Colt. She had missed her last period but she had irregular periods, which was one factor in her difficulty with fertility. So, a missed period was no cause for alarm when she had tried for years to get pregnant to no avail. They had only had unprotected sex two times early on in their affair and she had gotten her period after the first encounter.

"The red barn," Lee said in wonder, her hands pressed to her stomach. She had tried for years to get pregnant and then Colt managed to knock her up on a hay bale in the red barn?

"I'm sorry?" Dr. Shankar asked.

Lee didn't repeat it. The place of conception was not something she wanted to widely advertise.

"I fell off a horse a couple of weeks ago," Lee said, her eyes on her slightly rounded stomach.

"Then I would say, Ms. Macbeth, that you are twice lucky."

Chapter Fifteen

The night of Callie's engagement party at the Story Mansion in downtown Bozeman, Lee took extra care with her appearance. She had gone to Rebecca's Clip Art Salon to have her hair trimmed and styled. She treated herself to a massage and a facial so her skin would look dewy and fresh. Lee had spent countless hours shopping for just the perfect cocktail dress and then spent an even longer time trying shoes on her high-heel foot for her prosthetic. It wasn't easy to find a shoe that had the right angle to fit the prosthetic foot designed for high heels and she was often thwarted from buying the shoes that she truly wanted for the outfit. But in the end, she found a sexy pair of strappy black heels to go with her little black dress. Lee knew that Colt loved her silky brown wavy hair, so she wore it long and loose just for him. He also didn't like a lot of makeup so she was careful to have a light hand when she applied her mascara and eye shadow and lipstick.

"What do you think?" Lee asked Chester, who was watching her in the breadbox position from the bed.

"Will Colt like this?"

Lee spun from side to side and looked at her reflection in the mirror. *She* liked how she looked in the long-sleeved cocktail dress with the swirly short skirt that showed off her prosthetic leg and new strappy, sparkly black shoes. She ran her hand over her stomach, pulling the material more tightly over her growing bump. If someone saw it, they wouldn't assume right away that she had a baby on board. Soon, that wouldn't be the case.

Her video chat started to ring and she ran to answer it. "Hi, Tessa!"

"Let me see!" her sister said excitedly.

Lee put the phone down on the nightstand and stepped back so her sister could see her outfit. "Ooh, pretty."

"Did you see the shoes?"

"They're neato," Tessa confirmed. "You look beautiful, Lee. How are you feeling?"

Tessa was the only person who knew that she

was pregnant. After she shared the news with Colt, then the rest of her family and friends would be told. But for now, it was just a secret between sisters.

"I don't feel pregnant."

"That's a bonus."

"I know," Lee agreed. "The whole thing is blowing my mind. I'm like one of those old metronomes that Grandma Macbeth used to have on her baby grand—one minute I'm happier than I've ever felt in my life and the other minute I'm so sad about the embryos that Michael and I created. All I want to do is eat ice cream and listen to Sarah MacLachlan all day long."

"That sounds a bit pregnant."

Lee laughed. "I suppose."

"Is tonight *the* night?"

"I don't know. I hope so. I know he'll be there."

Lee had considered calling Colt and asking to meet but she wanted the moment to be more organic. The engagement party seemed like the perfect place to gauge how he was feeling about her. Did he miss her the way she missed him? She missed him so much, every day.

Colt put on his tuxedo, flipped his hair out of his face and then took a look in the mirror. His face was clean-shaven and the tux fit like a glove. The person he wanted to impress was Lee and he was pretty sure he would accomplish that goal with this getup.

There had been too many times to count when he had gone to pick up the phone to text her or video chat or call. He had stalked her on social media just to keep up with her day-to-day life he missed her so much. Yes, he had kept himself busy—his friends were glad that he was available to hang out again now that Strides wasn't taking up the lion's share of his free time. But Lee was never far from his thoughts. By now, she would have been to the fertility clinic. By now, she could be pregnant with Michael's baby. He hadn't been able to completely evolve on the subject but he was working on it. What he couldn't accept was living his life without Lee. If she was pregnant with Michael's child, then he wanted to be with a woman who was pregnant with her late husband's child. That was where it was at for him. Would he have chosen it—planned for it—wanted it? No. But he did want Lee. He wanted to be back with his sweet Lady Macbeth.

Colt checked the time on his phone, grabbed his keys, took one last look in the mirror and then headed out the door. He wanted to get to the party early and stake out a spot so he could greet Lee as she came in the door. She was supposed to be his date—why couldn't they still go together? If she walked in the door with another man on her arm, Colt was going to be flat-out devastated. Lady Macbeth was meant for him. She was his woman—his wife. His mind couldn't seem to accept any other outcome.

When he arrived at the Story Mansion, the majority of his family had already arrived. The main room of the historic mansion, with its dark wood molding and ornate light fixtures, was brimming with the excited energy of the Brand family. Everyone was laughing and talking and admiring the decor. Everyone was on a high of sheer happiness at the thought of Callie having a special night with her fiancé, Tony.

"Hey, it's good to see you made it back." Colt shook Tony Sr.'s hand.

"It was touch and go there for a while," the father of the groom-to-be said honestly. "Callie did not want to let go of the idea of them starting a family right away."

"I know it," Colt said. "Kate says she's wanted to have a baby since she got her first baby doll. How did Tony Jr. handle it?"

"Honestly—better than I did." Tony Sr. smiled. "He handled it like the man of the house, albeit with a very strong, very equal woman of the house on the other side of the issue. For now, babies are permanently on hold."

In the main ballroom, Callie was holding court with her fiancé, Tony, on her arm. Callie looked prettier, and more adult, than he had ever seen her before. His mother had hand-sewn a beautiful blue traditional garment with long fringe and sparkly beading that twinkled when she moved her arms.

"Congratulations to you both." Colt hugged his niece and shook Tony's hand. "Are you ready for the next step?"

"I'm ready." Tony squared his shoulders. He was standing so proudly next to Callie. It was obvious to anyone who saw them that these two people were genuinely in love. So in love that it had brought two families from completely different lifestyles together.

"I—I can't wait," Callie said and then giggled behind her hand.

"I'm looking forward to moving here," Tony said. "I need to find a good job so I can help support my wife."

"You can work for Lee," Callie said. "She said that she'll interview you."

"I don't know." Tony pushed his glasses to the brim of his nose. "I don't like horses so much."

"Ms. Lee!" Callie waved her hand wildly. The moment Colt heard Lee's name, he turned around so he could see his ladylove. Standing in the doorway, her wavy hair framing her lovely face, her cheeks flushed a pretty shade of pink, Lee was a vision in a figure-flattering black cocktail dress with matching high heels. He loved the fact that her prosthetic was on display; it showed her con-

fidence and her boldness. Lee knew who she was
and she was unapologetic about it.

Colt was relieved she was alone—that meant that
he at least had a shot of making her his date for the
evening. His eyes naturally drifted down to her abdomen—was there a baby already growing there?

Instead of waiting for her to join them, Colt crossed
the room to where she was scanning the crowd. He
couldn't wait another moment to speak with her.

"My lady," he greeted her. "You look lovely tonight."

Lee was quick to smile at him, a good sign in
his mind. "I like that tux."

He stood back, modeled a bit for her, falling into
their easy banter. "Why, thank you."

Colt waited a moment, looked into her eyes as
if to search for something intangible in the hazel
depths, and then offered her his arm.

"If memory serves, you agreed to be my date at
this shindig."

Lee hesitated for the briefest moment before she
hooked her hand to his arm. "Yes, I do believe I did
say yes, didn't I?"

Colt proudly escorted Lee across the main ballroom. This was the first time that the world was
seeing them together. No, they weren't officially
back together, but Colt just didn't care. He had Lee
back on his arm and that's all that mattered in the
moment.

* * *

The first person Lee saw was Colt looking so dapper and handsome in his black tuxedo. Knowing that she had a secret, it set her nerves at ease when Colt made a direct beeline for her and claimed her as his date. She no longer had to wonder about Colt's current feelings for her; he still loved her as she loved him.

First, they stopped by the spot in the room where Tony and Callie were holding court.

"Why are you holding Uncle Colt's arm like that?" Callie asked Lee with a curious, almost gossipy tone in her voice.

"She's my date," Colt answered the question. "Are you okay with that?"

Callie giggled behind her hand and nodded. "I—I think i-it's probably okay."

After they left the couple-of-the-hour, Colt led her over to the refreshment table.

"Can I interest you in sparkling grape juice?" Colt led her to the table where nonalcoholic sparkling white or red grape juice was being served instead of alcohol out of respect for Callie and Tony, who didn't drink alcohol.

It was the perfect excuse for her to avoid the alcohol question everyone would usually ask if she didn't indulge at a party. Now, she could drink nonalcoholic grape juice with everyone else in the room and never tip her hand about her pregnancy. Until it was time.

After the grape juice, Colt took her on a whirlwind of introductions with his family. Some of the family members, like Liam and Kate, she already knew. But so many of the Brand clan were new faces to her.

"I'm so glad to finally meet you!" Savannah clasped Lee's hand in her friendly manner. Bruce's redheaded wife actually had the most in common with Lee in that she had started a nonprofit organization after they had lost their son, Sammy, to an accidental drowning. Sammy's Smile was Rebecca's organization and, just like Lee was about Strides of Strength, it was her passion.

"I've seen videos of your Ted Talks—you are compelling to watch," Savannah said to Lee.

"Thank you."

"I would love for you to come speak at one of our fund-raising events. We have a silent auction twice a year..."

"I would love to donate my time."

"Oh!" Savannah's emerald green eyes widened. "That would be wonderful. So wonderful. You have no idea!"

Lee exchanged numbers with Savannah, and then she was relieved to find out from Colt that they had met all of his siblings and their spouses who were currently in attendance. She had also met Colt's lovely mother, Lilly, and his salty father, Jock, who did not have a social filter even on special occasions.

"Are you okay?" Colt asked, catching her off guard.

"Yes. Why?"

"You swayed into me, like you were going to faint."

Lee touched her brow and then her neck with her cool hand. "I think I might just need a bit of fresh air."

"Let's go."

Hand in hand, they strolled along the sidewalk, taking in the gentle breeze and the fresh evening air.

"I was worried about seeing you tonight," she admitted quietly.

"You shouldn't have been," Colt said. "I love you, Lee. I always have. I always will. No matter what."

She put her free hand on his arm and squeezed it. "It's so good to hear you say that, Colt."

He put his hand over her hand. "I've missed you."

"And I have missed you."

"We have a lot to discuss," he added.

"I believe we do."

"But not tonight. Tonight, I just want to enjoy being with you again."

She quietly agreed, leaning her head over so she could touch it to his shoulder. How wonderful it was to have tall handsome, sensitive Colt Brand walking beside her once again. How lucky she was to be carrying this man's child. Truly blessed.

"Are you feeling better?" he asked, concerned.

She nodded. The dizziness had subsided.

"Would you like to dance with me, my lady?"

A smile brightened her face. "I would love to dance with you, Colt."

Colt escorted her back inside and he led her to the smaller of the two ballrooms where a band had been set up for attendees to slow dance. Colt swung her gently into his arms and she felt at home. The feel of his hands, the scent of his skin and the memory of the sensation of his lips pressed tightly against hers overtook her senses. Every fiber of her being wanted to be with this man again, stripped down, breaths mingled, bodies connected as one.

Lee looked up into Colt's face and she knew that it was time. It was time for Colt to know that she was carrying his child—their child. It was time for Colt to know that he was going to be a father.

"I have something to tell you that I only want you to hear, Colt," she said, hoping that no one had heard even those words.

Colt obliged her, leaning his head down so she could whisper in his ear. "I'm pregnant."

Colt lifted his head, his deep blue eyes held no surprise and a bit of wariness. "I know."

"You know?" she asked loudly. In her surprise, she forgot to whisper.

He nodded, his expression serious. "You went to the fertility clinic."

She opened her mouth to explain but he continued, "I want you to know, Lee, that even though I'm still learning to get used to the idea, I want to be there for your child—Michael's child."

Lee felt tears form in her eyes. It was so touching to her that Colt wanted to be with her enough—he loved her enough—to find a way to accept her decision about the embryos she had created with Michael.

"Thank you, Colt."

This was important for her to know because she still didn't know what she was going to do with the embryos. Would she still opt to transfer them? Would she consider donating them to an infertile couple? She just didn't have any idea at this point. Her focus had to be on the child growing in her womb now. But it made her life so much easier to know that the embryos were no longer a deal-breaker for Colt.

"This isn't Michael's baby." She locked eyes with him to ensure that he was hearing her. "It's yours."

Colt stopped moving. He stared down at her face, then his eyes moved down to her belly. "Mine?"

She smiled at him happily with a nod. "Yours."

"How?" he asked dumbly. "When?"

"I have two words for you, Colt." She held up two fingers. "Red barn."

"Red barn?" He repeated the words and then the lightbulb came on for him as it had for her. "Oh— red barn."

Colt grabbed her hand and led her outside. They broke the rule and walked on the manicured green grass of the lawn in front of the Story Mansion. Beneath the giant oak tree, away from the prying eyes of his family and their friends, Colt captured her face in his large hands and kissed her deeply. She wrapped her arms around his body and didn't care who saw them kissing. This moment was theirs to celebrate. They were together. They were going to have a baby.

"I'm going to be a father." Colt was still holding her face in his hands.

"You are," she said, an emotional catch in her throat. "And I am going to be a mother."

Colt continued to stare into her eyes and then a flash of concern crossed his face. "Are you sad? About Michael? I know how much you wanted his child."

"I don't have just one feeling about it, Colt. I would be lying to you if I said I haven't felt mo-

ments of sadness about it. But—" she took his hand
and put it on her stomach "—my happiness cannot be measured, my love. I am so happy to be
pregnant with your child. I love our child as I love
you—without limits."

Lee had put off telling Boot about the baby. Boot
didn't say it much, but he had wanted to see her give
birth to Michael's child as much as she had wanted
to do that for all three of them. Now that Colt knew
he was going to be a father, it wasn't fair to expect
him to keep it a secret. It was time for her to tell
Boot before he found out from someone else.

Lee walked into Boot's shop and stopped in her
tracks. Boot was kissing Gilda—full, open-mouth
kissing like they had done it many times before.

"I'm interrupting," she said plainly, after decid-
ing not to skulk away unseen.

Gilda and Boot sprung apart as if they had received an electric shock. Gilda touched her short
hair, an embarrassed flush staining her cheeks.

"I should go."

"No, Gilda," Lee said. "You may as well stay. I
have news and this saves me the trouble of track-
ing you down separately."

"What's the news?" Boot moved back toward
Gilda and Lee wished it didn't bother her. But it did.
She liked the memory of Boot with Mama Macbain.

Seeing Boot with Gilda, as much as she really liked Gilda, was just plain weird.

"I'm pregnant," she blurted out. "Colt and I are going to have a baby."

"Oh, that's wonderful." Gilda hugged her and dropped a quick kiss on both her cheeks. "I have to see to the horses. I'll see you later, Boot."

"You bet," Boot said and gestured for Lee to sit down at his barrel table.

Lee sat down, now regretting that she had been so blunt in her presentation of the pregnancy.

"I'm sorry, Boot."

"Now what are you sorry for, Lee?"

"I'm sorry that this isn't Michael's child. He was your only son and we both wanted you to have a grandchild."

"Who says I don't?" Boot asked gruffly. "You're my daughter. That's my grandchild. I've been lucky in my life—I had one son and because of Michael, I gained a daughter. I've never felt like an outsider with you."

"Of course not."

"Then don't think I'm one bit upset about whose DNA is making up the pieces and parts of that grandbaby you're carrying. It's mine either way."

There was a moment of silence between them. Once Boot covered a subject, it was covered. Lee looked over at him and said, "So, you and Gilda, huh?"

Boot grinned a bit sheepishly. "Yeah—it's me and Gilda."

Chapter Sixteen

After the engagement party, Colt and Lee became inseparable. They wanted to make up for lost time. They wanted to make plans for the baby that was on the way. The Brand family was always ready to welcome a new baby into the clan and Lee was excited that her baby would have first cousins, twins, that were close to the child's age. When Colt, a bad boy cowboy with a horrible reputation for childish pranks had been assigned to Strides of Strength, Lee could have never imagined that he would be the man to make her most precious dream come true.

"We're almost to the peak," Colt said, holding out his hand for her so she could steady herself as she stepped onto an oddly-shaped rock.

Together Colt and Lee hiked to the highest peak on Sugar Creek Ranch. It was a blue-sky day in big-sky country and Colt wanted this to be a special moment they could remember. Lee deserved a proposal that was as special as she was. Perhaps this was going to be the perfect place and the perfect time to ask Lee to marry him. He had been ready since the day he met her. But it had been a journey for Lee to find her way to him. With his baby in her belly, Colt believed, finally, that Lee was ready to accept him as her husband. He believe that Lee was finally ready to be his wife.

"This foot is truly amazing!" Lee said of the foot attachment on her new prosthetic.

After the horseback riding accident, Lee had been awaiting the arrival of her new leg. Watching Lee receive her new leg was like watching a child receive their first bike on Christmas morning.

"I've never heard anyone get so excited about a foot." He smiled down at her affectionately.

Lee shrugged off his comment. "That's because you still have both of yours. For a BTK like me…"

"BTK?"

"Holy crow, Colt, you're with an amputee—get on board with the vernacular. Below-the-knee amputee," she explained. "For someone like me, this foot is life changing. It really moves like a real foot—just look how I can walk over these rocks!"

"I'm glad you're happy," Colt said. He meant it.

If Lee was happy, he discovered that he was happy. That was how plain and simple his life had become.

"Wow!" Lee stood at the edge of the cliff that overlooked the vast Brand holdings that made up Sugar Creek Ranch. "Is that the main house over there?"

Colt put his arm protectively around her. "That's the main house. Over there is where Bruce and Savannah live. Way over there is Little Sugar Creek, Gabe's corner of the world. And—" he pointed to the left "—if you look really closely, you can see Liam's cabin tucked away in those woods."

"It's impressive," she said, "what your family has amassed."

"This is our child's legacy now," Colt said. "We have to decide if we are going to use my land to build a house on the ranch."

Jock had carved up big chunks of Sugar Creek ranch to ensure that each of his children always had a home on the family spread. Jock had been turfed out of his father's cattle land, Bent Tree Ranch, just outside of Helena, Montana, and Jock had never forgotten or forgiven it. Jock was a tough breed of man, but he loved his family. And he wanted all of them to stay close.

"Do you want to live on Sugar Creek?" Lee asked him.

"I do," he said. "This is my home. I want this to be our children's home."

"I love this land." Lee breathed in the fresh air. "I could live here."

Colt hugged her more tightly. He had wanted Lee to love Sugar Creek the way he did—the way all in the Brand clan did. To hear her say that she could make this land her home was exactly what he needed to hear.

"I am going to build you the most beautiful house," he told her. "Whatever you want, you'll have it."

Lee smiled as she tightened her arms around him. "I already have everything I want, Colt."

They stood arm in arm, admiring the view. Colt gestured for Lee to sit down on one of the boulders nearby, far enough from the edge for her to be safer.

He joined her on the boulder, taking her hand in his. "Lee, this is the most beautiful spot on all of Sugar Creek Ranch."

"I love it here."

He kissed her hand. "You are the most beautiful woman I have ever met."

Lee smiled a bit shyly at him and tucked her head onto his shoulder. "I'm glad you think so."

"I do think so."

Colt left her side to kneel before her. It was the moment he had been waiting for. The sky was so blue and cloudless, the sun was warm on their faces and there was a gentle, fresh pine-scented breeze keeping them cool.

"I've known from the very first moment that I met you, you were my bride, Lee. From the very first moment, I wanted to marry you."

Lee's eyes were moist with emotion. "I love you, Colt. So much."

Colt reached into his pocket and pulled out a small ring box. He opened it and displayed the ring he had selected especially for her.

"Will you marry me, Lee? Will you be my wife?"

Lee stared at the ring for a moment and then with a nod of her head, she said the one word that he had been waiting to hear for months.

"Yes." She held out her ring finger for him to slip the ring on. "I will marry you, Colt."

Colt put the ring on her finger. It was an unusual ring—a miner's cut bezel-set with a platinum filigree setting.

"It's so beautiful, Colt." Lee admired the ring sparkling in the sunlight. "I've never seen another just like it."

"I've never seen anyone like you before."

They sat together in the quiet, holding each other while Colt imagined what it would be like to see his first child born.

"I want you to know that I will always understand how you feel about Michael…"

"Colt—"

"No. Let me finish, Lee," Colt said quietly. "I know how much you loved him. How much you still love him. I know you always will. If we have a boy, and you want to name him Michael, I will support you."

"No." She shook her head. "That's not want I want for us. It's not what Michael would have wanted."

He kissed her hand. "I used to be jealous of the love you had for him, because I wanted it all for myself. But I don't need all of the love, Lee. I just need what I have with you right now. Forever."

Lee held on to his hand tightly. "I always believed that we only get one forever. But that's not true. You are my second forever, Colt. And I am so grateful that we found each other."

Lee reached for her locket. "My Grandmother Macbeth, the original Lee Macbeth, gave this to me. It was hers and I cherish it."

Lee opened the locket. "Grandmother Macbeth always told me to carry what is most important to me close to my heart. Now, this is what is most important to me."

Inside of the locket, there was a picture of the ultrasound of their child. Colt wrapped his arms around her in gratitude and kissed her on the top of her head.

"I just want you to be happy, Lee. That's all I want."

Lee held on to him just as tightly as he was holding onto her. "I used to think that I was happy, Colt.

I thought that I was happy when I was invited to give motivational talks or when I had a successful summer session at Strides. I thought all of those things were making me happy. But it wasn't true."

Lee looked out to the horizon. "I was so painfully sad inside. I was holding on to a time when I remember being happy—when I was with Michael and we were planning a family together. But the truth was, Colt, I was trying to remake a moment that couldn't be recaptured. It's gone. I had to accept it."

Colt kissed her on the lips, wanting to comfort her with his love. She put her hand on his cheek so sweetly. "I haven't been happy for such a long time, Colt. But I am happy with you. Because of you, I am alive inside again. Because of you, I remember what it was to truly love. I am so lucky to have you." Lee put her hand on her abdomen. "And I am lucky to have our child."

"Are you ready?" Colt called out to her anxiously. "Everyone is waiting for us!"

Lee came out of the bedroom with an off-white dress she had purchased off the rack with a matching pair of sparkly off-white ballerina slippers that fit her favorite foot perfectly.

"I'm ready." She laughed at his nervousness. "I don't want to be an unwed mother."

"Hey." Colt had his long hair pulled back from

his face in a ponytail. "What about me? I don't want to be an unwed father."

"Tessa!" Lee called for her sister, who was getting dressed in their spare bedroom. They had thrown together an impromptu wedding at Sugar Creek and invited only family. Tessa was the only one who could fly out on short notice, so she was the representative of Lee's family from Florida.

"Here I am." Tessa came out looking beautiful in a sundress with a cinched waist, her dark curls framing her slender face. Tessa was the taller of the two sisters and her hazel eyes always turned bright green whenever she cried. Lee assumed her sister's eyes would be bright green today during the ceremony.

"I'm so glad you could come." Lee hugged her sister.

"Me too," Tessa agreed.

"Let's head over to the main house. Bruce has been texting me that everyone is waiting."

The three of them bundled out the door and climbed into Colt's Ford truck. Colt floored it and sped along the dirt road that would take them from the cabin to the main house.

"Meesh!" Tessa exclaimed when the sprawling main house, a mansion in its own right, came into view. "You guys sell a lot of cattle, don't you?"

"A bit." Colt swung the truck into a parking spot

and jumped out to come around to their side of the truck.

"I can't believe that we're late to our own wedding."

"It's not the real wedding though," Lee was quick to remind him. "After the baby is born, I want a real fancy wedding with all the trimmings."

"We didn't even get to go wedding dress shopping," Tessa pointed out. "I know that Mom and Grandma Macbeth will want to go wedding dress shopping."

"This is just a ceremony so our child is born in wedlock." Lee reached for her husband-to-be's hand. "Agreed?"

"As you wish, my lady." Colt opened the front door to the house and quickly led her to the backyard.

The family that had gathered in the outside garden all cheered when they arrived at their own wedding; Lee felt like she was always on a Brand merry-go-round when she was with Colt's family, moving from one person to the next to the next but never really getting anywhere. She was passed from Bruce to Savannah to Gabe and his fiancée, Bonita. Callie and Kate were there, as were Shane and Rebecca. Lee had grown up in a small tight-knit family. It would be an adjustment to integrate into a large tight-knit clan. It seemed like the Brand family always traveled in a pack.

"Take your places, everyone!" The priest at Savannah and Rebecca's church had agreed to officiate the wedding.

"Are we ready?" Gail Allen was sitting behind a rental organ that had been wheeled into the garden. "Well, I'm starting."

Gail began to play the wedding march. Colt walked quickly up the aisle to stand by his brother Liam, who was acting as his best man. Tessa followed behind him, smiling and curtsying until she made it to her seat right up front.

"Here we go again," Lee said to Boot, who was waiting to walk her down the aisle.

Lee's mind flashed back to her first wedding. Boot had been there with his wife and Michael looked so nervous, waiting for her at the end of the aisle. They had been so young, but everyone in both families hadn't objected. Perhaps it was because everyone always assumed that they would marry young, right out of college.

"I want to thank you, Boot, for always being here for me, no matter what comes our way. Even now, you're here, walking me down the aisle."

"Where else would I be?" Boot asked in his gruff way. "Hmm? You don't realize what you give me, Lee. Because of you, I'm good for something. Because of you, I am still useful."

Lee refused to cry before she walked down the aisle. Instead, she adjusted Boot's tie, linked her arm with his and began the walk down the aisle to her new life with Colt.

"I don't think either of us expected this," Lee said for Boot's ears only.

"That's what makes life so fun," her father-in-law said, "You never know what's right around the corner."

Lee had to agree with him there. Gilda was his date for the wedding, and even though she herself was marrying someone else, it was still difficult for her to see Boot move on. Not everything in life was cut and dry.

As she walked, she felt the baby moving inside of her belly. Lee put her hand on her belly and laughed. "The baby has decided to join in on the excitement."

At the end of the aisle, and when he was asked, Boot gave her away to Colt with his booming, fatherly voice. Lee's parents and grandmother were watching on video chat, which was being managed by Tessa in the front row.

Colt was there to receive her. He took her hands in his and stared into her eyes in such a loving way it almost brought her to tears. Why was she so fortunate to have this man love her? What did she do to deserve this wonderful man?

Colt mouthed the words *I love you*.

"I love you," she whispered back, squeezing his fingers.

"Dearly beloved, we are gathered here today to marry this man and this woman…"

The ceremony was simple and short, just like she'd wanted it. The real wedding would happen later. For now, she just wanted to bring their child into a marriage. It was important to both of them.

"Well," Colt said as they walked together down the aisle for the first time as a married couple, "you're mine now."

"And you are mine," she reminded him playfully.

"I haven't even asked you where you want to go on a honeymoon."

"Okay—I know it's not sexy, but I really want to see my family in Florida."

"I wouldn't mind stopping by Walt Disney World for a pair of those mouse ears," Colt said with a straight face.

"If you agree to go to Central Florida to see my family and meet my Grandmother Macbeth, I will buy you two pairs of those ears. That's a promise!"

Their first night as a married couple was spent in Lee's 1930s bungalow. Tessa was staying in the cabin and it just made sense that they have privacy on their wedding night. After Colt agreed to spend their honeymoon in Florida, Tessa found them seats on her flight and they all planned to fly together.

"Come join us, my beautiful wife." Colt was lying down on the bed, his shirt unbuttoned, his shoes kicked off. He was lying down with Chester, who was purring happily while Colt rubbed his belly.

"I'm just warning you. Tubby and I spoon every night. It's a tradition."

"If you're telling me that I am going to play second fiddle to this cat and all of your horses, I already know that." Colt smiled and held out his hand. "Come here."

Lee joined him on the bed, careful not to disturb Chester. "Have you ever made love to a married woman before?"

Colt made a face. "Now how do I answer that without getting into trouble?"

Lee hit him on the arm. "Okay—let me rephrase that. Have you ever made love to your wife before?"

"Now that I can answer without getting into trouble!" Colt said. "Not yet."

Colt gently put Chester down on the floor and guided him out of the bedroom. "Sorry, big guy. I need some alone time with the wife."

As was typical of Colt, he stripped out of his clothing, completely confident in his gorgeous skin.

"What are you waiting for?" He tugged her toward him, reached around her back and began to unzip her out of her dress.

"I just thought you might like the pleasure of unwrapping your wedding present."

Colt growled at the thought, helping her out of

the dress. Soon her bra and underwear followed and she was standing naked before him, wearing nothing at all except her prosthetic leg and her locket.

Colt leaned down and kissed her rounded belly, then he kissed a happy trail from her belly up to her swollen breasts. After sucking on her nipples until she was begging for him to kiss her all over her body, Colt swept her up in his arms and set her down on the bed. He reached out for her, but she stopped him. It was her turn to please him. She took his thick hard-on into her mouth, holding onto his thigh to keep him exactly where she wanted him. She played with him, loved on him until he couldn't stand a moment more.

"Enough," he said gruffly, guiding her backward on the bed. He knelt down between her thighs and loved her with his tongue and his lips until she was moaning and writhing and reaching for him.

"Please." She tried to pull him up so he would cover her with his heavy body. "Please. I need you."

Colt covered her body with his and slid deep within her. "Oh, yes, my love." He kissed her eyes and her lips and her cheeks. He rocked inside of her, long deep strokes, taking her on a journey that only he could provide.

Lee felt him so deep inside of her. She arched her back and felt like she was floating away on a cresting wave. She dug her fingernails into his arm and heard herself cry out his name, again and again. *Colt, Colt, Colt…*

Colt picked her up and spun her around so she was sitting in his lap. She wrapped her body around his and kissed his neck and earlobes and lips. She inhaled deeply, taking in the scent of him just as she had taken his body into hers.

"This is our forever, Lady Macbeth." Colt kissed her so sweetly.

"Always and forever, Colt." Lee captured his face in her hands, happy to get lost in his bright blue eyes. "Always and forever."

* * * * *

COMING SOON!

We really hope you enjoyed reading this book.
If you're looking for more romance, be sure to
head to the shops when new books are
available on

Thursday 28th May

To see which titles are coming soon, please visit
millsandboon.co.uk/nextmonth

MILLS & BOON

Coming next month

MARRYING HIS RUNAWAY HEIRESS
Therese Beharrie

'It isn't a boat. It's a gondola.'

'My mistake,' she said blandly, and made him smile. She did that a lot. And he was smiling more than he ever had before. That worried him, too. But it didn't stop him from smiling at her. Or from thinking about how different she was now, when she wasn't thinking about the decision she had to make.

What if she didn't have to make it?

He couldn't pay attention to the thought when the gondolier called for them to get in. He did, using the man's help, then gently nudged him aside to help Elena. She smiled brightly, and it became obvious why he'd wanted to help her. Apparently, he would do anything to get that smile. To keep it there, too.

It stuck as they sat down and the gondola began to float down the canal. It was a bright, sunny day, and the blue green of the water around them sparkled as it stretched between buildings. A gentleman began to sing, rich and deep, and Elena sighed at his side. She snuggled closer, not intentionally, he didn't think, but it made him hold his breath.

That might not have been the right description of it. It was more like someone was squeezing his lungs, so he had less capacity to breathe. He'd felt that way the entire day. When they'd been exploring the stores around St Mark's Square. Or when Elena had insisted on feeding the pigeons, then got alarmed when more and more of them came.

'What is it with you and pigeons?' he'd asked. 'I told you this wouldn't end well.'

'I thought you were exaggerating. You exaggerate.'

'You live in Cape Town, Elena. You've been to the Waterfront. You know what pigeons are like.'

'I thought European pigeons would be different.'

He'd laughed, harder when she hid behind him. She'd ended up giving the bag of seeds to a kid before running away, causing the pigeons to scatter. They'd eaten pasta and chocolate crêpes and taken pictures. Once, Elena had photobombed another couple, then apologised profusely and taken about twenty pictures of them alone to make up for it. Now they were here, on the canal, having someone sing to them.

It was a lot to process. Not the experience, but the emotions that accompanied it. And the thoughts. Those insidious thoughts that had popped into his mind all day, then scurried away before he could put his finger on what they were suggesting. They all pooled together now though, growing into an idea that stole his breath.

It was based on never wanting to see Elena as tortured as she had been the night before. To keep her as happy as she was now, as she had been all day. It was built by the memories of how she'd elevated his business banquet that night in Rome because she fitted so perfectly into his world. She went head to head with him when he did something stupid, forced him to think about the way he treated people, and made him feel more like himself than he ever had. If he'd ever encountered his equal, she was it.

She was it.

'This is so nice,' Elena said at that moment, as if sensing his confusing thoughts. And his body, as if confused itself, responding by putting an arm around Elena's shoulders.

He froze. Until she rested her entire body against him. Then he melted.

It was like the hug from the night before. Warm and comfortable. Except there was more now. She was looking up at him, smiling, and he felt himself stumble. Whatever part of him had been standing steady in the face of the onslaught that Elena was unknowingly waging against him broke down. Whatever sanity he had left that told him not to indulge his ridiculous idea fled.

The proposal spilled out of his mouth.

'Marry me.'

Continue reading
MARRYING HIS RUNAWAY HEIRESS
Therese Beharrie

Available next month
www.millsandboon.co.uk

LET'S TALK
Romance

For exclusive extracts, competitions
and special offers, find us online:

- facebook.com/millsandboon
- @MillsandBoon
- @MillsandBoonUK

Get in touch on 01413 063232

MILLS & BOON

THE HEART OF ROMANCE

A ROMANCE FOR EVERY KIND OF READER

MODERN

Prepare to be swept off your feet by sophisticated, sexy and seductive heroes, in some of the world's most glamourous and romantic locations, where power and passion collide.
8 stories per month.

HISTORICAL

Escape with historical heroes from time gone by. Whether your passion is for wicked Regency Rakes, muscled Vikings or rugged Highlanders, awaken the romance of the past.
6 stories per month.

MEDICAL

Set your pulse racing with dedicated, delectable doctors in the high-pressure world of medicine, where emotions run high and passion, comfort and love are the best medicine.
6 stories per month.

True Love

Celebrate true love with tender stories of heartfelt romance, fro the rush of falling in love to the joy a new baby can bring, and a focus on the emotional heart of a relationship.
8 stories per month.

Desire

Indulge in secrets and scandal, intense drama and plenty of sizz hot action with powerful and passionate heroes who have it all: wealth, status, good looks…everything but the right woman.
6 stories per month.

HEROES

Experience all the excitement of a gripping thriller, with an inte romance at its heart. Resourceful, true-to-life women and strong fearless men face danger and desire - a killer combination!
8 stories per month.

DARE

Sensual love stories featuring smart, sassy heroines you'd want a best friend, and compelling intense heroes who are worthy of th
4 stories per month.

To see which titles are coming soon, please visit

millsandboon.co.uk/nextmonth

JOIN US ON SOCIAL MEDIA!

Stay up to date with our latest releases, author
news and gossip, special offers and discounts, and
all the behind-the-scenes action
from Mills & Boon...

 millsandboon

 millsandboonuk

 millsandboon

It might just be true love...

MILLS & BOON

HISTORICAL

Awaken the romance of the past

Escape with historical heroes from time gone by. Whether your passion is for wicked Regency Rakes, muscled Viking warriors or rugged Highlanders, indulge your fantasies and awaken the romance of the past.

MILLS & BOON
MEDICAL
Pulse-Racing Passion

Set your pulse racing with dedicated, delectable doctors in the high-pressure world of medicine, where emotions run high and passion, comfort and love are the best medicine.